Merry Christmas,
Mr Larry

Merry Christmas, Mr Larry

LARRY HOLLINGWORTH

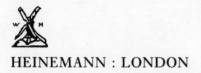

HEINEMANN : LONDON

First published in Great Britain 1996
by William Heinemann
an imprint of Reed International Books Ltd
Michelin House, 81 Fulham Road, London SW3 6RB
and Auckland, Melbourne, Singapore and Toronto

A CIP catalogue record for this title
is available from the British Library

ISBN 0 434 00290 9

Phototypeset in 11 on 14 point Ehrhardt
by Intype London Ltd
Printed and bound in Great Britain
by Clays Ltd, St Ives plc

To Josie, Sarah-Jo and Matthew, to the British Army, to UNHCR and to the people of Bosnia – Serb, Croat and Muslim – for giving me the opportunities which have shaped me and made me what I am.

Contents

Acknowledgements

Baroness Chalker of Wallasey with admiration and thanks.
Roger Courtier. For the idea of the book.
Mark Lucas. For the translation of idea to action.
Tom Weldon. For action to book.
Emily Kerr and Ilsa Yardley. For editing.
Kate Goodhart. From editing to publication.
Charlotte Mendelson for the final lap of the publication marathon.
Gordon Stevens. For encouragement.
Ron Redmond. For constant support.
Sylvana Foa. Without whom, no publicity. No me, no book.
Glynne Evans. Wisdom, support and advice.
Dr Gary McGrath, New England College. For a 'safe haven'.
Graeme Bateman. For advice and support.
Tony Beard. For help and advice.
Tina West. For technical support.
Vesna Stancic. For Bosnian translation and interpretation.
RAF Lyneham, especially the Herc crews.
Colonel Peter Williams and 1st Battalion Coldstream Guards.
Tony Birtley for Srebenica photograph.
Bernard Carrier, RICM. For photographs.
Anneliese Hollmann. For photograph.
Peter Kessler. Kris Janowski.
Martin Bell, Allan Little and Jon Snow. Masters of their medium.
My thanks to all who provided me with photographs. If you recognise
        yours and you are not credited for it, let me know. We will
        get it right in the paperback.

List of Abbreviations

APC	Armoured personnel carrier.
BH Command	UNPROFOR Headquarters in Bosnia-Herzegovina.
BiH	Government of Bosnia-Herzegovina.
COR	Commission for Refugees.
ECMM	Monitors under the auspices of the European Commission. Multi-national teams who wore white uniforms and were unarmed.
HDZ	Croatian Democratic Union. Bosnian Croat ruling party.
HVO	Croat Defence Council. Bosnian Croat Army.
JNA	Former Yugoslav National Army.
PTT	Post and Telecommunications Office. The UNPROFOR headquarters in Sarajevo and in Srebrenica.
SDA	Party for Democratic Action. Bosnian Muslim ruling party.
SDS	Serb Democratic Party. Bosnian Serb ruling party.
UN	United Nations.
UNHCR	United Nations High Commissioner for Refugees.
UNICEF	United Nations Children's Fund.
UNPROFOR	United Nations Protection Force.
WHO	World Health Organisation.
WFP	World Food Programme.

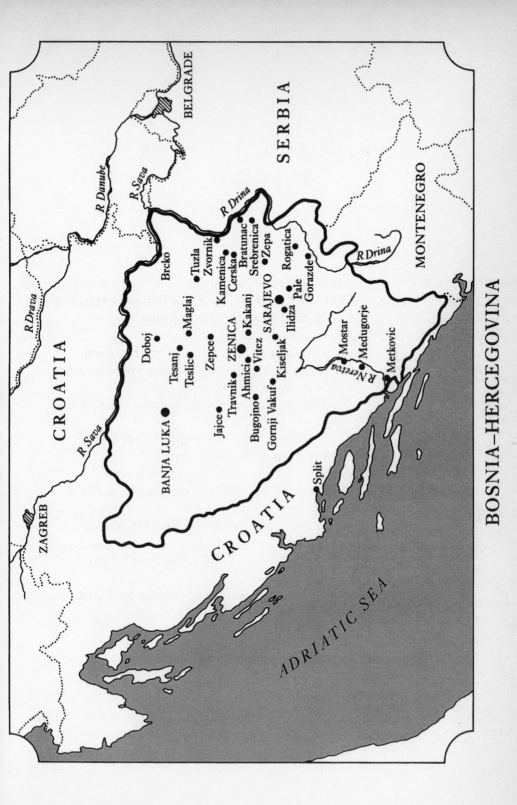

BOSNIA–HERCEGOVINA

Preface

This book will not explain Bosnia but it may explain what it was like to work in Bosnia with Bosnians. I hope it will make you laugh, make you cry, make you feel proud, make you feel ashamed. The journalists who have covered the war are writing books about the politics and the politicians, soon the historians will write and put the war into context with the previous history of the country and the region. The aim of this book is not to encroach on their territory. This is an account of two years in war-torn Bosnia working as an aid worker. It is a ramble through my mind and my memories. It is how I saw it and as I remember it. Dates may be wrong, names may be wrong but the events are right.

'Could it be that there is not room for all men to live in this wonderful world, under this fathomless starry sky? Is it really possible that in the midst of such natural splendour, feelings of hatred and vengeance, and the passion to destroy one's fellows can reside in the hearts of man?'
Leo Tolstoy, 'The Raid' from *A Prisoner in the Caucasus*
Raguda Publishers, Moscow, 1983.

PART ONE

I

Settling in

Bosnia, on the front line at Maglaj, 1993.

I wanted to share this first contact. I waved forward Ginge. He came up to join me. The leader of the defenders, a boy who turned out to be eighteen but an already established front-line veteran, shouted something from the trench.

'Come up and join us,' I said.

Vesna translated and he replied, 'We can't; they can see us.'

'No,' I said. 'The firing is parallel to the convoy. We are OK.'

He and his number two climbed up on to the road. A hail of bullets came whacking in from the woods on our left. These were not parallel to us. They were aimed directly at us. They smacked into the tarmac and ricocheted around us, some hitting the canopies of the trucks. The two Bosnians leapt back into the trenches. Ginge and I did a little dance, a sort of retired military two-step. Poor Serb Vesna dodged the Serb bullets by taking refuge in the UNHCR vehicle, her own little safe haven. I clearly remember screaming into the woods, 'Stop that firing.'

I have no doubt that my words had no effect whatsoever on whoever had fired. He had achieved his aim by scuttling the Bosnians. But shouting made me feel better. I stopped and turned to my big companion. 'Ginge. What are we doing here?'

Just what was I doing in Bosnia? How did I get there?

My grandfather ran away from home at the age of eight and joined the crew of a wind-jammer as a cabin boy. By the outbreak of the First World War he had sailed the seven seas.

My father left home at seventeen and joined the army. By the outbreak of the Second World War he had returned home after seven years in India.

My grandad's favourite hobby was to sit and drink and talk about the sea. I sat and listened and occasionally sipped.

My dad's favourite hobby was the cinema. There were two close to where we lived: the Regent and the Colosseum. The shows changed on Wednesday. Sunday there was a special film. Special, then, meant 'Sundayish', bland with a happy ending. My dad went three times a week. He sat in the one and nines and I went with him whenever possible. Cowboys were his favourites.

I was, therefore, brought up on tales of exotic places, of ports and harbours and seas and continents. I knew the geography of India better than that of England. My actual knowledge of horses was of the milkman's and the breadman's and the coalman's. But by ten I had ridden the length and breadth of the Wild West.

On Saturday mornings my school friends would go to the matinée. I rarely went. The children's cinema was not for me. It smelt different. I preferred the evenings, the smell of tobacco smoke as it curled and merged with the silver screen. Matinées were also noisier, goodies were cheered and baddies booed, which never happened in the evenings. Maybe there was the odd sob as the hankie dabbed the eye. Also, I hate coming out from the land of make-believe into bright daylight. You have to rub your eyes and in doing so you rub away the magic of where you have been.

Saturdays and Sundays were my days to 'skipper' my own craft.

The Birkenhead ferry plied from Woodside to Liverpool pier-head. One penny per trip. I was first on. The gangplank chains were still rattling as I raced to the bows to claim my spot. In the V of the bows there is a small metal shelf about one foot off the deck. Why it is there I do not know, but by standing on it I was able to see over the rails. Thus did I chart my seven seas. I was captain, engineer, look-out, pirate, marine, as the ferry boat thud-thudded its way across the Mersey. 'Land ahoy,' I would silently shout as the ferry came alongside the Liverpool landing stage. I watched 'my' crew as they threw out the hawser to be wrapped around the bollards. I listened to the rope straining as it pulled 'my' ship alongside, compressing the huge squeaking tyres fastened to the sides of the landing stage. Then, as all eyes were on the lowering gangplank, I ran to the toilets to hide, to re-emerge when the Liverpool passengers had embarked. Pennies from my paper round were short! Often I was not alone. If a fellow skipper emerged before me and claimed the bows, I went to the stern and watched the spume, the spray and the seagulls. Landfalls, shipwrecks, naval battles, occurred every weekend on this short stretch of the Mersey. And not a word reached the columns of the *Liverpool Echo*! No wonder that by the time I was eighteen I wanted to travel.

An obliging government had the solution. I was old enough to catch the tail end of National Service. I joined the Cheshire Regiment. The battalion was in Malaya, which would have suited me down to the ground. Basic training, however, was done in Chester. When it was over, the vicious bugger who had plagued my life for the twelve weeks it lasted called me to him. 'We've got you down for an NCO's cadre.'

'What's a cadre?'

'It's an army word forra course. You'll be an NCO at the end of i'.'

'Does that mean that I do not go to Malaya with the rest?'

'Kerrect.'

'Then I do not want to go on your course.'

'The army's norra picky organisation y'know. You'll do as yer told.'

'If I am going to miss Malaya and go on a course then I want to go to Sandhurst.'

'T'where?'

'To Sandhurst. It's the Royal Mil—'

'I know what it f***ing is.' He paused. 'Who d'ye think yew are? Have you got any munney? Is yer dad anybody special like?' He looked at me long and hard. 'You wanna settle for sumthin' real, you do.'

'Can you get me an interview with the platoon commander?'

'I will bu' he'll love you. 'E went to Eaton Hall. Couldn't even get to Mons 'imself.'

He was right. But eventually I got to see the company commander, who was excellent. And I went to Sandhurst. My first tour as an officer was in Berlin, with its Russian, French, British and American sectors. A city of intrigue and excitement. A great city to be in as a young army officer. I was there three years. By twenty-five, and serving in England, I thought I should leave and study to be a doctor. But at the last minute I stayed on. I next looked over the wall fifteen years later, wanted to be a television star then.

But it was to be another ten years before I finally left the army. After thirty years' service in many of the places I had first 'visited' by courtesy of the Mersey ferry: Far East, Middle East, Africa, Europe, but never India and never the Americas.

Life in industry and commerce was not to be for me. I wanted travel and fun and a challenge. I threw away my razor, bequeathed most of my suits and ties to the local charity shop, packed a suitcase and visited Geneva. I wanted to be an aid worker. Preferably with refugees. My overseas tours, especially those in Africa, and most memorably in Uganda, had left me with a secret wish to go back and do something positive and permanent. What and where I did not know. I only knew it had to be with people.

Long ago I had discovered that I am a 'people person'. When friends returned from holidays and got out the photographs I was interested if they were of people. Photos of parks, beaches, trees and buildings don't draw my attention in the same way. But snaps of men fishing, women working and children playing fascinate me. I knew that I did not want to save jungles, mend the hole in the ozone layer, or restore monuments. As meritorious as these projects are, they are not me. I wanted to work with people. Everybody wants to work with children, but I was more attracted to whole families, to whole communities. I had no idea what I could do but I knew that I could stand on my own in the middle of nowhere. My ideas were simple, naive and possibly romantic. But I felt that the time was right. I knew that it was now or never.

I travelled by train. I was very lucky at Geneva station. I asked the taxi driver for 'Refugees, s'il vous plaît'. He could have taken me to a soup kitchen; fortunately he took me to Avenue de la Paix, then the home base of the office of the United Nations High Commissioner for Refugees, UNHCR. I bluffed my way into the personnel branch, was interviewed by a charming, very professional and experienced lady, Sue Munch, who gave me the big break I needed. She sent me first to Cyprus, then brought me back to Geneva before sending me to Sudan to work for an outstanding man, John Horrekens, who put me in charge of a refugee camp of fifty-seven thousand Ethiopians and gave me lots of guidance, but who left me alone to do the job to his satisfaction. This was followed by trips to Ethiopia and to Eritrea, before I took over my next camp in a place called Liboi on the Somali border. Sixty-three thousand Somalis. A tough, tiring assignment. It was travel and a challenge but as my old sergeant would have said, 'Norra a lorra fun.'

In May 1992 I returned to the UK minus my Parker pen which I had had for more than ten years, my UN blue anorak which I had had for five years and twenty kilos in weight. The pen and anorak were 'liberated' by my Kenyan driver at a halt for a wee on my way to Nairobi airport. The kilos were lost as the result of bugs picked up in the bush.

My first two weeks at home were dictated by a simple time-and-distance calculation: at least twice an hour I needed to find a toilet. A time-and-motions study. Fortunately, the local military medical centre near my home had on its staff a graduate of the School of Hygiene and Tropical Medicine. He cured my loo dependency and I was then ready to move.

The situation in ex-Yugoslavia was the lead story in all the news-papers. UNHCR was the leading aid agency. Jose Maria Mendiluce was the Special Envoy. He and I had worked together in Geneva. A small, broad, urbane and elegant Spaniard, he is a brilliant linguist with an open charm which hides experience gained as a veteran of tough tours in South America and Kurdistan.

In just over a year he had seen a lot of history in the making. Slovenia had fought briefly and successfully for its independence, Croatia and Serbia had gone to war. The newly independent UN-recognised Republic of Bosnia-Herzegovina had been pronounced still-born by the doctor of medicine, Radovan Karadzic, who led the Bosnian Serbs. His diagnosis was faulty, as was so often to be the case. The infant state was not dead, but nor was it healthy. Its life-blood was regrouped and separated, its limbs stretched from their sockets. But it was alive. It was now in an incubator state, vulnerable and isolated; kept alive by infusions of rhetoric and promise and by occasional injections of aid. Sarajevo, its capital and seat of government, was battle-scarred and besieged, the population shelled and hungry. To alleviate the suffering, the UN Security Council had voted on 8 June to open Sarajevo airport for the delivery of humanitarian aid. The airport was in Bosnian Serb-held territory, their tanks and soldiers were on the runway. They protested. On 28 June President Mitterrand, in a bold, brave move, flew into Sarajevo. The airport was then deemed to be open. The Bosnian Serb forces withdrew under the watchful blue eyes of the newly appointed UNPROFOR Commander of Sector Sarajevo, the Canadian General Lewis Mackenzie.

Madame Sadako Ogata, the High Commissioner for Refugees, was determined that UNHCR, the organisation she directed, would run the airlift. Jose Maria Mendiluce, her Special Envoy, already had a man on the ground in Sarajevo. The task was to airlift humanitarian aid from Zagreb, the capital of Croatia, to Sarajevo, the capital of Bosnia-Herzegovina, to feed the starving blockaded population of three hundred and eighty-five thousand. The decision as to who should operate the airlift lay with the UN Secretary General, Boutros Boutros Ghali. He had an offer from the United States, who wished to undertake the task. With hindsight, an amazing offer, and one which, if he had accepted it, would have altered the UN involvement and maybe the whole course of the war. The Secretary General gave the task to UNHCR.

A new task needed more staff. I was called to Geneva. I was thrilled. The newspapers and the television were full of the story of the war. I had watched, nightly, Jose Maria giving interviews. The challenge that faced him was enormous, the scenes were horrific, as though from a previous age. The chance to be part of the team, in any capacity, was not to be missed.

In Geneva, the whole ex-Yugoslav operation was under the supervision of a senior UNHCR director, Eric Morris, a taciturn American, bright, direct and reserved. Eric quickly realised that the Geneva end was becoming larger than the sharp end. He decided that I should go to Zagreb and run the airlift. It was a great decision for me as I am not a corridors-of-power warrior. Eric told me to contact the UNHCR Chief of Operations in Zagreb, Tony Land, an Englishman who had just returned from Afghanistan. In a short, sharp call Tony made it clear that he was looking for 'a man who will fight for refugees in the most difficult circumstances. A man who will lie for them, cheat for them and be a rogue for them. You are ex-army, aren't you?' he concluded. 'You have the right background.' I was not too sure whether I was going to like Tony.

The office gave me my air ticket and, at the last minute, a huge satellite telephone. I struggled to the airport and arrived after check-in time. The Swiss, with whom time is an obsession, are not happy with late arrivals; the Swiss, with whom money also is an obsession, are very happy with excess baggage. The plane left without me, while I was still paying the surcharge. I took the next flight.

I love travel. As the aircraft approached Zagreb I was like a child, pressing my head against the cabin window trying to get an idea of the size of the place. It was dark and the myriad of pinpricks of light told me the city was big. I was met and taken to the five-star Intercontinental hotel. If this was war, I could take a lot of it.

The following morning I was briefed by Jose Maria and Tony. They gave me a run-down on the war so far. Jose Maria was anecdotal. He knew all the key players. Tony is like a housemaster who has a good brain but prefers to run the school sports. He was academic and aggressive. His arms swept over the huge map on the wall. He prodded at place names, followed the course of rivers with his pen, pointed at Corps headquarters, named generals. I tried to take notes, but in truth I could not have placed my finger on Belgrade on this huge map which Tony knew so well.

'What was the name of that man again?' I asked.

'Prlic,' replied Tony.

'And the General?'

'Hadzihasanovic.'

'Can you point out on the map again Biljana Plavsic?'

'She is Vice-President of Srpska Republika.'

The housemaster was getting irritable. The pupil had not done his homework. I was in danger of getting detention. I decided to nod wisely, pretend to write and ask no more questions.

After the briefing I felt part of the scene. I was excited and looked forward to my part in the action. The airlift was not only vital, because it brought in food, but was a symbol of the commitment of the world to the Bosnian crisis. The airport authorities offered us an office co-located with the airport fire brigade. It was on the tarmac. It was easy to see each aircraft and to ensure that every pilot reported in after landing.

Some aid arrived from donor countries by road and was stored at the airport for loading on to aircraft and flying into Sarajevo. Some aircraft arrived at the beginning of each day with aid loaded at their home airport. They reported into Zagreb, flew on to Sarajevo, then returned to Zagreb for further loads. Other nations parked their aircraft at Zagreb, where they were loaded from the ground stocks and flew to Sarajevo.

As the numbers of aircraft built up, so the numbers of sorties per aircraft diminished. Most of the crews were keen to fly and vied with each other for 'slots' into Sarajevo. None were keener than the Brits. They would ensure that their aircraft were loaded faster than others, they would watch like hawks for any delay in another aircraft's take-off and if there was the narrowest window of opportunity they would rumble along the tarmac, slowly lose contact with the ground and lumber into the sky. This tactic would throw out the plan and meant another nation losing a trip. The Brits were the worst for excessive zeal, but they were not alone. The poor UNHCR representative on the ground, initially me, would suffer the wrath of the pilot cheated out of his turn.

The enthusiasm of the aircrews was matched only by their bravery. Each and every landing, halt and take-off in Sarajevo was threatened. Many aircraft were to be pock-marked by shrapnel, penetrated by bullets and tracked by missiles. One aircraft, from Italy, was to pay the highest price. It was shot down with the loss of the crew.

After I had spent only a few days in Zagreb it was decided that I could be replaced and sent to Sarajevo. This was the answer to my prayers. It had been my intention to get to Sarajevo from the moment I left England. I knew it was the centre of the action, anywhere else was peripheral.

My first call was to the quartermaster stores of the Royal Engineers. 'Any chance of the loan of a British Army sleeping bag?'

'Who are you?'

'UNHCR.'

'Where are you going.'

'Sarajevo.'

'OK, but you will have to sign for it.'

The sleeping bag became a close friend. Thank you, RQMS.

The next day I handed over my airport responsibilities to a young UNHCR lawyer, who soon handed them over to Mike Aitcheson, a veteran professional airline man. From his arrival onwards there was no queue jumping by any nation, no disorderly behaviour, no nonsense. The airlift ran smoothly and efficiently.

As I was leaving, I heard that on the previous night there had been heavy firing across the airport. 'Damn,' I thought. 'I will arrive and it will be all over.'

I hitched a lift to Sarajevo with the British plane and had my first Khe Sanh experience. The flight from Zagreb to Sarajevo is dangerous for most of the way. A slow-moving, fully laden transport aircraft is an easy target to track and hit in a war zone where bored, trigger-happy, unaccountable brigands roam the hills. But the descent to land is the most vulnerable manoeuvre. The RAF crews adopted the descent procedure used by the Americans as they landed in Khe Sanh during the Vietnam War. This involves an extremely high approach with tight turns, then an almost vertical angle of descent with a sharp pull-out at what seems feet from the runway. It is a spectacular sight to watch from the ground, but to be honoured by the crew with an invitation to travel in the cockpit and to stand behind the pilot's seat during the flight and descent is a truly exhilarating experience. You feel that you can touch the sides of the hills. The navigator indicated that it was time to put on flak jackets. The pilot, Chris Tingay, a *Boy's Own* image of a pilot, bright-blue eyes, hero handsome, with a tight, tough smile, pointed out, with his yellow-chamois-gloved hand, Sarajevo in the valley ahead. Then the descent began. Chris pushed the stick forward, the nose went down. It was as if someone had taken away the floor you were standing on. Your ears blocked, your blood rushed to your head, your knees buckled. Your stomach, intestines, liver, kidneys, all never before felt, were now individual items and floating within your body. The airport was rushing towards us, surely we would penetrate the runway, not land on it. Chris pulled back on the stick, conversations passed over the headphones, the aircraft levelled, the body regrouped itself. The aircraft wheels hit the ground, we bounced, Chris and his co-pilot had their hands on the central controls, the aircraft was shaking, vibrating, the noise was deafening and penetrating, the huge tyres again contacted the ground, the aircraft raced along the centre of the runway, then the engines were reversed, the cargo lurched forward in the hold, straining against the bolts and straps. You yourself were holding on, knuckles white, to the back of the pilot's seat. The noise and speed subsided. The great overweight bird was now a slow-moving land vehicle controlled by a ridiculously small primitive wheel which was in the corner of the cockpit below the side window. It is parallel to the deck, not angled, and is controlled by the pilot's left hand, as if his craft were a trolleybus or a tram. You realised that your eyes were wide open, your face grinning ecstatically. The crew were folding maps, flicking switches, clearing up, closing down. They had entered the most dangerous airport in the world; they had parked their winged chariot on the pock-marked tarmac. They had made themselves the biggest target for miles. They sat and waited while they were unloaded, preparing for an equally spectacular Khe Sanh take-off. Chris was later awarded the Air Force Cross for his bravery, the first medal to be given for former Yugoslavia. 'It's a collective award for all the crews in the operation,' he modestly and generously said.

I thanked him and his crew, collected my bags and left the aircraft through the side door and took my first steps in Sarajevo. My initial view was of the damaged Air Traffic Control Tower. Broken sheets of glass looking as if they would fall to the floor to impale all below. I was taken to the UNHCR hangar. Outside were parked two Canadian APCs. The whole of the front of the hangar was open, in the top right-hand corner was the office. It was very makeshift and untidy. The rest of the hangar was either storage space or living accommodation.

Fabrizio Hochschild then arrived. He had been in Sarajevo since before the war began and was in charge of the office. He and I had last seen each other in Sudan. He is a young, extremely bright Oxbridge graduate, polyglot, thinker and a man deservedly earmarked for the top. He was wearing a jacket with a blue UNHCR tabard over it. He looked like a graduate engineer on a building site, part of the scene but slightly above it. He welcomed me, told me to settle in and outlined my tasks. I was to run the airport and the airlift.

The RAF invited me into the area of the hangar they had curtained off as an officers' mess, where I met Flight-Lieutenant Lee Doherty, a London-Irish workhorse. Lee had made himself responsible for the loading and unloading of aircraft. He was unbelievable. He could do every task, from driving the most enormous fork-lift truck to cleaning his shoes, quicker and better than anyone else. The French, Canadian and Norwegian teams who worked with him were overwhelmed by his energy. No man was more responsible for establishing the system of loading and unloading the aircraft at speed to ensure that they were on the ground for the least possible time and thus least exposed to danger from shell, mortar and small-arms fire. He was awarded the MBE for his efforts. Recently I met a Sarajevo driver and we talked about Lee. 'I remember three things about him,' he said. 'Hard work, cold showers and Jack Daniels whisky.' Lee, if ever you are looking for an epitaph that's not a bad one!

The team told me about the previous evening. There had been heavy firing across the airfield as the Serb-held Airport Settlement had fired on government-dominated Dobrinja. The boys told me exciting tales of the sky lit up by tracer fire, they pointed out from where shells had come and where they had landed. I have to confess that I secretly hoped it would last at least one night more, that I would see some action myself.

The night was quiet, the firing subdued. The hangar was dimly lit. It had the smell of dust and flour and diesel fumes. The military were in their uniforms, the local staff in shorts, T-shirts, overalls, all sorts of casual clothes. The girls were in jeans. All wore their flak jackets. Everyone was sitting at the benches around the dining-tables in small groups. In some the language was English, in others Serbo-Croat. I very much felt that I was the new boy, even though no one had been there more than a week. Each group made me welcome, there was a lot of laughter and shouting. I had expected a tense atmosphere but these were all old hands in this new war. Old hands and old friends. Danger had short-circuited the time normally taken to establish close friendships. I went to bed at about nine. I opened out my sleeping bag and discovered a bonus: the previous occupant had left a maglite torch in it.

I had learned that inside the hangar there were one toilet and two washbasins, to be shared between thirty people at night and maybe fifty by day. I established that most people got up at six thirty. I set my alarm for five forty-five. I wanted to have used the facilities before the others awoke.

I slept well and was out of the sleeping bag before six. Only one other person was up: Nonjo, the cook. While I washed, he made me a cup of tea. The next person up was no surprise. It was Lee.

I went across and talked to Nonjo. He is a tall, heavy, generous man with a warm, sincere personality. He was employed as a driver and was a typical, well-educated, street-wise city boy. He had a great sense of humour and had as one of his many party pieces a monologue about an old lady learning to drive an armoured vehicle. His timing was as good as Bob Newhart's and the story as funny with each retelling. Nonjo was to become one of my barometers. I was able to measure the morale of our staff by his mood and their reaction to him.

After breakfast I was taken to see the commander of UNPRO-FOR Sector Sarajevo, General Lewis Mackenzie. If ever a man looked the part he was playing, it was him. He is a tall, broad, film-star-handsome man. He is tough physically and cerebrally. A fluent speaker with an enviable vocabulary, he was without a doubt in charge. He exuded command and confidence. A brilliant choice. I learned that his hobby is racing cars. If I had had to guess it, racing cars would have been alongside sky-diving or big-game hunting as my first choices for him.

I took my virgin trip into the city, to visit the UNHCR warehouse at the Zetra Olympic stadium and to see the city authorities.
It was an opportunity to view the devastation already suffered in
the opening days of the war. The French soldier at the airport
entrance raised the barrier from the protection of his heavily
sandbagged guard post. Ahead were buildings put up to house
the competitors in the 1984 Winter Olympics and afterwards
occupied by the luckier residents of Sarajevo. They were not so
lucky now. This was Dobrinja. Every house, every apartment,
every building was battle-scarred. Shattered windows gaped open,
curtains flapped in the breeze. Here and there, tiles were missing
off the roofs like gaps in teeth. The narrow airport road was pock-
marked with shell and mortar craters.

This was one of the sniper alleys. It had claimed the lives of
some of the army of journalists who lived in the city and came to
the airport for briefings. I gave a reassuring touch to my flak
jacket; an action which became a habit like a nervous tic. We
sped recklessly along the narrow road, the wheels crunching over
cartridge cases and the tailfins of spent mortar bombs. 'Serbs on
the left, Muslims on the right,' said the driver, enjoying our wide-
eyed fascination. He sped over a small bridge, then with minimum
deceleration steered the vehicle through a sharp left-hand turn.
'Snipers,' he shouted. The squealing tyres and the violent lurching
of the vehicle shook the butterflies in our stomachs. We passed
the newspaper office of *Oslobodjenje* with the core of its tower still
standing – defying the Serb gunners who can see it, but whose
skills are not sufficient to demolish it, and symbolising to the
world the spirit of the *Oslobodjenje* staff, bowed, battered but not
beaten. Daily they produce a newspaper, regardless of the intensity
of the shelling, the appalling conditions or even the lack of proper
'news' paper. It had a multi-ethnic staff. Sadly it could not avoid
single-side propaganda, which on occasions demeaned its
excellence.

Next to *Oslobodjenje* is the garish building known as the Rainbow
Hotel, built to house old people but taken over by the UN as an
accommodation block, the location of one of the first ignominies.
It flew the UN flag but was shelled, the UN vehicles in the car-
park destroyed, the patches of white on the shattered and burned

vehicles to remind generations of UN soldiers of the first insult. On our right we saw the wires which had powered the trams. They were severed by shrapnel and dangled from their bent poles, littering the road.

We passed the PTT building which was the headquarters of UNPROFOR, the turning marked by an abandoned red tram. On the left is the TV building, a concrete monstrosity which pre-war attracted tremendous criticism for its prison-like exterior. In war it was to prove a gold-medal winner. Its windowless walls, solid exterior and construction rejected the Serb calling cards. It became office and studio to many international journalists, and home to some.

We were now on the other infamous sniper alley. This great boulevard, built, on Tito's orders, wide enough to drive tanks and to land aircraft, was now a principal taker of the lives of those who lingered. On the right were tiers of huge apartment blocks, some of which housed the scum who aimed through their sniper-scopes and murdered innocent women frantically shopping, men desperately walking to work or children recklessly playing. We saw few people on the streets. Those who were moved with the cunning of hunted animals.

Our first port of call was to the Municipality, a dark-brown stone building next to the Presidency, to pay a courtesy call on Mr Pamuk, the director of the city. His title initially confused me, but he explained that he was the senior civil servant in the city and the district of Sarajevo. A powerful post. He was glad to see me. My grey hairs pleased him. So far, he had been told how to run his city by men the age of his sons. We had an immediate empathy. I had neither youth nor solution. He was maybe forty-five. On a bad day he looks a little like Brezhnev, on a good day like Lord Healey. He has a craggy face, dark, thick hair, prominent eyebrows, eyes which laugh a lot and a voice honed and trained on rough tobacco. He wore a dark-grey party suit. He was a product of the party but had a mind which had easily adapted to the circumstances of today. I liked him and knew that we could work together. I promised to return later in the week when he would have in his office a committee of five senior citizens appointed to oversee the distribution of aid.

We then moved to the Holiday Inn hotel, home of many journalists. We were to meet Minister Martin Raguz, who was responsible for Refugee Affairs. The Holiday Inn was a magnet for Serb shells, in truth its hideous yellow outer walls would be the target of many a brickbat in times of peace. We were driven to the main entrance and made a quick dash to the front door which was part glass, part fresh air. To the right of the entrance was the reception desk where bored staff dealt with tired journalists. A notice board near the door attempted to answer the most routine enquiries. We crossed the reception hall. Our presence was noted by the cabals of media men pocketed about the bar area. We climbed the large but clumsy central staircase and turned to the right. The Minister was waiting for us in a private dining-room. Martin Raguz was a young man, perhaps thirty. He is a Croat, tall, dark and presumably attractive to women. He was accompanied by two very attractive secretaries.

We were served a meal: my first away from the hangar. It was called burek, a pie with meat inside it. They were war economy portions but it was more than I expected. The Holiday Inn survives because of its clientele. The journalists are paid well, many have a generous expense account and they pay in hard currency. The hotel management is therefore able to do deals with checkpoints to bring in food to satisfy customers as voracious at table as they are on the streets.

This meeting was very important to me. It was the first time I realised the significance of working in Sarajevo. Mr Pamuk and I had been talking about the needs of Sarajevo. Minister Raguz was talking about the needs of Bosnia-Herzegovina (BiH). The UNHCR man in Sarajevo was thus double-hatted: talking to the local authorities on Sarajevo and to the government on BiH. Martin Raguz wished to talk about aid to his nation. He wanted us to support computer links to the principal towns, to know how much aid had been delivered to each region, how much was planned. He talked as if there was not a war raging around us, as if communications were normal. I realised that he thought that we, the UN, were better organised than we were. He was presuming that we had a great plan and a system to match. He talked about aid to isolated areas. He mentioned Gorazde – the first time

I ever heard the name. He asked if we could send a convoy there urgently. I left the table realising that I had a lot to learn. Feeding Sarajevo looked as if it was only half of the job.

I returned, hot and sticky, to the airport and sat with the drivers and a map. They showed me where Gorazde was. They explained that it was in Eastern Bosnia, had been a multi-ethnic town with a 'Muslim' majority, but was now surrounded by territory which had fallen into Bosnian Serb hands. They patiently explained that to get there I would need Serb approval and that it was not in the interests of the Serbs to permit aid to enter Gorazde. The Serbs wished to starve the 'Muslims' into submission, then to move them out to Central Bosnia, releasing the whole of Eastern Bosnia to the Serbs. My drivers showed me two other places also besieged, Zepa and Srebrenica. Gorazde was enough for me in one night.

Now that I was aware of the dual role of UNHCR, I needed to know who was who in the government as well as in the city. I began to do battle with the names. The President of Bosnia-Herzegovina, Alija Izetbegovic, I could manage. The mayor of Sarajevo, Mr Kresevljakovic, was going to take some time.

My second evening was noisy. I stood with the RAF boys and the drivers outside the hangar and watched a battle begin. A tank on the Serb-held hill began firing into Butmir. Government-held Dobrinja replied from behind us, Serb-held Lukavica joined in over our heads and Butmir replied, Serb-held Airport Settlements fired on Butmir. The rounds flew above our heads, low enough for us to hear their passage, high enough to avoid frightening us. As darkness fell the tracer rounds flew like rockets across the sky. Following tracer shell is fascinating but macabre. The trace disappears at the end of the trajectory of the round, there is a delay, then an increasing rumble and slowly flames flicker into the sky. It is at first easy to be taken in by the event and to forget the reality of the action. Perhaps to begin with we see it as we see a movie film. Later, when I was close enough to see the action and to hear the screams, the fascination had gone, replaced by horror at the result and hatred of the perpetrators.

2

Moving around

The airlift was increasing. We were soon up to fourteen flights a day. On a rough calculation, we reckoned that we needed to bring in about four and a half thousand tonnes of food a month for the city to survive. Fourteen flights a day delivered about one hundred and sixty per day. With a bit of luck we might be able to win. The calculation, however, did not take into account medicine, fuel and other essentials. We needed road convoys as well as an airlift. Furthermore, we were not allowed to concentrate solely on Sarajevo, pressure was increasing by the day for a convoy to Gorazde. The government was whipping up enthusiasm among the journalists. They had become excited by the story line: 'Large city in the middle of Serb-held territory, tens of thousands of people besieged and starving.' The story was very similar to Sarajevo, but they had 'done' Sarajevo. The Bosnian government wanted action for the more altruistic reason that their people were dying.

UNHCR was asked to visit President Izetbegovic. This would be my first official visit. The Presidency is in the centre of the city. Normally the entrance is around the back, but for official visits the front door is used. My translator and I went by French APC. We parked outside the main door, the guards checked our identities – not too difficult in my case as there were very few Methuselah look-alikes in Sarajevo. We were ushered in and seated on a huge settee. The reception room was chosen well; it faced the front of the building and had two large windows which were open.

The President arrived. He looked gentle, confused and exhausted. His daughter, Sabine, was with him. She acts as secretary and sometimes translator. He understands English and in a one-to-one conversation is prepared to speak it, but he prefers to use a translator. He sat in the corner of one settee. The shelling began and there were two loud bangs very close to us. The President appeared not to notice them. He never even paused in his speech. He wanted to discuss aid in general and aid to Gorazde in particular. He had with him a senior officer, Hadzihasanovic. The Bosnian government were not strong on military ranks, so it was safest to address them as 'commander'. I was later to meet Enver Hadzihasanovic in Zenica and again back in Sarajevo. He is one of the ablest Bosnian leaders, handsome, silver-haired and charming.

We were briefed on the reports coming out of Gorazde, which were horrendous: a hospital with no medicine; a population with no food. The commander discussed the options for getting aid into Gorazde. The Bosnian army had a mule route, but it could take very little and was frequently attacked by the Serbs. 'I'll bet it is,' I thought to myself. It was an open secret that the mule route took in mainly ammunition for the defenders of the town.

The President was strong. 'There is not enough aid for Sarajevo, but Gorazde is of a higher priority.' I could see that it was. Strategically, the last thing the President wanted was major towns to fall to the Serbs. Also he was testing the strength and will of the UN and its agencies. It was a short meeting.

The following day was my second visit to the office of Mr Pamuk for a meeting with the five-person committee to discuss distribution. We had to pass through shelling which was heavy and dangerously close. It was my first trip at the wheel of the car. Leyla Hrasnica was my translator and guide. She is not yet twenty but has the maturity of someone twice her age, the missing years telescoped by war. She is tall and walks with great confidence. She wears skirts and seems to know everyone by their first name. Leyla is everyone's equal.

She showed to me the 'back route', the quieter one. We arrived at the Municipality a few minutes late. The building had taken a few hits and there was machine-gun fire bouncing off the walls. As I parked the car under the direction of Leyla I had two thoughts which I voiced: 'Leyla, if that was the quiet route, what would the other route have been like?'

'The shelling would have been a little closer, but . . .' she added with a smile, 'we would have been a little quicker.'

'Leyla, just as a point of interest, when are conditions considered to be too bad to cancel a meeting?'

'When the other side cancels.'

We passed the empty offices and arrived at Mr Pamuk's. He was there with two other people, two of the five. He introduced them to me. One was Professor Kljic, an economist who was to be the architect of the distribution plan after consultation with us. There was a tremendous bang as a mortar hit the base of the building. Leyla never flinched. We waited a few minutes more for the other three to arrive. The professor and I began to talk. He was hoping that I would have a blueprint for feeding the city. He was not to know that I was as confused and overwhelmed as he was. I explained that my own experience was with refugee camps, where I had been responsible for almost one hundred thousand people, a little exaggeration, but I thought acceptable in the circumstances.

Mr Pamuk wanted to know for how long the Sarajevo airlift was guaranteed. I was able to answer clearly and truthfully that it had been funded for one month. We began discussing the Berlin airlift. There was a knock at the door and the secretary to Mr Pamuk came in – we were not to wait for the others. They had been seriously injured by the shrapnel from the mortar that we had heard explode. I was disturbed by this, but the others were not; they were used to it. I needed more time before I too accepted the macabre as commonplace.

The professor wanted us to give him the aid as quickly as possible. Then he wished to sit on it until he had enough to be able to issue a little to everyone, or at least a little to everyone in a district, 'to issue by rings'. The first thoughts of UNHCR were to keep the aid in our possession until we knew the day of the issue, then to hand it over, so that we could see and monitor the issue. We wanted to see it given to the most vulnerable: the widows and orphans; the elderly; the homeless. We also wanted it distributed rapidly. The people were starving now and they knew that aid was arriving. Given a little aid, their morale would improve. Given no aid, they might storm the warehouses.

Not only was there a difference of opinion on method of distribution, there was the age-old shadow boxing between donor and recipient. I hate this mutual mistrust. It happens with every operation. Basically we believe that the only way to guarantee that all the aid will be distributed to the needy is if you yourself put the spoon into the mouth of the beneficiary. Clearly, this we could not do. We had to trust and use the local agents. Sarajevo was a Central European capital. The professor was a man of honour, but I've been ripped off by foreign royalty with degrees from Oxbridge, so I am cautious and tread carefully.

Nevertheless, the professor was someone whom, over time, I learned to like and respect. The job that he had been given was the worst in Sarajevo. He was criticised by everyone. The citizens never appreciated how little we were able to bring in and accused him of either stealing it or misappropriating it. The authorities accused him of being too honourable. We accused him of being too slow and weak. His task was Herculean and Solomonic. I was later to visit his home. He had far less than anyone else. His family suffered because of his position. Initially I gave him a hard time. I did not accord him the respect he deserved.

At the end of the meeting, while we were discussing the terrible plight of Sarajevo, both the professor and Mr Pamuk requested that we divert aid to Gorazde. 'The citizens of Sarajevo, who have little, wish to share that little with the citizens of Gorazde, who have nothing.' I reassured them that we were negotiating the entry of a convoy, but I knew that Fabrizio was having little success.

Having visited the government side, it was time for me to see the Serb side, to discuss their needs and their wishes. Fabrizio Hochschild had set the policy. He knew that aid to one side was morally wrong and practically impossible. There were many thousands of refugees in the Serb-held territory around Sarajevo, mainly Serbs, but also some Croats and a few Muslims. All aid coming into Sarajevo passed through Serb territory. There was no way the Serbs would allow aid in to feed the population of Sarajevo without a share going to them. He was put under pressure to choose the suburb of Ilidza as the Serb-side delivery and distribution centre, but he chose the quieter area of Rajlovac. Hence a percentage of the aid arriving in Sarajevo was to be sent to the Rajlovac depot for distribution by the Serbs to the displaced and vulnerable in those parts of what had been the District of Sarajevo which were now in Serb hands. Both sides referred to these territories by the same names: 'free Sarajevo' and 'occupied Sarajevo', but to each, of course, it had the opposite meaning.

So I took my first trip across the front line to Rajlovac which is, as the crow flies, close to Sarajevo airport. The warehouse is next to a huge railway yard and a small aircraft landing strip. I was met at the warehouse by the man responsible for distribution and his lady assistant. Milivoje Unkovic is an artist by training, a painter by choice. He was wearing an army uniform but like an artist. It did not restrict him. It was as if a Bohemian was wearing army surplus. He is a neat, gentle, handsome man. His assistant, Ljerka Jeftic, is the power. She is dark-haired with a commanding voice. Polite but firm. Also present was Ljubisa Vladusic, the Commissioner for Refugees for the Serb side, from Pale. He is young, very tall, heavy, with an open, friendly face.

Ljerka ensured we wasted no time, we were off to a strong start. The Commissioner began: 'The Srpska Republika government has set up this depot in co-ordination with the Serbian charity Dobrotvor, the Red Cross and UNHCR to supply aid to the Municipalities and to stop its manipulation.' He then added an important line: 'This is a civilian task. It has nothing to do with the army.' He beamed as I nodded approval.

Ljerka then took the floor. 'We would like a delivery of aid every two days, we are feeding two hundred thousand dependants. Forty-five per cent are refugees, women and children.' Very professional.

Then from Mr Vladusic came a very sharp question, asked with no emphasis: 'What is the population of Sarajevo at the moment, Mr Larry?'

Nice one. I thought. 'I think they are talking about three hundred and forty thousand.'

'Then we should get two-thirds of what they get.'

'I am not into numbers yet. I see the parallels and I see the tangents. Sarajevo is of course surrounded, besieged. You have access to rolling plains, open fields, woods, farms. So not all your people are entirely dependent on what the agencies bring in. Sarajevo is.'

'Why do you say Sarajevo is besieged?' Ljerka again.

'Because the roads to it are blocked by you.'

'We have opened the airport and a road for you. Also we have said that if the people want to leave they can do so.'

Both statements were true, but Bosnian truths. The road was not open to commercial traffic, the airport would never bring in enough to satisfy the total needs of the city. As to her 'also', right again. The Serb side were very keen on opening the road out of Sarajevo and permitting the whole population to leave. The Sarajevo government and UNHCR called this 'ethnic cleansing'. Sarajevans have the right to live in their own homes in Sarajevo. I went on to the offensive: 'The removal of the rightful inhabitants of the city is not an option, nor is "Stay and starve and be shelled" an option.'

Ljerka ignored this comment. I then carefully and naively explained how I, a recent arrival, saw the situation, emphasising how the Serbs were receiving a bad press for actions they could put right immediately. They were very polite and patient. Mr Vladusic and I were to become good friends. I found him always to be fair and honest, and professionally cunning.

Wiser, I returned to the airport.

A few days later we did bring in the first road convoy. It came from Split in Croatia. A team of British drivers pioneered the route. They were funded by the Overseas Development Administration (ODA). They were recruited and led by John Foster, the Emergency Planning Officer for the Isle of Man government, on loan to ODA.

The first deliveries into the city were to those people living in the Bosnian-government-dominated area. We were aware of the fact that the district of Grbavica was in Serb-held territory and that it had a large population of starving people. Furthermore, it could not be reached by the Serbs themselves from Rajlovac, so I spoke to Professor Kljic. He agreed that Grbavica needed aid. Painfully he told me that it was the area of the city where he had lived before the war. He had never had any trouble with his neighbours. He certainly felt it right and just that they should receive their share of the aid. This was a good start. He talked to his masters. They agreed. We therefore had approval to take aid out of the city into the Serb territory. We then approached the Serb side via the liaison officers. We agreed a date for a convoy and the Canadians agreed to escort it. It was to be UNHCR vehicles with UNHCR local drivers. At the last minute the Serbs vetoed this; they would not permit 'Muslims' into their territory. I should have given them an ultimatum: 'Aid food, aid drivers.' My Bosnians were prepared to go, but I compromised, which I regret. So we had to borrow drivers from the Canadians. It was a short trip and we ended up only a few yards from where we had begun, but on the other side of the river. The organisation for our reception was chaotic. There was a lot of sniper fire from the Bosnian government side. They had approved the convoy but could not resist the chance of taking shots at the reception committee. No one seemed to know where we were going to unload. If in doubt, slivovic out. They plied us with offers of drink, while they found the location and the keys. Meanwhile, we were parked out in the open, with sniper fire only a few metres away. The man with most initiative was a small, feisty priest, Father Vojislav Carkic. He ran the local Serb charity, was a parish priest and a military chaplain. He did a little shouting and a shell-damaged supermarket was opened. Then came the next crisis: there was no enthusiasm to unload. More words from the priest and a group of men were found. I forbade the Canadians to unload. It was not a precedent I wished to begin. The recipients of the aid must unload. It is difficult to restrain soldiers, especially when they, rightly, want to dump and run in the face of sniper fire.

I had been asked by Professor Kljic whether I could see if his precious books were still safe in his flat. I was assured that they were not. With a shortage of electricity, gas, wood or oil for kitchen stoves, thick, heavy economics books were especially useful. As we were leaving, Father Carkic gave to me a holy picture. 'I will give you a different one every time you bring aid. We have started off with the apostles. We need eleven more convoys for you to have your first set.' His toothless mouth stretched into a wide grin.

His companions laughed. I personally achieved only a quartet, but some of the drivers must have collected 'The Lives of the Saints'.

With the success of Grbavica, Fabrizio was determined to spread our sphere of influence even further. Dobrinja is a large suburb of Sarajevo very close to the airport. It was cut off from the city, but under the influence of the Bosnian government. The majority population are Muslims. Fabrizio decided to take aid to Dobrinja. Citing the Grbavica convoy as a precedent, he got Serb approval but took no chances. He took in a small convoy with a one-hundred-strong Canadian escort. It was successful. The irony of the day was that we achieved feeding Dobrinja but failed to get a single convoy into Sarajevo itself. 'Somebody' shelled the Canadian barracks.

That evening, Erik de Stabenrath, the French colonel, second-in-command of the French Marine Battalion in Sarajevo, came to see me. Erik is small and wiry. He has all the energy of a tightly wound watch spring. He has attended many courses in the UK and the USA and speaks excellent English. He is tough, but neither in the noisy, boorish paratrooper mould, nor in the silent, sinister SAS way. Rather in the manner of an aristocratic adventurer: an iron fist in a tailor-made glove. Erik was born to lead. I learnt to like, respect and admire him. Beating within his muscular chest is a sentimental heart. He was impressed with the convoy to Dobrinja, but believed that the key to our safety in the airport was for the combatants on all sides of the airport to see us, to know us and to be sure that we were impartial. He therefore proposed a 'Hearts and Minds' programme. He intended to nominate a liaison officer for the peripheral districts of Nedzarici and the Airport Settlements held by the Serbs, and Dobrinja and Butmir held by the government. The LOs would go into their territory every day and build up a close relationship with the community and its leaders.

'If they go in, why don't they take in aid?' asked Erik.

'Erik, this is music to our ears. We will find the aid. Good luck in getting the approval of the local commanders.' He succeeded and thus began a brilliant and vital programme.

Now that we appeared to be succeeding in delivering aid into and around Sarajevo, Fabrizio was working non-stop on organising a convoy to Gorazde. Suddenly it seemed to fall into place. The Serbs agreed to give him approval to try, UNPROFOR agreed to provide an escort, UNHCR found the trucks and we diverted the aid from Sarajevo. It was a gallant attempt. It was mined, it came under fire, it almost reached Gorazde. It lost one APC and one ten-ton truck. But it failed. On its return journey to Sarajevo it encountered more gunfire. The team returned safely but some were badly shaken and Una Sekerez, the UNHCR translator, had been lightly wounded.

When they returned, I met them at the PTT building. They were high on adrenalin. Fabrizio was pacing his office like a caged tiger. He wanted and needed a shower but could not relax, could not stand still. He told me the whole story in short bursts as he paced and turned, turned and paced. Thanks to his debrief, the next attempt would succeed, but not without incident.

After only a matter of days, Fabrizio was called to greater things, he was appointed special assistant to the Special Envoy and left for Zagreb. I moved into his office and behind his desk, which is where I was sitting when I was visited by Jeremy Brade, an Englishman, an ex-Ghurka officer, the recent head of the European Community Mission Monitors in Sarajevo and now Lord Carrington's man on the ground in former Yugoslavia. Jeremy knew everybody and everything. He knew the principal players, the splinter groups, the goodies and the baddies, and he knew the geography and the history of the place. By nodding wisely and listening intently, I was able to sketch in whole areas of deficiency in my knowledge. Jeremy is also an excellent mimic. His descriptions are accompanied by mini-portrayals. Before leaving, he warned me that there were two imminent visits from the UK: one from the Foreign Office and the other from a member of the Cabinet.

The first was from Dr Glynne Evans. She was accompanied by Andrew Pringle, a brigadier then working within the Cabinet Office. Glynne is diminutive in stature, formidable in intellect and gigantic in drive. Whatever a pentium chip does to a computer Glynne does to UN programmes. She is head of the Foreign and

Commonwealth Office UN section. A very attractive woman, she wears the most feminine of clothes, regardless of the environment. To see her alight from the rear of a Hercules C130 aircraft with flak jacket, high heels and ear-rings is an experience. She strode across the bullet-scarred tarmac as if it were a military catwalk. She is imperious, compelling and in charge. Her 'Tell me, Larry . . .' in a clipped, crystal-clear, aristocratic accent commanded undivided attention. She risked the bullets and the shells to visit the warehouse, then left Sarajevo and crossed three front lines to travel to Kiseljak to meet one of the earliest road convoys into Sarajevo. She fired penetrating, deadly accurate questions, demanding a rapid response; all delivered with charm. Tricky pauses were defused with a smile and a steely glint from her eyes.

One Glynne story should sum up her abilities. 'Larry,' she said at the end of the long tiring day. 'What would most make life easier for you here in Sarajevo?'

I had no hesitation, for I was running into the centre of the city and crossing front lines every day. 'An armoured vehicle of my own. At the moment I either waste hours begging lifts from a French APC or risk life and limb in a soft-skinned vehicle.'

'Right,' she said. The following morning she left. Three days later an armoured range rover rolled out of the back of a British Hercules. Glynne had located one in Madrid belonging to the embassy and persuaded the ambassador to loan it. She had it driven to London, serviced, then flown to Sarajevo. And remember, I am a UN employee, not a member of the Foreign and Commonwealth Office, not even on the staff of the ODA. This was to be only a minor miracle. She was soon to have three thousand British troops on the ground, fully equipped and fully trained.

The Cabinet minister proved to be the Foreign Secretary, Mr Douglas Hurd. He arrived on a very hot day. After a short meeting with General Mackenzie, he came up to our hangar and had a guided tour. He had been well briefed by Glynne. He knew about the request for the armoured car and was aware of my background. At a lunch in the PTT building hosted by the French, he had conversations with everyone. When it was my turn I was, unusually for me, a little tongue-tied, but then I don't meet Foreign Secretaries every day. In our hangar he had been in his shirt-sleeves and on the move, meeting people at their workplace. He was relaxed and easy-going. Now at lunch he was wearing his jacket and looked much more formal and formidable. I had prepared a few conversation pieces. I was going to ask him about his novel writing and if Sarajevo had given him any ideas. But on meeting him, this gem deserted me. He saved the day by talking about humanitarian aid. I liked him.

Having visited President Izetbegovic, I wanted to visit Dr Karadzic. All negotiation with the Serb side was done through the Serb liaison officers of whom there were three. Brane, a professional soldier, had served at the airport prior to the war. He is my height, with slightly greying hair, bright, warm, moist brown eyes, a neat toothbrush reddish-brown moustache, a voice which is deep, friendly and conspiratorial. He is a man of charm, humour and honour. Misha Indjic, slightly smaller, losing his hair, has lost some of his 'smiley' teeth. He has eyes like olives, dark and bitter, and a dark-brown moustache which enhances his smile and emphasises his anger. Misha is intolerably Serb and pathologically anti-Muslim. Both men speak excellent English. The third was a professor of geology, Dr Vlado Lukic, a Balkan intellectual who knows many subjects inside out but can only argue from one standpoint. Bright but inflexible, a tall, heavy man, shy to use his English, he was closest to my age. He was teased mercilessly by Brane. They lived in one room in the PTT building. They slept around the walls. Their job was incredibly difficult. When the city was shelled, UNPROFOR demanded that they contact their masters and stop it. All patrols and convoys were cleared through them. Dr Lukic was the most conscientious, the most pedantic. He would take ages to get a decision because he would process the request meticulously. Brane would pressure his masters for an answer. Misha was the most sinister – I reckon he made a lot of the decisions himself. On those he had to refer, he built in a delay factor. Both Brane and Misha spent a lot of time translating for the top generals. They both know too much. Watch your backs, boys! Dr Lukic went on to become Prime Minister.

I decided to approach Brane: 'I would like to see your big white chief. Can you fix it?' If you asked Brane a rhetorical question he answered not with words but with a smile. So he smiled and arranged an appointment at midday the following Sunday. I had only ever seen photos of Dr Karadzic, he always wore a double-breasted suit so I thought I had better wear mine. When I put it on, the cheeky Leyla wolf-whistled. It was the first and, with only one other exception, the only time they saw me wear it. They cruelly nicknamed it my Karadzic suit.

I arrived at Lukavica on time. Serb television cameras were waiting to record the event; not surprising, as the agency SRNA is a propaganda machine much favoured by the media-happy doctor. I was taken up the stairs and into the end room on the right. Dr Karadzic was there on his own. There was a buffet-type lunch on the table. He is an easy man to be with. He greeted me as if we were old friends. He asked me about the health of Jose Maria. He complained that Mrs Ogata had recently seen Izetbegovic but not him. He enquired where I was from, and through all this he helped himself and me to food.

'I'm from Liverpool.'

The inevitable happened – I got his favourite Liverpool line-up. We talked about the Sarajevo football team to whom he was the team doctor.

'Why do they need a psychiatrist? Do they keep on losing?' I asked.

'Liverpool humour,' he answered.

'I gather you are a poet,' I said as we ate (I was tucking in heartily; he had more food than we did). This changed the direction of the conversation completely.

'Do you like poetry?'

'Very much.'

'Who is your favourite poet?'

'Matthew Arnold,' I replied. Actually it is Kipling but he is after all a doctor and a president as my mother would have said. She always wanted me to keep up appearances, whatever that meant. He knew Arnold. 'Who is yours?'

'Njegos,' he answered. Actually I thought he had coughed.

It was much later that I discovered that Njegos was a famous Montenegrin.

He rummaged in his briefcase. 'I have a copy of one of my books here.' He found one. 'Do you read Serbian?'

'No.'

'Sorry, it is the only copy that I have here. I will send you a copy in English. Who is your favourite author?'

'It is a toss-up between Dickens and Tolstoy,' I replied, truthfully this time.

We talked about books. I watched his mop of hair bob about his forehead. He has prominent eyebrows. At times he looked like Lord Healey. Bosnia clones Healeys!

I was actually enjoying his company. But business is business. 'Dr Karadzic. What is your aim for Sarajevo?'

'Sometimes I believe the Muslims can have it in exchange for other areas. Sometimes I believe it could be an open city. We could have parts of it, like Jerusalem.'

He is a cartophile. He took out a map of Sarajevo and showed me the options. He then moved on to other maps, pushing the food out of the way as he spread them out. He did not do this as a general, more as a professor explorer, a Dr Challenger. He was not happy with Gorazde, a cancer in his midst. I watched and listened fascinated. I did not need to be there – he was talking to himself, to crowds, to parliament.

'Do you think it would be possible to stop the shelling of Sarajevo? At least of places like the hospital?' I asked.

'It is the Muslims' fault. They place their weapons behind the hospital and fire on us.' Sadly, I knew this frequently to be true. So I did not pursue it. We talked about the opening of the city. He would be happy to have corridors. He would be happy if all the Muslims were to leave. He would be happy for convoys to move. It was a happy day for Dr Karadzic. There was a knock on the door: his Corps commander from Ilidza.

My time was up. We shook hands. He promised me the book. I returned to Sarajevo and put the suit away. Everyone asked, 'What did he say?' I told them. No one was impressed. They'd all heard it on the radio, seen it on the tele, read it in the press, a thousand times. I went to debrief Jeremy Brade. He could do the script and the actions better than Dr Karadzic.

I never did get the book.

Meanwhile, back at the airport the RAF detachment supervised the building of a bunker to which we could race when the shelling became particularly heavy. It was tomb-like and claustrophobic. It rarely tempted the local drivers. It was a magnet to the self-contained Brits.

Our next visitor was Paddy Ashdown. This environment should suit him down to the ground. His office in London asked me if I could arrange for him an interview with President Izetbegovic. It was a hot, hot August day. Mr Ashdown got out of the Herc in shirt-sleeves and flak jacket. He was bundled into a French APC and taken to meet the French commander. Mr Ashdown is very popular, everyone wanted to meet him. He saw me and kindly recognised me, which boosted my ego. 'Larry, good to see you. When will we get together?'

'As soon as you are free.'

'I would like to stay with you and your men.'

'No probs.'

After a brief courtesy call he was back with us. He was delightful company, so easy to be with. I took him to meet General Mackenzie. Mack is in a little office in the control tower. He and Paddy speak the same straight language. The press were at his heels and he was not pulling any punches. He was highly critical of the Serbs and wanted to lift the arms embargo so that the Bosnian government could be rearmed. Taking him to see President Izetbegovic was going to be easy. Going to Pale would not.

We motored him at speed to the Presidency; front entrance, up the stairs and into the reception room. The President was waiting to see him. Paddy extended his arm. 'Hello, Mr President. Thank you for seeing me.'

He could not have predicted Mr Izetbegovic's reply: 'Hello, Mr Ashdown, I am glad to see you. I am told that you are the most handsome politician in the world.'

They got on very well. I started the meeting sitting close to

Paddy on the same settee. I then saw the Bosnian Sarajevo TV camera and heard Paddy's hard-line defence of Sarajevo, Gorazde, Tuzla, and his forthright condemnation of the Bosnian Serbs. The President was delighted. I was slowly and I hope surreptitiously sliding away from Paddy, out of the view of the camera. As noble as his views may have been, they were not the UN's, nor UNHCR's, and in parts not mine.

After the meeting he faced the international cameras. And told them exactly what he had said inside.

'Mr Ashdown, tomorrow you are going to Pale. Will you be as strong over there?'

'Yes,' he replied, not knowing what the result would be.

We returned to the hangar. The shelling was continuous and dangerous. We decided to spend the night in the bunker, where we had developed a routine and a system. Lee and his boss, Squadron Leader Willie Dobson, had the wall slots. I was piggy in the middle and Ron slept at the entrance. With Paddy staying it was going to be a little more cosy. I had with me a small hammock, so I gave my bed space to Paddy and slung the hammock from the supporting girders.

Paddy had brought some refreshments, we provided the mugs. It was a hot, sticky night, so we sat huddled around the entrance to the bunker and watched the battle rage between the Airport Settlement and Dobrinja. There was a sound-and-light show to rival Jean-Michel Jarre. As usual, we went to bed early. Equally as usual, I was up first. Reminding myself that I was in a hammock, I climbed out slowly and, in the dark, found my shoes, grabbed my towel and toothbrush – not for me the hassle of razor and brush. I clambered out of the bunker, paused at the entrance, then made a dash for the hangar, hoping that the snipers were not looking for an early kill.

Nonjo and Ploco were in the hangar but not at the tap, so I washed. As I dried my face, I looked down at my feet and thought to myself, 'That's a fine pair of shoes, Larry.' I then realised that the fine pair of shoes on my feet certainly did not belong to me. I raced back to the bunker. Paddy was still in his sleeping bag. I quietly put his shoes back in place and put on mine. If any of you

Lib Dems wish to step into Paddy's shoes I can tell you they are 11s.

Today was Pale day for Paddy. I was to take him to the Serb military headquarters in Lukavica. The Serbs had agreed to take him on to Pale. Paddy always seemed to enjoy the challenge of the Butmir 400, the exposed four hundred metres of front line between the Serb and the government troops guaranteed to increase the heart rate. The French have raised a memorial at the entrance in commemoration of those whom they have lost on its deadly tarmac.

At Lukavica we met Brane, the Serb liaison officer. They were ready for 'the distinguished guest'. They had laid on a BMW, the only time I ever saw them do this. They had also laid on an interpreter, a lady. We shook hands and Paddy left. The arrangements, confirmed by Brane, were that they would host him, give him an official dinner and return him the following morning.

Mr Ashdown was as forthright as he promised the press he would be. Dr Karadzic had not expected such a strong speech but he had the last word. When Paddy left the hotel to return to Sarajevo, there was no car and no translator. Paddy, in a none too friendly environment and without an interpreter, had to find a car for himself. This was no challenge to an ex-marine: he found a taxi. When he eventually arrived in Lukavica I was there to meet him. We returned to Sarajevo. He left for England. I next saw him in Sarajevo a few weeks later. He was to become a regular and very welcome visitor.

The airlift roared and rumbled on. At the end of each month donor nations pledged their aircraft. More nations joined, some for a token flight, others for the long haul. A few of the flights carried VIP passengers, many carried people who thought they were VIPs. An American Herc landed and out tumbled a large US senator who was a senior member of the Armed Forces Committee. He was accompanied by a press team from the forces newspaper, the *Stars and Stripes*. The Herc would be on the ground for a maximum of twelve minutes. The senator saw me and shouted, 'Here, sonny, over here. Stand by me and I'll make you famous.' I am not too sure who was more embarrassed, the photographer or me.

The Hercules crews deserve a very special mention. They did their job with great courage but always wanted to do more. They had a strict rotation pattern, crews and craft returning to Lyneham after a tour of four weeks. The new crews brought from the UK sufficient meat, sausages and beer for both international and local staff to have a good relaxing party. We never paid for this, they did. They did many other small kindnesses. They made phone calls for refugees, posted letters, changed money. I particularly remember Chris Tingay and his crew once finding me looking especially tired. On the next flight he sent up two crates of pot noodles with a little note: 'You look weak. Take one twice a day with water.' Water we had. They were delicious, nourishing and restored our strength. We did not always remember to say thanks at the time but a big thanks now may not be too late.

The one thousandth flight of the airlift came around quickly. It was on 2 September. We were all excited by it, it was touch and go which nation it would be. In Zagreb there was a lot of friendly rivalry and jockeying for the honour. Mike Aitcheson, the UNHCR airlift co-ordinator, was refereeing. We had no way of throwing a party but the event was marked by the boys who made a huge '1000 Flight' banner. When the plane approached, I could see that it was a Brit Herc. I was now especially pleased. The Herc landed, the crew got out and we shook hands; it was all a little flat and disappointing. Then Mike Aitcheson appeared at the door with promotion hats and banners from the brewery King and Barnes who, via Mike's local, the Plough at Blackbrook, had donated a lot of English ale to celebrate the occasion. Mike had it with him. The day was suitably celebrated. The local staff were thrilled. Well done, Mike, and thanks to Robin Squire, the landlord of the Plough. That day ended on a high, the next in disaster.

The airlift was running as usual. Zagreb informed us by sat-phone of the take-off of the aircraft, the tower in Sarajevo told us the arrival time. A well-established procedure after more than a thousand flights. Mike notified us of the take-off of the Italian plane and of the flight following it. The later plane arrived first. Unusual, but it had happened before. We waited for the Italian.

No news. Both UNHCR and the tower contacted Zagreb. No news. The aircraft was posted as missing. Eerily we kept looking into the sky, but it never came. In the early afternoon the rumours began that an aircraft had been shot down in the hills close to Sarajevo. Erik de Stabenrath took out a group of marines to investigate. UNHCR sent with him Ed Bishop, our immensely bright and energetic American Programme officer whose qualifications included holding a pilot's licence. Tony Land was visiting the Croat headquarters in Kiseljak on his journey back to Zagreb. The Croats told him of the downing of an aircraft and the discovery of wreckage. He set off to find it.

He met Erik and Ed at the crash site. The Hercules was carrying bales of blankets. It came down on a wooded hillside. The wreckage was spread over a small area. It had destroyed trees, small fires were smouldering, the smoke curling up to the roof of trees bedecked in blankets which were strewn for miles. The bodies of the crew were brought back to Sarajevo. The Italian government announced that the aircraft had been shot down by a missile. Morale crashed. The airlift was suspended. It was vital to Sarajevo but it was expensive in cash terms and now it had proved expensive in lives. Could, would, nations be prepared to continue to risk crews and aircraft? Should crews risk their lives to bring in food to feed all three sides when at least one side had men sick enough to shoot them down? Whenever the airlift stopped we always had the feeling and the fear that it would not restart.

The airport was strange and silent – like a school playground on a Sunday. With no airlift we had little aid, so we decided to empty the hangars, taking what sparse stock we had into the city. We chose a bad day. While unloading at the main warehouse, heavy shelling began and the compound received seven shells. One vehicle was badly damaged but there were no casualties. A local Jonah suggested that there would soon be a third incident. We adjourned and returned the following day, when fifteen rounds of sniper fire zinged around the trucks. Told-you-so Jonah was very happy. But wrong! There was a fourth incident. A narrow escape for Ed Bishop in the hangar. I was standing near my bedspace tidying up my corner, Ed at the desk speaking to Zagreb on the satellite phone, with Sejo, the driver, close to him. A single machine-gun round came flying through the hangar window above me on a downward trajectory. It missed Ed by an inch and hit the desk. Splinters hit Sejo. I thought of Jonah and wondered if this counted as a triple or if it was the first in a new cycle. As we were silently and reflectively cleaning up the slivers and splinters, there was a hearty 'Hello' at the door. It was cheerful, irrepressible Kate Adie from the BBC. 'Anything happening?' she asked.

All in all, not a good week.

3
Into Gorazde

My quest to get into Gorazde was given a strong push by the arrival from Geneva of Leon Davico, a Belgrade-born retired UN senior official, who globe-trots on missions of mercy and peace. He gave me an introduction to Mrs Plavsic. This was excellent news for me. She was a professor of biology at the University of Sarajevo and had a flat in Sarajevo, but most importantly, now as Vice-President of the so-called Srpska Republika she lived in Pale and in Belgrade, and was responsible for Humanitarian Affairs. I was to meet her at the Serb army headquarters barracks at Lukavica on the outskirts of Sarajevo. When we arrived it was obvious we were expected. We were taken upstairs to the main conference room at the end of the corridor and offered coffee, then Mrs Plavsic arrived. She is a tall, well-built lady with a very strong Slav face. She has a fine head of mouse-brown hair. Her English is slow and hesitant, but fluent. She was charming and calm.

While we were talking, shelling began. Mrs Plavsic said that whenever the 'Muslims' saw that Lukavica had a visitor they shelled. For sure, these were incoming rounds and they were not very far away. Suddenly there was an enormous crash; a shell had landed very close. We had heard the whistle and the thud, felt the windows rattle and the pressure change. A soldier who was outside the door entered the room and told us to get away from the windows. Mrs Plavsic, I noted, was unflustered. She picked up her notes and her coffee and moved towards the door. There was another great bang, but this was an outgoing reply to the 'Muslim' intrusion. The soldier suggested that we find a less exposed room, one with less glass. We moved down the stairs to a tiny room with a single window. It was also at the side of the building.

Mrs Plavsic took all this in her solid stride. We resumed our talk. I took the lead and explained that there was tremendous pressure on us to get aid through to Gorazde. 'UNHCR, led by Fabrizio Hochschild, whom I know you know well, has made one attempt but the convoy lost an APC and a truck in mine explosions.'

Mrs Plavsic confirmed that she knew Fabrizio well. 'I had supported the convoy attempt and was sad at its outcome. I have no objection to you trying a convoy, but before you attempt Gorazde I would like you to try to relieve two other "Muslim" villages which are cut off and desperate.'

This answer was not what I expected. Her magnanimity took me by surprise. She went on to say, 'There are Serb majority villages, isolated and starving, which I should also like you to attempt to reach.' This was good news for me, as I knew that all take and no give would not work in this environment. I showed great enthusiasm to learn the location of all these villages.

She was well prepared for my visit. She called in an army officer and arranged a further meeting for us with some military officers to pinpoint these other locations. She implied that a successful attempt on the easier targets would earn full support for an attempt on Gorazde. At no time did she say 'No' to an attempt on Gorazde.

I returned to Sarajevo and went to see Lt-Col. Erik de Staben-rath at the airport. His battalion had rescued the last attempt at Gorazde. Erik and I had spoken and were determined that we were going to relieve the siege of Gorazde together. Erik's background intrigued me. The name de Stabenrath is obviously not French. An ancestor of his had been secretary to one of the Louises who had ruled France. But Erik's father had commanded the French Foreign Legion at Dien Bien Phu. The parallels between the French position in besieged, surrounded Sarajevo and in Dien Bien Phu were uncanny. Erik's father had died in the closing hours of the battle. In an unguarded moment, the reserved aristocrat told me of the time, as a tiny child, when he had told his nanny that he no longer had a father. Long before the news was known, long before it could have travelled, he 'knew'.

Erik took me in to see his senior, Colonel Patric Sartre. Erik is the second-in-command of the marines, both he and Sartre are small and tough. Interestingly, they both have strawberry birthmarks on their faces, though they tell me that it is not a compulsory feature for promotion. We discussed the 'Plavsic' proposal. Colonel Sartre requested that he attend my meeting with the military, when I would learn about the Serb and 'Muslim' villages.

I returned to the PTT building to see the liaison officers; the government ones to tell them about the progress towards a Gorazde convoy and the Serb ones to arrange a meeting with the military. The following day Indjic gave me the details, Mrs Plavsic did not hang about! The meeting was to be at Pale, the capital of the so-called Srpska Republika where Mrs Plavsic had her Vice-Presidential office.

Sartre picked me up at the airport and we went in his APC. We had with us Svetlana, his translator. Before we got to Pale our APC was stopped by a Serb patrol and we were told that the venue was not to be Pale but Jahorina, the ski resort, the famous host of the 1984 Winter Olympics.

We pulled in with our APC at this great resort hotel and were met by Mrs Plavsic on the steps. We were escorted to the conference room; in attendance were Mrs Plavsic and some senior army officers. We were told what was expected of us. The 'Muslim' villages were Podzieblje and Godzenje. We were given grid references, timings, lunch and wine. Doing business with Vice-President Plavsic was a pleasure. Interestingly, she did not mention isolated Serb villages. This was a no-linkage offer. Armed with the grid references, we planned our movements. Gorazde would be on the following Thursday, the two isolated 'Muslim' villages we would do on the Tuesday before.

Tuesday's convoy was action-packed, but failed. We had a Serb military escort. We ended up in a clearing in dense woods. Our path was blocked by huge felled trees. We were very close to the villages but 'very close' does not fill stomachs. As darkness fell, Sarajevo ordered us to return. I was very disappointed and felt a failure. Fortunately Mrs Plavsic was still keen to permit an attempt on Gorazde. With Erik commanding the military I felt full of optimism.

We loaded the convoy the night before we set off. My Sarajevo drivers could not drive their vehicles; the Serbs would have given them too much hassle and the convoy was too important to risk on principles. Although they could not drive, they were still going to be part of it. They serviced, cleaned and loaded every vehicle with care and determination. The drivers would be Ukrainians. I had insisted that they sleep in the hangar the night before the convoy, as they were not renowned for their ability to be on time. I settled into my cosy corner with all the activity continuing around me. All sorts of thoughts raced through my head and kept me awake. Would we be mined like Fabrizio? Would we get shot at? Would anybody die? Would we get there? Try as I might, I could not drop off to sleep and when Nonjo came to wake me at five with a cup of tea I was wide awake. I got up, washed and kick-started the drivers. The Ukrainians were stretched out in their coarse uniforms, tall, stocky peasants, sound asleep. Nonjo then called me over to the table; very touchingly, he had cooked a special breakfast for me.

My own drivers were putting finishing touches to the vehicles, carefully stacking and loading vital medicines for a hospital with a daily intake of patients wounded by mortar shells and sniper fire, a hospital carrying out major surgery without anaesthetics. We lined up the transport and the French escort arrived. It was exhilarating. I felt proud and excited; the adrenalin was running. The dawn was bright, warm and still, Sarajevo was quiet. The local staff wished us every form of luck. The military call the start time of an operation 'H hour'. We crossed the start line at H hour; not a second before, not a second later. We were on French marine timings.

In the convoy was a contingent of the best of the press. Jeremy Bowen of the BBC, a seasoned war correspondent whose age has yet to catch up with his appearance. He is a tall, heavy man with a gravelly voice of authority. He interviews, without finesse, on a 'Your job is to be here, my job is to be here, let's get on with it' basis, which I like. His cameraman was Nick Millard from ZDF. From Reuters there was the terrier-like journalist Kurt Schork, aggressive and persistent, and the very attractive, efficient and brave Corinne Dufkas, one of the finest photographers in the business, who had started her career as an aid worker in South America. The smooth Patrick Rahir represented AFP and kept the French on their toes.

At Lukavica we were met by Brane. Always an honest, good man, he genuinely wished us luck. The tall Serb in the APC swung out of the Serb barracks, moved to the front of the convoy and led the way.

The road as far as Sokolac was that which we had taken on our unsuccessful trip a few days previously. Looking at it for the second time, it contrasted starkly with poor Sarajevo. The fields were green and full of crops. Houses were complete, windows intact, children played. Materially, these Serbs were untouched by war, mentally they were scarred by the propaganda pushed out from the TV and radio stations of Belgrade and Pale. They could not see the suffering that their soldiers were inflicting on innocent civilians in Sarajevo, they could hear only of the alleged impending atrocities about to be committed by 'Muslim hordes'.

We arrived, still following the Serb APC, at Rogatica. Here, outside a flour mill, the convoy was halted. Here it was to be inspected by the Serbs to ensure that it contained no weapons or ammunition for Gorazde. The inspection was carried out under the auspices of the Milicija, the police. The Chief of Police of Rogatica, who had held the post before the war, invited myself, Erik and some journalists to his office where we drank slivovic. His office was towards the far end of Rogatica, so we were able to see for the first time the damage done to a front-line town. Before the war, Rogatica had been a majority 'Muslim' town. There had been bitter fighting over it. The Serb army had driven the 'Muslims' out and they had fled into Gorazde. The centre of the town was destroyed, every shop window shattered, most buildings burned. The shopping centre is just one long, narrow street. The proximity of one side of the street to the other emphasised the destruction. Literally, the damaged buildings leaned over you and hemmed you in. Not a place for the claustrophobic. The Chief was very friendly. I gave him a bottle of whisky, he assured me that we would have no trouble from the Serb side but he was certain that the 'Muslims' would attack the convoy and put the blame on the Serbs. He therefore gave me a formal warning that as we left Rogatica the Serbs would no longer guarantee our safety and that we were proceeding at our own risk and against their professional advice. This was the first time I was given this speech, the first of many times. The bizarre, devious events that followed this convoy were an early lesson to me in the 'Balkan' factor.

We returned to the convoy; the inspection was going well.

I briefed the journalists and the drivers: 'If we are ambushed drive on like bats out of hell, if we are mortared keep moving, if a vehicle is hit and the road blocked get out and seek cover. If you get out in a hurry look before you leap. At some stretches the road clings to the mountainside with a sheer drop of a hundred or more feet. If we stop and you want to urinate do it at the roadside, forget modesty, to attempt to find a secluded spot may result in your genitals immodestly spread over the countryside if you stand on a mine. Any questions?'

'Can you show me where we are going on the map?' Kurt Schork of Reuters wanted my finger to trace the route. I was soon to learn that this was the most innocuous question that Kurt had ever asked. Normally he delivers the fast ball that dents the ground and smashes the wickets. Jeremy Bowen gave the map his full undivided attention. He was driving the press vehicle. If he was separated from the convoy, he wanted to know exactly who was where.

The Serb APC and the Chief of Police's car escorted us to the boundary of Rogatica, conveniently at the entrance to a gorge. We waved to the Serbs, took a sharp right-hand bend and were on a wide tarmacked road in a steep-sided valley. There were huge rocks on the road which had fallen from above: a peacetime hazard in an eerie area full of potential wartime evil. Since the outbreak of the war, only Fabrizio's convoy had travelled this far. Somewhere ahead we would find the debris of part of his convoy. We travelled at a slow speed in a strange silence. Birds must have twittered, the river was but yards away but we did not hear it gush and flow.

Turning off on to the mountain route, we could see our road ahead. It wound its way up an isolated mountain. Within a few hundred metres we encountered our first hazard, a rickety wooden bridge with a weight restriction of 2 tons. All our trucks weighed more than 10 tons. I decided we would risk it. Erik agreed to send an APC across to secure the other side. The APC is no test of weight for a bridge, as their enormous tyres and design specialities distribute their weight more successfully than a truck's. I marshalled each vehicle across the bridge individually, they paused about 100 metres before the bridge, then went at great speed. I waited for the vibrations to stop before sending another. The bridge was obviously grossly underestimated, it eventually took many a convoy. I was able to study the face of each driver. All sat alert and upright in their cabs. Tension was mounting.

Soon after the bridge there was a sharp right-hand hairpin bend. It was made negotiable by our trucks because to the left of it extended a rocky plateau at the base of a sheer, needle-like mountain. The trucks were able to swing wide on to the plateau. Up at the top of the needle were 'Muslim' forces. It was their outpost; high, safe and secure. They shared caves with mountain goats whose muffled, plaintive bleats travelled across the still valley. From these observation posts, the Bosnian army was able to report to Gorazde who was approaching. From their eyries they could also snipe at Serb patrols and at us. We felt very exposed. Dragon, my driver, was dividing his attention between the narrow track and the 'Muslim' outposts. His eyes darted from hilltop to track. I could sense that he was nervous. Justifiably so, for if the Bosnian troops stopped us, he might be the first unarmed Serb they had seen for many months. The French soldiers in the APCs were also reacting to the environment. Some searched the hills for movement, others the roads for mines. All held their weapons cocked and ready.

We passed this defile without incident. One hundred and fifty metres on, there was another bend, at which we found a small Serb position, three soldiers in good humour. Just before the next bend – another right-hander and exceedingly sharp – we came upon the debris of the APC from Fabrizio's convoy. I paused while I recollected his account of the events after the vehicle hit a mine, lost a wheel and overturned. We swung past the discarded APC axle, wheel and other debris and moved to the top of the mountain. We could just see Gorazde, way down in the distance. I was really excited, but still not sure if we would make it. We could also see a strong Serb military post and behind it the remains of the leading 10-ton truck from Fabrizio's convoy which had hit a second mine as he had bravely attempted to continue the morning after the APC explosion. I anticipated trouble from the Serbs. They looked a wild bunch but they gave me no hassle and the media some excellent pictures. From their positions on the summit, the Serbs could see the whole panorama of the city of Gorazde. Their guns were trained on the strategic points. They could be in no doubt where their shells were landing. Tenement blocks, the hospital, gathering crowds were all clearly visible. It needed no military skill to land a shell in Gorazde. I was never present on the hills around Sarajevo or Gorazde when Serb heavy guns were fired. I would like to have seen the faces of those who fired. Did they celebrate, cheer; did they smile, laugh, slap their thighs when their rounds landed? I suspect they did. Did any feel sick with sadness or shame? There was a story, which I was never able to prove but which I am sure is true, that bus-loads of Serbs motored from Belgrade to the outskirts of Gorazde to join the guns and to fire 'their' round into Gorazde. Men whose number one sport was hunting swapped their quarry from boar and bear to 'Muslims'.

The hilltop Serbs let us pass. We had one more check-point to go, half-way down the road into Gorazde. As we descended this road, you could touch, feel, our excitement. We could see Gorazde, so close. Surely we would reach her. We were stopped at the final check-point. The Serbs were not sure we had approval to advance. We must wait for a military commander.

Jeremy Bowen was out of his vehicle, ensuring that he got as much footage as he could, just in case we were turned back. I sat at the side of the road with Dragon, then walked over to Erik, who smiled, but I knew his smile hid as much tension and apprehension as mine. So close. Dragon was trying to avoid the Serb soldiers; he did not want any last-minute hassle with them.

The commander arrived, a small, grey-haired man aged about fifty. He confirmed that we had permission but warned me that ahead lay no man's land. He was certain the 'Muslims' had laid mines. He, like his senior counterpart in Rogatica, gave us approval to pass, but at our own risk. We passed his barrier and moved towards our goal. The road was deserted. Bricks, stones, fallen branches littered it. Ahead of me was one APC, then Erik's vehicle; behind me the press and the convoy. The first wave of excitement was when we saw the road sign 'Gorazde'. It was scarred with bullets but it meant we were there. Just after the sign was a gentle bend to the left and as we came out of it the roof-tops of a whole Gorazde street were on our right. Many of the houses were destroyed. There was no sign of life.

I halted the convoy. Erik stopped his vehicle and came over to me.

'Erik, I think you and I should walk in on our own from here.'

'My view exactly,' he replied.

We set off together. The APC and the convoy, including journalists, halted. God, we were so excited! It was a mixture of achievement, expectation and joy. As we walked down the hill, there were some large buildings on our right. Each was gouged with shrapnel. Bullets had sprayed up the walls. Window-frames were buckled, none were covered. In some, curtains flapped in the gentle summer breeze. I was wearing my white helmet and flak jacket, Erik his flak jacket. I tried to walk tall, with my shoulders back and my head held high. Erik was almost strolling. He was calm. He wore his pistol but his hands were at his side.

'It seems deserted, Erik.'

'I think there is some movement in the basement,' he said very quietly.

At the bottom of the hill there was a crossroad. There had been traffic lights and street lamps but the posts and the wiring hung awry. The shops on the corner were also windowless, glass strewn everywhere. We turned right towards where we thought the centre of town might be; we were still alone. There was absolute silence: no noise from the convoy behind us and complete stillness from the city around us. Now we were walking along a pavement and the buildings were within touching distance. They were drab blocks of apartments, each with a tiny concrete-encased balcony. The doorways to each block were open. We could see in. They were dark, dirty and deserted.

'There are people looking out of balcony windows,' whispered Erik.

Feeling foolish, I shouted in Serbo-Croat, '*Visoki Kome sarijat. United Nations.*'

A man appeared. He was in his fifties, small, jolly and very emotional. His clothes indicated that he had once been plump. He embraced Erik and myself. People now appeared in doorways, mainly women and children. Then balconies filled. The man told us that he was to take us and the convoy to the centre of the town. Erik and I turned to go back to the convoy. The journalists were on our tail, cameras thrusting, pencils gliding over notebooks. A wave of the arm was all that was needed for the convoy to move. As it entered the town, people appeared from everywhere, they clapped and cheered and wept and sobbed and embraced us. They placed flowers on the vehicles. I could see the faces of small children in the crowd. They were bewildered as they were jostled and pushed. Minutes ago their parents were apprehensive of these strangers, suspecting a Serb advance, now they were holding them and kissing them. We, to a man, were overwhelmed. I saw journalists and soldiers with eyes damper than my own.

At the centre of the town we were met by the man responsible for receiving the aid. The place was a carpet of broken glass. The people of Gorazde could not risk their lives sweeping it up. Your feet crunched as you walked about on it. Part of the aid was to go to the basement of a building in the centre. A chain of men was organised to unload those vehicles which carried baby food. Two more locations were decided upon. They wanted the food dispersed. They were convinced that the Serbs would shell wherever we unloaded. They were later proved right.

The mayor wanted to see us and we wanted to see him. We also wanted to visit the hospital to deliver the medicines we had brought. Dragon, my driver, who as a Serb had been really afraid about entering Gorazde, had been recognised by old university friends, smothered in kisses, cuddled, presented with flowers and now felt confident enough to lead off, on his own, one of the groups of vehicles to be unloaded. Erik and I went together to the mayor. His office was hidden in the back streets of the city, in an area comparatively hard to shell. We were led there, running across notorious sniper locations. It was a dingy, dark office. For our benefit the room was lit by a tiny bulb powered by a car battery. Erik handed out the cigarettes. Eyes glowed, there was a clamour to get one. That day I was to learn that if the first convoy into a besieged town carried only cigarettes it would be welcomed. They were desperate for a cigarette made from tobacco. They had their own, made from leaves and rolled in newspaper.

The mayor, Hadzo Efendic, I was eventually to know well. After the tragic death of Mr Tureljevic he was to become Vice-President of Bosnia. He welcomed us and told us the story of the city: the deaths, the deprivations, the despair. He was straight and blunt. He asked why we had taken so long to come to their rescue; why the United Nations had allowed the Serbs to block our access. When did we anticipate we would be back? What were we going to do for his sick and wounded and elderly? He pointed out that the contents of our convoy were sufficient to feed only some of the citizens for a matter of hours. Selfishly, childishly and innocently, I had actually hoped for some thanks and some praise. I left him with the diplomatic Erik, who patiently and sympathetically explained the limitations of the United Nations troops in Bosnia.

I left for the hospital.

Soon after our arrival the Serbs had dropped three mortar shells into Gorazde. In fairness to their promise, they had landed them on the far side of the river well away from us. They missed us but they did kill and maim some citizens of Gorazde. As we arrived at the hospital they were being brought in. One victim was a three-year-old girl whose mother had been killed outright. The little girl had multiple shrapnel wounds.

I arrived at the same time as Jeremy Bowen of the BBC. We entered the casualty department. The hospital had no electricity, the room was dark. The surgeon, Alija Begovic, was digging the shards of metal out of the body of the writhing child. There was no anaesthetic; the small amount we had brought was not yet unloaded. The girl's screams were piercing, sounds etched on my memory's tape recorder, later to be heard at unguarded moments. The surgeon saw the TV cameraman whose camera had a light attached to it. He called him over; he needed the light to work by, to remove the slivers from where the child was bleeding. We watched as the cameraman closed in on the girl held down by the nurses. We outsiders were stunned and silent. The Gorazde hospital staff had seen and done it so many times before, they were able to accept that this was Gorazde in 1992. To me it was a scene from centuries ago. It was not caused by earthquake, or accident. This orphaned child lay bleeding and screaming because some man had fired a mortar bomb into the heart of a city. I watched battle-hardened veteran correspondent Bowen. He was dark and silent as he prepared the words for his 'piece to camera'. As we left the room where the girl lay, we passed the other mortar victims waiting for treatment. My heart went out to them. To sit outside a room, to hear the screaming, to know that your turn is next.

I went off to the third location to see how the unloading was going. It wasn't. Or at best it was going very slowly. I started to get angry. 'I want this truck unloaded now. I'll give you thirty minutes to do it or I'll take it back.' I felt guilty because the men were as thin as rakes. God knows how weary and tired they must have been.

Opposite us was a police station. A policeman came over to me. 'Mr Larry, don't get angry. They are not lazy. They are taking their time simply because they do not want you to go. They know that when you go the shelling will start again and probably worse than before to punish us for your visit.'

I understood their fears, their hunger and their reluctance, but I had an obligation to my convoy. We had told the Serbs we would be out before dark. The road we had come along was bad enough by day. To negotiate it by night would be reckless. Besides, by now it might be mined. The locals were not interested in my problems, they proceeded at a very slow pace. I was not prepared to compromise nor was I about to take any of the food back as I had threatened. 'Right. We will dump the sacks straight on to the floor. This will make life more difficult for you. Instead of them going straight on to your shoulders, you will have to pick them up.' We began to unload them, in the hope that more people would help us. They simply called my bluff. We dumped the whole lot on the floor and had emptied the trucks in half an hour.

All three convoy sections met back at the town centre. We said farewell to the mayor. We promised faithfully to be back. Before we left, the French Marine Battalion Public Relations warrant officer, Bernard Carrier, took a photo of a very happy Erik and myself shaking hands. The photo I saw much later in a magazine when I was in Rwanda. It was captioned, 'Bravo, Erik. Well done, Larry.' So far so good. We now had to get the convoy back safely. We left the cheering, clapping crowd and headed back. We were late. We would at least clear the first check-point before dark, probably we could get beyond the summit of the hill. We would then need an unhindered run down the twisting road to make it to Rogatica, where we would stay overnight. It was a slow haul up the hill. The Serb check-points were interested in the conditions inside. The majority seemed genuinely concerned, but I remember one in particular who said, 'If the conditions are so bad why don't they surrender?'

In truth, having the image of the little girl fresh in my mind, I was not in a pro–Serb mood. By the time we reached the summit, Erik and I knew that we were going to need a lot of luck if we were to reach Rogatica that night. 'How far do you think we can go?' I asked him.

'We must still aim for Sarajevo,' he replied, then after a long pause, 'and hope we reach Rogatica.'

We passed again the remains of the 10-ton truck of Fabrizio's convoy. Now that we had been into Gorazde we could appreciate just how close they had been to achieving their aim. I silently saluted Fabrizio.

By now, night had fallen and we decided that I would travel in the leading APC, which was commanded by a really bright young French lieutenant who spoke beautiful English. We started the descent. The APC has a spotlight and the young officer stood in the commander's hatchway and swept the dirt road with the beam of the light as we motored along at a very steady pace. It was a dark night, the mountain was on our left and the hedge of trees delineating the track and preventing us from falling to the next level was on our right. Both mountain and trees captured the dark and enveloped the convoy.

As we approached the sharp hairpin bend which led to the foot of the sheer rise where earlier we had seen the 'Muslim' look-out, the lieutenant slowed the APC down to the pace of an escargot. On our way up he had fleetingly seen a suspicious pile of stones at the side of the road, the sort of location where a mine could be laid at short notice. As we inched forward, he caught the mound in the beam. He stopped the APC. Slowly he traversed the light across the track. In its beam, his sharp eyes saw a wire stretching from the mound of stones to the other side of the track. He was on the radio to Erik, who came forward. I got out of the APC and together we slowly, in my case somewhat clumsily, advanced to the wire. At Erik's order, the lieutenant held the gaze of the lamp on the pile of stones. There, clearly visible, was a mine, an evil mix of plastic, metal and high explosive. A few more feet forward and the APC would have set it off. It was so positioned that it would have done most damage to the officer standing in the hatchway. Erik spoke on the radio and soon we had a small gathering of experts.

'The end of a long day,' I said to Erik.

'*Non*,' said a warrant officer. 'We can shoot it and set it off. Then proceed.'

I was not happy with this. It may be the gung-ho marine answer, but it was not my recommendation. 'What happens if it is the first of a number of mines? Do we go down the road shooting at all mounds of rocks? Whoever laid it knows it is there. The side that didn't probably doesn't. Therefore, if we fire even a single round, let alone set off a mine, we could find ourselves in a fire-fight.'

Erik was in no doubt. 'We do nothing till dawn.' Sandhurst and St Cyr were in agreement.

By now, the press corps were happy snapping from a distance. For them the convoy was getting better by the minute. We gathered the drivers together, briefed them and warned everyone to make minimum noise. Mess tins rattled, cans were opened, bottles produced. I particularly remember a good single malt emerging from the bottom of Jeremy Bowen's bag. Whatever the drink, whatever the food, the conversation was the same in every group. 'Who has laid the mine and why?'

'The Serbs.' They usually were blamed for everything so it was natural that someone should start off with them.

'But why, what have they got to gain? Surely they would have mined the road on our way in to prevent us reaching Gorazde,' said someone applying logic.

'Yes, if they had laid it on our way in, the Serbs could easily have said that it was part of the "Muslim" defence,' added a man with a little more time in the Balkans behind him.

'It was the Serbs. They did it, knowing that we would blame the "Muslims".' An old Balkan hand talking.

During the long night, the answer partly became clear. Behind and above us there was a lot of noise. The French had deployed guards and listening posts. They reported that armed men were moving around us. The marines knew their mandate. If attacked, they could return fire. If not, they sat still and observed. Erik had great faith in their training. It could not have been easy for them. The armed groups were close enough to be heard and seen, but far enough away not to be identified.

At first we feared an ambush. We were in a perfect position. We considered moving the convoy back, but not seriously, as there was no room to turn and every vehicle would have to be reversed in the dark on a narrow road with a steep drop. Also, had we now been mined behind us? If you cannot go forward and you cannot go back, you make the best of staying.

At the height of the movement behind our position another clue as to who had laid the mine fell into place. A mortar bomb came whooshing through the dark sky and landed among the trees about one hundred metres behind us. The trees shielded the flash, the blast and the splinters. The mortar had undoubtedly come from Serb positions ahead of us in the direction of Rogatica. It was unlikely that the Serbs would fire on Serb troops. I was later to learn that this was not a hard and fast rule. Balkan forces could deliberately fire on their own in order to blame the other side. But this night we were convinced that the troops moving around us were Bosnian forces from Gorazde. They had mined us in and were using us as a screen while they moved. The mortar was a warning shot from the Serbs who knew what was going on.

'Erik, do you think the Serbs will fire any more?'

'No, I do not think they will risk hitting the convoy. But if I were you, Larry, I would sleep in one of my APCs.' So saying,

Erik stretched out in his flimsy little jeep. But I knew that before long he would be up, out and at the forward sentry posts. I have to admit that I took his advice and found a corner in an APC. Dragon slept in the back of a truck.

We were awake before dawn. We wanted to see the situation by daylight. Erik and I watched the sun come up. Accompanied by his lieutenant, we could now clearly see the mine and the wire. The APC moved back a few metres. We placed a branch across the road. No one was to move further forward than this. It was a necessary precaution as the lady and gentlemen of the press were dancing around and over the wire. I was worried that one of them might attempt to limbo under it.

Having decided that the mine was laid by the Bosnian side, we agreed that I would go forward with Erik to the clearing and would try to attract the attention of the Bosnian forces in their eyrie. This I would do with a United Nations flag attached to a branch from a tree, shouting my favourite words, '*Visoki Komesarijat.*' I did this, much to the amusement of the soldiers, the joy of the press and the embarrassment of myself.

While I was performing, Erik was looking at the clearing with his professional eye. 'Larry, there are more mines here. These are anti-tank.'

I stopped my 'Relief of Mafeking' semaphore act and joined him at the perimeter of a fresh pile of stones clearly covering a large green dish designed to tear the wheels off any of our vehicles.

'Very well placed,' said Erik. 'There is no way the convoy could have avoided it. To swing around the bend you had to go over the mine. It would have had a more devastating effect on our progress than the first one.'

'Erik, if we have two we may have more.' I returned to my cabaret act but attracted nothing and no one.

Erik got on his battalion radio net to Sarajevo, by morse, and told them of the latest developments. We were instructed to sit tight, a meaningful HQ decision in the circumstances. Sarajevo first asked the Serbs if they would clear the mines. Apparently they said 'Yes' until they realised where they were. They then said '*No*'.

Sarajevo then decided to send the engineers out from the

marines at the airport, from the same battalion who were escorting us. This all took time. We spent the whole day and the whole night in the custody of these mines. It was half-way through the next day when we heard that the marines were in the area. They arrived cautiously and slowly, which was just as well. At the bridge with the 2-ton limit they found more mines. It was late in the afternoon before they had made safe the mine with the wire and a little later when they detonated the anti-tank mine in the road. We were then free to move, forty hours after the sharp-eyed lieutenant spotted the wire. Incidentally, he was later to receive an award for his professionalism. We returned to Rogatica where we were met by an extremely agitated Brane.

'Mr Larry, get the convoy through here as fast as you can. You are not welcome here. The people may attack your convoy.'

'Brane, what has happened?'

'While you were mined in, the Muslims moved their troops, using your convoy as a shield. They came into Rogatica, there was a battle and twelve from the town are dead. This is the largest number of casualties in one battle in this area since the war began. They are very anti-UN, anti-UNHCR and especially anti-you, Mr Larry.'

I liaised with Erik and directed the convoy to speed through Rogatica. As I was talking to him, two Serb commanders from Rogatica came up to me, their faces black with anger. One, Captain Rajic, I would get to know very well. They began to threaten me, to accuse me of having aided a 'Muslim' attack, of having taken ammunition into Gorazde.

'That is ridiculous. You inspected the trucks. You know they were clean. We have never and will never carry warlike stores for any side.' I was becoming angry. Rajic, in particular, can look very menacing. He is about five foot two; round, podgy face; black, straight hair; stained teeth and unshaven. He was accompanied by a bandoliered bodyguard whom I was to antagonise on many occasions. Being in the company of Rajic was like being an extra in a spaghetti western, with Rajic playing Zapata.

The other Serb was a reasonable, almost kindly man. 'The Muslims moved, using you as a shield. We fired one mortar to warn them and to let you know that we knew that they were moving. We could have prevented their attack and wiped them out in the hills, but that would have placed you in extreme danger. We had given you our word that you would not be in any danger from us. Our word has cost us lives.' As we spoke a small open truck drove by, on it the bodies of eight of the victims of the battle. We were joined by a man who said he was the mayor of Rogatica. He had some very heated words with Brane. It was obvious that the Serbs in Rogatica were identifying Brane with us. Brane, extremely brave liaison officer that he is, had heard the situation developing and raced to Rogatica on his own initiative to assist us. His action was angering his own people.

'Mr Larry, they want you and the press to go to a makeshift mortuary and see the bodies unloaded. They want you to see close up what your convoy has done to their people.'

This convoy was turning out to be a real media event, a photo call at every phase.

'What do you think, Brane? Is it wise or not?' My fears were of meeting either angry soldiers or grieving women.

'Mr Larry, I don't think you have an option,' said Brane with a wry smile.

'Let's go,' I said, knowing that at least by now the convoy was clear of the town. I just hoped that Erik had halted it and was waiting for us to catch up. Rogatica was not the place for my landrover and two press vehicles. Brane was driving a VW Golf. He followed the mayor's car; we followed him.

Rogatica is a three-road town. We had come from one of them, the convoy was on another, we took the third, the right fork behind the flour mill. We caught up with the truck and formed a macabre procession. The truck turned into a small yard. We swung in after it. The yard was not large enough for more than the truck, my vehicle and one other. The truck parked in front of a small room with double metal-and-glass doors. To the left of this room was an office and a workshop. A group of men, some in uniform, some not, started to unload the truck.

I heard Corinne Dufkas say, 'My God, some of them are still bleeding,' from which I assumed that she was indicating that they were very 'fresh', straight from the battlefield which could not be far away. Corinne asked me if I could find out if she could take photos.

'Yes,' said Brane.

Corinne literally raced across to the truck and started snapping, close, bloody, gruesome shots. It's her job. She must have a steady hand, a good eye and a strong stomach. Taking the lead from Corinne, Jeremy and the TV men moved in.

Kurt Schork from Reuters endeared himself to me by saying, 'I'm staying right here. I have seen enough dead bodies in my life.'

I had no option. I had not been invited just to stand back. There were eight bodies, the other four were on their way, from some other location. The bodies were not neatly laid out, they had been thrown on the truck, probably in a hurry near where the battle took place. The initial view was of intertwined limbs. Some bodies faced upwards, with open, milky eyes; some lay sprawled across their neighbours, their open-mouthed, lifeless heads supported by blood-stained torsos. Some were indeed bleeding. As they were pulled and dragged off the truck they left red scuff marks on the corpses of their colleagues. Some were very heavy. None of these men had been professional soldiers. They were men from Rogatica. The heaviest had a large stomach – the men unloading his body had great difficulty. They attempted to lift him by his clothing, but a handful of shirt and trouser leg was never going to support his bulk. They succeeded only in pulling his trousers down, exposing his genitals. I remember clearly thinking: 'I hope his wife does not see him now.' The men unloading were forced to take hold of the bodies by their limbs. They sagged under the dead weights.

We were then instructed to stand back and wait. After a short time we were told to enter the room where they had been taken. Each lay on the floor, head to the left, feet to the right. The eighth body was so close to the door that we had to step over his feet to enter the room. I walked the eight paces to the end and stood still. The sun was streaming in through the open door. In the room were myself, the mayor and Corinne. I slowly looked at each of the dead. Some seemed hardly marked, one had lost half of his head and face, and part of his hand was missing. He must have been close to a mortar round, may even have been hit by a passing shell. Whatever, he was not a pretty sight. The youngest of them was probably thirty, the oldest fifty. Yesterday they were alive, somebody's father, brother or boyfriend. Today they were dead. And I was accused of being to blame. I, who had set out with a convoy of food for starving people. Like so much in this war, the facts were correct. Judged by them, I was guilty. Judged by the motives, could I be any more innocent? But these accusations do not go away. Once sown, they burst and bloom. I have often wondered if there is some mother, the wife of one of those eight, who tells her children that their daddy would be alive today if it had not been for the aid convoy which they allowed to pass. I know it is not true but . . .

We left Rogatica. Brane led us to where the convoy was parked. 'Mr Larry, we must move. It will not be safe for you in Srpska Republika tonight.'

Erik had done a quick time appreciation and was not happy at us going back the way we had come. One stretch of the road had active gun positions which nightly shelled Sarajevo. He did not want us to pass close to these, as they frequently attracted fire as well as delivering it.

'Leave the route to me,' said Brane. This we did. We moved fast and used a new 'tank road', a track carved out of the hill by the Serbs for the safe movement of tanks and heavy artillery.

It was soon dark, but as we were so close to the front line and as neither side's front-line troops knew of our presence, we had to travel with convoy lights only; one cowled, measly little bulb in the centre of the rear bumper lights. The going was not easy. To complicate matters, a French APC had broken down and was being towed by the last vehicle in the convoy, the huge, lumbering, crane-carrying recovery vehicle. In order to monitor and keep in touch with the progress of this, our slowest vehicle, I dropped back to escort it. We kept in contact with the convoy, but only just. On a few occasions the little convoy light of the vehicle in front of me disappeared as it turned a sharp bend or crested a hill. Whenever this happened there was a moment of panic. Are we driving straight on when everyone else has turned? Are we about to go over a cliff, rapidly followed by a huge recovery vehicle towing an APC? Are they so far ahead that we are lost?

We descended a very steep hill and the convoy came to a halt, itself a tricky movement when you are relying on only convoy lights. We seemed to be moving forward a vehicle at a time. I got out and advanced towards the front and found the problem. The track we were on was basically single track, wide enough for a fast-moving ammunition resupply convoy or a troop of tanks or towed guns. In the middle of the dip at the foot of the hill was a four-wheel-drive vehicle, an ex-German army UNIMOG. It had been part of an ammunition convoy but had broken down. It was facing the opposite way to us and could have been closer to the edge to give us more room to manoeuvre past it. However, the driver had been there some while and had had as his sole companion a one-litre bottle of slivovic, now empty. He was aggressive. I watched the trucks negotiate around him and knew that when it came to my little packet we were going to have some fun. At last it was time for the recovery vehicle and its APC. No way would it work. I asked the drunken driver politely to get into his cab and we would gently nudge him closer to the edge. He replied.

'Dragon, what did he say?'

'Er . . . he said no.'

'No?'

'Well, the gist of it was no.'

'Dragon, tell him to get in his vehicle.'

The driver's response was unexpected. He pulled a hand grenade out of his pocket, put his finger in the ring attached to the pin and spoke to Dragon.

'He says that if you come anywhere near his truck he will pull the pin and blow us all up.' One of Dragon's more superfluous translations.

The commotion had not gone unnoticed. Erik and Brane arrived. Brane talked to the driver but he was not to be placated. Erik is a long-serving marine officer and a very hard man. Calmly and quietly, he drew his pistol and placed it at the side of the driver's head. 'The grenade, put it away.' A time-stopping moment. Which action is quicker, the pulling of the pin or the squeezing of the trigger? Even after one litre of slivovic the driver knew that the pistol would win. He gave in, with a drunken, leery smile. He put the grenade back in his pocket. Brane persuaded him to get back in his cab and we nudged his vehicle to the very edge. We could then pass. At Lukavica we said a heartfelt thanks to Brane.

It was past midnight when we drove on to the tarmac at Sarajevo airport. Outside the UNHCR hangar all the staff were standing waiting to greet us. The marvellous Willie Dobson had organised a barbecue. He had kept in touch with our progress through the French ops room. It was a great party. I was called to the phone twice, once to talk to my alma mater, the BBC World Service, and once to the irrepressible, dynamic Deputy High Commissioner of Refugees, Doug Stafford, who was not only a great boss but a good friend. He has got me out of many a scrape by his loyal support.

The Sarajevo drivers all wanted to know what it had been like inside Gorazde. Dragon, Serb Dragon, was able to tell it as it was. After a little time at the party I crept away to my hidy-hole. I wanted to be alone; to take in slowly all that we had seen and done. I lay on top of my sleeping bag, the pleasant sounds of the party humming in the background, and I felt good. Really good. I had been into Gorazde. I was back safe and sound, mainly thanks to Erik and his boys and to Brane. I thought of the people in Gorazde, and of Efendic. He was correct. The United Nations delivering aid from besieged Sarajevo to besieged Gorazde could not be right. We were the most powerful organisation in the world and yet we allowed ourselves to operate under conditions imposed by madmen and bandits. But, Mr Efendic, we were betrayed by the very people we had gone to help.

4
Rajlovac

The Ukrainians informed us that they were to receive some new APCs. I did not pay much attention to this information but the Serb liaison officer came to see me and complained about the imminent arrival. 'We have not approved of them.'

'Since when does the UN need your approval?' I asked, with a conviction I still felt in those days.

The following day the APCs arrived. It was late so they were parked outside our hangar. The RAF boys, who knew a thing or two about APCs, pointed out that these new arrivals were different from the normal ones. These had an additional dome near the turret.

'They are artillery-locating devices.'

'Which means?'

'They can pinpoint from where shells are fired.' Hence the Serb disapproval. Maybe the UN would locate the position of the Serb guns and knock them out. Maybe the UN would locate the guns and inform the Bosnian government, who would take them out. Maybe the UN would simply accurately pinpoint the weapons and apportion blame correctly after a shelling incident. Whichever, the arrival of these vehicles and the parking of them outside our hangar was to prove dangerous and expensive. That evening, when the convoys returned the drivers parked their vehicles outside the hangar, parallel to it and in one long line. They were slightly further away from the hangar than usual because of the Ukrainian APCs.

Ploco, our architect turned cook, designed the evening meal. There was a battle brewing outside. The rounds were zipping around the hangar. We decided that it was not safe to sit in the open air even though it was oppressively hot in the hangar. We went to our respective beds early. The night got noisier. I heard a group of the drivers decide to race to the security of the French hangar. The rounds were certainly close. I heard RAF radio expert Ron Bagnolo set off for the bunker. Squadron Leader Willie then told me that he was off and suggested that I came with him. I was comfortable and felt safe. He went. I sensed that I was alone in the hangar. The noise seemed to increase. 'It's because I am on my own,' I reassured myself. But as a concession to my feelings I pulled on my trousers without lifting my body a centimetre off the bed. A bullet flew through the hangar. Then there was an enormous bang.

I heard Willie's voice. 'Larry, it's time to go.' He had come back to get me out.

I heard Ron's urgent voice. 'Come on, Larry.'

The action was very close; the rounds sounded near enough to touch them. Willie and Ron were checking that everyone else was out. I picked up my sleeping bag and ran. At the door I saw Willie and Ron.

'You OK?' Willie asked.

'Yes.'

'Let's run . . . *now.*'

As we ran there was a terrific thunderous boom with a great flash of light. We would have beaten any Olympic sprinter to the bunker. Shrapnel was whanging through the air. I could smell burning. We reached the bunker, breathless but elated. I located my spot and climbed back into my sleeping bag. 'Good-night, guys, and thanks.'

Sleep was slow to come. The night continued as it had begun. The earth shook as round after round thudded in, we could hear metal on metal as bullets ricocheted above us. The bunker felt good, strong and womblike. I said a quick prayer of thanks to the RAF boys who had seen it as a priority when others had mocked. I felt really safe and was able to listen to the battle as if it were a sound-track on a film.

The following morning I was up first. It was quiet. I ran on to the tarmac. Our vehicles had taken a hammering. Five were badly damaged. They sat there with their tyres punctured by shrapnel, their windscreens shattered by blast. They lay in a pool of their own oil, spilt as their engines were hit. The vehicles were as much a part of the team as we were. The shells had bounced off the APCs. I asked, 'Why my vehicles?' I was annoyed with UNPRO-FOR for jeopardising them. I picked up the tails of nine mortar bombs. I walked into the hangar and around our bed spaces. There was no damage to them, but we had lost a few more windows during the night. As I stood at my own bed, as undamaged as it was, I was glad that Willie had come back for me. There is something very special about being part of a team in a crisis.

The excitement was not over. The Ukrainians came to look at their APCs. At least one was going no further. Various military came to view and to pronounce. None came to remove the offending APCs. So at about nine the shelling began again. This time it was much easier for the Serbs. It was daylight and last night they had zeroed in. We were quick off the mark. At the first loud bang we ordered everyone into the shelters. Willie and I did a quick check of the hangar and were on our way back to the bunker when the Serbs put one shell straight through the roof of our hangar, our home. We had to wait more than an hour before it was calm enough to go back.

Shrapnel had shredded many of the bed spaces of the drivers. There was a large hole in the roof. There was shrapnel and what looked like cotton wool everywhere. The 'cotton wool' itself was a health hazard. It was asbestos used to line the roof. Nonjo took a few photos. Within an hour he had established himself as the guide and was conducting tours around the hangar. He had many visitors, senior officers, journalists and aid workers. He quietly restored morale. The incident became a battle honour.

A few of the drivers moved permanently into the main airport lounge where the French soldiers slept. All of the expats stayed. Nonjo, of course, stayed. Three of the drivers, Dominiko, Franjo and Veseljko, came to see me. 'From the five vehicles that are damaged, if you will agree to us cannibalising, we reckon that we can get two back on the road.'

I had reported the damage and the spares required to Zagreb. They told me that they would get the spares needed as quickly as possible. Within hours they were asking: 'Do you want an xyz1235 or an xyz1234?' I could see that this would run for ever. Logisticians with catalogues are like train spotters. 'Dominiko, cannibalise.' It took them more than two weeks but they did it. What I marvelled at was their enthusiasm and their ability to get dirty. They were covered in oil and grease. It did not help that we had no water.

We did have some excellent liquid soap. A fact I discovered by accident. A few days prior to the hole-in-the-hangar saga it had been a disturbing night, but mainly with small-arms and machine-gun fire. At one stage a few rounds had passed through the hangar. This had caused a thinning out of the residents, but some of us stayed. I reckoned that I was OK as it seemed to be passing up the centre of the hangar. I fell asleep. The battle stopped, but before dawn they started again. I heard the whistle of a round and a thud which I knew was inches from my head. Most rounds flew through the building at about three metres high, meaning that it was safe even for basketball players, of whom there are many in Yugoslavia and we proudly had our fair share. This last round was either fired by a midget, from a weapon which was pointing in the wrong direction or from one so far away that the bullet was at the end of its trajectory. Any of these possibilities could be repeated, so I decided to move.

I pulled myself out of the sleeping bag and put my bare feet on the floor. It was sticky. I put my finger in the sticky and brought it before my short-sighted eyes. The sticky was red. 'Oh my God,' I thought. 'Is it me? Where am I hit? No, it can't be me. Ugh, ugh, there may be someone sleeping on the other side of my little barrier wall. Journalists often did.' I got up and trudged through the sticky around the other side of my bed. There was no one there. I was now much bolder. I was almost standing up. Then I saw the source of the sticky. It was pouring out of a box. The box contained 'Hibiscrub', a medical liquid soap. The box said, 'Hibiscrub saves lives.' It had stopped the bullet at the height of my head. The bullet had been slowed down as it passed through six containers of the stuff.

'Hibiscrub saves lives.' It saved mine. Five litres of it cleaned up our mechanics.

*

In late October the drivers had a bad day. The convoys moved through the city slowly, children gathered at the side of the road, especially at corners and junctions where the convoys were at a walking pace. The soldiers threw sweets and food to the children. There would then be a mad scramble as the kids rushed to gather up the donations. Often, standing behind them and encouraging them, would be their parents. I was against the practice, if some of the sweets bounced along the road the children chased after them. On this tragic day they included a little toddler of about three. Sweets were thrown, the children pushed and pulled each other. The little one chased one sweet. It bounced back into the road and the toddler followed it under the rear wheel of our first truck. The driver, whom I dare not name, heard the crunch as the wheel passed over the infant. He knew exactly what had happened. He stopped the truck and was sick. The driver of our escort vehicle was Sejo, the brother of Nonjo. The driver of the second truck, who had seen only the closing moments of the accident, was Zlatan, a doctor of medicine. They raced out of their vehicles and approached the child. Zlatan could see that it was dead. The truck was soon surrounded by the child's parents and a group of neighbours. A minute ago they had been cheering and clapping the convoy as the escort threw sweets. Now their mood had changed. They were violent. They kicked Zlatan away from the child, they stoned the vehicles, they beat up the driver of the truck which had hit the child. A very brave Sejo picked up the messy body of the child and carried it to his vehicle. He then sped away to the nearest First Aid post. Our driver was badly cut and bruised. We were never able to use him again on city convoys. The practice of throwing sweets never stopped. Innocent, generous soldiers placed innocent, needy children at risk, innocently.

Despite the good work they did and the risks they took, our local drivers were not liked by everybody. The men of Sarajevo who were in uniform considered our drivers to be draft dodgers. To the Karadzic Serbs, our Serbs were traitors, our 'Muslims' and Croats spies. Many of the citizens of Sarajevo saw them as opportunists and capitalists, and believed they were part of the black market. One or two of them were. We did dismiss some.

The lives of the drivers changed drastically with the arrival of a Norwegian army officer on loan to UNHCR. Dag Espeland was a captain in Norway, a tall, lumbering man with a heavy boxer's face. His hair never looked combed. Dag was not a man for the front rank on a big parade, but he was the finest logistician I have ever come across. He did all his calculations with a pencil on a dog-eared pad. He wrote simple notes in a primitive hand. But he could see the centre of a problem and come up with a solution faster than anyone I know. He reorganised the warehouse, the distribution programme and the amount of aid coming in. Delivering aid in Sarajevo was dangerous but easy. The problem was the amount of aid we received. Dag hit on the idea of sending the Sarajevo drivers out of the city to Croatia to collect more. More convoys, more aid.

To my surprise, the drivers were delighted. They were prepared to risk the Serb check-points as they both departed and entered the city and to risk motoring unescorted along damaged roads close to front lines. A risky enough task with an empty vehicle in a war zone where banditry and hijackings are commonplace events. An heroic task when the trucks are filled with highly desirable food worth a fortune on the black market.

Dag divided the convoys into two, one to be led by Svabo, whose hair was very fair, and the other to be led by Milan, whose hair was jet-black. Thus the convoys became known throughout Bosnia as 'Boss White' and 'Boss Black'.

Ever cautious, Dag led a trial convoy out of Sarajevo to the warehouse at Vitez. The Serbs were told clearly that more convoys meant more food for them. The first convoy had no trouble at the Serb check-point. Three days later Dag decided it was solo time and the Boss White convoy set off on its own. It succeeded. The drivers were teased by the Serbs but not hassled.

Meanwhile I made my first two attempts on breaking the siege of Srebrenica. The reports from the amateur radio were describing an horrendous scene. The town was overcrowded, its population doubled, there was no food, little water, heavy shelling and no medicine. The government had made Srebrenica its top priority. But despite careful negotiation and much hard work, these attempts failed. My first effort reached Milici, where the police chief with great sincerity persuaded me that we had been re-routed via nearby Bratunac. Foolishly I believed him. But at Bratunac we were blocked by a huge demonstration of angry women. Even more foolishly I returned to 'my new friend' in Milici, to ask him to clear a path to Srebrenica. To greet me and meet me the chief had laid on a reception committee of Milici women, as vociferous if not as angry as those in Bratunac. They blocked our entrance to the village. We had no option but to go back to Sarajevo.

The second attempt was equally hopeless. The women of Bratunac attempted to overturn my car. They insisted that I visited the graves, all freshly dug, of their husbands and sons, killed by a raiding party from Srebrenica.

'Why should we allow your convoy to pass? Why should you take food to those who have killed our men?'

I tried to explain that the men from Srebrenica had attacked because their families were dying of starvation and shelling caused by the men from Bratunac. This they did not want to hear. If only I could have made the women on both sides see reason.

We turned the convoy around and left. The Serbs had found a new cheap and plentiful weapon.

I returned to Sarajevo from these failed attempts depressed, but there my depression was increased. Both UNPROFOR and UNHCR were not happy with me. UNHCR because in my enthusiasm I had apparently not informed Zagreb of my intention to take a convoy to Srebrenica. UNPROFOR because I had changed the aim of the convoy. I had approval for an attempt via Milici which was loosely in the working domain of Sector Sarajevo. I had then added Bratunac and a return to Milici, both involving stepping into a country, Serbia, where we had no approval to operate. I was summoned to Zagreb to take a rap on the knuckles. I was replaced in Sarajevo by the outstandingly pretty and intelligent Izumi Nakamitsu. I was very unhappy with this.

My new brief was to open an office in Mostar and to negotiate locally the freedom of the road for our convoys, especially those of Boss Black and Boss White. The proposal by Dag to increase the tonnage into Sarajevo using the local drivers had gone well.

They had successfully done the Vitez route. They now wanted to do Sarajevo–Split. The problem was that the road was closed. The crucial bit was in Bosnian Croat hands, who at that time were supporting the Bosnian government; but the Serbs, who in effect held the east bank of the road, regularly shelled the road and even more regularly shelled Mostar.

My point of contact in Mostar was Minister Bruno Stojic. He was professional and co-operative. My first request was for accommodation. 'Minister, where in Mostar do you recommend I stay?'

'Sarajevo man, do you like shelling?'

'No.'

'Then why live in Mostar?'

He fixed me up with accommodation in Medjugorje, famous as the place where the Blessed Virgin Mary speaks regularly with a few chosen locals; a Yugoslav Lourdes or Fatima. I sometimes worry about what heaven is going to be like. The Holy Family seem to hang around some terrible places. If heaven is as dull and as dismal as Medjugorje I shall be very disappointed. Furthermore, I hope heaven is not full of cheap souvenir shops run by relatives of the apostles selling rubbish blessed by the many resident popes.

I discovered that the problem on the road was not just shelling. There were a number of Croat soldiers who were freelancing, setting up spurious check-points and ambushing passing vehicles. Sometimes loads disappeared, sometimes trucks, sometimes people. With the help and encouragement of the Minister I spent many days liaising with the local warlords. Through the good offices of Geoff Beaumont, a Brit in the ECMM, I was able to get some sort of safety assurance from the Serbs. I informed Zagreb and Sarajevo that I thought we could risk the route.

I took the first convoy through without incident. Dag then had the extra convoys he needed, but only thanks to the tenacity and bravery of our Bosnian drivers. It worked well for a while, but they were particularly at risk after January 1993 when the warring factions realigned. Put simply, the Croats abandoned the Bosnian government and allied with the Serb side. This meant that the convoys with their multi-ethnic mix were at risk in three territories, not just two. The days of Boss White and Boss Black were over. It was too dangerous, even for them. But that was yet to come.

Now, many miles away, Lord Carrington had given up the task of peacebroker and handed over to Lord Owen, who wanted his own staff. Jeremy Brade was therefore offered to UNHCR, who sent him to Sarajevo as Head of Office. I was asked to go back as Chief of Operations. I was delighted. I soon picked up where I had left off.

We were looking for an assistant to work with Leyla in the new warehouse. She recommended Suad, a friend who before the war had been a croupier. He was a dark, oilily handsome man, a meeter and greeter oozing charm who spoke excellent English. We took him down to the old warehouse in Zetra. No one was on the streets. There was no shelling, but a strong foreboding of danger sharpened a torpid day. We left the centre of the city and headed out to Zetra. We were the only car moving. We were in the unarmoured landcruiser, clearly marked UNHCR on the doors and the roof. We could sense that the Serbs in the hills were watching us. I had a feeling that perhaps we should not go. It was not absolutely vital. But tomorrow might be no better. Life must go on.

I was driving and conscious that we were alone. There were no pedestrians, no other cars. We reached Zetra and I turned right, swung across the road and entered the stadium. The huge steel door to the tunnel road where the storehouses were located under the stadium bowl was closed. Those inside were taking no chances. I hooted on the car horn and stopped at the steel door. I heard someone approach and asked Leyla to shout out that we were UNHCR. I felt very exposed and kept the car engine running. The heavy door began to open. One guard was pulling it from right to left. I shouted 'Good day' to him. He smiled. Suddenly there was one huge explosion. It felt as if it was on top of us. There was pressure on my ears. We were enveloped in a cloud of grey-brown smoke. Through it, I could see that the door was open probably wide enough to get through. I gunned the engine and sped through. A second bang, louder than the first, reverberated to our right. Another shell had exploded on hitting the outside wall. It sounded louder because it was echoing off the walls of the underground tunnel we had entered.

I did not stop the car until I was deep inside the tunnel road. We got out and all smiled at each other. Ten minutes ago Suad was a new outsider, now he was part of the team. Leyla, not yet twenty-one, was ice-cool and calm. We walked back to near the entrance. A shell had smashed through the top left-hand corner of the door, then bounced off the concrete wall. The guards were attempting to clear up the debris of glass and wood and metal. The door was buckled, the guard room was raked with shrapnel which had knocked out the security camera monitors and console. The man who had opened the door was dead. Shrapnel had hit him in the chest. We stayed for an hour or more while I psyched myself up to risk driving the car out through the same door we had come in.

A few days later I was motoring into the centre of the city again with Leyla, but this time Dragon was driving. It was one of our first trips in a newly arrived armoured range rover. We were approaching the entrance to the barracks of the Ukrainians when a shell hit the road no more than fifty metres ahead of us. It left a small crater in the road. It baptised the range rover. I was always happy to be out with Leyla. Lucky Leyla. So young, so wise, so brave, so pretty. She hated being out with me.

The sniper fire along the airport road was considered too severe to risk my return to the hangar, so I decided to stay the night in the PTT building. I had also heard that General Morillon was visiting. He was the commander of all the UNPROFOR forces in Bosnia-Herzegovina and was then a four-star general. He was a hero in France for previous campaigns and was now covering himself with glory here in former Yugoslavia. He was a soldier's soldier. I was looking forward to meeting him. No one could confirm if he was in or if he was free. In the middle of the evening heavy shelling began. It drew closer to the building, then one round hit the entrance, slightly wounding a French soldier. The alarm was sounded and people began to make their way to the cellar when a second round slammed into the room occupied by the UNPROFOR police. No one was there. The last man had just left. The room was destroyed. Girders were bent, large chunks of masonry from the outer wall smacked against the inner walls and as the mortar had exploded, fragments of the shell case from splinter-sized slivers to the ash-tray-sized solid base had pock-marked the walls and torn through the woodwork.

Two rooms were wrecked and one badly damaged. Their occupants were on the landing and on the stairs outside when the shell landed. The explosion at the entrance and the scream of the wounded Frenchman had caused them to leave their rooms to see what assistance they could give. Their sense of duty saved their lives.

Down in the basement, at the foot of the stairs, I had my first view of General Morillon. He was in his grey fatigue uniform. He was wearing his blue beret which was shrunk to fit his head, a trick learned early in service by all soldiers. If you do not shrink them they flop on your head like a cow-pat. Beneath the line of his beret I could see his close-cropped silver hair. The General was smoking. He is a walking advert for Davidoff cigars. Not only was he smoking but he was pacing up and down the confined space of the basement stairwell like a caged tiger. A few paces, then a quick turn. He was accompanied by fellow Frenchman Colonel Davout, the acting Sector Commander. Tall, angular, straight-backed Davout, an aircraft pilot, although how he ever fitted into a cockpit I will never know.

I watched the tiger. Apparently he should have returned to his headquarters but now he was caged here. Was he prevented from moving by 'aggressor' Serb provocation, as the Bosnian government would want him to believe? Or had his return to the city initiated a touch of Balkan intrigue? Was the shelling of the building done by government troops, attempting to make General Morillon believe that the Serbs were antagonising him? Whatever, I had watched enough, it was time to make his acquaintance. I introduced myself directly. He was instantly charming. He exuded calm command. As he talks to you he squares off to face you. His voice is unmistakable. Every word begins in his throat and swirls over the back of his tongue, reaching his lips as a growl. He is every inch the professional soldier. He has served in the most illustrious of French regiments including the Spahis and has commanded the Foreign Legion. We had only the shortest of conversations but I knew that I was going to get on well with him. After a while Colonel Davout decided that everyone could return to their rooms and offices. I went back to the HCR office. Una and Leyla slept in the outer office on mattresses on the floor. I slept in the inner office on a mattress against the wall furthest from the entrance door. There was a communicating door between the girls' office and mine. I was tired, so I went straight to bed. Outside in the corridor I could hear people discussing the extent of the damage done by the shells. With these conversations in my ears I fell asleep.

I am a very light sleeper. I heard my office door open. I looked up and saw a soldier enter. He was tall and thin. Because of the association of the last conversation I had heard before I went to sleep I thought that he must be checking the rooms for damage. I closed my eyes. However, he moved from my room to where the girls were sleeping. I still thought that he was inspecting the rooms. He made little noise. I suddenly realised that it was far too late for anyone to be inspecting anything. I leapt out of my sleeping bag. I was wearing only my underpants. I entered the girls' room. They were fast asleep and the soldier was standing over them. He had not heard me. I watched him as he began to undress. I moved quickly across the room, grabbed him and forced him towards the door. He was a wiry man, taller than me, but he offered little resistance. I pushed him out of the room and into the corridor. I yelled at him and shoved him out through the double doors on to the staircase. I thought he was French. I had shouted at him in English anyway. He had not spoken to me, not a word. Perhaps he was drunk, but I could smell no alcohol on his breath and far from being unsteady he gave the impression of being rigid and isolated. I returned via the girls' room. Leyla murmured to me. I told her everything was OK and went back to my mattress, thinking that it had been a busy day and making a mental note to tell the girls to lock their door at night. I was soon asleep.

I heard footsteps in the corridor. They stopped outside my door. I unzipped my sleeping bag. I heard my door handle turn, saw the door slowly open. The soldier entered my room. He came straight towards where I was lying. In his hand he was carrying a bayonet. I was on my feet in a flash. I met him half-way across the room and bundled him back to the door. I was trying to hold down the hand in which he held the bayonet. As I got him against the wall I realised two facts: first, that the bayonet was very long and that it was a most unwieldy weapon; second, that he was much stronger than me. I pride myself on being strong. I am not running fit but I am able to shove and push as well as the next man. This fellow was not the next man. Up against him, I was able better to assess him. He was maybe twenty-nine. He was tanned light brown, had an angular face, a pointed nose, mean, thin lips. I think his eyes were brown. His breathing was imperceptible. I felt that mine was like a steam train by contrast. Most significantly, he never uttered a word.

I was about to lose this contest. It was taking all my effort to keep his bayonet hand pinned to his side. If he had been carrying a knife with a shorter blade I would have been in big trouble. Discretion is the better part of valour, so casting my pride to the wind, I yelled out, 'Girls! Girls!' This diversion spurred on my assailant and he very nearly put me through the door. To me it was vital that I hung on to him. I continued, 'Girls! Girls!' I heard no response, no movement, but suddenly was joined by my good friend the WHO doctor Nedim Jaganjac, who, apparently short of a mattress, was sleeping in the outer office near the girls. He was a little sleepy-eyed but he saw the struggle and the bayonet. He bearhugged the soldier, thus pinning his arms and the bayonet to his side. I then had a brilliant idea: I would knee the soldier in the genitals. In films it always seems to drop the assailant to the floor. I expected that it would at least make this fellow's eyes water. What actually happened was, as I drove my knee into his groin, I drove my toe on to the pinned-down bayonet. We both winced, but he dropped the bayonet. He then seemed to lose the will to fight.

One of the girls went to the duty operations room, which was only 40 metres down the corridor. Nedim went upstairs to the damaged rooms to get Sergeant Jim Hull, the Canadian RCMP, who was the Sector Commander of the Civilian Police in Sarajevo. I bundled the man out into the corridor for the second time. He resisted, but in a non-violent way. I was able to shove him along whenever he stopped. As we were close to the ops room door he stopped and we scuffled. From his pocket a pistol fell to the floor. I went cold.

By then there were other people about. He was taken over by them. Then Jim arrived. Jim is the man who should have dealt with him. He is not your tall, handsome, moustachioed Mountie from the posters, who can yodel, ride horses and lance pegs. Jim is a balding, stocky, street-wise muscleman, in the image of Yul Brynner. The soldier would have met his match with Jim, without 'Girls, girls'. Jim arrested him. I returned to my room, still in my underpants and incidentally, God, if I have to hand-to-hand again, please may I be wearing my trousers and my shoes. Traumatologist Dr Nedim looked at my bleeding toe with little interest and even less sympathy. The girls were fast asleep. On the violence scale of Sarajevo this had been for them a very minor incident.

The irony of the evening was that the soldier was a Ukrainian and a policeman. He worked for Jim. He was one of the occupants of the room destroyed by the shell earlier in the evening. The theory is that the closeness of the event shocked and numbed his mind, hence his strength and his behaviour. He was sent home. Which pleased me. What did not please me was the departure of the RAF team who were given their marching orders. They had to return to the UK. A great loss.

I then had the bunker to myself. I was very happy there but the summer ended, the weather broke and the rain came. One night it was pouring down. I was stretched out on the floor about to go to sleep when I heard a creaking and a cracking. The metal support bars were bending under the weight of the now rain-sodden sandbags. The last straw was a rumour of a possible invasion across the airport by the Serbs using tanks. If they came they might not see my lone, solitary bunker. If it was not holding up to the pressure of wet sandbags it might not take too kindly to the weight of a tank. Enwombed I liked, entombed I didn't. I moved to the PTT, a French colony. We in UNHCR had been in the PTT before the French arrived. Fabrizio had laid claim to quarters befitting his station. When I arrived the French were drawing up new borders. We in UNHCR were to move from the first floor to the ground floor. All civilians were to be in the one corner. Civilians meant UNHCR, UNICEF, WHO and the local liaison officers.

I had this strange idea that the military were in support of the humanitarian agencies, an idea encouraged by the mandate written in New York. The French, however, considered civilians a nuisance, to be put in a corner where an eye could be kept on them. In a corner on the ground floor near the exit as a constant reminder. Furthermore, the French insisted that civilians national and international must produce proof of identity on entering the building and must submit themselves to a body search by a French conscript. Military of any shade or hue were exempt from this inconvenience. There were no more than thirty of us civilians, no more than ten internationals, but exempting us from this humiliation was beyond the wit, the power or the inclination of the French. I was body-searched up to thirty times a day. I appealed to the better nature of the senior of the French officers, only to discover that he did not have one.

I had the small office, the girls the larger. We worked, slept and played in them. By day they housed nine or ten, by night they slept four or five. The whole building heaved with humanity. If there was water, we washed. If there was no water, we didn't. The greatest inconvenience was the conveniences: no water and they stank. Jerrycans of water were placed in them daily, but as often as not the jerrycans were empty and the toilet bowls full. Living cheek by jowl, both sexes together, was fun. It created a team spirit among those who were clubbable and madness in those who were not. Despite the living on top of one another, there was the opportunity for living on top of one another. Liaisons were formed, relationships flourished. Where there is a willie there is a way!

Once again we had trouble with the delivery of aid to the Serb-held territories surrounding Sarajevo. The Bosnian government military were preventing our convoys delivering to the Serb warehouse at Rajlovac. They refused to accept that our charter was to feed all sides. More importantly, they refused to accept the reality that if we did not give aid to the Serbs, they would prevent anything from entering the city by road and could disrupt the airlift.

I went to see our government link, Mugdim Pasic. He politely gave me the party line. Sarajevo was besieged by Serbs. The Serbs were not besieged. Why did we give any food to the 'aggressor' Serbs? Was the UN a party to bribing the Serbs? Did the world know what was going on? Each line was given to me as if it were fresh and new.

'My dear friend, no more rhetoric. Does my convoy go through or not?'

'Not,' was the answer.

So I had to go to the Serb liaison officer and get myself an appointment with the Serb hierarchy to try to keep them sweet so that they would let convoys into Sarajevo.

I left with my driver, Pepe, a Bosnian Sarajevo Serb, my faithful translator, Meliha Hadzic, a Bosnian Sarajevo Muslim, and two visitors from Zagreb: Wycliff Songea, an African protection officer with a great sense of humour, which was about to come in handy; and Boi Lan, a Vietnamese-born American. At the Bosnian checkpoint, the soldiers gave us the usual hassle, but agreed that we could go through.

At Rajlovac depot we were met by Ljerka, the liaison officer. She took us into the conference room, where a large group of people waited for us, including the mayor of Ilidza and the aggressive military commander. On the table there was slivovic; it was going to be a long, hard session. My radio crackled and Sarajevo asked if I could send Pepe back as they were short of vehicles. Foolishly I said 'OK'. As we were on Serb territory, I did not feel unhappy about sending Serb Pepe back alone and he was quite happy to go.

The meeting was as tedious as I expected. The military commander, a very difficult man, began by accusing me of 'favouring the Muslims', and 'delivering low percentages to the Serb side', and the usual, but always infuriating, 'and you are smuggling ammunition into Sarajevo'. I refuted the wrong accusations and tried to explain the accurate ones. The commander would not listen. I tried to be patient. He tried my patience, I raised my voice, he his. It was a well-tested formula. The mayor, a gentle, wise man, did his best to keep the bile and venom down. Ljerka and the Serb humanitarian workers then came in with another old chestnut. When we were able to get a convoy to them, could it also bring in the contents of the convoys that had failed to arrive? This argument I have heard wherever I have served. My answer is always the same: 'You cannot eat yesterday's food.' By four o'clock I was worn out and they were not too happy. We shook hands with them all, left the conference room and discovered no vehicle.

I got on the radio. 'Where is Pepe?'

'Don't know,' was the reply. 'He did not return.'

'Then you have two problems: find Pepe and find me transport.' We ourselves had a problem as there was shooting and shelling not too far away.

It is embarrassing to say farewell, shake hands and reappear. Ljerka took us to an outer office; her conference continued and we waited. After about five minutes I was back on to the Sarajevo office. Pepe had been arrested at the Bosnian check-point. Some of the soldiers had recognised him and knew he was a Serb. They would send another vehicle 'soon'. Ljerka's meeting had ended, more handshakes, off they all went, leaving Ljerka and us.

I was back on the radio. 'What the hell is going on?'

'There is a vehicle on its way. Be with you in five minutes.'

'Ljerka, is it inconvenient if we stay here until our transport arrives?' She was honest, it was; if she did not leave in the next few minutes she would not be able to get home that evening and at home she had two children. I got back on the radio and was assured that the vehicle was approaching me, so I made a decision. 'Right, folks, we will leave Ljerka so that she can get away and we will walk to the warehouse gate, by which time our vehicle will have arrived.'

Ljerka was pleased and away she went. We walked towards the depot gate with the distant rumbling of shells in our ears. Ljerka's car overtook us. At the gate the guard waved us through, then locked the gate and he too set off for home.

It was a strange feeling to be alone in Serb territory with the sounds of war in the distance. I began to feel that I had not made the right decision and I got back on the radio. 'Any news about the car?'

'It should be with you now,' was the reply. There were two choices open to me: stand outside the locked exposed depot or walk along the road where the car would come. I chose the latter. The first hundred or so metres were fine. Then we turned into the main Sarajevo road, it looked lonely and the light was now beginning to fade. I tried the radio, my voice was not as demanding as before. I needed them.

'Definitely on its way, should be able to see it from where you are.' More decisions! Stand and wait, or walk. We were wearing our flak jackets and our helmets; it was obvious who we were. I decided we would walk, twenty paces between each of us and we would make as much noise as we could. The distance in case we were mortared: better to lose one of us than to lose all of us. The noise to ensure that we did not suddenly startle any guards or check-points. Off we went.

I was uneasy. I knew I had made one bad decision, that of leaving the depot. I was not sure if I was now compounding it. When we got very close to the Serb front line, we were opposite the entrance to a Serb army barracks. We walked in single file, as high-profile as possible. Suddenly all hell broke loose. Bang, bang, bang, rounds flew over our heads. The sentries on the front line did not know who the hell we were. In the failing light we could have been anything or anybody, so they opened fire. Time stopped. I was at the back of the line. I saw the tall, beautiful, elegant Meliha trying to get into a ditch in a ladylike way, so as not to get her overcoat dirty. My African friend turned to me, his eyes bright and white. Calm Boi Lan asked me, 'What do we do?'

'Down, down,' I shouted, somewhat unnecessarily as I was the only person standing.

I turned and walked towards where the shooting was coming from. I had my hands above my head and shouted, '*Visoki Komesarijat*. Humanitarian Aid. HCR. United Nations.' The shooting continued but I realised that it was above our heads and not at us. As I walked towards the barracks I could see a man of about fifty. I shouted to him, 'Stop shooting.' He shouted something back at me. I was then very close to him. He turned to his troops and, I think, gave the order for the shooting to stop. I called my group forward and they began to run towards the barrack entrance.

Then we had a complication, the outgoing Serb barrage caused a response from the 'Muslims' and they started to fire into the Serb barracks. Not surprisingly, the Serbs returned fire. We were now in the middle of a fire-fight. I was yelling in English at the Serb to stop. He understood not a word and was otherwise preoccupied. My little group needed no more leadership from me. They raced towards the guardroom. The Serbs let us in and the shooting stopped. Meliha explained to the Serb soldiers why we had been walking along the main road. They were incredulous. They accused me of being reckless. I do not want to absolve myself but the whole episode did stem from innocence.

In the guardroom, Meliha was very worried. Meliha is Muslim. Meliha is a very Muslim name. All the soldiers in the guardroom were Serbs. Quietly she asked me what she should say if they asked her name. 'Meliha,' I said. 'Let's play it by ear.' I then realised that I had called her 'Meliha' quite openly. I also realised that my priority was to ensure that Sarajevo knew that we were now in Serb army hands. I contacted Sarajevo very publicly. Fortunately Tony Land was now back in the office. Tony never panics. I felt a lot better when his voice came on. 'Pepe was recognised as a Serb. He was arrested at the Bosnian check-point. He is in jail. We have sent a United Nations armoured personnel carrier to get you out. In it is Captain Jan Segers. It is held up at the check-point because there has been a mini-battle which you obviously caused.' He concluded with, 'Stay where you are,' a totally unnecessary piece of advice. We were now happy. Well, happier. I was certainly pleased that Jan was involved. He is a Belgian officer whom I have had many dealings with. He is a bulldog. He never gives up on a problem and never lets go.

A young Serb officer then arrived and demanded that I go with him to be interviewed by his commander. To divide our group would have been a great mistake. So I declined the 'invitation' and sent the reply that I would be delighted to see the commander in the guardroom. This reply did not go down very well.

While we waited we handed out some cigarettes. One of the

soldiers asked Meliha where she came from. She replied, 'Sara-jevo.' He asked her, 'Where?'

She answered very reluctantly.

The Serb soldier brightened up. 'I don't live very far from there,' he said. 'Tell me, have you seen . . .' They then began to discuss neighbours, school friends, university friends. They chatted as if they were what they actually were: twenty-five-year-olds swapping stories about friends and neighbours.

Meanwhile, I was back on the radio to Tony. We could hear the APC. We could also hear the shooting. Every time it moved forward it was fired upon. It received direct hits. The tough little Irish APC driver from the French Foreign Legion did his best, no doubt encouraged by Jan. They were persistent and brave. But they could not get through. Then our radio battery died. We heard the progress of the APC and watched the tracer bullets bouncing near it. It was pitch dark. We heard the APC leaving. I asked the commander if he would be so kind as to come and see me. He did. He was not friendly. He told me that we would stay in the guardroom until it was considered safe to move us to Ilidza, where we would be taken to the sector commander, my adversary of the afternoon.

Meliha was happy, she was the centre of attraction, a fount of knowledge giving some of these men the first news of their homes and their relatives. We other three were cold, bored and hungry. After a couple of hours we were taken in the freezing cold night to Ilidza, to the mayor's office. He was with the military commander. They were amused by my predicament, in which the Serbs were blameless! They took us to the Hotel Ilidza, produced a bottle of wine, some hot soup and a good meat meal. We slept little. It was too cold. We left the hotel at six and were picked up by a French APC and taken to the airport. All our UNHCR colleagues were present. I had forgotten that it was the day of the visit of Madame Ogata.

The majority were pleased to see us. Karen Landgren, the Chief of Mission, was not. She came across to me with ice-cold blue eyes and an ice-cold manner and informed me that I had been totally irresponsible and had hazarded the lives of her staff.

On the tarmac I saw Pepe. Tony had managed to get him out of jail. He was none the worse for his experience. I never again let myself be separated from my vehicle.

5

Students

The pressure to get 'Third Country National Students' out of Sarajevo was increasing. Every day a delegation was in the office with some tale of woe. The majority of them were Arabs and they had enlisted the support of the UNPROFOR Head of Civil Affairs in Sarajevo, Adnan Al Razak. He is a Palestinian, so he is well qualified to understand refugee problems. He is also a hell of a nice guy, very efficient at his job and most supportive of HCR.

The majority of the students were from the medical faculty of Sarajevo university. In fairness to them, they were not going to learn a lot in the classrooms. If they wanted to be hands-on medical workers, then a Ph.D. of experience was at their disposal. In truth the majority did not see this as their war and wanted out. A bright young Sudani was their principal spokesman; whenever one of his fellow students was wounded or killed he was banging on my door demanding that we get the students out.

Adnan and I decided to try to do something. After a lot of effort, a lot of hassle and many false starts we were in a position to say 'Go'. The Bosnian government agreed to release them. The Serbs agreed to them transiting through their territory. The Croats agreed to their entry into Croatia as long as they had the means to move on and did not stay.

The number of students had swollen to eighty-nine. Adnan laid on three buses. It was a bright, sunny day. We arranged to be at the PTT building at 0700 hours. The buses would arrive, with all the students. We would check their passports, ascertain that they were self-sufficient and away they would go, escorted as far as Kiseljak by one UNPROFOR APC under the command of an

UNPROFOR military policeman, who turned out to be from Poland: Warrant Officer Andrzej Buler, a short, stocky, smiling cube of a man, with a great sense of humour and, as the day was to prove, a lot of courage. Jim O'Neil, the Head of Office of UNICEF in Sarajevo, a good friend and a great supporter of UNHCR, would also accompany the convoy. I would monitor its progress from the Serb HQ at Ilidza.

Contrary to the arrangements, the students started arriving at the PTT building at about 6 a.m. As ever, this taxed the thin patience of the French guards, who in the main were conscripts, did not want to be in the army and certainly did not want to be in Bosnia. The buses arrived at seven. Adnan and I went out to meet the crowd. My task was to ensure that they were all 'foreign' nationals, all students, all eligible to go and that they all had the means to get themselves home. We had given their names to the Serb liaison officers and they had sent a Liaison Officer Momcilo (Momo) to observe. Right from the start it was obvious it was not going to be easy. There were far more than eighty-nine. Some of the students had local wives, girlfriends, associates, and despite all the warnings they had brought them along to try to get them out. I understood it but did not appreciate it.

So task one was to separate those who could go from those who could not. This meant tears, breaking down luggage, farewells and hassle I could do without. Task two was to line up everybody who could go and to check passport against holder. This also proved to be fun. Many of the students had not renewed their passports and they were out of date. A very good question which they put to me was how could they renew their passports when their embassies were in either Zagreb or Belgrade and they could not get out of Sarajevo? Momcilo, the Serb LO, thought that out-of-date passports would be OK as long as the students had arrived originally with valid ones. As I walked along the ranks of the students checking their passports, I rapidly realised that many of them were 'professional' students. One or two had birth dates as old as mine. Some were 'Economics' or 'Social Studies' students, on their third degree. Quite a few looked nothing like their passports. Two were eliminated because there was no way, even with the passage of time, that they could be the person in the passport.

Some of the passports were written only in Arabic. I could see the Serb check-point enjoying these. The compliant Momcilo thought they would be 'OK'. He just wanted the show on the road. He had no idea what would be accepted at the check-point. It would depend on the whim, the fancy, the mood of the soldiers who, I suspected, had spent all night drawing lots for the fun of ransacking this exclusively Muslim convoy.

Many of the students had letters of support from their embassies, all told me that they had money. Eighty-seven passed the test and were motioned forward to join the buses. I went over to see the drivers, who were in good humour. The buses, however, were typical of the Sarajevo scene. They were battle-scarred, ramshackle, creaking, groaning hulks on shattered springs and bald tyres. The chance of them reaching Split was zero. The drivers assured me that the buses were the best in the city. My impression was that the drivers did not give a damn how far they got, as long as they themselves got clear of Sarajevo. Two of them were young men and one was middle-aged. We got everyone on board; I stood by the door of each bus and counted them on. The APC growled into life, the Polish policeman stood in the turret and away they went. Adnan and I shook hands and breathed a sigh of relief. We now had eighty-seven fewer problems. I motored to the Serb headquarters with Momcilo, to be on hand when the convoy went through. We were in the petrol-driven armoured range rover, which I noticed was short of fuel. So I got on the radio and spoke to Dag. He was at the airport, there was an acute shortage of petrol, but the other range rover I had loaded for our next attempt at Gorazde was full. He would come into Ilidza and we could swap vehicles. I concurred, better a ten-minute delay now than hours later. Dag arrived in record time. We swapped vehicles and Momo and I set off for the check-point.

When we got there, there was trouble. It was manned by a particularly unruly, drunken bunch. One of them I knew very well, a giant with the rustic looks, the ruddy complexion and the enormous hands of a farm labourer. He was well fuelled, swaying and giggling, taunting and mocking with that unpredictability of the man of limited intelligence, violent tendencies and local power. His fellow Serbs were humouring him, a bad sign. They too were frightened of him. The situation was grim. Some of the Serb soldiers claimed to have seen one of the bus drivers, a Muslim, fighting in the front line against them. Another Serb then claimed that the bus driver was a known murderer and furthermore was responsible for the death of his brother. All three drivers had been taken to the building we had left, one under arrest, the other two under investigation. Apparently the Polish policeman and Jim O'Neil of UNICEF had fought hard under a lot of pressure and threats for the release of the drivers but without success. The Serbs had provided three Serb bus drivers who were to take the students to Kiseljak, where they would be unloaded, and the buses would then return to Ilidza. They claimed that it was reckless to risk those buses on a trip to Split. I noted that they said the buses would return to Ilidza, not to Sarajevo. The Serbs would therefore gain three buses. The Serbs then harangued me about the numbers: eighty-eight, not eighty-seven students. I was adamant that eighty-seven had left the PTT building and explained that I had counted them on. I volunteered that it was possible that the bus had stopped outside the PTT and that someone could have jumped on, but I doubted it. The Serbs were insistent that eighty-eight had left the PTT. The more I insisted the more did they. Just before I went into my usual anger overdrive I sensed that their anger was as 'staged' as mine, that I was being set up.

The Serb female interpreter was called across. She confirmed eighty-eight students, but with a big smile. I was then let in on the story.

The three buses arrived at Sierra One, the Serb check-point. They were halted and checked bus by bus. The drivers were told to report to the check-point control room, a dirty, sparse and spartan room in what had been a roadside shop. Two soldiers and the girl got on to the first bus and checked the passport of each student. The students were, at first, subdued. They had left Sarajevo on a high, they were escaping, fleeing from the shelling, the sniper fire, the hunger, the deprivation. Here for the first time since the war began they were face to face with what the Sarajevo government was calling 'the aggressor'. The majority of them were Arabs and some were viewed by the Serbs as mercenaries, as 'mujahedin'.

It was a hot day. The first bus was crowded with twenty-nine students. In the hold of the bus was the bulk of their kit, spread around them on their seats were their more valuable and their more personal possessions, including the compulsory one radio per person without which students from the Middle East seem unable to travel. There was not a lot of room for the Serbs to move but they did their job. They frightened some students, awed others. The majority were too high on the imminence of their freedom to be intimidated.

The students in the second bus were a little more fractious. They had had longer in the sun to bake and they were apprehensive. They had watched some problem develop over the drivers. The girl got on. The passport check was carried out. The soldiers rummaged through some of the bags. Relations were strained between the Serbs and a couple of the older students. There was some accusation of them being 'Turks', although none held Turkish passports.

The third bus was the most overcrowded. The Serb team were cantankerous. There was kit everywhere and Arab students everywhere. The coach was hot, sticky and smelly. The girl, by now, knew how many students were on the other two coaches so it was a cumulative count. She worked her way from the front of the bus to the rear seat, checking passports, adding the total. She was quicker than in the other two coaches because this one stank. As she and the soldiers reached the end of the coach they counted the last two students, eighty-six and eighty-seven. Next to these two, lying on the rear bench seat, was a large cardboard box.

'What is in the box?' one of the soldiers asked.

'My friend,' the Arab student replied.

Student number eighty-eight had died three weeks before. His fellow countrymen, believing that they were close to leaving, had decided that he was to go home with them and be buried in his homeland. They wrapped him up and kept him in their room. They had put him on the bus without the driver's knowledge. I had happily inspected passports, counted them all on, but had not inspected the empty vehicle. The Serbs were right. There were eighty-eight students. One of the Serb soldiers could verify this. He had insisted that the Arab opened the box. The interpreter had attempted to intervene. Her nose told her what her eyes did not need to see. Big brave Serb managed to hold his vomit until he had left the coach. The Serb commander summarised my problem. I needed to get to Kiseljak quickly. I had to find three coaches and arrange for the transportation of eighty-eight students, eighty-seven living and one dead, from Kiseljak to Split. The circus of the early morning had become comic opera.

Leaving Serb Momcilo behind, I therefore moved off to Kiseljak, a Croat town in the hands of the Bosnian government. In doing so, I made a great error of judgement. My mind was on the students. Time was precious. I needed to hire drivers, coaches and get the students away before dark if I was not to have the problem of trying to accommodate eighty-eight Arabs in Kiseljak. In my haste I left behind the three drivers; three Muslim drivers, one of whom was accused of the murder of the brother of a Serb soldier. I abandoned them in a Serb stronghold. So simply are nightmares foaled.

I arranged for the Sarajevo coaches to stop at the warehouse in Kiseljak used by UNHCR. When I arrived the students were all standing around their coaches. As I got out of my vehicle, quite unexpectedly they broke into a great round of applause. Many came across and hugged me. They felt free and safe. This threw me a little as we had only fought half the battle. I called together a group of the student leaders. I asked them about the extra passenger. They were not at all contrite. They felt they had a duty to take him home. I explained to them that I would try to arrange other coaches. I almost said fresh coaches. This proved to be a challenge. I went to the bus company and saw the manager. Kiseljak is a small town. He had heard the story, but not all of it. He knew that he had a captive audience. He wanted two hundred dollars a coach. If I agreed quickly he could find drivers and they could leave this evening. I did not have that sort of money. I promised him that I would return the next day with the cash but he was adamant, cash now. I understood, he had to buy fuel and pay the drivers and in a war zone everyone wants money up front, as they say.

I went back to the leaders and explained that we needed money. They were incensed. They had paid in Sarajevo and they could see no reason why they should pay twice. At times, refugee work can be unrewarding. I patiently explained that without money they were going nowhere. One of the leaders was most reasonable. He explained to me that many of the students genuinely did not have any money. They intended throwing themselves on the mercy of the embassies when in Split. So much for their assurances earlier in the day. I lined them all up and told them that I needed two hundred dollars a coach. After a debate it was agreed that we could squeeze everyone on to two coaches. So the demand was for four hundred dollars. I led the way, putting in all I had, a mere twenty dollars, an emergency note I had in my back pocket in case I came upon any shops selling wine. After a lot of murmuring we raised just under three hundred and sixty dollars.

I went back to the bus company. The manager agreed to do it with two coaches for three hundred and sixty, providing I would do him a favour. His family were in Sarajevo, he wished me to take a parcel of food to them. I agreed. I still knew something he did not know. One of the passengers needed more room than the others. We agreed that the coaches would arrive at five. I returned to the students. They were very happy. We unloaded all the bags and the box and waited.

When the two Croat coaches arrived I met the drivers. They wanted an UNPROFOR escort to Split. I explained that this was impossible. I agreed to contact both UNPROFOR and the European Monitors ECMM and warn them that they were on their way. It was then load-up time. I asked the students' leaders to put their recumbent colleague in the luggage hold. This we managed to do unobtrusively without the driver noticing. However, when the rest of the students came to put their kit in the hold there was not enough room. So out he came. I was standing next to the driver when *opéra comique* became *opéra bouffe*. The students were struggling with the box, trying to get it up the steps and into the coach.

'What the hell is that?' asked the driver.

Everyone looked at me. 'A box,' I replied.

Then he caught the smell of it. 'It stinks,' he said. 'What is in it?'

Riddle time. 'What is six foot long, two foot wide and stinks?'

Riddles do not translate easily. 'I am not taking that,' said the driver. 'Get it off.'

Off it came. I told the driver that I would go and sort things out with the manager. At his office I met him heartily and asked him if he had the parcel ready for me. He did. It was an enormous box; tins, fresh fruit and vegetables, cooked meats and three or four bottles of spirits. We loaded it into my car. There was a letter with it. I took the precaution of taking the letter out of the box and put it in my pocket. As I was leaving I asked him if he would come around to the coaches as one of his drivers was being difficult and refusing to take one of the passengers. He came immediately and I watched as he began to remonstrate with his driver. After a second or two he turned and looked in my direction and laughed and laughed and laughed. I had a Croat with a sense of humour. The driver was still not happy. I asked the manager if he had any other suggestions? Had he any ideas as to what he could do with it? Was there a left luggage office or anywhere we could leave it? The driver now began to see the funny side and eventually agreed to take it. The students insisted that he travel in the coach on the back seat. By this time I was fed up with the whole saga. I told the students that when they get to Split the late student would travel in the aircraft hold back to his home. He would not be permitted to travel on the bloody aircraft seats. The driver also had had enough. He wanted to get away. The box travelled passenger class.

I took my farewell of the students and was impressed that they were all very concerned for the safety of the drivers who had been arrested by the Serbs.

Throughout most of the afternoon Jim O'Neil had been around and about giving support and assistance. He could easily have left me on my own and returned early to Sarajevo, but that is not Jim's style. Despite the delays, the confusion and the chaos, Jim was determined that we see the whole task through together. I really appreciated this and we set off for Sarajevo together, me in the lead in my armoured range rover, Jim following in his soft-skinned landcruiser. My own troubles were just about to begin.

At the Croat check-point we were very rarely stopped and checked. This evening we were. I was confident, I opened the back, they hardly looked in. But I realised that, in addition to the bus manager's parcel, by swapping vehicles because of the shortage of fuel, I now had with me all my kit for Gorazde. I was going to need a bit of luck at the Serb check-point.

We arrived back at the Serb check-point. Momo was waiting for me where I had left him. So were many of his colleagues. Two in particular I recognised as Ministry of the Interior; hoods, threatening hoods. They were waiting for me. They demanded to search the vehicle. I told them 'No'. They could look in but they were not rummaging through my possessions. Often I was bloody-minded for the sake of the principle, today I was genuinely concerned. By having swapped vehicles I had no idea what was in mine. I called our Serb Liaison Officer Momo over and reminded him that we had come into Serb territory to facilitate the passage of the convoy, which they had agreed, and had left Serb territory at their request to organise the coaches. The contents of the vehicles were as at this morning. I had no intention of permitting a search.

Jim watched fascinated as I did a little war dance. They lost interest in his vehicle. One of the Ministry of the Interior men pushed me away from mine and a soldier removed the bus manager's box. Their eyes lit up with this. I was now genuinely furious. I pulled away from my vehicle the secret policeman, a little runt of a man. I slammed the doors of the car. The contrast between white beard and red cheeks must have been alarming. I felt that I was close to bursting a blood vessel. One soldier removed my briefcase from the far side of the car and was about to take out letters from it when I assaulted him. At this stage they decided that I was under arrest. The Sarajevo girl translator was embarrassed at the hassle I was getting. She advised me quietly to agree to follow their car to the police station. 'Either that or they will throw you in theirs.'

I got into my car with Momo, locked the doors and windows and followed the police car. Momo was very upset and ashamed. He is an honourable man. He respects age and position. In me he overestimated both aspects. I noticed that the ever faithful Jim followed. They were happy for him to return to Sarajevo but he would not.

Whilst we were stopped at the check-point, we had heard a lot of shells falling on Ilidza. When we arrived at the police station there was a lot of noise. The shells were landing not too far away. I thought about not leaving the car. This would certainly embarrass them. They would have a hell of a job trying to break in. However, I had Momo inside with me. Locking him in with me would be a real test of his Serb loyalty. So I let him out, got out myself, locked the car and followed my escort. I shouted to Jim that because of the shelling he should go on to Sarajevo. He replied that he would wait. And wait he did. I followed the girl into the police station, and was led through the door, down to the area of the cells. There we awaited the arrival of an investigator. He was a tall, gaunt pre-war professional. He spoke exceedingly quietly. I had to strain to hear him. He was courteous and determined. He told me that in my briefcase there were letters addressed to Gorazde. He wanted them. He was right. Before I attempt to enter any besieged area I let it be known that I am prepared to take in mail. If I am successful, the news I bring in is often the first for many months. The exchange of mail boosts morale immeasurably. The letters in my briefcase were, however, special in that they had been given to me to hand to the mayor of Gorazde. In my opinion he was as entitled to mail as anyone. We examine carefully everything we take in. We do not handle parcels; we do not even accept bulky letters.

Back to the investigation. All I had to do was hand over the mayor's letters and I could go. I politely told the investigator that if he had mail for anyone in Gorazde I would happily take it and that he could rest assured that once he gave it to me it would be either delivered or returned. He smiled.

Meanwhile outside the shelling intensified. Poor Jim was still sitting in his soft-skinned vehicle, his ears ringing and the ground shaking. He decided on action. He marched up to the desk and asked if he too could be arrested. He reckoned it would be safer than sitting outside. His request was turned down.

Inside, I was told that the investigator had to leave. If I gave him the mail then I could go. If not, I must stay. I asked them to prepare a place for the night but reminded them that I was a UN official and a formal complaint would be made. The quiet investigator reminded me in turn that I was a neutral UN official, not a 'Muslim' postman.

Touché.

He left the room. The girl was not sure what was going to happen next. We sat and waited. The investigator returned. He was sorry but I must hand over the letters. If they turned out to be innocent I would be released immediately. If not, I might be held as a spy.

Ouch!

I had an idea. I proposed to him that I return to Sarajevo with Momo and the mail and that we take it to the Bosnian Muslim liaison officer together. There, it would be opened in our presence. If it contained anything nefarious, Momo would report it and the Serbs and report me to the UN and I would be labelled whatever they believed to be appropriate. The girl thought this a great idea. The investigator thought it childish. He left the room.

Once again, I was fed up. When he returned it was contrasting-colour time: red face on white beard. The investigator was genuinely shocked by my outburst. He attempted to reason with me in a quieter voice than before. Actually, I was genuinely annoyed, mainly with myself. He might have guessed this, because he then summarised the day's events and outlined my failings. I had attempted to smuggle a body out of Sarajevo. I had attempted to smuggle food and drink into Sarajevo. I had attempted to smuggle mail into Gorazde. I was a senior representative of a United Nations agency. Was this the conduct they could expect from me? This man was twisting the blade. He then said that I could go. No more mention of mail, no nothing, just go.

Outside, it was dark and very noisy. Jim was sitting patiently in his soft-skinned vehicle. He told me that he was glad to see me. Not half as glad as I was to see him. We had a quick debate. Should we ask the Serbs for accommodation or risk a quick dash back to Sarajevo? There would be a certain pleasure in demanding a bed for the night on my terms, but to be frank, I was at a low ebb and whenever that is the case there is no bed like home, wherever home is and however humble.

Momo, by now thoroughly embarrassed, sat in with me, and with Jim on our tail, we set off for Sarajevo at breakneck speed, no lights, no stopping. Ten breathless minutes later we were back in the PTT. My arrival was reported to the General, who had Adnan with him. He asked me to give him a full briefing and I recounted the day. The Bosnian government was furious about the arrest of the drivers. The General promised to see Dr Karadzic the following day to obtain their release. But circus turned to tragedy: the drivers were never seen again.

6

Sarajevo suburbs

'It's a small world' is a trite expression, but it is often proved true. Enesa and Aris Sparavalo had a beautiful daughter, Ana. When the baby was very young she was diagnosed as having a heart problem. In the very early days of the war Enesa got herself and Ana away, first to Slovenia, then to England. They were sent by the Immigration authorities to Bourne End in Berkshire, where they lived next door to the parents of one of my closest friends. It was impossible for Enesa to keep in touch with her husband. The normal telephone lines between Sarajevo and the rest of the world were down. My friend is a man of great initiative and a large heart. He contacted my wife in Salisbury, she was able to contact me by satellite phone and asked if I knew how to get in touch with a family called Sparavalo. Alma, standing next to me in the office, saw me writing down the name and said, 'I know the Sparavalos; they are friends of mine.' Two coincidences. Small world. My wife passed messages to me, I gave them to Alma, she passed them on to Aris. The news was always good. Ana was happy and strong. Enesa lived with a wonderful family. The man of the house idolised Ana, who looked upon him as her grand-father. She was awaiting an operation at the Royal Brompton hospital.

Meanwhile the demand for fuel for Sarajevo, be it coal, diesel, wood or whatever else burns and produces energy, was a constant nightmare. The media could never understand why we were not able to bring in at least sufficient fuel for the generators in the hospitals. The answer was simple – the Serbs refused. They believed that if fuel was brought in, it would be used by the government to support the war machine. They very carefully monitored the amount of fuel brought in by UNPROFOR for its own use. We, the civilian arm of the UN, were the poor relations. We had to beg from the UN military for our domestic fuel. The military did allocate a small amount of its fuel to the Bosnian government hospitals. I discussed with my masters in Zagreb and with the Bosnian Serbs ways of funding and transporting sufficient fuel to keep the vital functions going.

The Bosnian Serb attitude was simple: 'If you bring in fuel for the Muslims you must bring in fuel for us.' This sounded fair until you looked at it. Firstly, the Bosnian Serbs were getting plenty of fuel from Serbia, which itself was blockaded but with sieve-like barriers. Secondly, no Bosnian Serb town was besieged. UNHCR was therefore very reluctant to spend money on fuel for Bosnian Serbs as a bribe to permit vital humanitarian fuel into Sarajevo. There was a justifiable element of 'What will the donor nations say? What will the media say?'

The Bosnian minister responsible for fuel and energy was Rusmir Mahmutcehajic. In addition to his jaw-cracking name he had the strange title of Minister for Energetics. He is a small, dark man who possesses a formidable intellect. He has a fiery temper and a short fuse. He also has a serious problem with his eyesight, which he hides well. It is obvious only when greeting him. You extend your hand, he extends his, but you have to find his as he cannot see yours. His secretary is his eyes. She is also his ears. She sits in an outer office where visitors wait and she understands English, especially indiscreet comments. Her total loyalty to the Minister is unquestionable. She is his wife.

I was first summoned to see the Minister on a very cold day. The ministry is in the centre of town in a narrow street. I drove myself and had Meliha with me. We parked on the corner of the street and walked to the office entrance in an old building. There was a policeman outside with the inevitable gun. The building was freezing cold. We went up the stairs, turned right and we could smell the warmth. Unbelievably, this little corner of the building was heated. Not excessively, but enough to be able to stay and work in.

I met Mrs Mahmutcehajic, and the deputy to the Minister. They asked me to wait, as the Minister was on the phone. The phones rarely worked so when they did he took full advantage. I could hear him through the wall; he was not happy with whoever was on the other end. With each sentence his voice, which was deep and resonant, rose. He was warming someone's ears.

'Would you like me to come back?' I politely asked his wife.

She is a fair-haired, attractive lady with a pale face, bright eyes and a friendly smile. 'No. No.' She then entered his office without knocking.

'Meliha, what is the conversation about?'

'He is on the phone. I can only hear half of it. He is angry.'

Sometimes I wondered why I had an interpreter. But before I could probe further, the door opened and the Minister was gently guided towards me by his wife. She is taller than him. He welcomed me profusely. He had a conversation with Meliha, I am certain in order to establish how open he could be with me. Old habits die hard. He took his seat at the desk, which was at the head of a long conference table. He began immediately and brusquely. 'Mr Larry, we have many tonnes of fuel in Split in Croatia. I want you to bring it into Sarajevo.'

'Minister, your request should be simple but unfortunately the Serbs will not allow the fuel in.'

This triggered a tirade. The Minister gave me a lecture on the Charter of the United Nations, the sovereignty of Bosnia-Herzegovina, the mandate of UNPROFOR and the needs of the people.

'Fully understood, Minister. But no Serb approval, no fuel.'

'Why does it depend on the Serbs?' he asked in a menacing tone.

'Because, Minister, so far, they have won the war. You are not besieging Pale, they are besieging Sarajevo.' The Minister did not like this. But I continued, 'So if you want fuel in, you, or more accurately, we, have to do some deal with the Serbs.'

I expected apoplexy. But Rusmir Mahmutcehajic is a solver of problems. 'What do you think they will want?'

'I know exactly what they want. They want forty per cent. They will permit a convoy of five vehicles, three for Sarajevo, two for them.' Prior to meeting the Minister, I had paid a visit to Pale to meet my old Serb LO friend Dr Lukic, who was now prime minister for the so-called Srpska Republika. We had discussed fuel at great length. My homework visit was beginning to pay off.

'That is too much. We cannot agree to give them that much of our fuel.'

'Dr Lukic tells me that the fuel in Split was paid for with money which belongs to Serbs as well as Croats and, dare I say it, Muslims. He says it is Bosnian money and a share of anything it purchases must go to the Serbs.'

'If we agree,' said the Minister, 'how does the fuel get here and what happens to it when it arrives?' Two crucial and complicated questions.

'Well, Minister, UNHCR is prepared to hire a tanker and we have the strong possibility of the loan of a fuel tanker from the British Army contingent in Split.'

'We also have tankers in Sarajevo and in Split,' said the Minister. 'I offer them to you.'

'Excellent. Are they fit for the journey and can we paint them white?'

'No problem. We can also provide drivers. What about my second question, the distribution of the fuel?'

'Minister, when the fuel leaves Split it will become UNHCR property. It will come into the city, be stored and distributed under our auspices.'

'Where will you store it?'

'We will park the tankers at the airport in a secure location.'

We both smiled. He knew that UNHCR had lost at least half a dozen trucks to shellfire at the airport. A fully laden tanker would surely earn a Serb mortar man bonus points.

'We have underground fuel tanks in the city. Why can you not store it there?'

'Because if it is not under our direct control, you will issue it to the Army.'

'You do not trust us?'

'Correct.' I then added 'Correct, sir' for courtesy.

The Minister looked at me coldly. 'To whom will it be issued?'

The correctness of 'To whom' suddenly made me realise that so far this conversation had been held in English.

'We will issue it according to priorities drawn up by you. We would hope that the hospital and the bakery will be the top priority.'

'And any fuel that goes to the Serbs. How do you control that?'

'Easy. We insist that the fuel comes into the airport from where we issue their share. Same priorities.'

The Minister had heard enough. 'OK. I will speak to Split. My deputy will liaise with you. Thank you for your co-operation.' That was the end of the subject of fuel for the day. He then changed topics. 'Mr Larry, I have heard that you are keen on art. Do you know the work of Dzavid Hozo?'

'The lithographer,' I replied.

Rusmir was pleased. 'Yes. Have you met him?'

'No.'

'Then I will arrange a meeting.' I found his hand, shook it and we left. Both of us had much work to do if this conversation was to lead to the arrival of fuel in Sarajevo.

The Brits had indeed offered a tanker and, more importantly, the loan of a logistics team. But there were a few deployment problems. The Brits had their own sector, Sarajevo was not part of it. The only Brit in uniform in Sarajevo was the Chief of the UN Military Observers. There were a number of 'turf' problems to be sorted out. There were also a few UNHCR questions. Would the Brits be in uniform? Would they be armed? To whom would they report?

The team arrived on a reconnaissance, in uniform and with weapons. Commanded by Captain Peter Jones, it included Don Hodgson, a warrant officer from the REME, Alan Knight, a staff sergeant from RLC, and surprise, surprise, a girl from the Adjutant General's Corps, Caroline Cove. In a quiet, efficient way, they were to transform our operation.

Rusmir Mahmutcehajic was pleased with the speed of response. True, there was no fuel, but he could see that we had fuel experts on the ground. He invited myself and Meliha to have tea with him, his wife and the artist Dzavid Hozo. The venue was to be the artist's house. We agreed to meet outside the Presidential building. We arrived a little late. Despite the danger from shelling, the Minister was waiting in his car. His wife was with him and he was driven by his bodyguard.

The artist lived in a house on a very attractive small estate on one of the hills in Sarajevo. The road was narrow and the artist's house at the top. We arrived as darkness was falling. The Minister left his car quickly and his bodyguard ushered him rapidly to the house. I could see as I parked the UNHCR vehicle that the front of the house was overlooked by a hill which must have been in Serb hands. Hence the speed and caution. There were cars parked in the road. Some looked OK, others had been victims of the war. I parked off the road facing the hill and noted that we would have to go back the way we had arrived. The top of the hill went nowhere.

The artist and his wife were marvellous hosts. I was always embarrassed when people who had so little were so generous. The house was small, crowded and very much an artist's home. The room used for entertainment was up a flight of stairs and was lit by candles. We had a super evening: good food and wide-ranging, provocative conversation. I also had the pleasure of seeing a lot of Hozo's work. In particular, he was assembling a book about art which was in the proof stage before the war began. The project was shelved until life could return to normal when paper, ink, printers and publishers would be available.

With great reluctance, at around nine, Meliha and I said our farewells. I had to take her home, then get myself back to the PTT building. Dzavid kindly gave to me a book about his art. Rusmir and his bodyguard escorted us down the stairs. The latter opened the door and Rusmir and I were about to shake hands when there was a burst of gunfire in our direction. The bodyguard bundled the Minister back up the stairs. Meliha and I followed. The bodyguard explained that a sniper had seen us arrive, recognised the Minister and had waited for him to reappear. Just wait a minute or two, then try again, but without the Minister. 'OK,' I agreed.

After a few minutes standing in the dark behind the door the bodyguard opened it, wished us luck and out we went. 'Move quickly and with no lights,' he said unnecessarily. Meliha and I moved very quickly out into the dark night and across to the car. I opened the doors. Meliha jumped in. I got in, put the key in the ignition and paused. So far no shooting.

I was used to driving at night in Sarajevo. Move fast. Stop. Move fast. Stop. I had parked the car off the road. It was narrow and I was unfamiliar with it. The night was very dark and there seemed to be parked cars everywhere. I sat in the car and waited. If anyone had seen us move, they would now be up in the aiming position. Wait a while and they might come out of it. After a couple of minutes I turned the key. The engine sprang to life. I engaged reverse and the reversing light, bright and white, lit up the street. 'Jesus, Lord.' I quickly disengaged, the light went out, and a burst of gunfire whistled over our heads. I sat, thinking. My first thought was the most ridiculous: 'I will get out and remove the bulb.' My second was to drive forward and swing around in front of the parked cars, but this was the side of a hill, the edge of which I could not see. My third thought was to see if the car would roll back. It would not. I engaged reverse, swung back like a car on a movie set and hammered off down the hill. There were no more shots. On reflection, I believe the sniper was after the Minister. When my illuminated vehicle reversed, he fired, but then realised that it was a UN vehicle and decided against further action. By ten, I was in bed with my new book.

The Brits got a fuel run going. It was never enough, but it was better than none. Peter Jones was awarded an MBE for their extraordinary efforts.

Rusmir wanted fuel, Kosevo hospital in Sarajevo was forever pleading with us to bring in cylinders of oxygen. Driving a truck-load of highly explosive cylinders of oxygen is exceedingly risky. There are more uses for a cylinder of oxygen than just medical ones. It took a lot of negotiation with the Serb side before they would agree. Their terms were that oxygen cylinders must be provided for their hospitals as well. It took at least a month of negotiation to get the first convoy moving. The transportation of the oxygen was a small success, but we were proud of it. Well, so we thought, until Tony Land was summoned to the operations room. We had a convoy blocked at the Serb check-point. It contained a truck of oxygen bottles and the oxygen bottles contained gunpowder!

Tony was taken to the check-point. The Serbs were not annoyed but ecstatic. Since the beginning of the war they had accused us of smuggling weapons and ammunition on behalf of the 'Muslims'. Now they had proof. Tony had taken with him UNPROFOR policemen. Together they were shown oxygen cylinders which, when the top was unscrewed, revealed a black powder which the Serbs said was gunpowder. They were right. We were furious and lost faith in a number of people. We delivered the cylinders direct to the hospital, so some of the doctors must have known what some of them contained. We felt betrayed. It put our reputation at risk. It put our drivers at enormous risk. Not only were they carrying oxygen through active front lines, but oxygen and gunpowder. Furthermore, they could have been arrested by the Serbs. This incident gave the Serbs a big stick with which to beat us. It was followed by an increase in their vehicle search techniques and the constant gibe that we had smuggled ammunition to the 'Muslims'. An accusation we could not deny.

The gunpowder plot was not the only time we knew we were used. The delivery of food to the areas around the airport was progressing brilliantly. The French battalion containerised the aid and took the container on a trailer to the 'Muslim' areas of Butmir and Dobrinja, and to the Serb area of the Airport Settlements. The trucks and the containers were not specific to each area. The 'Muslims' in Butmir, who had access to ammunition from the Bosnian army, quickly realised that there was a space between the base of the container and the platform of the trailer. This they filled with ammunition, mainly Kalashnikov rounds, and waited. Sooner or later the trailer would end up by chance in Dobrinja. There the container would be lifted up and the ammunition removed. If the container and trailer went to the Serb side it made no difference. They did not know about the space, and never looked for it . . . until one night. Tony was called again, to be shown the evidence of our treachery. This time it was the turn of the French to be furious. The French liaison officers who risked their lives identifying themselves closely with their sectors particularly felt the betrayal of trust.

These were scams which were discovered. God knows what took place without us finding out.

Journalists were in and out of the office. Many had with them a local translator who not only knew the language but also knew who would give interviews, who wouldn't and how to get to those that would. Alma is an outstanding translator. Diminutive, attractive, full of energy and with a wide circle of influential friends, she is a favourite with journalists, especially those from the international cerebral broadsheets. The first time I met her I did not know who she was. She breezed into my office with two Spanish reporters. Her English was excellent. All three sat in the available chairs and fired questions at me. There was an equality among them. I presumed that she was an international journalist. I had just come from the dining-room and had collected an apple and an orange. They were on the sandbagged window-sill behind me.

As the interview came to an end the girl said, 'Is the orange yours?'

'Yes.'

'May I have it?'

I was a little cold. I thought she would be here for a few days and then move on. We rarely had fruit. I was about to say 'No', when I noticed that the two males were a little uncomfortable. I suddenly realised that the girl was not an international. 'Are you Bosnian?' I asked.

'Yes.'

'OK,' I said very ungraciously, and to my shame I turned, picked up the apple and the orange and threw them towards her. She caught them and, with a big smile, put them in her coat pocket. Still seated, I said goodbye to them.

When they had left, I thought over the incident. My attitude and action had been arrogant and ignorant. I tried to find Alma's telephone number to ring and apologise, but the phones were down. It bugged and niggled me for the remainder of the day.

It was a month later before I saw her again.

'Remember me?' she asked.

'Oh yes. And I owe you an apology.'

'Let me tell you about the orange,' she said, riding straight over my reply. 'I took it home and gave it to my mother. She longed for fruit. She was dying. It gave me so much pleasure to find fresh fruit for her.'

'Look, I want to apologise for throwing the fruit at you. I should have got up and handed it to you. I'm sorry. I thought you were a cheeky, greedy journalist.'

'And not a starving Bosnian.'

I blushed. 'How is your mother now?'

'She died. That is why the fruit was so special. It was the last treat I was able to provide for her.'

The battle for the Sarajevo suburb of Otes lit the sky day and night for four days. The drama was intense and vicious. In four days the two square kilometres were hit with more than fourteen and a half thousand shells. Four days and much of four nights the ground shook, as shell after shell pounded in, one every thirty seconds. The families who lived in this pretty modern village, which had the misfortune to become a strategic target, first took to the basements of their buildings. When it became clear to them that they were locked into a battle unto death and destruction, a lot of the husbands persuaded their families to attempt an escape into Sarajevo.

Many of the women, children and elderly left by night and crossed the icy water of the River Bosna. Most survived, some drowned. Meanwhile their men fought on. There were many deaths. While the battle raged, we in UNHCR frequently attempted to gain access to the area to assess and to assist. On the last day of the battle we visited the Serb Army Corps headquarters in Ilidza. It was located in a large old house down a magnificent boulevard designed in the days of the Austro–Hungarian Empire, lined with huge poplar trees, which reached to the sky. In better times, carriages drawn by horses had trotted tourists up and down its length, viewing the splendid houses of an earlier era while *en route* to the nearby source of the River Bosna. More recently it was a venue for weekend cyclists. Now the road was scratched and scarred by tank tracks and the country homes scuffed and stained by the boots of soldiers.

The wary Corps commander greeted us and handed us on to his sector commander, a long, lank, battle-weary professional soldier, whose eyes were rimmed with grey-black circles caused by lack of sleep. His neck was bandaged; he had been wounded in a recent battle. His office had been a small bedroom. The bed had gone but the heavy furniture ingrained with polish applied by generations of maidservants remained. He had recently been visited by the French battalion commander, his calling card, a box of six bottles of red wine, stood on the side table.

'What does he want?' he asked my translator, whom I had chosen with extreme care.

Vesna Stancic is the most fluent simultaneous translator at headquarters. 'To enter Otes,' she translated.

'What is your name?' he asked her. She told him. Both her Christian and surname are Serb. 'Where are you from? Who was your father?' He wanted to know if she was Serb. 'What was the maiden name of your mother?' He wanted to know how Serb she was. Satisfied that she was Serb Serb, he relaxed. 'What does he want to go to Otes for?'

'To see if he can help the families in there.'

'Does he think the war will stop for him?'

'No.'

'Come back tomorrow, the battle will be over.'

That night the noise eased. The following morning we returned. Three of us: myself, Vesna and the Chief of the UN Military Observers, Lt-Col. Richard Maule, a British Army officer who had taken over the job from a gung-ho, exceedingly brave and excessively caring New Zealander, Lt-Col. Richard Grey. The Brit led equally as successfully, but by calm example.

The sector commander agreed to see us. I placed my single Johnny Walker card next to the still untouched box of wine. The commander had with him an officer, a small, sincere, chubby-faced pre-war schoolteacher with warm, soft brown eyes. 'He will be your guide.'

The conversation was finished. As I rose to leave, I looked carefully at him. He was a thorough professional. The battle was over and he had won. But there was no elation, swagger or bravado. He had gained ground but lost men and the war had not ended. Before we could leave he shouted to our guide. 'What did he say?' I asked Vesna, then looked at her for the answer. The blood had drained from her face.

'He said, "Do not let them see the bodies." '

We took the guide in our car from Ilidza to Otes. As we passed under the bridge which had separated the two districts we met a large group of soldiers. They were returning from looting the houses. They had boxes, bundles, prams full of household items, televisions, videos, pictures. One stopped and hung up on the wall of the bridge a magnificent mounted head of a wild boar. They were not embarrassed by our presence. These were the spoils of war.

Our guide was. 'Look at them. Look at that one.' He pointed to a young man with a pigtail. 'He thinks he is Rambo. But he is a tourist.'

'A tourist?' I asked.

'Look at his eyes. Look at mine. He has not been here fighting over the past days.'

I looked. The eyes of Rambo were bright, alert and laughing. Our guide's were sad. Deep pools of sadness. 'Did you lose many troops?'

'Too many. We underestimated their ability and their resolve. I think we lost more than they did.'

We left the car at the entrance of the village and walked. First we saw a small block of apartments. The ground floor had been shops. The walls, windows and doors had been shattered by heavy gunfire, the stock stripped by looters. The floors above were like a doll's house. The outer wall, the complete front wall of the building, had fallen away, pulverised by tank shells. The rooms were open to view. Beds with linen, tables with cloths, chairs with cushions, stood open to the elements. Water gushed from wash-basins, toilets and fractured pipes. Our guide let us wander. We went down a street of small detached houses. There were groups of civilians, mainly older couples, going from house to house, looting.

'What is going on here?' I asked.

'These are people who have returned to collect their possessions from their damaged homes,' our guide replied inventively. The civilian looters did look guilty as we watched them. I suspect they were the parents of the front-line troops and were getting the 'first pick' of this war harvest.

We wandered along the interconnecting network of trenches built by the defenders: deep, narrow burrows leading from street to street. Bodies lay where they had fallen, some from each side not yet collected. One was close to where we stood. A young man. He was lying against the wall of the trench as if he were standing. His face was turned towards us, his eyes open, his skin a strange dark green. I hate looking at bodies when I know that the next of kin have not been informed of the death. The knowledge alienates you from them and in some strange way allies you with the body. I dwelt too long for Vesna. She gently tugged on my sleeve.

'Where are the civilians?' I asked.

'Gone.'

'Gone where?'

'Some left during the fighting. Others have left now. Some to Sarajevo, others to Kiseljak.'

'Where are the bodies you are not allowed to show us?'

'They are in different corners.'

'Are they civilians?'

'Yes.'

'Why can we not see them?'

'Because the commander said no.'

'But why? Are they mutilated?'

'No, they are just bodies.'

'Women and children.'

'Some.'

We walked back to our vehicle. I was not going to press this man to see bodies. They had cleaned up the area. They had gathered together the bodies. My seeing them was not going to alter the world.

'Come and look in the Bosnian army headquarters,' said our guide.

We went into a ground-floor room of a well-protected building.

It had been a military headquarters. There were maps, pencils, manuals and, stacked to the ceiling, UNHCR aid.

'That is what happens to your aid. It goes to the army.'

'I am sorry, my weary friend, but I do not buy your self-righteousness. When we issue aid to your side in Rajlovac it is stored in a military warehouse. It is distributed on military trucks.'

At the car, I took a last look at Otes. It was a bright, crisp December day. This time last year it had been Otes with Christmas in the air. Now it was still, almost silent Otes, just the sounds of trickling water and creaking, squeaking carts laden with goods stolen from the dead and the dispossessed. We passed the bridge under the beady eye of the boar's head, dropped off our host, thanked the commander and left. I slowly realised that I had no animosity towards them. I knew that if Otes had defeated Ilidza the carts would have tumbled in the opposite direction.

I received a message to meet the Brit Hercules. There were some parcels on board for me. I was very excited. Even more so when the plane landed. There was a large box and four sacks. The box was wrapped in Harrods paper. Like a squirrel, I collected my goodies and raced back to my bed space. I opened the box. It contained a Father Christmas outfit minus the beard! The sacks were full of toys. It was all from Harrods. The Al Fayed brothers had donated them to be given to Sarajevo children at Christmas, a really spontaneous and generous gesture. Peter Kessler, the UNHCR spokesman, and I handed them out over Christmas to the children's wards in the hospitals. Well done, Harrods. By the way, I still have your suit.

From England I received news that little Ana was now in the Royal Brompton hospital, which had agreed to waive the fourteen-thousand-pound cost of the operation normally charged to overseas patients. As is the custom of this outstanding hospital, Enesa was allowed to stay close to her daughter. Aris eagerly awaited news. Ana had the operation and began to recover. Being a very pretty little Bosnian refugee, she was the darling of the ward. The surgeons were pleased with her progress.

I then received a phone call: 'Larry, I have just had a phone call from Enesa. Ana is dead.'

My eyes filled with tears. I felt numb and cold. I had never met Enesa. I had never met Ana and I hardly knew Aris. But I felt part of the family. I knew that the death of one little child was insignificant in this great unfolding tragedy, but I had become involved. I could feel the isolation and loneliness of Enesa.

I asked Alma to send a car to Aris's flat and bring him in to see me. I rang the hospital and was put through to the children's ward. The sister was very pleased to hear me. They were at a loss. Enesa was alone. There were many private questions to be answered. They had asked Enesa where her husband was and where she wanted to go.

'Sarajevo,' was the answer to both.

There were many practical questions. What was to happen to the body of Ana?

'Let me talk to Enesa,' I asked. She came to the phone. I was her link with home in this, her loneliest hour. 'Enesa. I am so sorry about Ana. I have sent a car for Aris. He will be here soon. When he arrives I will tell him what has happened, then I will ring you and you and he can speak.'

A soft, stunned, 'Thank you.'

'Enesa. You need people around you now. Have you informed the couple with whom you live?'

'Yes. They are coming here.' Then, thinking very clearly and bravely she asked me: 'What will happen now to Ana and myself?'

The question had already run through my mind. 'Enesa, I am sure that I could arrange for you and Ana to fly back to Sarajevo. I do not think that would be right. I am sure that I can work out a way for Aris to come to England so that you may . . .' I fumbled for a word ' . . . look after Ana together. Just think about it and discuss it with Aris when he arrives.'

'Thank you.'

Aris appeared. He had not been told. I met him in the corridor of the busy, scruffy, chaotic PTT building. He looked so vulnerable. His face was grey, his eyes tired. He looked at me as if I had a way of influencing the news that he was about to hear. As if I could make it better. Amira translated for me. I put my arms round him and held him to me as he sobbed. I left him with Alma for a few minutes, so that she could console him in his own language. Then I returned.

'Aris, I am going to ring England now and put you in touch with Enesa. You must be very strong. She is there alone. She will want to know what is happening to herself and to Ana. I must therefore ask you some insensitive questions so that we can help Enesa.'

'I understand.'

I confirmed that he would want Ana to be buried and I explained to him my thoughts on where. 'Aris, I believe that you should go to England. You have suffered enough here. Think it over while I put through the call.'

I rang the hospital and put them in touch with each other. Amira kept everyone else out of the office. They spoke for a long time. From where I stood it was obvious that Enesa was the stronger of the two. But Aris had endured six more months of war. Aris finished the conversation and we then spoke. 'I would like to go to England.'

'No problem,' I replied, lying heavily.

I rang Mr Sparrow, the British ambassador in Zagreb, and explained the situation. He was marvellous. Understanding, kind and considerate, he promised to have a visa for England waiting at Zagreb airport for Aris. So far, so good. I rang the hospital to see how things were and to keep them in the picture. The Bourne End family had arrived and were with Enesa. I spoke to them. We talked about arrangements, then I spoke again to Enesa. She was emotionally very strong.

'I have one worry,' she said. 'The funeral will be expensive. We have no money.'

'Leave that to me,' I replied. I asked to speak to the Bourne End family and we discussed funeral expenses. The cost of dying in the stockbroker belt is as dear as the cost of living.

I then had a brilliant idea. Jeremy Bowen, the BBC journalist who was with me in Gorazde, had returned to London. His producer, Vin Ray, had gone back with him. I rang the Beeb. Jeremy was out but Vin was in. I explained the problem.

'Leave it to me,' he said.

UNHCR got Aris on the next British Hercules to Zagreb, where he was met by Mike Aitcheson, the UNHCR airlift chief, and a man from the British embassy. Aris was given a visa and moved on to England. Little Ana was buried in a plot provided free by the Wooburn Green cemetery. The funeral was paid for by F. G. Pymm and Son of Maidenhead, a remarkable company whose policy is not to charge for the funerals of children under sixteen.

During the Second World War the British government issued a poster warning servicemen against discussing military affairs in public. The slogan was 'Careless talk costs lives'. The peace negotiations in Bosnia were going very badly. Every five minutes Lord Owen was heard on the radio and seen on television with his maps of ethnic majority cantons. His proposal was rejected by the Bosnian government, supported and rejected by the US government and killed by General Mladic imposing his iron will on the Pale government. The media wanted a comment on the post-Pale situation.

I was very busy, but was tracked down by the BBC. In the middle of a 'What is the aid situation?' type interview, the smooth, measured tones asked, 'Apropos the rejection of the Owen Plan, what do you think Lord Owen should do now?'

'I think he should get himself a new colouring book and a new set of crayons,' I replied, surprising myself with my spontaneous wit. The BBC repeated it on the hour every hour for what seemed like days. If I walked into a room it was always news time and there it was. If I sat in a car with someone and they had the radio on, it was news time. An unfair remark became a trite remark. It did not please Lord Owen and it did not please my masters. I was rebuked soundly by Mr Stoltenberg. Careless talk almost cost my UN life.

Conferences and meetings took up a lot of our time. Tony took the brunt of them. They were mainly heavy and serious, but just occasionally they were fun.

'The next item on the agenda is "Bull semen for cows in Sarajevo",' said Deputy Prime Minister Zlatko Lagumdzija.

Tony Land was leading for UNHCR. 'Er, Deputy Prime Minister, firstly I have seen only one cow in Sarajevo. Secondly the transportation of bull semen is not easy, unless you happen to be a bull.'

Zlatko Lagumdzija replied: 'To answer your first point, there are few cows. There will be even fewer if we do not get semen. To answer your second, bull semen needs to be transported in temperature-controlled containers.'

Tony drew on his Chemical Engineering degree and his Sarajevo knowledge. 'Mr Lagumdzija, the containers need to be nitrogen cooled. There is no way the Serbs will allow such containers in.'

'There you go,' said Lagumdzija petulantly, 'back to what the Serbs will allow.'

Tony then said, only half in jest, 'Maybe we can negotiate that the Serbs have thirty per cent of the semen.'

Back came the Deputy Prime Minister's reply: 'The Serbs can go and f*** their own cows.'

More often than not, these conferences were just hard work. In January 1993 Zlatko Lagumdzija came to the meeting in a fighting mood. When we arrived there were TV cameras set up in the conference room. Always a bad omen.

'Mr Hollingworth, you are failing, in Sarajevo, in Srebrenica, in Zepa, in Gorazde. Let me give you some solutions.

> Model one: Give us the means to solve the problem ourselves.
>
> Model two: Give us air drops.
>
> Model three: You use all necessary means.'

Zlatko was clever. What he said was true but it wasn't news. His bluntness was designed to annoy me. The cameras were turning. Whatever was said would be on local TV that evening. I began to seethe, but held my temper.

'Mr Hollingworth, are you aware that in Zepa two hundred and ninety-one people, including a hundred and sixty-six children, have died. You told us that you were going to take a convoy in on 21 December. You said that the Serbs told you it was impossible because of heavy snow. There was no snow. You told us that you would go in on 6 January. You said that the Serbs told you it was impossible because of heavy fighting. There was no fighting.'

This was cruel. He knew how much effort I was putting into

convoys for the enclaves. The local camera crew held the lens on my face. I let him continue.

'Mr Larry, what is the role of UNHCR? What is the role of UNPROFOR?' These were rhetorical questions. He left no time for a reply. 'Believing you, we have been promising the people aid. But all of the UN institutions have done nothing . . . Nothing . . .' A long pause. I thought about interrupting but he continued, 'Why do you not adopt the mandate you have been given?'

He paused again. The camera was again on me. I wanted to shout out, 'Look, you ungrateful bastard, we are trying to operate in your war. We are stopped by you Bosnians; be you Serbs, Croats or Muslims, it is Bosnians who are preventing us from carrying out our task.' But a sound bite from me would have been cut out of the programme and Zlatko knew the situation.

But he was not yet finished. 'Negotiating with the Chetniks [he always referred to the Srpska Republika leaders as Chetniks] is a waste of time. Go on, admit that UNHCR and UNPROFOR cannot achieve their aim.'

He paused long enough for me to get in, 'Zlatko, we do our best. We . . .'

But he was quick. This was his speech, not mine. He cut me off. 'Mr Larry, your best is not good enough. Tell the donor governments that it is not possible to provide aid to the enclaves. Tell the governments that hundreds are dying of cold and star-vation. Continue the way you are and all will die. The Chetniks started this war to annihilate these locations. They are close to finishing what they started.'

At this stage the Deputy Prime Minister stopped and amazingly – yes, that is the right word, amazingly – began to cry. These were genuine tears of frustration and emotion. I am sure that they took him by surprise. His emotion devastated some of his col-leagues. I was not prepared for it. I had until the moment of his tears thought that I was listening to a carefully prepared and rehearsed speech.

In the pause, a doctor from Zepa whose brother was practising there stepped in: 'Why haven't you reached Zepa? The road is clear today, there is no fighting today. Go now.'

This was not my day. No sooner had he stopped than my friend Murat, the ex-mayor of Srebrenica, who knew how much effort I had put into attempts at reaching Srebrenica, began, 'There is no fighting near Srebrenica. Try now.' He caught the 'Et tu, Brute' look in my eye and mellowed. 'Try. If you have to return, it is OK. At least they will know you tried.'

These interjections had given Zlatko time to recover and back he came with a vengeance. 'So we agree we cannot enter anywhere because the Chetniks do not let us. So whatever happens it is because the other side will not let us. Then let us inform the media that it is the Chetniks' plan to kill all these people. You, the UN, have the mandate to relieve them. You, the UN, are holding cities under siege. At the airport meeting the Chetniks agreed to allow convoys. They clearly did not mean it. So, UN, with your mandate there is no solution. We demand air drops. Please try again, this time with adequate air drops. If you cannot respect the UN resolution we will do something on our own. It will clearly be suicide but we will do it.

'Mr Larry, inform Geneva that the people of Bosnia believed in the United Nations. But you have not carried out the mandate it gave to you. We must now do it our way.' Then, cleverly, he left. No farewell; he just swept out of the room.

Zlatko, if I had been in your shoes I would have said exactly the same. You were not normally a passionate man. You were on that day and I admired you for it. But you hurt me. You scored well on TV that evening. You were right about your expectations of the UN. That was our biggest problem. We were there. Our presence implied a commitment, one we were unable to fulfil. However, at the next meeting I was able to defend myself better.

'Mr Hollingworth [a bad sign], we have received from your office in Zagreb all the paperwork for all the aid that has arrived at the airport. There is a thirty per cent deficiency between that which was put on the aircraft and that which was distributed. Who is eating our food?'

'Mr Deputy Prime Minister, you cannot eat aircraft pallets!'

In the Serb enclave called Nedzarici, only a few hundred metres from the airport, there is an old people's home. I knew it was there. I had heard that it was in an appalling state. It was absolutely on the front line. The Bosnian government forces said that it was a sniper post for the Serbs. This was certainly true. On one of my visits the French took me up to an end room. Pulled close to the window was a chair, on the floor were the cartridge cases of rounds from a high-powered rifle. The Serb side said that the home was the regular target of Bosnian small-arms and mortar fire. The aid that we were able to get to Nedzarici was minimal. I doubted if any of it reached the home. In the summer we heard that the home wanted food and medicine. I was told that it contained a hundred and three patients. We were unable to get sufficient essential supplies to the main Sarajevo hospitals. The old people's home was forgotten. As winter began we were again reminded of the home. It had no heating. It had no fuel. It had no food. There were now only seventy-five patients.

I discussed the problem with Erik de Stabenrath. Nedzarici was one of the areas his boys were visiting regularly. We agreed to go together to see the place. I took with me little Mica as my translator. A tiny girl, she was wound up with intense energy and had a rapier-sharp wit. Her parents lived in a huge block of flats where the floors above and below were burnt out by shellfire, but they stayed. Mica is a deceptively tough little girl, always in scrapes of one sort or another. She was reluctant to come with me. 'My English is good enough for conversation but not for translation.' She must also have been worried about going to Nedzarici. Not only is she outspoken, but she is married to a well-known Bosnian satirical journalist. Despite her size, she cannot merge or blend into the background; there is something about Mica that lets you know she is there even when she is still and silent. But Meliha was not available, Mica it had to be.

The French escorted us in. It was a bitterly cold day. The approach to the home is along a very narrow road, with destroyed houses on both sides. Fifty metres before the end of the road, the vehicles mount the kerb and swing around a barrier. The home is on the right. It is Serb territory, but the first Bosnian rifles are no more than one hundred metres away. This is a most active front line. We parked. Both sides knew we were visiting, but both sides were firing at each other. This was not a place to linger. The staff were waiting to meet us at the side door they used as the entrance. It was almost midday. They had a huge wood-fired cauldron by the door. I opened the lid, steam rose and hit our nostrils. I dipped in the ladle and swished it around. All that I could see was greasy water. 'Mica, is this washing-up water?'

Her black eyes flashed back. 'It is soup.'

We were introduced to an old man who lived in Nedzarici and was helping at the home. He looked old enough to need some care and attention himself, but he was alert in mind and body. Apparently he was invaluable to the staff. No job was beneath his dignity.

The 'safe' way to the wards was through the kitchen, which had not been used as a kitchen since the war began. Then out into the 'day room', an open area flanked by broken windows.

'Move quickly across this room. You can be seen by Muslim snipers,' said one of the soldiers we had with us. They were Serb. One was young and pleasant, the other rough and offensive. Mica kept close to me. We moved quickly. I watched the care assistants cross this room. They must do it twenty times a day every day, but they were as apprenhensive as we were. Sniper fire had often killed patients in the hospital. This day room was one of the death spots.

We were not prepared for the 'wards'. The home was badly damaged by shell and mortar rounds. The wards used were chosen because of their relative safety: the rooms least likely to be hit. There was, of course, no electricity, no running water, no central heating.

The first ward was on the ground floor. The insides of the windows that remained were covered in ice. The room was refrigerator cold. The beds were close together. On them there were bundles of what looked like blankets. The nurse approached the first bed. By rearranging the bundle, she revealed an ashen face with deep-set dark eyes. The nurse spoke and the response was a silent opening and closing of the thin-lipped, toothless mouth, as if a little chick was waiting to be fed. We visited each of the bundles. The blankets were damp, the sheets frozen. The source was urine. The smell was strong. In this ward there were eight human beings for whom death would be a warm relief.

We moved upstairs where there were smaller wards and a large
room with a stove which was the gathering place of the patients
who could leave their beds. They were a lively bunch. Like
patients in all old people's homes they were holding conversations
at different levels, at different angles and at different times. There
was an elegant old Serb officer, a little lady who spoke English,
another who thought I was her son. In this room there was
life. The wood-burning stove warmed the room to a temperature
sufficient for it to be a magnet for these ambulant patients. They
stayed by the fire as long as they could, before returning to the
ice boxes that were their wards.

The small staff of six were saints. They had little food, lived
on the front line and attempted to dispense care in these appalling
conditions. If they handled a patient, fed a patient, changed a
patient, laid out a dead patient, there were no rubber gloves, no
hand-basins with the elbow taps and the sterilising soap. The
smell of the patient, the touch of the patient, lingered on their
flesh. None of these women had received any salary. None had
the prospect of salary. Why did they do it? Mica asked them.

'Because it is our job. We can't leave them.' They could not.
We had to. But we left food, some medicine and stoves. Enough
stoves for each room. But they needed installing and they needed
wood.

We returned to Sarajevo depressed. Not over what we had seen
but because what we had seen was shocking but not unique. I had
been in Kosevo hospital after a mortar attack, had seen patients
brought in like damaged sheep, carried by their limbs, laid on the
floor. I had seen the operating theatre with no electricity; stressed
and tired surgeons without instruments, without plasma, fighting
for the lives of young children. There were sick and dying patients
in the hospitals. There were other old people's homes. There were
lunatic asylums. There were pacemaker patients without batteries,
diabetics without insulin. There was no electricity for dialysis
machines, for incubators, for X-ray machines. We had limited
resources, yet we had access to unlimited resources. We could
only bring in a fraction of what we had and a small portion of
what was needed.

I did try to get the patients out to alternative accommodation,

but the Sarajevo authorities were not enthusiastic. They wanted a
cease-fire around the home. They reminded me of the situation
within the city. Finding space for another seventy would not be
easy. The Serbs were more helpful. They would take the Serbs
and possibly the Croats. We would have to fund their upkeep in
their new location.

The Bosnian government authorities did not agree with this:
'They are all Bosnians.' The problem was taking too much time.
It was buried under more pressing and more urgent matters. More
pressing and more urgent unless you happened to be a patient in
a living morgue. My attention moved on to other issues.

A week or so later, the media, on for them a quiet day, visited
the home. Nine had died since our last visit. Some of the stoves
we had taken were still lying in a corner waiting to be installed.
The media went for our throats: the military for not installing
the stoves, UNHCR for not . . . for everything else. 'Why are the
patients still there?' they asked me to camera.

'Because to move them I need places elsewhere.'

The media interest focused the attention of both the Serb and
the government authorities. The Serbs offered accommodation
at the nearby Serb hospital to the worst of the patients, 'Muslims,
Croats and Serbs'.

I got hold of the Serb doctor from the hospital, I took him
away from his Christmas lunch in his hospital staff room. It was
6 January (the Serbs still use the Julian Calendar). The doctor
was brave – our journey involved him crossing Bosnian government front lines. He assessed the worst of the patients. I agreed
to donate to his hospital food, blankets and fuel for heating. On a
great media circus day a convoy was arranged and with difficulty
some patients were moved. We did not shift the worst, but those
who would benefit most from the move. They all had to be
volunteers. Some were so unaware of the war they could not
understand the significance of the question, 'Are you prepared to
go to a Serb-dominated area?'

On this occasion the Serbs were magnanimous and noble. Their
side of the operation went without a hitch. The facilities they
offered the patients were magnificent. The Bosnian government
annoyed me. Bosnian TV accused me of having 'ethnically

cleansed' the home. The journalists did not leave the story. On the farewell visit of the Special Envoy, Jose Maria Mendiluce, they raised it again. I can take criticism but I took more than my fair share over this home. I did not put the patients there. I did not keep them there. I took to them what I could when I could. It was not enough and it was not quick enough. True, I did not check on the progress of the installation of the stoves which we had delivered. Maybe twenty of them died who could have lived.

Some bastard shot dead the little old man who assisted the staff. Right outside the door of the home he had done so much to help.

7
Zepa

Of all the convoys that I did, the one that gave me the most satisfaction was to small, intimate Zepa.

Zepa is a village at the bottom of a steep valley. The valley is dotted with small groups of houses all dependent on Zepa for direction and support. The nearest town is Rogatica, the nearest city Gorazde. Zepa is almost unique in ex-Yugoslavia. Because of its location and the tenacity of its occupants, it alone during the Second World War managed to keep the invading Germans out. Not a single German soldier entered Zepa. Convoys and patrols often entered the valley, but their vehicles were blocked on the narrow twisting roads by obstacles natural and unnatural, and they were easily and accurately picked off by sniper fire as they attempted to recover them.

As the Bosnian war progressed, Muslims from Rogatica fled to Zepa or Gorazde, and Serbs from Zepa and Gorazde to Rogatica. Blood was spilt on both sides. Outlying and isolated groups of houses were attacked and burned. The Zepa valley was encircled, Serb forces prevented the access of vehicles and more than ten thousand people were besieged.

Reports described an ever increasingly depressing scene within Zepa. The media had heard a rumour that conditions were so desperate, some had turned to cannibalism to survive. I was determined to get there. I bombarded Pale with requests. I pleaded with all my Serb friends. 'Come on, what difference does it make to your great war plan if I get one convoy into Zepa? I'll just take medicine. Just one convoy, once.'

After the usual delays and rejections, I eventually got a tentative 'Yes'.

HCR Zagreb, Tony Land, UNPROFOR, all swung into action. The escort was to be Ukrainian, the drivers from the joint Belgian–Netherlands battalion base in Pancevo near Belgrade. Risto Tervahauta from the World Health Organisation would accompany me. Risto, a world expert on cold-weather survival, also ran his own hospital in Finland. Coughs, colds, heart attacks, major and minor surgery were all his daily fare. A good man to take to a clinic performing major war operations without anaesthetic. He is a tall, square, extremely fit man with a tanned, craggy face. He has short, dark hair. His English is accented but absolutely fluent. He has a very keen sense of humour, a rare quality for a Finn. If I were forming a team to go anywhere I would try to get Risto. He is a quiet, stubborn organiser.

As the roads were covered with snow and ice, the French volunteered a recovery truck and a heavy vehicle with a snowplough blade, which I was delighted to accept. My driver and interpreter was to be engineering graduate Predrag Blagojevic, 'Pepe', a quiet, polite, tall, handsome, laconic Serb, who I am convinced was cured of a stutter as a child by speaking to the beat of a metronome. His conversations were preceded with a pause as he tensed his stomach muscles. He would then fire off staccato sentences, like the chatter of a hot machine-gun. When translating he would never look in the eye of either party. He bowed his head, paused, shifted his weight from foot to foot, appeared to balance word against word, then delivered his translation – like a philosophy don or a divorce lawyer.

The press were extremely interested in Zepa. The dean of a large corps was John F. Burns of the *New York Times*. John is a big man, physically and mentally. He is bearded, with a shock of curly dark-brown hair. A Pulitzer prize winner, he is feared by those who know his talents. Not a man to annoy.

We left the PTT building at 6.45 a.m. on Friday, 15 January and arrived at the airport ready for a seven-thirty start. The French were lined up and ready to go by seven. The Ukrainian escort were nowhere to be seen. They eventually arrived at 8.45 a.m. and we left immediately after I had berated the officer in charge. Why the hell we ever feared these people for forty years I will never know.

At Pale we met with the convoy, which had arrived the night before from Belgrade. The commander, Captain Dirk, was a small, thin Belgian captain. He looked like a young boy, but in a quiet way, he had the total respect of his soldiers. UNHCR Belgrade sent François Seurat. We moved on to Rogatica and arrived there at midday.

The Serb military commander for Rogatica was Major Radomir Furtula. He is an ex-Yugoslav National Army regular officer. He was then about thirty-eight, open-faced, dark-haired and slightly portly. He is a decent and probably an honourable man, but he was caught up among soldiers of fortune, profiteers and gangsters. Examining his conscience later in life may be a bitter experience for him. His home village was just outside Gorazde, so he was a local boy. He went to school with the leaders of the community in Zepa and in Gorazde. His home was in Muslim hands, he worried if it still stood, who lived in it, would he ever see it again. And, because he is a sensitive man, whether his old neighbours would understand what he was doing now. I liked Furtula.

Our convoy contained two truckloads of medicine. The local doctor, Radomir Bojovic, a civilian now in uniform, was to inspect the medicine. I knew him from Gorazde convoys. Small, officious, bumptious – a man with a nervous giggle. I have long ago learned to beware of men who giggle under pressure. He began with the first vehicle. I was hoping that he would accept the vehicle manifest, which stated the number of cartons of medicine. Not this practitioner of medicine; he wished to open the cartons.

'What the hell are you doing?' I asked him as politely as I could in the circumstances.

'Firstly ensuring that there is only medicine in the cartons and secondly that the box contains only that which is on the manifest.'

'Doc, each box contains medicine for Zepa, for a clinic which has grown into a hospital, which has no drugs.' I wanted to add 'because you have besieged it', but it was, as yet, too early in the proceedings for me to be rude. I had to keep some powder dry for a possible final volley. The doc and his henchmen, some brutish soldiers, whom I had clashed with before and who were storing up their score-card awaiting the day when they could collect, ignored me.

WHO Dr Risto got the task of supervising the 'medical inspection'. It stretched his faith in fellow doctors but then he had not been tainted, nay, discoloured, no, stained, by racism. It went badly. The doctor found some boxes which had more tablets than they should have had, even some which contained items substituted for brand names not available at the time of dispatch. Sadly, initiative in the medical warehouse in Copenhagen was not appreciated by this warrior doctor in Rogatica. His eyes gleamed, his giggle increased. He wanted to 'confiscate' the non-manifested items. Now I want to make it clear here that I was not being anti-Serb or excessively cynical but this seemed to me to be hindering the passage of vital life-saving drugs to a desperate medical team serving a hideously deprived community. I knew that the people of Rogatica were short of medicine. I knew that this doctor was short of medicine himself. I approached him. 'Doc, I have given you medicine. On every trip through here I have told you, if you want medicine, I will bring you what I can, based on needs, not on desire. At no price will I go along with your covetous eyes. More importantly, I will not be robbed by you.'

Poor Pepe, his verbal machine-gun jammed. 'Mr Larry, do you really want me to translate, "I will not be robbed by you." They will not like it.'

'Pepe.' My eyebrows were raised, my voice stentorian. Pepe concentrated on his diaphragm and translated. He was right. They did not like it. For revenge, they opened every box and put the 'excesses' and the substitutes to one side 'for confiscation'. After much hassle and a large waste of valuable daylight, the paper-qualified healer cleared the convoy for Zepa.

Patient Risto negotiated a division of the 'spoils': some for Zepa, some for Rogatica and some to be collected on the way out. If the Serb medicine man ever applied for post-grad training in generous Finland I suspect Risto would have him blackballed.

Furtula had hidden during this blot on Serb humanity. With the convoy now ready to roll, nothing untoward having been discovered during the inspection of the food-carrying vehicles, he reappeared. There was a small dispute over the two French vehicles, especially the one with the snow-blade. Neither was on the convoy list approved by Pale, but Furtula agreed to let them go. He provided an escort vehicle to the Serb front line at Borike. I felt confident. Pepe did not. 'Mr Larry, the Serb soldiers are looking forward to you meeting Captain Kusic in Borike.'

The road to Borike twists and turns, the steep, steely blue mountain is on the left and the deep valley on the right. We passed isolated houses, some burned, some shell-damaged, some untouched. After a few kilometres we rounded a bend and the road was blocked by a barrier. To the right of the barrier there was a small hut. I stopped the convoy. It was late in the afternoon, if I was to proceed with any safety I needed no delay here. The escort vehicle disappeared. I got out of my vehicle with Pepe. The man on the barrier was a simple soldier, aged about fifty. He looked at us as if we had come from the moon.

'Convoy for Zepa.'

'For where?'

'For Zepa.'

'Zepa,' he said unbelievingly.

'Tell him to get his commander,' I wearily asked Pepe.

The poor soldier was now surrounded by press. 'What's the score, Larry?' Reuters TV asked me.

For a brief moment I wondered if I should say, 'I don't know. I've just arrived here myself.' But I did not. 'This gentleman is going to get his commander to lift the barrier so that we can proceed,' I lied.

A green Yugoslav army jeep arrived from a village the other side of the barrier and stopped. The first out was a small, round, unshaven man with a Zapata moustache. I recognised him as the Borike commander, Captain Rajko Kusic. He was carrying a weapon, but he probably didn't need to, for he was quickly followed out of the vehicle by two bodyguards. One looked normal, the other was the classic image of a Chetnik – the Serb mountain fighter. He was of medium height, with long, dark, lank hair and a raven-black full beard. On his head he wore one of those upturned boat-keel-shaped hats, the shapka. His eyes were like shiny black olives. He carried a heavy machine-gun and crossed over his square chest were two bandoliers of brass-cased bullets. He wore a thick leather belt from which hung a long sheathed knife. He moved to the side of his leader. The soldier who was initially at the barrier quickly briefed 'Zapata'. I moved forward to introduce myself and my task. I had to force my way through journalists who believed it was their show.

'Commander. It is good to see you.' I had my hand outstretched.

'Mr Larry,' he replied with a slight smile as he shook my hand. His eyes were bright.

'Hello,' I said to the walking armoury by his side. I offered my hand. He moved half a pace forward, took it in his and attempted to crush it with a vicelike grip. Fortunately I have a firm grip myself and I had been caught out by these macho, masonic-like competitions before, so when I offer my hand I widen my palm and try to lock my thumb against the other man's. If these hand crushers can take just your fingers or, worse still, the lower joints of your fingers, they can drop you to your knees. We squared off. I looked not just into his eyes but into his soul. I was slightly taller than him. Our faces were separated by no more than ten inches. I could smell him. Peripherally, I could see the shining bullets and was aware that in order to shake hands he had trans-ferred the heavy machine-gun into his left hand and had the butt pressed against his side by his elbow and forearm. I held my gaze until he broke eye contact. This he accompanied with a slight body shuffle. I could see I had an enemy. Kusic and the other bodyguard sensed the outcome of the confrontation and seemed amused. Pepe, I could tell, was worried.

I turned to Kusic. 'Commander, I have brought the convoy for Zepa. As you know, it has been inspected in Rogatica. It is getting late and I want to move before it is dark. Please have your men remove the barrier and guide us on the road to Zepa.'

Kusic looked pained, as if he had a naughty child in front of him. 'The way to Zepa is dangerous. There are reports of fighting on the road. At the moment it is not safe for you to go there.'

'Commander, the convoy has approval, it has been inspected, we were permitted to leave Rogatica. I intend taking the convoy there tonight.'

Poor Pepe. He recognised the anger in my voice and attempted to convey the message and the tone. 'Rambo', the bodyguard, repeated the almost imperceptible body shuffle. It was a twitch, a tremor in his upper body. It was enough to make Pepe move back slightly.

Kusic was crafty. He changed the subject. 'Who are all these people?' he asked, pointing to the notebooks, the pencils, the cameras both still and TV.

'John Burns, *New York Times*,' said the Pulitzer prize winner seizing the initiative from his unruly colleagues. 'Can the convoy go forward?' he continued.

'Who gave the journalists permission to be here?' Kusic asked me. A clever way of attempting to make me feel guilty.

'We have approval from Pale,' said Burns, pulling from beneath his coat an accreditation card. This was like a signal from the chairman of the Magic Circle. Accreditation cards were produced with a flourish from the pockets, the chests, the necks, of his acolytes. Most correspondents have their cards on a chain around their necks, the 'ID discs' or 'dog tags' of journalists. The cards are therefore extended only for a quick viewing. Just as well, as many are out of date, others forged and some very spurious. Why fashion magazines and canine newspapers should have a Bosnia correspondent I never could work out. Kusic had achieved his aim. More of my time and, more importantly, daylight time, was being wasted. The journalists were keen to impress him. They knew that only he stood between them and Zepa. There was a babel of sound as their translators vied for the ear of the commander. They were a press corps, but a corps of individuals with an eggshell-thin veneer of loyalty to each other. 'Please, Captain Kusic, let us all go through. If we can't, then at least let me. Nice, kind, friendly, insistent me,' seemed to be the message.

This show was slipping away from me. Time for a little initiative. 'Commander, may we go to the office?' I asked, pointing to the hut near the barrier. Kusic agreed. Pepe, myself, the commander and Rambo headed for the hut. It was crowded. The Ukrainian officers had been much quicker off the mark; they were huddled around the stove and were handing round slices from a huge sausage they had brought. In return they had been given a bottle of slivovic. I should had been pleased if I had known this initiative was to win over the locals in order to further our immediate advancement, but I was certain the Ukrainians had decided that it was too late to move forward and were negotiating the best option for the night. Kusic was delighted to see them. There is a rapport between the Serbs and the Ukrainians. They have enough common words to keep a conversation going and they share the same attitudes to communism and orthodoxy.

I was now attempting to run a three-ring circus: the convoy, the press and the escort. The hut was too crowded, so I steered Kusic outside. 'I want this convoy moving now.'

'There is no approval for the press,' replied Kusic very calmly. 'They must leave.'

'It is the convoy that is important, but I think you are making a mistake. If you send away some of the best reporters in the world you will receive bad publicity. If you let them accompany the convoy you will get good publicity for letting them go forward. If they find that conditions in Zepa have been exaggerated by the amateur radio, the Bosnian cause will receive adverse publicity.'

Like many local commanders, his reply was simple: 'We do not care what the press say.'

'Why don't you just allow a pool of reporters? Or just one to represent them all?'

Then another standard local commander statement: 'The orders are no press.'

I had my own battles to fight and was fed up with this one. 'So do I go forward or not?'

'I am waiting for orders.'

I left him and briefed the press. They were upon him in seconds, each pleading his cause. The interpreter with a TV company thought he had been clever: he asked the Ukrainians to negotiate on his behalf.

The light was failing fast. Kusic was both flattered and irritated by the attention he was receiving. He was surrounded by the press when I asked him once again to raise the barrier.

'The convoy cannot go forward tonight.'

Ah. 'Tonight.' A key word. That meant hope for tomorrow. And once again, as it was dark and the unknown lay before me, I was in truth happy to park up and begin again at dawn.

Then came the punch-line: 'So you will have to leave here and go back and return tomorrow.'

'I am sorry, Commander. The convoy cannot return. It is too late.'

Rajko Kusic then upped the stakes. 'You cannot stay here. There are bandits. I cannot guarantee your safety.'

'Too right there are bandits,' I thought to myself. But, on an isolated hill, with the shared responsibility for a fair number of lives, I felt that the truth might be just a little too provocative. 'Then let me go forward.'

'Impossible.'

It was now dark, so I added a new ingredient: 'Commander, the road is very narrow. I cannot turn the convoy round. It must stay here.' I was determined that the convoy would stay. If I agreed to go back, where did we go back to? Me to Sarajevo? The trucks to Belgrade? What would happen tomorrow, a new inspection? The approval for the convoy was for today. Tomorrow they could tell us we have no approval.

'It cannot stay here.'

'Then it must go forward.'

'It has no permission to go forward.'

'Then it must stay here.'

'It cannot stay here.'

This could have gone on all night, which would at least have achieved my aim. But Pepe, reading the vibes, quietly told me that I had gone too far.

'Commander, I cannot go forward, you are right [said with great sincerity]. I cannot go back [pause]. I cannot stay here [resignation]. Tell me, Commander, what can I do?' Over to you, Pepe. Here I caught the eye of John Burns. He was close to laughter, which might not help matters.

'The press must leave now,' said the captain. Which implied that the rest of us could stay. An admirable face-saving non-decision. Well done, Captain.

'Thank you, Commander,' I said, losing not a moment to cement the agreement. 'Sorry, boys,' I said to the press. I then briefed Dirk. 'We are here for the night.' Next the Ukrainian commander – who already had his boots and socks off and was preparing for the night.

The press stayed and pleaded their cause until they had totally exhausted the patience of Kusic.

The great John F. Burns was one of the last to leave. 'I am off to Pale to get approval. See you tomorrow. Good luck.'

Kusic then came to see me. 'I want all the drivers and crews to stand by their vehicles and to show me their identity cards.'

'OK.'

Dirk gave the order and his men lined up. Kusic and his soldiers then walked the length of the convoy, checking each soldier. They looked at the identity card, at the face of the soldier and at the list approved by Pale. My first thoughts were that he was just making sure that all the journalists had gone. Poor naive me. He reached the last two vehicles, the French recovery vehicle and the truck with the snow-plough. They were not on the approved convoy list. They were offered as a bonus and I had gratefully accepted them.

'Mr Larry, what are these vehicles?'

'Snow-plough and recovery vehicle, Commander.'

'But they are not on the list!'

'Quite right. I offer my humblest apologies. They were included at the last minute because of the road conditions.'

'But they are not on the list.' Kusic was using his 'Got you by the testicles' voice. Rambo was twitching, imperceptibly but ecstatically.

We reached yet again the part I hate. The temptation was to say: 'Look, you little pillock, I have here a convoy which has to go through ice and snow on tracks not used for months. I need a snow-plough and a recovery vehicle. I need them. I have them. And I am taking them with me.' But he knew all this. He was there to stop or at least delay the convoy. His credibility, in the eyes of both his seniors and his subordinates, was at stake. Furthermore, in the old communist days, if you turned up without the correct paperwork, you were sent back.

So it was grin and bear it. 'Commander, you are once again right. The vehicles are not on the convoy paperwork but [time for a little fib] they are approved. When it was realised that the roads were so bad we contacted Pale and asked for approval. They gave it verbally. If you can contact Pale they will tell you that they are approved.'

Kusic shook his head. 'They must go back.'

Stalling tactics time. 'OK, but it is too late now. They can return tomorrow.'

'OK.'

The French, who were fired with enthusiasm for reaching Zepa, were delighted. I was optimistic that Kusic would allow them to go, Pepe was not.

As we walked back to the barrier Kusic began a strange conversation. 'The Muslim commander in Zepa is an old colleague of mine. I was his pupil on a military course. His name is Avdo. He is a good man. I want you to give him a message from me. Tell him that I will not attack Zepa. In return he must not attack us.'

'Commander, why not write him a letter and I will deliver it personally to him?'

'Good idea.' This was a different Kusic: reflective, deep and sincere. At the barrier he smiled, shook hands and went into the hut. I returned to my vehicle to prepare for the night.

In the good old days of touristy Yugoslavia the bleak but rolling hills around the village of Borike were an attraction for horse riders. Some visitors may well have pitched their tents or parked their caravans where we were now laagered. But today we were near a front line. It was isolated. We were in a Serb stronghold, the home of Rambo and his friends, and we had a convoy with attractive items destined for the very Muslims whom local propaganda blamed for a catalogue of evil. The Ukrainians, our escort, did not fill me with confidence. But they were cavorting with the local troops, which is better than antagonising them. Dirk briefed his boys 'Minimum movement' and posted sentries, correctly assessing our 'escort'. It was a black, moonless night and the nearby hilltop loomed like a dark monster. Sleep would bring security.

As dawn broke, Dirk had his soldiers up and about, but we had to wait until eight before Kusic returned. He was adamant that the French vehicles had to go back. Arguing with him was delaying the start, so most reluctantly I agreed. The French were very

unhappy and disappointed with me. I asked Kusic to provide me
with an escort or guide up to the Zepa road, but he refused. He
ordered the barrier to be raised and the convoy moved forward.

'OK, Pepe?' I asked.

There was a pensive pause. 'OK, Mr Larry,' was the apprehensive reply.

I never give the bravery of these translators enough credit. I
had been pushing and stretching the courage of Pepe with Serbs.
That in itself was a test. The Serbs did not like what I asked him
to do and said they were not pleased by the fact that a Serb
worked for the UN. Now I was about to stretch his courage
further. I was about to take Serb Pepe into ten-month-besieged
Zepa, a Bosnian 'Muslim' enclave. They could not know that Pepe
is a Yugoslav, a Bosnian. They might see him as one of those
Serbs who had holed them up, shelled them, raped them, murdered them. I looked at Pepe, pensive, apprehensive Pepe, and I
gently touched his arm. Sometimes the best sentences contain no
words. I hope he realised how much I admired him.

The road from Borike to Zepa is well defined on the map but
not clear on the ground, especially when it is, in fact, a track and
is carpeted white with snow. We moved down the hill to deserted
Borike village and swung left. The map indicated a few kilometres
before we took a right turn. There were some Serbs on the wooded
hill rising to our left. I could see no one ahead or to our right.
The convoy was moving very slowly. The track was no wider than
one vehicle. The Ukrainian commander was looking back to me
for direction. To the right of the road at a distance of about one
hundred metres and running parallel to it there was a snow- and
ice-covered river bed. Beyond this rose a steep-sided hill. After
moving for about ten minutes I could see many of the convoy
vehicles stretched out behind me. Mine passed the hill to our
right. The track was then bordered by a small open plain, rising
to more hills in the middle distance. Suddenly, there was a burst
of machine-gun fire. The Ukrainian APC stopped. The whole
convoy came to a halt. The machine-gun was joined by the crack
of individual rifle fire. As the convoy had just started out and I
knew that we were some distance from Zepa and still in Serb
territory, I was not as alert as I should have been. I got out of my

vehicle and took cover behind it. Risto was quicker than me. He was out, but assessing the situation. 'It's outgoing,' he said, meaning that the rounds were not coming in our direction. Dirk had left his vehicle and joined me. I now switched on and realised that four of our vehicles were exposed – two trucks, Dirk's vehicle and mine – and that Risto was right. There was a lot of noise. Many rounds were flying but not in our direction.

Just then, Kusic arrived in his vehicle. He swung in front of mine. He was furious.

Pepe translated. 'You idiot!' he said to me. 'What are you doing here?'

'I . . .'

'You are killing my soldiers and risking your own!'

I was still crouched behind my vehicle when I replied: 'You let me move along this road. It's the road to Zepa.'

'It is not the road you have approval for. You have missed the turn and the Muslims are attacking.'

'Where is the turning off then?'

'Too late, too late, you must now go back. Some of my men are dead. You cannot go forward.'

The gunfire increased. Kusic continued to hassle me.

'Just leave us alone,' I said to Kusic.

'Larry, I must get my vehicles into cover,' said Dirk.

The track was too narrow for anything to turn. The snow was so deep it was not possible to delineate the sides. Nor was it possible to reverse rapidly. Ahead, about fifty metres into the firing zone, was a track to the right. Dirk spoke to each of his drivers in the two trucks which were exposed. He calmly walked in front of the first, guided it around his and my vehicles and led it to the highly exposed track junction. Here he supervised the reversing of the truck. This brave action he repeated with the leading four trucks, thus giving his second-in-command time and space to reverse and turn the others under cover. During this action the sound of gunfire intensified. It was impossible to know if the Serbs were firing at nothing just to scare us, or whether they had located a party from Zepa and were keeping them away from us. This lack of knowledge made Dirk's brave actions even more courageous.

Eventually the convoy was facing Borike, from where we had set out. Kusic was alongside my vehicle and shouting that we must go back to Rogatica 'until the Muslim attack is over'.

I was not buying this suggestion at all. 'Where should we have gone, which way should we have taken?'

He pointed to a narrow track off to the left. A small vehicle had recently disturbed the snow and left its tyre marks. The track seemed to cross a stream, then rise quite steeply for fifty or so metres. It then disappeared around to the left of the hill.

'OK,' I said to Kusic. 'I am taking this track.'

He argued, but not as forcefully as I expected. I realised that he had either received orders to let us advance or he had a surprise waiting for us somewhere *en route*. The track was extremely narrow, the snow was deep and there was ice. The APC, my vehicle and Dirk's swung around the turn to the left with ease, but we were then into a sharp S bend and on a steep slope. Our wheels spun and the vehicles slewed, but we made it to the brow of the hill. Not so the first truck. It spun its wheels deep into the snow and ice on the S bend.

Dirk and I left our vehicles and went back. Dirk ordered chains on tyres for all those trucks which carried them. Fitting chains to any vehicle is not easy, fitting them to trucks up to their axles in snow and ice is time-consuming, skin-scraping, oath-issuing work. The heavy chains are taken out of the coarse sacks, laid on the ground near the wheels and the struggle commences. The vehicle is moved either backwards or forwards, so that the tyre moves on to the chain. Not easy when the wheels are spinning, the vehicle is sliding and hands are numb with cold. Once on, the chains must be pulled tight, a job demanding brute force and determination, as spinning wheels shed loose chains with speed and anger. A chain thrown by a wheel can stun or maim. Even with chains, the ascent up this, the first incline of our journey, was slow. Kusic could well wave us on, he must be enjoying this. I cursed him for not letting us have the snow-plough. I cursed myself for not fighting him over it. I had wanted to save minutes, now I was likely to waste hours.

At the brow of the hill I was surprised to find a crossroads with a few houses. They were inhabited by Serbs; we were still in Serb territory. Kusic could have escorted us this far if he had wanted. The occupants of the houses were old and friendly. They waved and smiled. Beyond the houses the track dropped away down a long persistent decline. There was nothing on either side of the track. The wind pushed and sucked snow from the hills on one side and deposited it on the other. The descent was fun. The APC slipped and slid, the little military jeep was fine, my land-cruiser covered large sections without any guidance from Pepe. The trucks made progress, sometimes bunched together as one came to a sudden halt, sometimes hundreds of metres apart. After a couple of kilometres we came to another sharp bend with a clearly visible but unused track off to the right. Was this the way to Zepa? We stopped. It was eerily calm and quiet.

Risto, Pepe and I decided to check the track to the right, before looking at the left-hand one. We walked into the woods in single file. We found a set of footprints which wove their way in and out of the trees and never led on to the track and these we followed. They led to a huge barrier. Felled trees blocked our way. We carefully walked to the edges of the barrier and found wires leading into the snow. Wires do not grow in woods. They led somewhere, probably to anti-personnel mines. We retraced our steps to the vehicle where I radioed Tony Land in Sarajevo. I told him about the tree-felled barrier and the mines. There was a pause from his end.

'Larry, are the trees Serb trees or Muslim trees?'

Risto and Pepe laughed.

'Tony, am I now some sort of ethnic dendrologist?'

Tony praised the intelligence of my backside and asked directly, 'Are you in Serb or Bosnian territory?'

In truth, Tony had hit on my number one problem. From the moment that we had turned left after reversing the convoy we were not able to follow the map. The track we had used was not on it. I could not therefore pinpoint our position. I did not know where we were. 'Tony, we are on the front line,' I said positively. A reply vague enough to permit him to brief the press.

Risto and I then took the track to the left which led into the woods. There were no tyre-tracks or footprints. There was no sign of anyone. The snow was so thick its carpet could cover all sorts of hazards. Should we go ahead, left, right? Go back? The Serbs would love us to return voluntarily and unsuccessfully. I felt really down. We had come this far, right through the Serb lines, and could not find Zepa. I felt lonely and panicky. 'Come on, Larry,' I said to myself. I quietly cursed the Bosnians for not being here to meet me. 'Risto, where the hell are we?'

Risto, in addition to being a doctor and a cold-weather expert, is a Finn and therefore an ace orienteerer. 'Larry, I think we are here,' he said, pointing to a spot on the map.

'Think we are here or know we are here?'

'Give me the map. I will return in half an hour and tell you exactly where we are.' He then set off alone in no man's land and raced up to high spots and took bearings. Within the half-hour he was back. 'We are here.' He pointed on the map. 'No question. This is Boksanica wood.' Then just to clinch his certainty: 'We are now at an altitude of 1100 metres. Zepa is at 500 metres.' If Risto was right, we were half a kilometre from the track to Zepa. Somewhere ahead of us in the woods was a path which would take us to the track we would have been on if we had not been re-routed by the shooting. This path had to be wide enough and safe enough to take the convoy.

It was now the middle of the afternoon. Our first indication that Risto was right came from the Serbs. They landed a mortar bomb in the woods to our left. One lone noisy round. Its shrapnel was contained by the branches of the trees. Its only effect was to scar a few pine trees and to confirm that we were on the right track.

We did not have much daylight left, so I rounded up the principal players. 'We are in the right place. We have made enough noise for the people of Zepa to know that we are here. If we try to advance into the woods without a Bosnian escort we may be in trouble. Also, we have no more than ninety minutes of light left. So there are two alternatives. One: stay the night here in no man's land and hope the Bosnians make contact. Two: return to Borike and try again tomorrow. Comments?'

The Ukrainians wanted to return to Borike. Dirk was not happy with the trucks stuck out in the open but was even more reluctant to move them under the cover of the woods because of the danger of mines. I was alone in wanting to stay. My reasons were that I hate going back, the Serbs might not let us return, darkness would be an ally to the forces from Zepa who would find it easier to contact us in the night. In fairness, I pointed out the snag in this scenario. If the Bosnians did appear, the Serbs might attack them and we could be stuck in the middle. I obviously painted this picture too graphically, as it produced a strong consensus to return to Borike. No sooner had we finished our powwow than a Serb vehicle appeared with my favourite heavies. Our discussion had been purely academic, they were here to turn us round and take us back. Turning the convoy took an age, the journey back even longer.

By the time we arrived at the outskirts of Borike it was almost dark. There was a reception committee awaiting us: Major Furt-ula, Captain Kusic, the captain from Podromanija and a number of Milicija vehicles. I stayed in my vehicle but wound the window down to speak to them.

Furtula spoke first. 'You did not meet with the Muslims?'

'No.'

'That is very strange.'

'I will try again tomorrow.'

'Yes, you can, but tonight you must return to Podromanija.'

'Podromanija? You are joking, Major. I am going no further than here. We park where we parked last night and I move off at dawn.'

Pepe obviously translated well as the usually calm and charming Furtula suddenly became furious. Maybe I was insulting him in front of his colleagues, maybe he felt he was losing face. 'You will do as you are told!'

Now this is something I have never been very good at. 'Major, I do not like your attitude or your tone.'

'You will follow these Milicija vehicles which will escort you to Podromanija.'

'I will not.'

'Then I will arrest you,' said Furtula. At this Rambo moved towards my door.

'Major, I will immediately inform Geneva of your threat.' A

blatant lie if ever there was one. There were times when the radio could not even contact the vehicle behind me, let alone Geneva.

I picked up the handset and called Sarajevo. Miraculously, Tony 'The Trees' was able to receive us. I informed him of Furtula's proposal and threat.

'OK, just sit tight. I will speak with BH command.'

I looked Furtula in the eye. Geneva are contacting New York.'

Rambo was kicking our tyres. He had obviously done the short mechanics course.

'Stop that at once!' I commanded. Poor Pepe translated, making, I am sure, a mental note to emigrate as soon as possible.

Rambo stopped. He spoke to Pepe.

'What did he say?' I asked.

'He said that one day he wants to get you in the sights of his weapon.'

Furtula then approached again. 'Move this convoy *now*!'

'I am awaiting instructions.'

'I will put you under arrest.'

'My friend, me, or all of us?'

'All of you.'

Just then the radio came to life. It was Tony. 'It has been agreed you go to Podromanija. They are guaranteeing that you can try again tomorrow.'

'Tony, that is not the answer I wished to hear.'

'Send me a postcard from Podromanija.'

I got out of my vehicle and approached Furtula, who was with his fellow officers. 'Major, the United Nations agrees for this convoy to go to Podromanija. The Serb authorities in Pale have given their solemn word that it returns here at dawn.'

We fell in behind the Serb escort and motored back through Rogatica to Podromanija. I do not know what the views were of the rest of the convoy, but as we travelled along the dark, isolated roads, following the rotating blue lights of the escort vehicles, I was convinced that we would enter Zepa the next day. I analysed our day. The Serbs were surprised we had not made contact with the 'Muslims'. I felt that their high command wanted us to go in. In effect, we would be doing their reconnaissance. They wanted to know if the road was mined, was it easy to clear them or were they dug in? Where and what were the barriers and the obstacles. By watching our progress they would find out.

At Podromanija we were parked by the Serb police. They were very efficient. The Podromanija captain, a straight, honest man, reaffirmed that we would leave there at seven. He also told me that the Serbs could not understand why I had not met with the 'Muslims' from Zepa. They were convinced that I would have been in Zepa this night. 'The convoy has maximum Serb co-operation,' he concluded. I briefed the leaders and returned to my vehicle. Pepe was with two relatives from nearby Sokolac. They had recognised him on our outward journey, heard that the convoy had returned and come to take him to their house. I was not happy and overruled it, much to Pepe's delight. He had no desire to bump into Rambo on this very dark night. A reporter came up to me and told me that he had heard on the BBC World Service that the convoy had been returned to Podromanija but would make a further attempt tomorrow. Well done, Tony Land, keep the pressure on!

That night I slept very little. At first I accepted the captain's statement that the convoy had had maximum Serb co-operation and that I had failed to get it in. I then remembered that maximum co-operation had included a little shooting and a bit of shelling. What was keeping me awake was the prospect of returning to the same place tomorrow, not finding any Bosnians and having to find a route through the snow in the woods. I could flounder around in those woods for days. My poor little brain swirled and reeled as I held conversations with myself. If only I had the vehicle with the snow-plough. I would ask for it. It was now back in Sarajevo. It would take hours to get it up here. Better to wait and have success than go early and fail. But the Bosnians might be there waiting for us. Concurrent activity. Ask Tony to get the thing on the way as early as possible, to join us *en route*? Rubbish, it would not arrive here before early evening, by then I would either be in or back here.

Dawn broke. The Serbs were as good as their word. The convoy lined up and we left with a police escort at seven. They took us to the barrier just before Borike, to Kusic's kingdom. He insisted that the convoy stopped, that all drivers stood by their vehicles and produced their identity cards. The vehicles were cursorily inspected, the barrier raised and we were off again. This time along a road we, at least, knew. However, knowing the road did not improve the conditions. We reached the mouth of the woods at about ten thirty in the morning. The convoy was lined up behind me. I got out of my vehicle and began to walk up the snowy slope, Risto and Pepe behind me. I said a quick prayer. 'Please God, let there be some Bosnians here.'

Yesterday the woods had 'felt' empty. Today I knew they were not. There was an electric feeling. My whole body was alert and tingling.

Pepe whispered: 'There is someone by the tree on the left.'

I looked up and saw a stocky figure in uniform. I smiled and shouted out that we were United Nations. He stepped out into the open. I saw the blue Bosnian badge with the fleur-de-lis on his sleeve. He was a Bosnian. We had made contact. We looked at each other from a distance of about fifty metres and I could see that he was smiling. My own smile was warm enough to melt the snow. I felt light-headed, exhilarated. I moved towards him with my arm out to shake his hand. I don't know if we ran or walked to each other. We did not shake hands, he threw his arms around me, kissed me and cried. I remember his cold, stubbly beard and his warm tears. I am sure he will remember mine. He was a great barrel-chested bear of a man. We hugged and laughed and cried. As I came out of his embrace I saw others stepping from behind trees, some in uniform, most in civilian clothes. Soon there were ten or more of them. Risto, Pepe, Dirk, François, each had his own group around him.

I took the 'Bear' to my vehicle and informed Tony. I could tell that he was as excited as I was. I gave a bottle of whisky and a packet of cigarettes to the Bear. He was like a child at Christmas. We both had a swig from the bottle, then he put it in his trouser pocket. For the rest of the day I saw him sharing his bottle and his cigarettes with his special friends. Whenever our eyes met his face beamed.

More and more people arrived. They had left Zepa at dawn and walked the whole way to meet us. Some had been in the woods yesterday, but had arrived too late to make contact with us.

They were bitterly disappointed as they thought that we would not return. But back in Zepa they heard on the radio that we were to try again. Well done again, Tony, for keeping the media informed. After so long without contact they were happy to chat and smoke. They had had no commercial cigarettes for months. We offered cigarettes, they took them, lit them, puffed on them and passed them around. These were magic moments for them and for us. For me it was a scene from a Robin Hood film. Deep in Sherwood Forest I had met the bandits who were really the goodies. They would have been happy to stay there all day but the convoy was still 20 kilometres from the centre of Zepa.

I spoke with the Bear, my Little John, and he told me that there were ten sets of barricades on the road to Zepa, all huge felled trees. The Ukrainians were now in their element. They used the APCs to winch, push and shove. Our aim was to clear a path wide enough for the convoy. Branches had to be cut, snow shovelled away. Once again I cursed Kusic for the loss of the plough and the heavy recovery vehicle. The main work-force for this mammoth physical task had to be the men from Zepa, men who had been besieged for ten months. God bless them, they were like rakes, as thin as laths. They were enthusiastic but so weak. It was cold and many were in flimsy clothes. Few had boots. Their weapons were pathetic. We had left Rambo, who looked like an arms manufacturer's Christmas tree, and joined *Dad's Army*. There were hunting rifles, First World War rifles, home-made weapons.

The military commander arrived, Avdo Palic, the colleague of Kusic. He is a gentle, innocent man. He was unarmed and had no bodyguards. I gave him the letter from Kusic. He was really touched. It brought a little humanity to the war. He promised me that he would write a reply. Avdo may have been the commander of the troops but the true protector of Zepa is its terrain. The track is narrow and these primitive barriers, if protected by even the lightest of covering fire, would delay a Serb advance.

More help arrived from Zepa including the mayor, Benjamin Kulovac, a doctor of medicine who is the son of the man who is in charge of the Zepa hospital. With him was a young girl, the best speaker of English in Zepa, our Maid Marian. Benjamin had had the responsibility for the preservation of life and morale in

Zepa during the ten months of the siege. He is tall and thin, painfully thin. He is bearded and has tired but bright eyes. He wanted to know what we had brought. He told me that he had twenty-nine thousand people to feed.

'Sir, I have brought ten trucks, maybe eighty tonnes.'

I was embarrassed. The men from Zepa were breaking down their barricades, making way for a convoy which would provide a maximum of two kilos of flour to each person after ten months of siege.

'We will give what you bring to the most vulnerable,' said Benjamin with a genuine, honest smile and warmth in his voice. 'You being here is more important than the food.' He then asked about medicine and Risto was able to brief him. When he heard that we had brought anaesthetics his eyes welled up with tears. To appreciate the full significance of this I had to wait until we reached Zepa hospital.

Benjamin's translator was a pretty girl called Denisa Kulovac, probably a relative of his. Her English was good but she was tired, and relieved to see Pepe and give the translation task to him. She had lovely eyes and a very gentle voice, but she was weak and her face was very white, milky white. The younger women in the besieged areas often have ashen complexions. Because they menstruate they lose blood. In a normal world this is no problem, but when food is scarce and vitamins scarcer, they soon lose their rosy cheeks. Eventually they stop menstruating, which is traumatic for differing reasons. Some falsely believe they are pregnant, others fear they may never be pregnant.

One of the men from Zepa had brought a chain-saw. It had not worked for almost a year, no fuel. We syphoned some from a truck and the woods soon filled with a buzzing and a burping as this resurrected machine trimmed branches and cut through tree trunks. Eventually we had a path through the obstacles. The convoy set off for our goal, Zepa itself. In my vehicle we took with us Benjamin, his interpreter and the Bear who, God bless him, was now high with excitement and awash with whisky. The APC led the way with at least fifteen passengers sitting on top of it. I hoped the Ukrainian officer had explained to them where the exhaust pipe is, since it is highly visible, highly touchable and very tempting to hold on to. If they touched it they would get a nasty burn. At night it can glow with heat.

Soon we cleared the woods and were on the main track. We had travelled no more than one hundred metres when we met the first hairpin bend. The twenty-four-foot-long APC had to have two goes at getting around it. During its manoeuvring one of the men from Zepa fell off the APC; another, in attempting to grab him, accidentally pulled the trigger of his rifle. A lone bullet whistled through the air as the one who fell off was hauled back up. He seemed none the worse for the experience. Both incidents provoked only laughter. As we rounded the bend we saw a small group of houses. All the occupants were standing outside and waved and cheered as we motored past. This was the first of the forty-eight villages dotted around the Zepa valley. The view beyond the houses was spectacular and frightening. To my right and above I could see back up the track where the first of our trucks was shunting around the bend, to my left and below, way below, was the River Zepa. The icy road twisted and turned, series after series of scary bends. Half-way down, I was able to look back and see the whole convoy, each vehicle clearly pinpointed, some travelling from left to right, others from right to left. It was easy to see how Zepa kept the Germans at bay. It was also thrilling to see our convoy. We were going to make it.

I was very pleased that the Ukrainian APCs had wheels and were not tracked. If the Brits had been escorting us, their magnificent tracked machines on this surface could easily have become thirty-tonne sleds. Not a pretty sight to follow; a rampant, snorting nightmare if they are behind you. At long last we reached the bottom of the valley. We crossed a small bridge, then saw Zepa itself, a tiny one-street village.

We passed the graveyard on the left and the hospital on the right. The narrow main street was lined with the whole population. The road is so narrow we were in danger of running over their feet. They had watched our progress during our descent. Their first reactions were already spent. Their smiles and waves were returned as much by Benjamin and the translator as by us. The Bear gurgled and grinned. We stopped close to the hospital and Benjamin and Risto got out. Benjamin gave me instructions. The convoy was to unload at a group of buildings which stand at the end of the main street at the top of an unbelievably steep slope which was a sheet of ice. Only one vehicle at a time could unload and then only after it had negotiated the slope. I took the convoy on and halted it at the foot of the icy incline. We all got out of the vehicles. The people moved forward. First there were polite waves, then handshakes, then hugs, then cuddles. This was an isolated valley, more reserved than Gorazde. The Bear was out on his unsteady feet, backslapping and handshaking. The people looked much weaker than in Gorazde, thinner and paler. I tried to walk up the slope. It was impossible. I tried again and ended up on my bottom, much to the amusement of the assembled crowd. Having broken the ice, I left the marshalling and unloading to Dirk and François and went back to the hospital. I had to walk, as the road was blocked by our convoy. I walked alone through the crowds. Some squeezed my hand, others clasped my shoulder. Little children ran from me. I was well wrapped but cold. None of these people was wearing an outer coat. It was a sharp, crisp day. The houses, all single-storey, were still and stone cold. No smoke from chimneys, no glow from lights. As I passed each of our trucks, the drivers gave me a big warm smile or a thumbs up. They were delighted to be in the convoy that had made it. Risto had already manoeuvred the medicine vehicle out of the convoy to the side of the hospital. When I arrived, Benjamin was waiting for me with his father, who before the war was the medical technician at the hospital. With them was Dr Ibrahim Heljic whose brother, another doctor, I had met in Sarajevo. The amateur radio had broadcast horrendous reports about the hospital and both Risto and I wanted to see for ourselves how bad it really was.

The hospital was never built as such but as a clinic. In days recently gone by, if anyone from Zepa was ill, it was Zepa for diagnosis and Rogatica or Gorazde for treatment. We entered by a small door which led into a corridor. Where there had once been consulting rooms there were now wards. Outside it was very cold, inside it was oppressively hot. What they lacked in drugs they were trying to compensate for with heat. I have learned in Bosnia a little formula, a scientific equation, Heat plus Emergency

Hospitals equals Gagging Smell. Each 'ward' contained more beds than space. Each had a wood-burning stove, with pipes and funnels leading to ill-fitting holes in window-frames. Smoke, heat haze and the smell of putrefaction mixed and swirled and assaulted the air. The bouquet of death and fear and despair attacked the nostrils of the visitor.

If under pressure, attack. Anything to take your mind off the sickness lying on the stomach waiting to be thrown up, to embarrass and to shame. 'Benjamin, how many people have died since the war began?'

'We keep very accurate records, Mr Larry. Nine hundred and one have died in the last ten months.'

'All from the war?'

'No, no. There is both war and civilian trauma.'

Benjamin's father, maybe my age, handsome, fit, lined and war-weary, interjected: 'We have lost four hundred who have died from hunger and cold; four hundred and thirty who have died from war trauma, war wounds, and seventy-one from diseases.'

Armed with these facts we walked from ward to ward. Images of bent and broken and bloodied people flashed across my vision. Risto, being a professional, was interested. He was asking the right questions. Technical jargon, medical mumbo-jumbo was exchanged. Words I could not distinguish. I was hanging on, hanging in . . . just.

It was now dark and in these cubicles, so grandiosely termed wards, lights were being lit. I was suddenly fascinated and nauseated; fascinated because the lights were some sort of wax held in a glass container, nauseated because the pungent smell of the burning fat added to the already noxious cocktail which I was forced to swallow. We moved to a small room, dominated by an old kitchen table.

'This is our operating theatre,' said Benjamin with pride.

Attack, Larry. Attack.

'We have heard that you have had no anaesthetics for months. Is this true?'

'We have carried out thirty-six amputations without anaesthesia.'

Oh my God!

'Twenty-seven were major. Twenty-two legs and five arms.'

I imagine myself on this table.

But he has not finished. 'Seven were on children, of whom three died. We also had to try to operate on two patients with stomach complications. But we lost both of them.'

'Show him our instruments,' said Benjamin's father.

'OK,' said Benjamin.

Whilst he got them out his father spoke: 'There are three doctors in the hospital, none of whom are surgeons. None have done any surgery since medical school. There were no medical instruments here. This is what we have.' His son produced two scalpels and, I swear on the Bible, a carpenter's saw. A wooden-handled, serrated-edged saw. These instruments had carried out thirty-six operations without anaesthetics. In the nineteen nineties, a two-hour flight from London.

'How did you calm the patient during the operation?' Risto asked Benjamin's father.

'It depended on the patient. If they were male we made them drink as much alcohol as possible, mainly slivovic. If they were women we gave them the option to have alcohol. If they were children we gave them no alcohol.' He then added poignantly, 'That is why we lost three of the seven.'

Perhaps I dwell too much. 'Benjamin, what are your thoughts, what are the patients' thoughts, when you begin to saw? Do they scream, do they keep still?'

These questions, I am sure, would have been Benjamin's ten months ago. But now, thirty-six operations down the line, he answers them a little wearily. 'We encourage the patient to shout out prayers or to scream. We have helpers who hold the patient down. We work as quickly as we can.'

I am stunned; speechless and stunned. I can hear the echoes of the screams which are embedded in these very walls. I can feel the first cut, the scratch, the scrape, the ripping and the rasping.

Benjamin, sensitive Benjamin, can feel my shock, my horror. 'Mr Larry, we do not like doing it. That is why we are so pleased that you have brought anaesthetics. Let me show you a man who must be operated on soon, a man who if you had not arrived would tomorrow have lain here without anaesthetic.'

We left the operating theatre and returned to a ward.

We had seen the man before but I had made him a blur. He lay in bed with a gangrenous leg. A leg which, I am sorry, looked hideous and smelt nauseous. It was explained to him that he would be the first operation for months with anaesthetic. He looked at us and thanked us. I wondered what had given him the greater loss of sleep: the smell and the pain from his leg or the thought of the amputation.

We had spent time with the living, they now wished us to spend some time with the dead. The majority of the war victims were not buried in the graveyard near the hospital, but were in a cemetery on the banks of the River Drina at a place called Slap. We motored in my vehicle the ten or so kilometres. Slap is a tiny village situated where the River Zepa joins the Drina, which at this point is wide and deep bottle green.

The history of burying citizens of the Zepa valley at Slap is recent, mystic and symbolic. The burial site is exclusively for victims of war. They are buried on the banks of the Drina in the hope that the great river will wash away from the valley the shame and the pain and the anguish of such an ignominious and unnecessary cause of death.

Slap by day is idyllic, a beauty spot, a tourist's dream, a fisher-man's haven. The steep sides of the Zepa valley rise out of the dark-brown banks of the deep green river. But when visiting graves on a cold winter evening, with the fading light casting long, dark shadows on the rippling, shimmering waves, Slap is melancholy and haunting. There is no path to the graves. We scrambled along the narrow undulating bank of the river. At one point centimetres from the icy water, at another it was metres below us. The bank was slippy, our guide sure-footed, my boots were not gripping the surface. I fell behind the others and worried about sliding into the river. When I caught up with them they were at the graves. It was like a Trappist cemetery. The path, bordered by the almost vertical hillside, had little room to spare for resting souls. The graves lay parallel to the river, two or three side by side with little space between them. They were fresh graves. The bodies were not buried deep, a mound of moist earth

covered each of them. They were there to be purified by the
Drina. It could not have been closer to them. I have no doubt
that tiny tributaries of this ancient river were seeping through the
soil and offering nature's condolence for man's aggression. We
stayed only a few long, soul-searching minutes. Then we struggled
back to the vehicle. I took one last look at this mythic place. The
emerging moon was silvering the surface of the river and I half
expected to see a hand rise from its depth. There are too few
knights in shining armour and too many Excaliburs.

We returned to Zepa and were invited to the home of Benjamin's
father, which adjoined the hospital. We climbed a cement staircase
and came to the front door of the flat. Everyone removed their
shoes and we were invited in, where we met Benjamin's mother,
his fiancée Selma, a very pretty, vivacious dentist practising as a
doctor for the duration of the war, and another doctor colleague,
Nijaz Stitkovac, with his wife and children.

Our host produced a bottle of slivovic, our hostess some bread.
There was no flour in Zepa. She had made it from the floor
sweepings of the barn. Offering it to us was a great honour. It
looked dark brown and wholesome. I could see ears of corn and
stalks of grass. I drank the slivo with no difficulty. I, who have
eaten snails, slugs, raw fish, insects, beetles, all in the service of
Her Majesty, failed to eat the bread. I took it in my mouth but
could not swallow it. I gagged on it. I admitted defeat. My hostess
was not surprised but nor was she amused. 'It is what I give to
the children as a treat,' she said, gently rebuking me.

'I am sorry. But I cannot eat it. I must spit it out.' And I did.
Fortunately I had brought a small stock of food, which included
chocolate and whisky and, most importantly, cigarettes. We handed
them over.

Benjamin's father called me out of the room and on to the
balcony where he had hanging by skewers in a wire cage long fat
slivers of dried meat. He chose a choice piece and we returned to
the table. I knew that I should raise the subject of cannibalism. It
would be high on the agenda of questions when I returned. My
host was offering hunks of dried meat from a large stock, surely
now might be the time to ask. But it is not exactly a subject which
trips off the tongue. 'Ah, doctor, tell me, do you eat people?' Or

even a light-hearted: 'Doctor, there is a silly rumour that there has been some cannibalism in Zepa. Ha ha ha.' So I settled for a very lame: 'What meat is this then, Benjamin?'

'Lamb,' he replied.

Lamb. I must confess I have seen no sheep but it must be sheep country. End of subject. But just in case, I ate very little. The star of the evening was Pepe. Shy, worried Serb, Pepe was the source of all knowledge on the war, the situation in Sarajevo and the world in general. He was delightful company.

Midway through the evening the doctors rigged up a car battery to a radio and we listened to the nine o'clock news. The World Service announced that the siege of Zepa was over and that a UN convoy was in the town. We clinked glasses and hugged and kissed. I can honestly say it was one of the proudest and most emotional moments in my life. It brings tears to my eyes as I write.

By ten o'clock I could take no more slivo. I told them that I was off to bed. They were most insistent that I should stay and sleep in the house, but I could see that it was already overcrowded and that there was a shortage of beds. Risto needed no persuasion. Pepe was offered accommodation with a friend. But I firmly refused and tottered back to the convoy. In truth, my head was spinning. Whether it was the slivo, the bread, the hospital or the anticlimax, I do not know, but I was up most of the night and was as sick as a dog. Thank God I had not accepted their hospitality. All around me there were sounds of fraternisation, as the people of Zepa celebrated our arrival.

The following morning Benjamin collected me for breakfast. Risto was looking particularly bright and chirpy. Breakfast was tea. Risto did a final tour of the hospital, gave advice on how to remove the gangrenous leg using the anaesthetics we had brought and made a list of medicines and medical instruments needed. The doctors requested a book on surgery in Serbo-Croat. Risto went to a lot of trouble to get them all that they needed.

I spoke to a woman who was one of thirty who had had an abortion last June. She had been raped in the early days of the war. A doctor had walked from Srebrenica with the medical instruments, assisted with the abortions and walked back.

Our final task was to syphon some fuel from the vehicles. They desperately needed fuel for the hospital and they had one vehicle which they used as an ambulance. The sick and the wounded from the thirty-three remaining villages were brought down to the hospital by horse and cart. One of the doctors did village calls on horseback to respond to emergencies. Because we had been forced to leave our jerrycans in Rogatica and because of the road conditions, we were able to spare very little. Commander Avdo gave me two letters, one for Kusic and one for Furtula. With hugs and kisses and promises to return soon, we left.

Back at Borike, we were met by Kusic. He seemed genuinely pleased that we had been to Zepa and was concerned about the condition of the people. He invited Risto and myself into the smoky hut. He read the reply. It was an exchange of greetings and the assurance from Avdo that he commanded only citizens. Men who had no intention of attacking but who would defend to the last man.

In Rogatica the convoy halted while we recovered the medicine and the jerrycans that the Serbs has removed. Major Furtula came and sat in our vehicle. We gave him the letter. He read it and was silent. His eyes were moist. He gently shook his head and sighed. Apparently it was a letter from a friend to a friend. No bitterness, no blame, just a wish for peace and a return to former times.

8
Kamenica

Srebrenica, Srebrenica, Srebrenica. Every conference, every meeting, every discussion was punctuated with demands for a convoy to Srebrenica. The latest reports from the amateur radio station were quoted. They were sickening. Starvation, severe cold, lack of doctors and medicine, heavy shelling. We kept on applying to the Serbs. They refused, blaming the 'Muslims' for attacking Serb positions from within Srebrenica. General Morillon, fed up with travelling from Sarajevo to Pale, called for a meeting between General Mladic and his Bosnian counterpart, General Sefer Halli-lovic, to discuss a cease-fire. A cease-fire at least long enough to permit a convoy of humanitarian aid into Srebrenica. It was to be in the conference room of the French battalion at the airport. General Morillon was to be in the chair. Victor Andreev, the Chief of Civil Affairs on Morillon's staff, attended.

Tony Land and myself represented UNHCR. The conference began at twelve. We were there by 11.45. The room was laid out with four long tables forming a square. We entered and sat at the table on the far left. Behind us on the wall was a detailed map of Sarajevo. Petite Vesna was next to arrive, her red hair drawn back tightly to her head. She was to translate. She was very nervous. She had not met Mladic before. Mladic arrived on time with the Serb Liaison Officer Misha Indjic. General Morillon and Victor Andreev met him at the door. There was no sign of Hallilovic. General Mladic sat opposite us. On the wall behind him were detailed blown-up photographs of the various check-points and French positions. Mladic removed his hat and we exchanged greetings across the table. General Morillon, Victor and Vesna sat at

The bunker at Sarajevo airport during shelling.
Fabrizio Hochschild is sitting on the far right of the picture.
General Mackenzie said he could tell how long I had
been in Bosnia by the length of my beard. These were early days!

The office inside the hangar at Sarajevo airport

Our bedspace after a shell hit the hangar

Outside our hangar. Lee Doherty is seated in the centre;
standing behind him is 'Boss White'; to the left of the photo
is 'Boss Black'. Front 'bookends' are Nonjo and Ploco, with Amra
in the middle. My driver Dragon is centre right standing.

Vesna

Deputy prime minister
Zlatko Lagumdzija

The Serb Liaison Officer
and my good friend
Brane Luledzija

Professor Kljic, the man
responsible for the distribution
of food in Sarajevo

Serb besiegers of Gorazde

Muslim defender of Gorazde

Convoy to Gorazde (*courtesy of Bernard Carrier RICM*)

Bravo Larry. Merci Erik. Erik de Stabenrath after he reached
the centre of Gorazde (*courtesy of Bernard Carrier RICM*)

A later convoy to Gorazde. Stage 1: Contact with defenders.
My driver Zlatan Oruc stands on the right; John MacMillan,
UNHCR spokesman, is on the left (*courtesy of Risto Tervahauta*)

(*below left*) Stage 2: Defender removes mine from our path (*courtesy of Risto Tervah*
(*below right*) Stage 3: The convoy can progress (*courtesy of Risto Tervahauta*)

Neill Wright, Glynne Evans, me and Jeremy Brade in Dobrinja
(*courtesy of Glynne Evans*)

Back at the base. Jerri Hulme is on the left; Tony Land on the right,
flanked by (anti-clockwise) Mica, Una, Leyla and Meliha

Earning my holy picture unloading the convoy in Grbvica
(*courtesy of Rajko Poštar*)

Serb refugees leaving Sarajevo (*courtesy of Rajko Poštar*)

the table nearest the door between ours and that of the Serb contingent. Behind them was a map of the whole of Bosnia. For fifteen minutes we sat and drank coffee. Aides whispered messages into the ear of Morillon. There was a problem. Hallilovic was refusing to come. He wanted to send his deputy, Colonel Siber. General Morillon explained the situation to Mladic.

Mladic stood up as if to leave. 'I am a general and a commander. You are a general and a commander. We will deal with their general and their commander.' General Morillon agreed that he was right and persuaded him to sit down again. Victor Andreev went to sort it out, leaving us with Mladic.

I decided on some small talk. 'General, who is your favourite author?'

'Clausewitz, then Sun Tzu.'

'Ah, what about generals then, who are your favourites?'

'I have many. Some you will know, some you will not. I like Rommel and Montgomery.' He smiled, having given me the easy ones. 'The Russian Marshals Suvarov and Zhukov. There are many.'

He then turned the tables. 'We have seen each other before when you were a soldier. I have been on many military courses. Where did we meet?'. I ran through my career, which includes neither Staff nor War colleges. He was not impressed.

But it gave me the chance to observe him. He sat at the centre of the table, his distinctive peaked hat to his right. He was square to the table. He is a broad bull of a man. His face is slightly too fleshy to be handsome. It is ruddy and moist with sweat. He has piercing steel-blue eyes. His mouth is small but too full-lipped to be mean. His hair is greying and *en brosse*, exposing two deep peaks of tanned scalp. His hands are small, with fat fingers. I asked him who was the most important influence in his life and his reply surprised me.

'My mother. She brought me up. My father was murdered by the Ustasha. She cared for us and gave us our values.'

While talking, he took an orange from a fruit bowl placed in front of him by a French soldier. Then in silence he took from his pocket a clasp knife, opened it and began to peel the fruit. He started with a surgically precise incision at the top and ran the blade along the circumference of the skin. The peel came away cleanly as one long, crinkly snake. I watched fascinated. I expected the orange to bleed. I realised that he had mesmerised us with this action. The room was silent and electric. I looked at Vesna. Her mouth was open and her eyes were wide – wide with fear.

Mladic went on the attack. 'Do you like Hemingway?' he asked me.

'Yes, I do.'

'You look like him.'

'I hope I do not end up the way he did, committing suicide at sixty-three.' Mladic held the knife in his hand. He stared straight into my eyes. 'You will not have to worry about that if you stay here much longer.' He closed the knife with a loud click and laughed as his words were translated by Indjic.

Hallilovic did not turn up. Perhaps he lacked the courage to face Mladic. The conference was postponed, but not before we had the chance to discuss a convoy to Srebrenica.

'General, we need to send a convoy to Srebrenica. We have discussed this before. I have tried and failed. I wish to try again.'

'You always want to try to reach Muslims. Have you ever thought about giving aid to Serbs?'

'That is unfair, General. We deliver aid regularly to Rajlovac, to Banja Luka and to many other Serb-dominated areas.'

'But you specialise in Muslim convoys. Tell me, where have you taken a convoy to a Serb town?'

'Grbavica, Rogatica.'

'*En route* to Muslim towns.'

I began to notice Mladic's attitude to Vesna. At the end of a reply he looked directly at her and just perceptibly nodded his head. When he was making the point he concluded with 'mala', which is a diminutive, 'little girl' or maybe 'lass'. But she was the instrument by which he was conversing, not the person through whom he was conversing. As his steel-blue gaze fixed her you could see her shrink away from the table, like a mouse in the gaze of a cat.

'OK, General, tell me where there are besieged Serbs.'

'I will tell you where you must do convoys before you enter Srebrenica.'

'OK.'

'You must do three convoys, the first to Slovici–Vlasenica–Han Piesak–Milici.'

I really liked that one. Han Piesak is the Serb Aldershot.

'The second to Bratunac–Skelani–Srebrenica.'

That I was happy to do.

'The third to Kalinovik–Miljevina–Neversenje.'

Another beauty. Kalinovik is the birthplace of Mladic, Neversenje a Serb corps headquarters. 'Thank you, General. May we do the second first?'

'No.'

By now he had had enough. Indjic was given the sign. They were on their feet. Hands were shaken. They left.

The last word belonged to Tony. 'Orange anyone?'

Vesna shuddered.

The father of Zlatan, my driver, had put his life savings into an attractive house in the country between Kiseljak and Visoko, not too far from Sarajevo. The house was built to his own design. There was a bedroom for each of his children and their partner and a bedroom for his grandchildren. It was built with retirement in mind. His children and his grandchildren loved it. It was second base for them all. For Zlatan and his wife it was a weekend escape from the rigours of the busy hospital where they were both doctors.

When old Mr Oruc bought the plot for the house he bought it for its beauty. It never occurred to him that Kiseljak had more Croats than Muslims or that Visoko had more Muslims than Croats. When the Bosnian war first broke out his house was comparatively safe. It was within range of Serb machine-gun fire but there were no artillery guns or mortars to threaten its substance. But as the conflict spilt over and pitched Croat against Muslim, his retirement haven became a front-line target. It lay equidistant between the land dominated by the Croats fighting out of Kiseljak and the Muslims out of Visoko. The Serb machine-gun became a side show. Mr Oruc fled ahead of the heaviest fighting. He and his wife could take little with them. The road was full of fighting patrols ready to strip and loot and rob. He had some money in the house and was tempted to take it with him. His wife said: 'No. If we are stopped we will lose it. We may be killed for it.' The calm grandad crept out to his patio, lifted a paving stone and dug the money deep into the ground. One quick tour of the house, a peep into the bedrooms, a flood of memories. They then left, passing the orchard so carefully planted, the trees beginning to fruit. Muslims by name, they turned right for Visoko.

Months later we were asked to send a small convoy from Sarajevo to Visoko via Kiseljak. Within minutes of the request I had a volunteer driver, Zlatan. Nonjo agreed to go with him. The convoy passed, with only a little hassle, through the Croat checkpoint and sped towards Visoko. It made an unscheduled halt midway between the two towns. Zlatan and Nonjo ran through the orchard. The house was destroyed. There was no time to linger over that. Together they lifted the paving stone and dug away the earth. The money was where the old man had hastily placed it. Zlatan recovered it and together they sped back to their trucks.

A few days later I needed to go to Visoko. I took Zlatan, just the two of us and the landcruiser. We tucked the vehicle into the gateway of the orchard and made a more leisurely tour of the remains of his father's dream. There was no roof to any part of the house, but the central staircase still stood. The ground floor was an uneven jagged carpet of shattered tiles and burnt beams. We carefully picked our way up the staircase. Zlatan pointed to where each room had been. He cursorily searched through the debris, looking perhaps for teddy bears, photo albums, favourite pieces. But he and his family will have to rely on their memories. There was nothing recognisable. We went out on to the patio to see his daddy's improvised but reliable safe. Machine-gun bullets whistled past us. We had woken up the Serb gunner. We left. Zlatan, on behalf of the family, had exorcised the ghost.

Later I was to find out that the house had been burned to the ground, not by Croats seeking to drive out Muslims, but by a group of Visoko bandits who had looted it and wished to lay blame on the Croats. A bitter pill for Dr Zlatan to swallow.

*

The Sparavalo family invited me to lunch at their flat in central Sarajevo. Sasha was to be my guide and interpreter.

'Please, Mr Larry, if you say you will go you cannot cancel,' he had warned me. We arrived at the block of flats where the Sparavalos live. The family were at the front entrance waiting to greet us. Mr Vjelko Sparavalo was a famous TV and stage actor and looked the part. He was wearing an immaculate pair of slacks with a knife-edge crease, a tailor-made blazer and an elegant cravat. He is tall, very handsome, with a neat moustache. Quite debonair. His wife, Kira, is a very attractive lady, slightly taller than he is, with close-cropped hair and a neat, elegant appearance. Their younger son is a student of music, tall and gangly. He looked seventeen but was twenty-two. They were embarrassingly effusive with their welcome. We climbed the stairs to their flat. On entering I could see that they had gone to enormous trouble. There was nothing in Sarajevo, but they had laid a table which creaked and groaned with food.

'I am sorry, but I could find no wine,' said Mr Sparavalo.

I had brought with me a selection of the food available to me, which included wine. We were all delighted. The meal and the hospitality were outstanding. Young Denis played the guitar brilliantly. I had great pleasure at looking through a photo album of the most notable performances of my host. He was desperate for the war to end so that he could return to the stage. We toasted Enesa and Aris and left, having had a super time.

By early February Srebrenica was truly a fixation. The nightly reports from the amateur radio were unfolding a horror story, even allowing for the inevitable exaggeration of the operator.

I had tried the two direct routes and failed. The Bosnian government were putting tremendous pressure on us. They told us that the villages of Kamenica, Cerska and Konjevici Polje, which were to the north of Srebrenica, were in danger of falling and that if they did, their populations would move to Srebrenica, thus swelling an already intolerable situation. We therefore decided to attempt a convoy to Cerska. If at all possible, we would drop off some aid at Kamenica. If we were really lucky we would attempt a reconnaissance into Srebrenica.

There was a grave shortage of food in Sarajevo, so the trucks and drivers would come from Belgrade from the Dutch–Belgian battalion. The French Foreign Legion were to be my escort. The press interest was confined to the intrepid Jeremy Bowen and his BBC crew, Pepe was translator and driver, Risto Tervahauta, who guided us into Zepa, was our medical expert and companion.

We were scheduled to leave Sarajevo at midday on Saturday, 13 February, but there was a fire-fight between the Serbs and the government troops across the airport which delayed our departure for two hours. We did not get far. After half a kilometre we were stopped at the first Serb check-point as the battle recommenced. We parked in the open for an hour as the battle raged over our heads. At the Jahorina crossroads near the principal site of the Sarajevo Winter Olympics we met up with the escort and together moved on to Pale. When we arrived there it was too late to go any further so the French parked up in a secure fenced compound near the Serb administrative buildings. We moved on to a small 'pension' recommended to us by Brane, the Serb liaison officer. It was a large three-storey house, owned by a fascinating two-story owner. The place had sufficient parking space at the side to permit small convoys to overnight in safety.

The entrance was up a set of concrete stairs. The door was wood and glass and led to a steep staircase, also concrete and uncarpeted. At the top of the stairs there was a mini-mountain of shoes, reminding the visitor to take off his muddy footwear and put on slippers from the stack of all shapes and sizes. This house was run by Novka Savic, a lady who likes cleanliness. She is tall, well-built, attractive, with warm, smiling eyes which welcome guests. Her husband, Nenad, is obviously a hunter, the walls are covered with trophy heads and stuffed birds. He is of medium height, but barrel-chested, with huge forearms, wide wrists, massive palms and a crunching handshake. It must be part of the curriculum at school for Bosnian boys. His open, handsome, rugged face carries a war wound. He has lost the sight in one eye.

'Welcome, Mr Larry, Brane has told us about you.'

'And I have heard all about you, my friend. They tell me that you are one of the most famous hunters in the whole of ex-Yugoslavia.'

'I used to hunt with Marshal Tito. Come with me.'

He took us out of the dining-room, past the shoe mountain to a staircase leading to the bedrooms. On each of the walls on either side of the staircase was stretched the skin of a bear. The one on the left wall was big, but the brute on the right was enormous. He pointed to it. 'The second largest bear ever shot in Yugoslavia. Shot by me.'

He showed me a photo which was of Tito standing over the fallen carcass of a bear. 'That was the largest ever. Shot by Tito, after we had hunted it down together.'

He produced an array of weapons, one of which had robbed the bears of their lives. He patted the head of the larger bear and stroked its paws which had long, thick, slatey grey nails. 'We came very close to this one. It was on all fours near a bush. I took aim, pulled the trigger and hit it here.' The gun barrel touched the still visible hole in the skin. 'It reared up on its hind legs and screamed, then fell with a thud.' The words were accompanied by the actions. The weapon was raised, his cheek rested on the butt, the sight aligned with his now blind eye. He copied the action of the stricken bear drawing himself to his height and extending his arms. He mimicked its cry and dropped his arms as the bear, vivid in his memory, collapsed to the ground.

Our hostess, an outstanding country-style cook, produced a great spread of home cooking, soup, hams and cakes. Our host provided bottles of slivovic. Local visitors came to see our hosts and we were joined by Jeremy Bowen and his crew. We all shared in what to us, direct from Sarajevo, was a feast.

We had heard the story of the bear, there was still another story to tell.

'Nenad, how did you lose your eye?' I asked.

He was sitting, squat and powerful, to my left at the dining-table, his wife was standing behind him. She lightly placed her hand on his left shoulder, his right hand moved and covered the tips of her fingers. Mummy bear and Daddy bear.

'Last summer, we Serbs organised a food convoy into a Serb village near Zepa. We had negotiated it with the Muslims. I was a driver of one of the trucks. Because we were on a humanitarian mission I was not armed. We had just a few guards with us.

'It was a hot day, the windows were wound down in the cab and even though we had negotiated approval, we knew from the moment that we entered the valley that things could go wrong. We were all tense and alert.

'Deep in the valley, as the convoy was spread out by the twists in the road and at its most vulnerable, the firing began. Some of the vehicles were destroyed, there was noise, flames and screams. I got out of the vehicle to find cover. I could see our attackers, they were so close. They could see me. The bullet hit me in the face. I ran and ran. There were bodies everywhere. Fifty-nine Serbs died that day. I hid. I could hear the Muslims around me, hear them in the vehicles, hear them killing. As night fell they left. I was bleeding and I knew that I had been hit in the eye. In my aiming eye. Fortunately the bleeding stopped. The pain didn't.'

The hunter survived. For four days he used his special skills to avoid capture and to move back into Serb territory. Meanwhile the world heard of the 'massacre'. All those who had not managed to escape were presumed dead. One of the survivors had seen the hunter hit in the face and fall to the ground.

'So you thought he was dead,' I said to his wife.

'Yes. There was a memorial service for them which I attended. His death was announced on the radio and the television.' Her eyes were moist. 'Then he just came back through the door. Back from the dead.' I looked at him and his eyes, too, were moist, one bright and moist, the other dull. Later he told Risto that he had had treatment in a Moscow hospital. He told me that he was learning to shoot left-handed. He reckoned he was now at least as good a shot with his left eye as the average man. He accepted that he would never again be the great hunter that he had been.

In one of the bedrooms the son of the hunter was sleeping. He was ill. Risto was asked to do a house call. He diagnosed tonsilitis and dispensed antibiotics. Baby bear.

We from Sarajevo took advantage of the bathroom, the flush loo and the shower. I slept well.

Even though we left before seven, our hosts insisted on giving us a good breakfast. They became good friends and I stayed with them often. They never resented our convoys to 'Muslims'. They took care of us on our way into and back from trips to 'enemy' territory. The hunter guaranteed that our vehicles would not be touched while parked outside his house. They were thoroughly decent people behaving admirably in bad times.

I once asked them, 'Do you hate Muslims?'

Novka was horrified by the question. 'Not at all. We had neighbours who were Muslims, not Muslims who were neighbours.'

His reply was a little different: 'Only the one.'

We joined the escort and the BBC at seven and left to meet the convoy at Zvornik. We passed through all my least favourite places, Podromanija, Sokolac, Han Piesak and through the 'Valley of Death' where the danger was from wild bands of Bosnian soldiers up in the hills who sniped on anything that passed through the valley.

By two o'clock we had arrived without incident at the Karakaj check-point on the outskirts of Zvornik. We parked our vehicles just before the bridge which spans the River Drina and separates Karadzic's so-called Srpska Republika from Milosevic's Serbia. The bridge was controlled by Major Vlado Dakcic, the king of the bridge, a reservist lawyer, a very tall, heavy, chubby-faced man with a drooping moustache – a blubbery walrus, responsible to the local authorities for the heavy traffic crossing the bridge. He controlled a police post, a customs detachment and liaised with his true masters, the army. I called in on his office, a tatty hut containing two desks, a telephone, one comfortable chair and a few rickety typist's chairs.

'Mr Larry,' said the Major, rising from the comfortable chair. 'How are you? Going to Belgrade?'

'No, my friend, I am here to meet the convoy from Belgrade.'

'There is no convoy from Belgrade here,' he said, looking for approval from his colleagues, who dutifully laughed.

'There soon will be, my friend. We are on our way to Kamenica.'

This seemed to bring the house down.

'Ah, the Kamenica convoy. There is a convoy from Belgrade on the other side of the bridge, Mr Larry, perhaps it thinks it's for Kamenica.'

More laughter. The game had begun.

I always hated this bit. At the beginning you never know how tough to be. Too tough and you blow it. They just disappear. You cannot find anyone to answer anything. Too weak and they send you away. But it is bloody hard to smile and to shake hands and to laugh when it is all at your expense.

'I'll go across and see if the convoy has arrived and return later.'

'Sorry, Mr Larry, but you cannot do that.'

'Why?'

'You have no approval to enter Serbia and if they refuse to let you in, you have no approval to come back into Srpska Republika, you may have to live on the bridge.' More laughter accompanied this threat. This was going to be a difficult mission. However, the immediate problem was solved by the arrival of the single jeep of the Belgian commander. I went across to meet him.

'Captain Dirk Van Bruck,' he said. I knew immediately that I liked him. Tall, broad, fair, he had excellent English and a big smile. He turned out to be an ace leader and a very good companion. He had a visa to enter Srpska Republika so he could come across as often as he liked. He had parked his convoy facing Zvornik, 50 metres from the bridge, which was causing chaos with the traffic, but he refused to move. He meant business. I introduced him to our French escort commander, who was unhappy with the escort parked so close to the bridge. The road is near to a barracks with soldiers constantly passing by, also we were parked opposite the town's main cemetery. Zvornik at war is a spooky enough place without having its dead as your neighbours. So we decided to move back to the check-point at the entrance to Zvornik. I told Dakcic what I intended to do. He then showed traditional Serb hospitality which is so often at odds with the situation. He sent a man with us and by the time we reached the check-point, a civilian was waiting to direct us to a nearby office block where at least some of the escort could sleep. There was a toilet and a couple of the rooms had wood-burning stoves. Dirk returned to spend the night with the convoy on the other side of the bridge. Risto, Pepe and myself slept on the floor in the office block. We chose one of the rooms with a stove. The overcrowding, the fumes, the smoke and the aroma from the much-used-by-many-persons sleeping bags soon filled the room with a fug and a smell that even pigs would reject. I decided that another day, another location.

We were up and out at dawn. We moved off to the bridge. The Major was nowhere to be seen. Some European Community Military Mission observers were looking for him, but could not find him. The French escort lined up by the bridge and the BBC set up its camera for the grand entrance of the convoy. After a lot of hassle I found the king of the bridge. He was in a very jovial mood.

'There is no approval for the convoy. Therefore it cannot enter Srpska Republika.'

'There is approval. We have approval from Pale, from General Mladic himself.'

'He has not told us. If you have approval be our guest. Just wait until we are informed, then you can go.'

I made many calls to Sarajevo. Tony Land visited Pale. Sarajevo made calls to Zagreb, Zagreb to Geneva, Geneva to New York. The temperature was minus five and we were back parked alongside the cemetery, which as a result of the war had extended beyond its fence. Three lines of graves had advanced towards the roadside. We watched as a grave-digger took many hours to pick and shovel and spade ice-cold clods of earth from the frozen ground.

As the day progressed it became colder and bleaker. Dr Risto decided to light a fire at the side of the road. He asked a young boy who was watching the convoy from a discreet distance where he could buy wood. The boy raced away to his home, the house nearest the bridge, adjacent to the cemetery. He returned with a wheelbarrow of firewood. Once Risto had taken the initiative everybody wanted to join in, BBC cameraman, French soldiers, Pepe. But Risto is a Finn, a cold-weather expert and a solitary fire maker. He has a system. With his trusty Finnish sheath knife he took branches and lightly slivered the surface, the white strips of wood curled like watch springs, still attached to the branch. These were the first twigs to be lit. The fire grew, slowly, slowly. Larger branches were put on only when smaller pieces were ablaze. The Brits and the Bosnians were impatient and wanted to throw on logs at the first sign of flame but Risto treated the fire as his baby and was possessive. His ritual and success drew an admiring audience among whom was the young Serb boy who had provided the wood. Pepe talked to him, found out that his name was Milenko. Jeremy Bowen shared some sweets with him. Soon the boy was joined by his grandfather, Slavko Sikimic. We talked about our task. He pointed out his house from where a large black flag was flying. His eldest grandson had recently been killed while on a Serb action near Kamenica, one of the places we were hoping to reach.

The man invited us to his house for coffee. UNHCR and BBC went together. His wife, Bojka, was lovely. She had been very pretty but she now looked older than her husband. She gave us coffee. There was no venom in her voice as she explained to us what had happened to her grandson. 'He was my favourite. He went out on a patrol to Kamenica. There was one single sniper shot. It hit him and killed him instantly; the only casualty on that patrol.'

We talked a lot about the war.

'What do you feel about us wanting to reach Kamenica where your grandson was killed?'

'The people there are like us. They need food, we understand that. It is not their fault.'

They were joined by their other son, the father of Milenko, and their daughter-in-law who told us that they had applied to go to Australia. They would soon be away.

They asked where we were sleeping. When we told them in the vehicles they offered to accommodate and feed us in their house. There were only two extra rooms and two extra beds but we were welcome. The offer was spontaneous, the hospitality free. Jeremy knew that they had little and that we could easily outstay our welcome, so he insisted on us staying only if they would take some payment, at least for our food. They reluctantly agreed.

The day passed without any positive news from Sarajevo. I occasionally saw the Major whose bonhomie was wearing really thin. I tried to see the local military commander, Major Pandoro-vic, but was told he was out 'at the front'. He eventually arrived for a brief visit with a group of soldiers.

'Major, I am here to take a convoy to Kamenica.'

The Major was polite but off-hand. 'There is no approval. When approval comes you can go.'

Pandorovic left as abruptly as he had arrived, but not before one of his soldiers infuriated me. There was an outbreak of laughter from amongst them. 'What was that about, Pepe?'

'One said that if the convoy gets through they will be killing fat Muslims, if not then it will have to be thin Muslims.'

By dark we had achieved nothing. The escort went back to their overnight laager, where they had made good friends with the locals. They soon had a large fire blazing without using the Tervahauta method. Jeremy Bowen, great professional that he is, was filming campfire and fraternisation footage. His experience told him that this was the best he was going to get this day.

Dirk returned into Serbia and briefed his convoy. He himself was sleeping in the tiny confines of his soft-skinned canvas-topped jeep. It meant that he could keep in contact by the vehicle radio with Belgrade. He had chosen his driver well, a man with a sense of humour and a sense of priority. The vehicle had enough food in it for a fortnight. He also had a copy of *Playboy*, which guaranteed him a steady flow of visitors.

We went straight to the house of Milenko, where the BBC crew were already well installed. The family had cooked us an excellent meal. During it, Dakcic, the king of the bridge, arrived. I hoped that it was not to intimidate our hosts. It wasn't, it was more Serb paradox, he wanted to offer his apologies for not being able to accommodate us himself and to pass on the order from Pandorovic that we were not welcome and we were to leave Zvornik and return to Sarajevo in the morning.

'What are you going to do?' asked Jeremy.

'Stay,' I replied.

Jeremy and his crew filed their 'UN convoy ordered back' piece.

We returned to the table and drank a few glasses of our hosts' slivovic, punctuated with a few nips from Jeremy's whisky bottle. Unlike at Gorazde, this was a blended bottle. The BBC must have cut down on his allowances. We were next disturbed by shooting close to the house. We had parked both our vehicles close to the side of the house, but they could still be seen from the road. After a sensible pause we went out to investigate and found no damage, but the source was still there, some drunken Serb soldiers were weaving their way home and firing into the air.

We returned inside the house, had a nightcap and reluctantly left the warm living-room for the morgue-cold bedrooms. Being the oldest, I qualified for one of the beds. Being the most handsome and because he was paying, Bowen qualified for the other. Our fellow team-mates slept on the floor, all of us wrapped up in our sleeping bags with only our noses peeping out.

The next day was no better. Dakcic was very unhappy when I refused to move. He ordered Dirk to return the convoy to Belgrade. Dirk refused to cross back over the bridge into Serbia, knowing that if he did he might not be permitted to return. Despite Serb intimidation, the convoy remained on the Serbian side, close to and facing the bridge. To show aggression and to prove our determination, we again lined up near the cemetery facing in the direction of Cerska. Milenko played truant from school and attached himself to Pepe and Risto.

Our persistence paid off. Pandorovic came to see us. He was more amenable than on the previous day and stayed longer, which gave me time to assess him. He is an ex-regular Yugoslav army officer. He is about five foot ten, stocky, with ginger hair and freckles. He has green eyes and is about thirty-eight. He stands square, looks fit and decisive. I would guess that he is a good leader.

'Major, why can't we proceed? We have approval from your masters in Pale. You know that. If we had not, we would not have got this far.'

'I have received no orders to let you go through. Besides, there is heavy fighting in Kamenica. Can you not hear the shelling from here?'

This was true, the distant, muffled rumble of artillery was ominously audible.

'But surely, Major, if there is shelling, you must be doing it. Kamenica is a small village. There are no heavy weapons there. I suspect that you are delaying us here, while you take Kamenica.'

'You can think what you like. Why should I let you into an enemy position to feed them?'

'Because, Major, you are mainly besieging women and children, starving women and children.'

At every check-point I had at some time or other to have this same conversation. This was slightly different, because Pandorovic may not have had the power to let me proceed, but he certainly had the power of life or death over those people I was trying to reach.

'If there are only starving women and children there, then starving women and children are killing my soldiers.'

'Major, I just want you to know that I am not taking this convoy back. I am taking it forward to Konjevici via Kamenica and Cerska.'

'Then I will meet you in Kamenica,' he replied cockily. His entourage roared with laughter. He left to their applause.

By six it was dark and cold. Reluctantly we had to admit that there was nothing else we could do. Dirk went back to the convoy, the French to their fires, and we to Milenko's. More hospitality, more slivo, more subdued.

The next day Major Dakcic surprised me by suggesting that I attend a meal with Pandorovic in Loznica. I asked him to arrange it. This he did. Pandorovic was very late. I had almost given up on him coming. Loznica is in Serbia but he arrived in uniform with his bodyguard. The meal was very interesting. He understands English but is shy to speak it. He told me about his wife and children, about life in the Yugoslav army, about the great country it recently had been.

I listened to yesterday but was more interested in today. 'Am I going to get into Cerska?' I asked him.

'Not before me,' he replied.

'Konjevici?'

'Maybe.'

'Srebrenica?'

'Never,' he emphatically replied.

'What about the women and the children?'

'They are not my problem. If the Muslims want to save their women and children they can lay down their arms and surrender.'

'How can you shell villages and towns where the majority of

the occupants are women and children cowering in the basements of their homes?'

'Their men are firing at us.'

'But, Major, they are firing at you because they are being attacked by you. They are defending their homes.'

He responded with the litany of the few villages and towns where the 'Muslims' had fired on innocent Serbs.

'Major, you are a professional army officer. Are you not afraid of being branded a war criminal?'

'I have never killed anyone. I do not even carry a weapon.'

Around us people ate, drank and a band played.

My last memory of the evening was of Pandorovic dancing in one of those Yugoslav folk dances where people hold hands, skip, dance and bob in a huge circle around the tables. He danced elegantly.

After a wickedly cold night, we were up at dawn. Before joining the escort I sat in the vehicle at the side of Milenko's house and contacted Sarajevo. I was told that there was intense activity on the political front. Having the BBC with us had kept the story in the public eye. Their presence had attracted other journalists. Madame Ogata, who was about to leave for a tour of Africa, was contacting New York and Belgrade, demanding progress for the convoy. General Morillon was in Pale, berating Karadzic and Mladic.

Although cold and weary, I felt that all we had to do was stick it out. Dirk and his drivers were cold but never miserable. They were as determined as we were to get through. Disturbingly the noise of shelling was more intense. We were racing against time for Kamenica. A lot of military trucks carrying ammunition raced past our position. The Serbs were determined to take Kamenica before world pressure allowed our convoy to proceed. The king of the bridge became cockier as the day advanced. He was getting news from the front. We were getting little or no good news from the rear echelons.

UNHCR convoys crossed the bridge for Tuzla, for Sarajevo and for Gorazde, but ours was blocked. Dakcic requested my presence at his office. I went in an aggressive mood.

'Soldiers of Srpska Republika have captured Kamenica,' he told me with a huge smile. I left his scruffy office deeply depressed and briefed Dirk, the escort commander, and the BBC.

Kamenica had fallen. While we had waited so close, the Serbs had overrun the village. Homes were burning, families fleeing as we spoke. I relayed this bitter news to Sarajevo. We waited for the world reaction and hoped that it would be condemnatory and that the Serbs would have to let us into Cerska, a naive, momentary thought. Jeremy Bowen had been telling the world nightly of the impending fate of Kamenica. It is not as if they did not know.

They. Who are they? Whom am I really angry with? Pandorovic to start off with. Mladic. The doctor Karadzic. But who could have stepped in? Clinton's answer to everything was, 'Lift the arms embargo.' They have no bread, give them cake . . . tomorrow. If we had gone straight down that road, would the Serbs, would Pandorovic have fired on us? We were doing this all wrong but I did not know which way was all right. I felt really miserable because I knew I could have done more.

I went to the barracks to find Pandorovic. I was told with arrogance that he was 'at the front'.

I wanted to know about refugees. 'Where has the population of Kamenica gone to?'

'We do not know,' said the only officer I could find.

'For Christ's sake let me forward so that I can at least see where they are going. These are women and children, and they will need help. Now.'

'No. I have orders that you are not to move.'

I pressured Sarajevo. Sarajevo put pressure on Zagreb.

I went back to the Serb headquarters. 'Can I go forward without a convoy to see where the civilians are?'

'No, but I can tell you that most of them have headed for Srebrenica.'

'Srebrenica is starving and overcrowded now. The last thing it wants is more people.'

But I got nowhere. The Serbs I was talking to were not going to let us go.

The French escort commander asked his headquarters if we could try to advance without permission and without the convoy.

The answer was a predictable 'No'. I knew that if the Serbs had taken Kamenica it would only be a matter of days before they continued their push on to Cerska. Jeremy Bowen was equally desperate to get into Kamenica but was having no luck. He knew that the longer the Serbs kept him out the more 'sanitised' the place would be.

Then the Serbs sprang a surprise on us all. They had found a mass grave in Kamenica. Risto suggested that WHO should be present at the exhumation. Dakcic thought it would be a good idea but said that he would have to get approval. He then vanished and did not return.

The day ended with us getting nowhere. We were depressed, frustrated and angry. Within a few kilometres of us men, women and children were trudging through the snow across the hills wearing little and carrying less; their lives, like their homes, destroyed.

That night I hid in my sleeping bag. I could not sleep. In the morgue in Gorazde I had seen the bodies of those who had frozen to death on the walk from Srebrenica, black, contorted human blocks. How many innocents were shivering and shaking in the hills so close to where we lay? Too weak to move, too scared to stay. I could see fathers carrying bundles, mothers hugging babies to their bosoms as they slipped and slid in the deep, damp snow, older children urged to keep up. I could hear the panic cries of the separated and the lost. We were so close and so far. That night I felt hatred.

The long night eventually ended. Within minutes of waking I contacted Sarajevo. Madame Ogata apparently had announced that if we failed to get into Cerska today she would have to withdraw the convoy. General Morillon was encouraging us not to give up. We did not intend to. I went with Risto to see Dakcic. I was subdued but seething. As we were speaking to him a busload of international journalists crossed the bridge. They had been invited to see the mass grave. Jeremy Bowen and his crew joined them. Risto was refused. Risto and I then heard that the majority of the bodies had already been removed and were in a warehouse in Zvornik. It was suggested that we we could go and see them. Risto runs a hospital in Finland and does everything from medical consultations to major surgery, with a touch of forensic medicine thrown in. He said 'Yes'.

When I was about seven, an aunt of mine took me to the Claughton picture house in Birkenhead to see a version of *Dracula*. It frightened the life out of me. For months at night I could see faces in the grained wardrobe in my bedroom. I vaguely remember scenes from the film of stones creaking, graves opening and bodies emerging. Now, many years later, I was being asked if I voluntarily want to see exhumed bodies. My true answer was 'No'. But if I said 'I do not wish to go' the Serbs would accuse me of wanting to see only massacres by Serbs.

We found the warehouse in a small street. A man appeared wearing rubber boots and heavy rubber gloves.

'We have approval to see the bodies from Kamenica.'

'I do not have the key.'

'Where is it?'

'With the military.'

'Risto, we could be here all day. Let's go.'

Surprisingly, Risto rapidly agreed. Perhaps, as a child, he had had a wardrobe with faces in the wood.

We returned to the convoy to meet Jeremy Bowen, who began to give us a spade-by-spade account of the exhumations.

'Jeremy, we have just come from the warehouse where the bodies have been transferred,' I said nonchalantly and truthfully.

'Did you see the one without its head and one with wire around the neck? The Serbs were saying that it proved that the one had been strangled and the other had his throat cut,' continued Jeremy. I made a mental note not to find the military man with the key. Headless, exhumed bodies were even worse than the Claughton picture house.

Tony called me from Sarajevo. There were all sorts of rumours. Madame Ogata was reported to be furious. She was on her way to Africa but the plight of the convoys was uppermost in her mind. There were rumours that General Morillon was on his way to us. The Gorazde and the Tuzla convoys that had passed us yesterday were stuck. We were definitely stuck. At least with the other convoys the escort and HCR vehicles were together.

The press corps, fresh from the mass graves and *en route* to

Belgrade, descended on us. I remember Dirk and myself giving an interview to both the BBC and to Penny Marshall of ITN. 'We are not turning back,' I said.

'We are only going forward,' said Dirk.

At six in the evening we received the news from Sarajevo that Madame Ogata had ordered the recall of all convoys. The French escort commander, Dirk and myself sat together. We were devastated. We had told Dakcic and Pandorovic that we were not going back. We had told the media that we were only going forward. We had a convoy less than a thousand metres from the population of a town which had been routed. We could see the smoke. We could see the soldiers returning from the front who had done the deeds. Surely we could not walk away.

The escort commander was told by his headquarters to stay, Morillon had indicated that he would come personally to Zvornik. The transport battalion headquarters ordered Dirk back to Belgrade. Tony in Sarajevo sympathised with my wish to stay, but reminded me that the decision was a UNHCR directive from Madame Ogata herself. Fortunately it was too late to move, so we had the night to sleep on the situation and to see what developments dawn brought. Another night at Milenko's. Sombre and sober. I was angry, ashamed and cold.

Dawn brought more confusion. General Morillon was determined to intervene personally; New York wanted him to stay aloof.

Tony brought me up to date on the UNHCR front. Madame Ogata was in Africa. Her decision to halt the convoys was causing chaos. No convoys could mean no aid. No aid meant no reason for UN troops to be in support of humanitarian aid. Therefore her decision questioned the need for UN troops on the ground. He also told me the latest news from Sarajevo. Zlatko Lagumdzija was calling for the suspension of the airlift and for a halt to convoys entering the city. The city was going on a hunger strike in sympathy with Srebrenica!

'Tony, you are pulling my leg.'

'I am serious. They are not accepting our food, so we have had to stop the delivery of aid in the city. We will keep the airlift going until we bulk out in the warehouses.'

This was one of those moments in the war when I wondered

what the hell I was doing there. We were cold, tired and hungry, doing our best to reach those who were much more cold, tired and hungry. The pilots were risking life, limb and aircraft with each sortie; the convoy drivers were hazarding their lives on dangerous roads and at violent check-points. And one of the sides was now saying, 'You are not doing enough. Therefore we are going on a *hunger strike*.'

'Tony, tell me this isn't true.'

It was.

I went to see Pandorovic, and I levelled with him. 'Look, Major, your action in stopping this convoy looks as if it might be the end of the humanitarian aid. You do not want that to happen. We are feeding hundreds of thousands of Serbs. Break the deadlock, let this convoy through.'

'I do not have the power to do that.'

'OK, what about a gesture, a humanitarian gesture. Let me go forward without the convoy to see what is happening to the refugees.'

'No, it is not safe. Also the Muslims may take you hostage.'

'I will take my chance on that.'

'You cannot go. That is final.'

'OK, then one gesture of goodwill. At least let the convoy cross the bridge.'

'No.'

By ten thirty Belgrade, Sarajevo and Zagreb were all singing from the same song sheet. The attempt was over. The convoy was to return to Belgrade, the rest of us to Sarajevo. Final. No arguments; no discussions.

At ten forty-five I shook hands with Dirk. He had been a tough, loyal companion and a great leader. He had kept the morale of his men high through five bitterly cold days and nights. We said farewell to Milenko's family. God bless them, they had become so much a part of our team that they were as disappointed as we were. With heads low we pulled away from the bridge. I did not dare call in on Dakcic or his men. If any of them had cheered or jeered I am certain I would have knocked them to the floor. I took one last look down the Cerska road. I vowed to myself that I would be back.

Meanwhile countless women and children were forced to flee their homes, to run in the snow to Konjevici where Serb troops pounded them again, forcing those that lived to slip and slide through the metre-high snow and the treacherous ice to join the already overcrowded, besieged and starving Srebrenica where conditions rivalled the worst images of the Middle Ages.

As we passed through Podromanija we were told that the Gorazde convoy was still at Rogatica. We arrived back at Sarajevo at 5.20 p.m. I went straight to the UNHCR office and was told that events were still moving. General Morillon had negotiated an agreement with the Serbs for the Gorazde convoy to be divided in two, half for Gorazde and half for Zepa. The convoys could move in the morning. I was to go to Rogatica and lead one of them.

But first there was the matter of the hunger strike. All my frustration and fury was channelled against it. I tried to track down Zlatko Lagumdzija but failed. I quickly contacted the mayor of Sarajevo, Mr Kreseljakovic, who agreed to see me. I took Meliha with me. I told him how angry and disappointed we were. The mayor was honest. He supported the principle of the hunger strike but understood mine. I told him how close we were to being pulled out. He promised to see Zlatko and to do his best to get the policy changed. Some time later, I had the opportunity to ask Zlatko what had made him pursue such a destructive policy. He told me that it had been conceived in order to deflect a proposal put to him by a delegation of Srebrenicans that in order to draw attention to the plight of Srebrenica, the Bosnian government should collude in the murder of a Serb living in Sarajevo each time a Muslim in Srebrenica was killed. Zlatko had stamped on the proposal with the message that he personally would defend the life of every Serb in Sarajevo. But he had to do something. I was stunned. I had not realised how difficult a position he had been in.

Back at the PTT, I slept like a log. No recriminations. Normally failure gave me days of depression and nights of sleeplessness but this opportunity to follow up the failure with the immediate chance of another crack at either Gorazde or Zepa kept my adrenalin going. I returned to Rogatica. One of our vehicles hit a mine, cratering the Gorazde road. I took the combined convoy to Zepa. I spent another evening in Benjamin's home receiving the same warm welcome as I had on my first trip. This time I summoned the courage to raise the subject of cannibalism: they laughed at my discomfort. They were not shocked by the idea of cannibalism occurring in their starving villages but they did not believe that it had happened. I was glad that I had fulfilled my promise to return.

9
Konjevici Polje

Some days after my return from Zepa the phone rang in the UNHCR office. 'Larry, come and see me now.'

I hotfooted it to the Residence where General Morillon had his office.

'I want you to accompany me to Cerska. No convoy, just an assessment. And bring a World Health Organisation doctor.'

'Have we approval?' I asked somewhat incredulously.

'I have told Mladic. He will find it hard to refuse me freedom of movement.'

Back in the office I rang Michelle O'Kelly, our protection officer in Tuzla. Eire born, a lawyer who had practised in Dublin, a buxom girl with a gentle accent, a big smile and a warm personality, she had excellent links with the Bosnian government Military Corps Headquarters, but more importantly, recently she had been invited to talk to the amateur radio stations in Srebrenica, Konjevici Polje and Cerska from the amateur station in Zivinice.

'Michelle, what is the latest information from Cerska?'

'Grim. My last contact was yesterday when the Serbs were attacking. Some of the civilians have already left for Konjevici.'

'Can the Bosnian government force prevent it falling?'

'No way.'

We had a race on our hands.

The arrangements made by General Morillon were swift and simple. The British doctor, Simon Mardell, and myself were to make our way to the BiH Command headquarters at Kiseljak immediately. Simon is a very special person. He is in his late thirties, tall, with receding dark hair. He has dark, demanding eyes. He is a rock climber and a yachtsman – not a dabbling dilettante but a serious sailor and climber. He has practised trauma medicine in many of the world's hot spots. He is a stubborn, independent man. But he has a heart of gold and is also sentimental. One of the very best. We arrived as self-contained as could be: rucksacks, sleeping bags, some tinned food and some high-protein biscuits. Whereas Sarajevo had nothing, Kiseljak had a small duty-free shop, so Simon bought ten bars of chocolate and gave me five.

On a nearby football field there were two helicopters. The General; his Military Assistant, the polyglot British Major Pyers Tucker; Mihailov, the General's bodyguard; Victor Andreev, the Russian-born Head of Civil Affairs; Simon and myself all climbed in and travelled the 150 miles to Tuzla. There we were met by Major Alan Abraham who commanded the resident squadron of the 9th/12th Royal Lancers. He was to take us to Zvornik. After ten miles we reached the first Serb check-point at Kalesija and crossed quite quickly. This could be a good sign. At Zvornik, however, we waited for hours. We sat in a conference room and were politely hosted. We were joined by Laurence Jolles, my UNHCR colleague from Belgrade. He is a bright lawyer, an outstanding linguist and an excellent companion in a difficult spot. We were all given coffee and slivovic to drink and fed on crumbs of information at infrequent intervals.

'We are waiting for a Serb escort.'

'The road is mined.'

'There is fighting on the road.'

General Morillon kept the pressure on. They could tell that he was not going to go away. Eventually we were told, 'You will be escorted to the village of Drinjaca, the Serb front-line village. From there on we give you no guarantees. We know that the Muslims have mined the road. We expect you to be back tonight.'

The first part of the journey was along a reasonable road, then we turned off on to a narrow road which stays in the valley and runs alongside the Drinjaca river. This I knew only from the map. There were five of us stuck in the back of the armoured vehicle, the usual crew and us passengers. We took turns to sit near the rear door from where we could at least see where we had been.

The road was bordered by the sides of steep, snow-covered mountains. It was rarely used and was thickly carpeted with snow, ideal ambush territory. I hoped that the Bosnians knew we were coming. I would have felt a lot happier without the Serb escort.

At Drinjaca we stopped at a Y junction just before the bridge leading to Konjevici. We all got out to stretch our legs. The Serbs moved freely and confidently. There were two routes into Cerska: one via Kamenica, which I knew from my recent long stay at Zvornik was now in Serb hands, and the second via Konjevici Polje. From Drinjaca we were to enter via Konjevici, which was only a couple of kilometres ahead of us but was shielded by a high col. Cerska lies about three kilometres to the west of Konjevici.

The Serbs did a quick head count in each vehicle, then the commander said, 'Good luck. We will meet you here at 2000 hours.' He then departed, not the way we had come but by the road to the left.

Major Abraham placed one armoured car to the front, followed by his own with the General, then ours, then an escort and finally an armoured recovery vehicle. It was a slow move forward. In my opinion, when travelling over thick snow in a possible minefield, luck plays a bigger part than skill. I particularly hate being on a dangerous road, in the back of a vehicle I cannot see out of, accompanied by people I do not know. If it is your own team you keep each other's spirits up. With a strange team there is more silence, more time to think, more time to worry, more time to pass on or receive fear. Also I hate not being in charge. My fate here was in the hands of Major Abraham. I trusted Alan implicitly but I just wished that I had been travelling with him, then at least I could have had an input. We stopped regularly, on each occasion opening the rear door, but we did not get out. It was tempting but would have been unprofessional. The valley was very quiet and still. The snow hung heavily on the branches of the trees.

After a couple of hours we reached the beginning of the Bosnian barriers. The road was blocked by felled trees. By now it was dusk. While we were working out how to tackle the problem, the Bosnians arrived. Unlike in other situations, these boys were not overjoyed to see us. They were not impressed that we wanted to tear away their barriers on the very road the Serbs could race along following our tracks. They were tired, tetchy and nervous. 'You cannot do anything until we have spoken to the commander,' they said. This made sense. Their commander is Naser Oric, a tough leader who rules with a rod of iron. General Morillon was impatient. 'Take me to see Commander Oric,' he demanded. They told him that he and we were going nowhere and doing nothing until they had their instructions.

The leader of the group was a tall, thin, mean, lean man. 'Why are you here?' he asked. 'Have you brought a convoy?'

'No,' we replied. 'We want to go and assess the situation in Cerska.'

'Cerska has fallen,' he said curtly.

'When?'

'Late yesterday.'

Mladic had played with us. He had delayed us in Zvornik while his troops were cleaning up Cerska. He had sent us via Konjevici when he could have sent us via Kamenica. He had made us take this route in order to clear the way for him. His troops would have observed our progress, they would now know there were no mines. We would have the barrier removed. These weary soldiers would never have the energy to replace it as it was. No wonder the Bosnians were not overjoyed to see us. I had sat and listened to the death of Kamenica. I was now a guest at the wake of Cerska.

Naser Oric sent a vehicle to pick up the General. The rest of us struggled for hours, forcing a gap wide enough to let our vehicles pass. It was a bitterly cold night. The Brits worked like Trojans pulling and pushing on the huge logs which were intertwined. They were designed to delay visitors. They were successful. I felt particularly sorry for Victor Andreev. He thought we were on a one-day visit. He had no kit with him and being a good United Nations senior official he was wearing a suit and shoes. He was very cold and very damp. Simon, good soul that he is, dug out of his bergen some spare socks and a Gore Tex sleeping bag outer cover.

It was late when we entered Konjevici. None of us gave a thought to the Serb deadline of 2000 hours. The General was in the municipal building with Oric and the local authorities. Major

Alan Abraham, Simon, the ICRC man, Laurence and myself joined him.

'You have heard about Cerska. The wounded from there are here. I have agreed with the commander and the authorities that we will try to evacuate those with the greatest injuries. We will stay the night. Tomorrow, Larry, will you organise an assessment of the situation here and the needs?'

'No problem, General. Simon can do the medical assessment.'

The conversation then moved to medical matters. They discussed the situation in Konjevici and the terrible plight of Srebrenica. Simon then said, 'I would really like to get to Srebrenica.' This was no surprise statement; we all wanted to go to Srebrenica. Konjevici was a half-way house. But the Bosnians said, 'We can take you tonight.' I saw Simon's dark eyes light up.

'No,' I said. 'It is important that he assesses here first.'

'No, Larry, no. It is good if he goes to Srebrenica,' said the General.

'No, General, he has not got the equipment and the initial requirement is here.' Simon by this time had got his bergen on his back and was standing near the door. There was no doubt about his feelings.

'I think he should go. He is fit, he has the boots and he has some medicine. No?'

'Yes,' said Simon. True, he had his doctor's bag with him which was packed with emergency medicine including a lot of ketamine. Also, Simon, excellent mountaineer and yachtsman, would have no fitness problems. Besides, by now he was out of the door with his guide. But I did not agree.

We were taken to a house. It was occupied by ladies. Three twenty-somethings and a couple of forty-somethings. We all threw in some food and a meal was prepared. It was then time for bed. The ladies all disappeared. It was a sharp, freezing cold night. Somewhere close to us were the refugees and the wounded from Cerska. Somewhere out there Simon was trekking through snowdrifts. Victor was in Gore Tex, suit and socks. I thanked God again for my sub-zero sleeping bag and was soon sound asleep.

I was up at dawn. I wanted to see Konjevici Polje. It was a bright, crisp, dry morning. The house we were in was at the end of a track on the top of a small hill. We were actually in the self-contained top half of the house. The ladies, whom I could now hear, were in the bottom half. From the doorway I could see the whole of Konjevici. It seemed to be just one long street with two or three rows of houses on either side of it. Everyone was up and about. I was soon joined by the ICRC man, Andreas Schiess, another old friend from my days with Somali refugees. We were to do a tour of the town, see all the wounded and identify those who needed urgent evacuation. I hated doing this. I am a complete charlatan. At least Andreas was Swiss and wearing a Red Cross badge. It mattered little that I knew that he was a lawyer. The sick would look imploringly at us. I did not know what I was looking at and if it was too gruesome I would end up looking greyer and sicker than any of them.

We were joined by a medic from the Brits, and two locals: Huso Unvalic, a medical technician, and Almira Mombera, a nurse who had three children with her in Konjevici. In the absence of qualified people these two had performed some major surgery. I had great confidence that they would guide us through the day. The first task was to find someone who spoke English. I was told that there was a young girl in one of the houses. I was taken towards the house by a young man. When we got near to it I saw a large group of fifteen- to twenty-year-olds. They were playing on a slide they had made on the slippy slope to the house. Such simple fun, such happy laughter. The girl was delighted to work with me. She was tall and pretty, which made up for her limited vocabulary.

There were two main locations of the sick and a number of houses where one or two were billeted. Naser Oric had told the General that there were seven hundred who needed evacuating. We did not see many more than a couple of hundred in total. Maths was not Oric's strong point. We reckoned that seventy needed urgent treatment. Some of these might not even survive being carried to the vehicle. I was particularly worried about a little boy with tubes and drains who had been hit by mortar shrapnel.

While we were doing this job, General Morillon had left us and gone back to Zvornik. He had been told by Naser Oric that the conquering Serbs had committed a massacre in Cerska and that many homes had been burnt. The Serbs were initially angry with him because we stayed overnight in Konjevici. The General, however, went on the attack and challenged them to disprove the stories about the massacre by letting him see for himself. They agreed and took him to Cerska where he saw a few burnt houses, one wounded Muslim, one pregnant woman and no evidence of a massacre. He arranged for the two Cerskans to go to Zvornik hospital, where he later visited them. On his return to Zvornik he was told that we should have left the previous night and must leave now. For diplomatic reasons he agreed and the message was passed by radio to Major Abraham that we were all to leave. We were to be at the bridge by two.

This message was passed to us by Brit soldiers. I was confused and went to the vehicle of Major Abraham. 'What about Simon?'

'I know,' he said. 'I think the General may have forgotten about Simon or it is part of a bigger plot. I will try to talk to him.'

We both agreed that any such conversation would have to be guarded. We did not wish the Serbs to know that Simon had gone into Srebrenica.

Soon we had an answer from the General. We were all to be out by two. He would meet us by the bridge. Major Abraham had already warned the local authorities that we had to leave. They were displeased but understood that we would go out and then return with a convoy to collect the wounded. I went to see their leader. 'Look, I need to speak urgently to Simon. How can I do it?'

He arranged for Laurence and myself to go to the amateur radio station which was in a small house on the top of a hill. The living-room was comfortably furnished. Along one wall was a desk and on the desk was the 'ham' radio where a young man in uniform sat.

'I want to speak to Simon in Srebrenica. Is he there yet?'

'Oh yes, he got there early this morning. He is in the hospital now.'

'Can you get him for me?'

'I will try. But do not forget the Serbs can listen in.'

After a lot of tweaking and crackling we got through to Srebrenica and a message was left for 'the visitor' to come to the radio.

Within a few minutes I was told that the visitor was there. I passed a short and simple message: 'We are off. Will be back. Get back here when we tell you.'

I felt very bad about this. Abandoning one of your team is not in the handbook. I was pretty certain that Simon would feel low.

We went down the hill and found a Brit armoured vehicle waiting to collect us. 'The convoy is ready to go. The locals are upset. The General wants us out.'

My kit was in the house where we had slept, so we had to go back for it. I was still troubled about leaving Simon. He was alone. The place had no food and was regularly shelled. 'Ask Morillon if I can stay,' I said to Major Abraham.

'I have already asked and he said no.'

We left. We waited at the barrier while the logs were pulled back into position. We arrived at the bridge late. The General was not there. There was a small group of Serb military policemen. I was quite worried. If they counted us they would find one missing. They asked for the vehicle door to be opened.

'Are you the last out?' they asked.

'Yes,' I replied truthfully but not accurately.

'Is Father Christmas there?' shouted one Serb.

'Yes,' his colleague replied.

'Then let them move.'

Back in Zvornik, we discovered that the General had returned to Sarajevo. We also heard that he had given his famous press conference.

'General, was there a massacre in Cerska?'

'*Non.*'

'How do you know?'

'*Je n'ai pas senti l'odeur de la mort.*' Which my O-level French tells me is, 'I did not sniff the smell of death.' The journalists were not impressed. The mainly Muslim authorities in Tuzla were decidedly unimpressed. They declared him *persona non grata*.

We all agreed to keep quiet about Simon being in Srebrenica. We would get back into Konjevici as quickly as possible and pull him out. Not having a vehicle, I went to Loznica in Serbia with Laurence.

We booked into a hotel. I lay on my bed and switched on my radio to hear the World Service news. 'Simon Mardell, a British doctor, has walked into Srebrenica' was the first item. The manure had hit the fan. I took off my jacket and discovered in the pockets five bars of chocolate. I knew someone who was going to need these more than me.

The next few days were dominated by the Simon saga.

SIMON SAYS . . .

Simon had left us in the municipal building. He was given an escort of three soldiers, who shared the task of carrying his rucksack, leaving Simon to carry his literally vital airline-pilot-type doctor's bag. The night was cold and dark, the track narrow; there were Serb patrols to be avoided, huge snow-drifts to be negotiated; there was indiscriminate unaimed fire and there was shelling. It took them six and a half hours to reach Srebrenica.

He was taken straight to the hospital and introduced to the army captain, Dr Nedret Mujkanovic, who had been sent into Srebrenica by the Bosnian government. Nedret spoke English but was tired and weary. His first words to Simon were, 'I am so glad you have come. There have been so many patients. I could not do any more than I have done.' An explanation to a fellow professional, an apology to his patients, living and dead, from a trained paediatrician who had carried out more than a thousand general operations without equipment, without drugs, without lighting, while being shelled. Nedret gave Simon a quick tour of the hospital and confirmed Simon's worst fears. There was no food, no medicine and twenty deaths a day.

Simon was given a bed in the hospital and started work immediately. He shared his ketamine, an anaesthetic administered by needle, with the doctors. Besides Nedret, there were five others. They were all trained with gas anaesthetics, none had used ketamine. Trauma surgeon Simon trained them as quickly as he could. Some were quicker than others. After working in the wards he returned to the operating theatre. A mortar victim was being operated on.

'Did you use ketamine?' asked Simon.

'Yes,' said the doctor with pride.

'Is the patient unconscious,' asked Simon.

'Not yet,' answered the patient.

As Simon discovered, when you have had no drugs for so long and then you receive some, the temptation is to use them sparingly. To make them last.

Simon rapidly realised that a priority was a translator. Srebrenica is not a university town. There was only one English speaker and he was there by accident.

Almir Ramic had left the suburb of Dobrinja in Sarajevo with his mother to attend the funeral of a relative in Visograd. It was to be a one-day round trip by bus. Whilst in Visograd the Bosnian war erupted. The Bosnian Serbs drove the Bosnian non-Serbs out of Visograd. Buses were burnt or stolen. The exodus headed towards Srebrenica. Sarajevo was cut off. Almir and his mother had less to carry than most of the other refugees. They had just the clothes they stood in. Almir was too young for university, was not a language student at school but had been an avid TV fan, especially watching English and American films. He became the resident translator and Simon's shadow.

I was right to think that when Simon received my call telling him we were off he was not happy. He had come on an assessment mission. After a few hours he had learned what he had come to find out. Srebrenica needed all the aid it could get. It needed a medical evacuation programme. It did not need an international doctor with no medicine and no food. He knew that his place was out of Srebrenica shouting for them, not inside screaming with them.

The question was how to get him out. General Morillon was racing around trying to get approval to go to Srebrenica. He had the support of his senior, General Wahlgren. He was also trying to arrange an evacuation of the wounded from Konjevici.

I went to see Pandorovic. 'I would like to go into Konjevici to bring out Simon Mardell.'

'He is not in Konjevici.'

'I know. He is in Srebrenica. You know he is in Srebrenica. It has been on CNN, Sky and Serb tele.'

'No. If I believe you, he is not in Konjevici, nor is he in Srebrenica. You told my police that you had all left. If you had all left then Mardell cannot be in Konjevici or Srebrenica.'

'If you had not insisted on us all being out by 1400 hours, he would have come out with us.'

'But you only had approval to stay until 2000 hours. You stayed overnight. You had no approval to send anyone to Srebrenica.'

I was on a loser here. 'OK. Can I collect him when he returns to Konjevici?'

'Ask me when he is in Konjevici.'

I left, furious. We were obviously expected to eat a large humble pie.

Getting Simon back to Konjevici was the first task. Michelle O'Kelly became a key link in this. She could talk to Zivinice, they could arrange for a message to be passed to Simon. But there was a snag. The authorities, the doctors and the patients in Srebrenica, did not want him to go. They did not know about the alphabet of letters after his name, but they did know that he was a switched-on, hands-on saver of lives. They also knew that he was fresh, enthusiastic and an international.

We asked for him to return to Konjevici by 1400 hours the following day. Simon got the message. He asked his translator to accompany him.

'How much time will you need to get ready?'

'I'm ready.'

'But you will need to pack.'

'I have nothing to pack. I have nothing.'

He asked Oric to provide an escort.

Simon and Almir were ready to leave at seven the following morning as instructed by Oric. No escort turned up. Over the next four days, Simon was ready to go on six occasions. Each time the trip was delayed and an excuse produced.

'There is no escort available to take you to the front line.'

'There is heavy Serb patrolling.'

'The front line has moved.'

'There is increased shelling in Konjevici.'

Michelle regularly confirmed to us that Simon was not in Konjevici. The Mardell story was now a big media event. Back in the UK his parents and his fiancée were reluctantly in the spotlight. I myself was also getting a fair bit of attention.

'Why did you permit him to go to Srebrenica when he was on an assessment to Cerska?' asked my own masters.

I received a wonderfully polite letter from Sir Donald Acheson, the head of the World Health Organisation in former Yugoslavia, a man whom I admire and like enormously. The gist of the letter was: 'You got him in. You get him out. And quick.'

From somewhere came a plan: when Simon reached Konjevici he was to be escorted by the Bosnian troops to their front line, then he was to walk along the no man's land valley road towards the Serb front line carrying a white flag. I did not like it.

Then there was a Plan Mark Two: when Simon left the Bosnian front line carrying a white flag, L. Hollingworth Esquire was to leave the Serb front line carrying a white flag. We were to meet in the middle. I liked this plan even less.

Meanwhile, back in Srebrenica Simon was worried. Almir had overheard conversations. 'Simon, they are not going to let you go. They need you as a doctor and as a focal point, a hostage.'

We were blissfully unaware of this. Via the amateur radio we informed him that he must, must, must be at Konjevici at 1400 hours the following day. 'Last bite at the cherry,' he was told.

Simon was determined that this was going to be his last day in Srebrenica. He had already studied the map. He had learned all the village names and had worked out all the routes. He had decided that the following day, with or without an escort, he would leave. To be at Konjevici by 1400 hours, he had to leave Srebrenica by 0800 hours. He worked hard for the remainder of that day, seeing as many patients as he could. He then packed and went to bed early, not difficult in Srebrenica without light and with a temperature nearing minus twenty.

He was up early. By eight there was no escort but he did have with him his faithful Almir. True to his plan, he set off without them. He headed north, the road was wide and good. He passed many refugees. He passed the football stadium, then the factory housing more refugees. After walking at a cracking pace for more than a mile, his progress was suddenly halted by shelling; direct hits on the road immediately ahead of him. He and Almir took cover in a building and waited for it to stop. While they were waiting the escort turned up and strangely the shelling stopped.

They set off together, still travelling north but looking for the track to the west which leaves the road close by the hill of Caus which was in Serb hands. It was a clear winter's day. The Serbs could see the birds in the trees. Spotting Simon, his translator and escort was too easy. They sent down a hail of machine-gun bullets which zinged about their ears. Once again it was stop, take cover, wait, then move. Each delay was placing extra pressure and strain on Simon. His deadline was 1400 hours. They waited a few minutes, then moved quickly to the turning off to the left. Here they were a little safer. The escort began to saunter, they had no convoy to meet. Almir was cold, hungry, tired and inadequately dressed. Simon decided to step out at his own pace. He gave his rucksack to Almir and strode off. He knew he was on the right track when he hit a wall of refugees, fleeing Konjevici. They helped his map reading but hindered his pace. He forced his way through family group after family group, all struggling in the deep snow carrying babies, holding on to toddlers, dragging bundles.

Simon eventually reached the outskirts of Konjevici. He had fifteen minutes left. On foot he was not going to make it. He saw a refugee with his possessions draped over the crossbar of an old bicycle. 'How much?' he asked.

'*Molim*, please,' said the Bosnian uncomprehendingly.

Simon took a fifty-dollar note from his pocket. 'Me the bike, you the dollars. OK?'

The refugee could not believe his luck. His possessions plus bike would not fetch ten dollars. Fifty might find his family accommodation in overcrowded Srebrenica.

Simon mounted the bike and pedalled with fury, forcing the ancient buckled wheels through the deep snow. And so passed into the brief remaining folklore of Srebrenica the story of the sight of an international doctor, pedalling an old, expensive bike, clutching, with one hand, a heavy bag against his chest and steering with the other, against the flow of traffic and *towards* a town being shelled.

Near the centre of Konjevici he almost collided with Naser Oric. 'Have you seen UNPROFOR?' he asked him.

Oric knew everything that went on, but he pretended not to understand. 'UNPROFOR?'

'Yes, have they left?'

'They left the day after you arrived.' Simon did not have time to waste amusing Oric. He pedalled on to the municipal buildings. It was after two. There was no UNPROFOR. He asked around. There had been no UNPROFOR. Simon sat at the side of the road exhausted, bitterly disappointed. He felt desperately thirsty. He had been running or pedalling for more than six hours. He asked for water and a lady brought him a litre jug. Simon put it to his lips and drained it, then a second and a third.

He left the bike and walked back two kilometres and up the hill to the amateur radio station. He asked for Tuzla and for Michelle.

While he waited, Almir arrived with the rucksack.

When Michelle came on the radio he did not want to hear the news she gave him. 'Simon, can you go back to Srebrenica. General Morillon and Larry with a small convoy are on their way there now. They will stay the night, pick you up and bring you out tomorrow.'

'No,' said physically and mentally exhausted Simon. 'I'm staying here in Konjevici.' Almir and Simon wearily made their way to the Medical Centre. With Almira and Unvalic, he did a ward round. He stitched and patched and cut and sewed.

He found the young boy whom I had marked on my list. He drained his chest. While working he considered his options: go back to Srebrenica; stay; walk out of Konjevici Polje the way he had come in through Serb lines. He decided that for today he would take the middle route. He stayed a further few days in Konjevici Polje, living through Serb shelling and doing all he could to help the wounded and the sick. He was finally evacuated by Major Abraham only minutes before the town fell to the Serbs.

10

Srebrenica

We left for Srebrenica on 11 March, by which time General Morillon had the full support of General Wahlgren and the agreement of Milosevic and Karadzic.

We were a small convoy. General Morillon with his British aide, Major Pyers Tucker, and his Macedonian bodyguard, Adjutant Chief Vangel Mihailov, a Legionnaire; a Canadian tracked vehicle and crew; a team of UNMOs; a duet of American military communicators; a trio from Medecins sans Frontières, Eric, Muriel and Branko; a jeep and two trucks from the Belgian transport company, under the command of my old friend Dirk, who had spent so much time with me trying to get into Kamenica; and finally the UNHCR vehicle, with myself and Laurence Jolles. We had started out with a much larger convoy but approval for the rest was not granted and it was parked at the side of the road on the Serb side of Zvornik.

We crossed the green River Drina at the Bratunac bridge and were waved straight through to the centre of the town, where we met a covey of dignitaries including the local military commander who told us, surprise, surprise, that the direct route to Srebrenica was not possible as the 'Muslims' had destroyed the bridge during the night. Why they should choose the day of the arrival of a desperately needed life-saving convoy to destroy the route confused me. Why the commander should think for one moment that we believed him I also do not know.

We were, therefore, to take the convoy through woods which had not been used for months, along a narrow mountain route, thick with virgin snow, which might be mined. In addition, thanks to the delays, we had about an hour of light left.

We moved on to the track with caution. We agreed that the Canadian armoured vehicle should lead the way. Tracked armoured vehicles have an excellent weight distribution and can often go where heavy trucks cannot. The UNMOs followed the tracked vehicle, MSF next, then me and finally the two Belgian trucks. The going was tough. Beneath metre-deep snow there was ice. The road twisted and climbed. It was picturesque, bordered by high, steep hills from which tall, snow-laden pine trees reached for the sky.

The General decided that our progress was too slow. He therefore zoomed ahead in the tracked vehicle. The MSF vehicle failed to negotiate a bend. The convoy was stopped and all the experts had a go at trying to extricate it. They succeeded in digging it in, up to its door sills, in thick snow. The wheels spun as if they were sitting in butter. We decided to abandon it. MSF joined the UNHCR vehicle. We set off again.

Suddenly there was an almighty detonation. The valley reverberated. I leapt out of our vehicle. The Belgian truck behind had hit a mine. The cab was shattered, the front wheels blown away, the snow stained black. A grey cloud was rising. There was a strong firework smell. My first thought was for the drivers. I yelled for Eric, the MSF doctor, and we raced towards the truck. I fully expected to find the bodies of the drivers. I did. But they were picking themselves up out of the deep snow. The vehicle was the only one in the whole convoy which had a Kevlar mine-proof lining inside the cab. The Belgian government had the foresight, the generosity and the concern, to ensure the safety of the drivers. As the cab disintegrated, the Kevlar cocoon protected the crew from the initial and deadly effects of the mine. They were thrown out into the white cushion of snow. Their ears were ringing, they had the odd bruise, but they were alive. The Kevlar had absorbed the impact, the blast and the slivers of metal. The truck was dead. It was a write-off. The cargo in the back seemed to be all right. It contained sugar and medicines. The sugar protected the medicines.

The doc examined the drivers; they were suffering from shock but were otherwise fine. The damaged truck was blocking the road. The one behind it would have to go back. The two crew from the destroyed vehicle wanted to travel on, but they had had enough excitement for today. As I walked past the damaged truck I saw the tyre track of the left-hand wheels of my own vehicle. They had passed over the mine. My vehicle was not heavy enough to set it off. Just as well, as it had never heard of Kevlar.

All this activity took time. I expected any second to see the tracked vehicle with the General return to see if we were all right. It did not happen.

Abandoning the remains of the truck and its precious cargo, we proceeded and eventually caught up with our gallant leader. He had made contact with the front line of the Srebrenica troops.

'General, we have lost a truck.'

'Is everybody OK?'

'Yes, General.'

'*Bon.*'

'Not bloody *bon*, General. You didn't come back for us.'

'Larry, I was negotiating here. It is their mine! They planted it! They never expected us to come this way. The Serbs lie. There is nothing wrong with the bridge. Let us go. We will soon be in Srebrenica.'

I remembered that 'Maintenance of the aim' is a principle of war.

We were still a long way out from the centre of Srebrenica. It was now very dark. The Bosnians put a guide in the armoured vehicle and away we went. The track is downhill and the incline is one in eight. We moved dangerously fast, but for all of us there was the exhilaration of being almost there. At the foot of the descent we were stopped at a check-point. A voice challenged us. I heard the reply which ended with 'Morillon'. I could feel the excitement of the soldiers as they repeated 'Morillon'. I could imagine how pleased the General was feeling. At the check-point we turned right and moved along a fairly wide dirt road. It was very dark, if there was a town ahead of us there was no indication of it. I could see no lights and hear no noise. The road narrowed. Suddenly I saw the dark silhouette of a building on the left, then I could see shapes moving in the street. One, two, then many;

huddles of people, bundles of people, little children. It was late, but visitors were rare; mobile visitors rarer.

My heart rate had increased. I was huddled against the window, squinting and peering. This was Srebrenica. The name was known in Washington, in New York, in London. Known because no one could get in. We were in! WE WERE IN SREBRENICA! My eyes were sparkling brighter than any star in the sky.

The armoured vehicle was stopped, we bunched behind it. On the left was a double-storey building; on our right another, but smaller. From the building on the right a group of men appeared. Our guide leaped from the armoured vehicle. Again I heard the word 'Morillon'. It was uttered as if it were a greeting. Then it became a mantra as it was repeated and passed on. I could see the man himself. He was out of the vehicle and shaking hands. He was wearing a parka with the hood down. He was half turned towards me. I could see his big smile, the smile of success. He had made it. He was in Srebrenica. On the faces of the reception committee I could see awe. They too could hardly believe that they had in their midst in Srebrenica the Commander of UNPROFOR. Morillon.

We joined the boss in the doorway of the building where it was dark and cold and smelled of damp. We went through the open double door. If it is midwinter and a building has had no heating, there is nothing to gain by keeping the door closed. Our guide knew the way and moved quickly, we stumbled and bumped into each other. We laughed, we were euphoric, but we tried to show each other that we weren't. There was a small landing, then another flight of stairs. At the top we turned left and were taken to the end room on the left. The door was opened and a warm, thick fug wafted towards us. There was a small stove in the left-hand corner of the room. It had the most wonderful red glow. The blanket of warmth enveloped us. Each of us was drawn to it. I can understand why fire is an earth sign, so primitive and important.

Our guide, a small, very friendly man, was in uniform and was introduced as the military commander of the town. That he may have been, but we knew that the real defender of the region was Naser Oric whom we had met in Konjevici. We were then introduced to the mayor of Srebrenica and other dignitaries. They looked very tired and thin. Their clothes were dirty and inadequate for the cold. Each and every one had deep, dark rims under his eyes. Their faces were grey and drawn. They were all overwhelmed by the presence of General Morillon who introduced us, his team, to them. Mihailov, his bodyguard, did the translating. We sat down at a long, narrow table. The room was tiny, long and thin. The table took up most of it. The chairs were basic and sitting down behind the table was a tight squeeze. I scrambled round to sit on the far side. I noticed that in front of me were windows. I looked out, but Srebrenica was a wall of darkness.

The talk was short. General Morillon told them that we had come to look: UNHCR to see the refugee situation, MSF the hospital, the Americans the air-drop sites and the UNMOs the security situation. They welcomed us and told us in brief outline the terrible plight of the town. It was agreed that we would meet early in the morning and have detailed discussions.

The MSF team left for the hospital, which was the dark building on the opposite side of the road. Laurence and I decided on a walk-about. We left the building, checked that the vehicle was still there and was still locked, then turned left, away from the hospital. The street was pock-marked, whether by shelling or disrepair I could not tell. Huddled on both sides of it were family groups. Some sat around the dying embers of smoky fires, others just snuggled together for warmth. The temperature was minus twenty-two. These pavement plots were home to these, the latest refugee arrivals. Those who had arrived earlier in the day were in the better positions in the doorways of buildings. We asked many groups, 'When did you arrive? Where are you from?' The majority had arrived in the past twenty-four hours from Konjevici. Some recognised us from our visit there. They told us stories of heavy shelling, many deaths and a mass exodus. We asked about Simon. Those who knew of him were full of praise. They told us that he had now left.

The pattern of conversation in each group was similar. All would answer our greeting. A man would be their spokesman for the initial questions, then the women would begin to answer, then they would cry, always drying their tears on scarves which they all wore around their necks. Few of the refugees wore coats. One or two had no footwear. The tiny children were bundled in the middle of the circle in whatever blankets, rags, newspapers were available. The elder children, those over seven or eight, were treated like adults; they took their place in the outer circle. We saw none with food. They were cold, hungry, tired, bewildered. Some were originally from Zvornik, the unluckiest had been cleansed from Zvornik to Kamenica, from Kamenica to Cerska, from Cerska to Konjevici and finally from Konjevici here. No wonder they had no winter clothes. Their misery had begun in April one year ago.

We walked back in silence. We had a little food we could give away, but to whom? To the largest group? To the one with the most children? To the one with the oldest couple? How could we give to one group without being mobbed by others? How could we favour one and ignore another? We returned to the building. The Canadians and the UNMOs with the General and his team were preparing for bed. They were all in one large room on the top floor of the building. I suggested to Laurence that we would be much warmer and more comfortable in the vehicle. We went to the car, opened it and decided that we would give a bar of chocolate to the nearest group. This we did clumsily and guiltily.

I got back into the vehicle and into my sleeping bag, removing only my boots and jacket. We were in Srebrenica. I was metres away from families like my own in size, maybe also in background. I wondered how I would cope, snuggling my children to me, attempting to ward off the bitter cold. I know that I would have felt humiliated, impotent, so I came to the conclusion that I would have stayed and fought. I then realised that these people had been driven out not by an advancing army – that was not the Mladic way – but by shellfire. You cannot stay and fight shells. They land and kill and maim indiscriminately. You can run like a headless chicken, you can stay in the cellar like a mouse or you can quietly and resignedly join the throng and leave. Perhaps that is what I would have done. I felt close to the refugees but not close enough really to understand. Even if I had sat on the pavement with them it could not be the same. I could escape, they could not. For me here was now, but for them here was now, tomorrow and maybe for ever. Sleep came.

Dawn broke, revealing ice inside the windows of the vehicle. Unzipped sleeping bag, put on boots. Opened door and out on to the snow. We had an audience already. I looked down at the huddles. They were all awake. Too cold to sleep, they had started patrolling the streets. First task was to clean my teeth. Used saliva and spat into the snow. I had a bottle of water but it would be so cold it would crack my teeth. Brushed my hair, brushed my beard. Always brings a laugh. But what else do people expect me to do with it?

The Canadians were in good humour, but the big attraction was the American Sergeant Chappel, he had a circle of admirers around him. He is big, black and has a great sense of humour.

Laurence and I entered the building and went up the stairs. In the big room everyone was up, some were shaving. The General had found a small annexe to the main room. He was there with his team. Laurence and I went to the room we were in last night. The fire was out and it was freezing. Damn. Next to the stove on the window-sill were bits of radios. Someone was trying to make one out of many. MSF arrived. They had spent the night in the hospital.

'How is it?'

'Unbelievable. Not possible to describe,' said Eric the doctor. Soon we would see it for ourselves.

A man from Srebrenica arrived with a burning piece of wood. It was to get the stove going. The General and the Srebrenica authorities arrived. With them were two journalists: Tony Birtley, the Englishman with ABC, and Philip von Recklinghausen, a German photographer. Tony had been there a short while with an Hi-8 video camera and had taken, and was to take, some fantastic exclusive film. He had arrived in Srebrenica on a Bosnian government resupply helicopter which flew in at hedge-hopping height straight across Serb lines. The pilots were mad but had no option, the wounded they took out had no option, Tony felt he had no option. He is a dedicated journalist. He was to leave Srebrenica with no option, as a casualty in a helicopter. Philip was a strange loner. He had been in Srebrenica for a long time, longer than many of the refugees. He had walked in. By now he had few rolls of film left but had captured on still film the history of the siege. He was as lean, as dirty and as hungry as any Srebrenican. Not a man to stand too close to, he was wounded three times while I was in Srebrenica.

The Director of the town, the senior administrator, appointed by Sarajevo, Hajrudin Ardic, began the briefing. He was about forty, had once been stocky, had a greying beard. He had carried the responsibility of the problems of the town on his shoulders throughout the siege. He probably never had been a talkative man, now he spoke wearily and almost without interest. 'The town had a population of six thousand five hundred. It was an undeveloped rural spa, famous for its water and its rehabilitation centre. The population was seventy-four per cent Muslim and twenty-four per cent Serb. In the whole region we had thirty-seven thousand. Now we have twenty thousand people in the town and eighty thousand in the region. All property is damaged. In the town eighty houses have been burnt, more than one hundred destroyed by shelling. The hospital has one hundred beds. It has one hundred and sixty patients. Twenty die every day. In the town we have one thousand children under one year old; two thousand under seven and four thousand five hundred under fourteen. The birth rate is up. We have had three hundred children born in the hospital; many more in the flats and houses and God knows how many in the streets. Four thousand people are living on the streets. They have had no food for five days. We have an emergency stock of tinned food of about seven tonnes. That is it,' he ended abruptly.

General Morillon thanked him, then divided our tasks. UNMOs to check out if the bridge was down. UNHCR and MSF to assess the hospital, the school and the refugee centres. We would be back by twelve and leave at one.

We went straight to the hospital. It is directly over the street but the entrance is at the back. We walked up the slight hill, which was icy. On the right is what used to be the clinic and lab building. Standing outside the main entrance to the hospital was a large crowd, out-patients and visitors waiting to be allowed in. A group of soldiers were controlling who entered and who didn't. Opposite the entrance was a long, dismal building with an incongruously blue door. It was unmistakably the morgue. We entered the hospital, turned left and climbed the stairs. At the top of the first flight there were patients on beds in the corridor and on the landing. We were met by the surgeon, Dr Nedret Mujkanovic, who was a captain in the army. He is a tall, heavy man in his late twenties, with limited surgery training. He had done some pathology and some paediatrics. By this time he was an experienced war surgeon, but a troubled man with deep, dark rings around his eyes. A man who moved in wild, jerky bursts. He spoke with great warmth and admiration about Simon Mardell, concluding with ' . . . I have his patient assessment list here.

'There are one hundred and thirty-one patients who need urgent evacuation. Ninety-six are men of military age. The staff know who they are. There are a further three hundred and five elderly who should be taken out. There are more than two thousand in the town, including many amputees, who have infected wounds. The hospital is overworked, overstretched and underequipped.' Nedret continued: 'Ninety-nine per cent of our patients are war casualties. Most wounded are from shelling, then gunfire, then mines. Since 12 July, nine months ago, there have been more than fifteen hundred patients in the hospital.'

In and out of the wards, packed with beds on which lay the wounded, we went. There were bandaged heads, bandaged legs, bandaged arms; blood, pus and the sickly, clawing smell. The bandages were a mouldy green. I later learned it was a wound infection bacteria called pseudomonas. We walked amongst a blur of bandages and smell, but each bandage wrapped a person: a soldier, a child, a woman, each reacting to our presence. Some smiled, some implored our help, some cried; some were bewildered, some dying. I tried to smile, to touch, to reassure. I tried not to swallow the smell. I wanted to spit it out.

Nedret took us to the operating theatre. It was a war invention; there had been no operating theatre before the war. Ragged and stained bandages were drying around a stove. A pan of water, in which lay the surgical instruments, was bubbling away attempting to sterilise the overused and blunt surgical implements. The operating lights stood by the operating table, two lamps lashed to a frame which stood on wheels, connected by a thin cable to a car battery.

'I need blankets, mattresses, bandages, plastic sheeting,' Nedret was firing away. 'We have no food for the patients, no milk for the babies.'

This desperate litany had been bottled up inside poor Nedret's head. It was unleashed with passion and desperation. 'Yesterday we lost five children, four women and eleven men. All casualties of the war.'

Mercifully we were now back out of the hospital. I took in a deep, deep gulp of ice-cold air. 'Thank you, Nedret.'

He held me to him. 'Please, Mr Larry, come back soon.'

We walked to the school. I needed the wind and the snow to blow away the clinging film of death and disease. The school is a short walk down the main street. There are small grey terraced houses on each side of the road. If I had been a tourist they might have been picturesque. They were now cold, overpopulated sanctuaries. The houses on my left backed on to the river. They were stained with damp.

The road was full of people, some perambulating up and down with purpose, passing the time. Others had a spring in their step and madness in their eyes. They were not able to understand what had happened to them and to their world. Yet others, the new arrivals, distinguished by the bundles they carried or pushed or pulled on wheelbarrows or sledges, were looking for somewhere to stop and park and live. We passed the empty tail section of a huge aircraft bomb, evidence that the town was bombed from the air.

The school is on the left side, the entrance set back from the road. The school playground is a large concrete square surrounded by a high wire-mesh fencing. It has stands with basketball nets. Football goalposts are painted on the wall. The school is large but bitterly cold and dark and damp – these words are becoming the motto of Srebrenica. The classrooms were full of refugees, there were huge dormitories, mattresses everywhere, pots and pans, blankets, old couples, young children; noise and clatter, but no laughter. The younger children were silent and soulful, the bright innocence of early childhood dimmed by the shadows of war and upheaval. The early teenagers were running about, pushing and barging, more able to cope. The middle teens stood in groups. They were all males. All war-wise, far more malevolent than street-wise contemporaries living in peaceful locations. The girls were somewhere with their mothers. No one was cooking anything. They all asked for food. Women appeared with babies, tightly wrapped like dolls; they had heard that there was a doctor 'from outside'. They wanted to show their babies to him, to discuss some problem, some illness. We patiently explained that our doc had the knowledge but not the equipment. A mother explained to me by gestures of the hand that her breasts had no milk. She wanted milk for the baby she thrust before me. The mother was younger than my daughter. 'We will be back soon with doctors, medicine, food and milk,' I promised her. Once again we were dispensing hope. In the school playground some of the children were kicking around a ball made from a bundle of rags.

Time was running out. We wanted to visit a small annexe to the hospital where the recent amputees recovered. It was near the municipal building: a couple of houses with the rooms converted to wards. We stayed only a few minutes. There were many young men who had lost legs, some above the knee, some below, some only the foot. One man had lost his right leg and his right arm. He was lying on his bed. I wondered how he would be able to walk. He had a crutch, so presumably he could. Their crutches were home-made. The men all asked only one question: 'When can we leave Srebrenica?' They wanted rehabilitation, they wanted artificial limbs. They had heard that the earlier they are fitted, the better, the easier, the more comfortable. They all seemed psychologically well adjusted to their loss. Presumably this was because there were so many of them.

It was time to return.

Murat Efendic was the mayor of Srebrenica before he moved to Sarajevo to represent the town's interests in the capital. He had asked me to visit his sister and his brother-in-law and to have a peep at his house to see how it was. His brother-in-law had come to the PTT building the night before and left his address, asking me to visit them. The house was close by, so we decided to call upon them to see if they had any message for Murat. A neighbour in the street pointed out the building. It was a small old block of grey-stoned flats. On the ground floor was a shop which belonged to the brother-in-law. It had been destroyed by shelling. The neighbour shouted out the man's name. A lady appeared at a window on the second floor. She was the image of Murat. There was no doubt she was his sister. She was thrilled to see us and called us up the stairs to her flat. It was immaculate, with lace tablecloths and heavy furniture. She wanted to offer us coffee. Here I could help as I had brought a small jar as a gift. Mainly by smiles and sign language we arranged that she would quickly write a letter for Murat and get it to the PTT before we left. We returned to our vehicle, restowed our kit, contacted Jeff in Kiseljak and told him we would soon be on our way.

The General wanted a 'wash-up' conference before we left. We assembled in the same small room. The stove was lit. The atmosphere was light and happy. General Morillon asked us all to give an outline of what we had done and what we intended to do. He promised we would all soon return; there would be land corridors for the convoys and air corridors for the evacuation of the sick. He told them that he was leaving with them the team of UNMOs and he promised them two more teams. They told us that they had recovered the load from the vehicle destroyed by the mine, which was great news. They wished us a safe journey and a speedy return. We all hugged, shook hands and joined our vehicles, which were surrounded by a huge crowd of people. Amongst them were Tony Birtley, camera whirring, and Philip von Recklinghausen, camera clicking. Murat's sister was there, she cuddled me and handed me a letter and began to cry. The UNMO vehicle was in the lead, the Canadian armoured vehicle next with the General waving enthusiastically to the crowd. My vehicle was at the rear. I waved to Dr Nedret and he gave me a great warm smile. The Canadian started the huge diesel engine. It belched out a black cloud of smoke, the tracks engaged and the great metal beast inched forward.

'Careful,' said the General to the women in the crowd who were dangerously close to the tracks.

I shouted, 'Make sure no one touches the exhaust pipe or they will burn their hands.'

It may have taken only seconds before we realised that the crowd were not waving us off. They were preventing us from going. They were blocking the path. The women were shouting to Morillon, '*Zasto bi ti isao kad mi ne mozemo?*' ('Why should you leave when we cannot?')

Our polite hosts, seconds ago so diligently waving us away, were nowhere to be seen.

Mihailov was next to the General, translating his words: 'It is vital that I go. I have to arrange the convoy and the air evacuation.'

The women did not move. Hajrudin was sent for; he joined the General on the armoured vehicle. He talked to the crowd but to no avail. The women were joined by others with children. They formed a human barrier across the road. Some even lay in the snow. 'You are our only guarantee,' they told General Morillon. 'Only you can break the siege.' The words were flattering and final. We were going nowhere.

I motored back far enough for the armoured vehicle to return to its place outside the building. I parked in my usual spot. The crowd remained in the snow. We returned upstairs to the small heated room. The attitude of our hosts had changed. The General appealed for them to intervene; they refused, saying that they had no power.

We were then told that we were not to wander around. We were to stay in the building. They knew that I had slept in my vehicle and also that our radio link was there, so I was permitted to go to it but not to leave the car-park. Pyers came with me. We briefed our respective headquarters.

Jeff in Kiseljak was calm and very professional. 'I will keep this channel clear and manned twenty-four hours a day. OK?'

'Thanks, Jeff.'

BH command were also calm, in the circumstances. 'Are you saying that you are prisoners? Are you telling us that the General is a hostage?'

Pyers reassured them that he was not. 'No, no, no. The road is blocked by women. We are just not allowed to leave.' Semantics! A rope barrier was now across the car-park, keeping the crowd at a distance, and preventing us from talking to them to find out the real depth of feeling.

I had often been warned by the Serbs that I would be taken as a hostage. It made sense. I think that if I had run Gorazde or Zepa I certainly would have considered it. I had thought about it and realised that it did not bother me. I lived in a city, Sarajevo, which was surrounded and shelled, so what difference did it make? Not a lot. For the General, it was another matter entirely.

We returned upstairs. By now the others had been told that we were all to stay in the one large room. We had lost our liberty. I looked at the General. He was outwardly cool and calm, but I knew his mind must be in a turmoil. There were many who had opposed his 'mission' to Srebrenica, who had said that he was abandoning his whole command for a small corner of his patch. There were many detractors who, when they heard that he was a hostage, would say with perverse pleasure, 'I told you so.' The Serb and the Bosnian Serb leadership would be saying not only 'I told you so' but 'We told you not to trust the Muslims'. To my mind, the worst event that could happen would be for him to become both a central bargaining chip and an impotent onlooker. Various scenarios flashed across my mind: between the Bosnian government and the UN: 'Lift arms embargo. We release General'; between the Bosnian Serbs and the United Nations: 'You obtain release of all our prisoners or we shell Srebrenica with your General inside.' Or between the Bosnian government and the Bosnian Serbs, with the UN in the middle: 'You allow convoys in and our sick and wounded military out and we release Morillon.' For a brief moment he looked troubled and vulnerable, but only for a moment. He was soon fast asleep, stretched between two uncomfortable chairs. Pyers and I had our evening schedule. Our masters were not impressed with our predicament. Pressure was being applied at all levels from New York to Sarajevo.

But the old dog had a few tricks up his sleeve. Unbeknown to most of us, he asked his team to wake him at 0200 hours. The man of action had a plan. At two, he quietly left the building wearing his parka jacket with the hood pulled over his face. He walked along the street to the far end of the town, where he waited for Tucker and Mihailov to join him. They were to take one of the jeeps, to convince the women that they had to make an urgent radio schedule and that they needed to move the vehicle in order to get good reception. The General hoped that without him in the jeep, the ladies would agree. They did not. The vehicle did not move and the General waited in the dark, freezing cold until 0400 hours, when he returned. This was not the end of his plotting. When he got back he placed his bed on the floor in a small room annexed to the large room where everyone was still sleeping. No one had seen him go. No one had seen him return. Perhaps if they did not see him they would think that he had gone. He kept the initiative.

For most of the next morning we stayed in the room. The authorities of Srebrenica visited more frequently as the morning progressed. They were looking for a glimpse of the General. They were obviously worried when they could not see him. He sat in his annexe with dignity. Maintaining his aura of absolute leadership, he sat and thought. Then he emerged. 'Larry, do you have a flag?'

'Yes, General.'

'A UN flag?'

'Yes, General.'

'Do you have a megaphone, a tannoy?'

'No, but I am sure we can find one.'

He sent for the Director of the town. 'I want to speak to the people. Get them outside the window. Also I want to use your amateur radio to send a message to the Serbs and to the Sarajevo government.' Hajrudin, relieved to see that he was still with us, agreed to arrange all this.

The General then explained his plot to me. 'I am going to tell the Serbs that they must allow corridors for the wounded and for aid. It is a matter of honour for them to open them. I am going to speak to the people of Srebrenica. I need a translator and a tannoy and I want you to have the flag ready on a pole.'

Hajrudin produced a large crowd outside the building. The General stood in the room on the top floor overlooking the entrance. He opened the window. The crowd fell silent.

'I came here voluntarily to be with you. I have decided to stay. I am placing you under the protection of the United Nations.'

This was my cue. I pushed the pole with the United Nations flag attached to it out of the window. The words matched the flag. The crowd clapped and cheered. The General beamed. At the beginning of the speech he was a hostage, at the end a hero, all because he had decided to stay! We were now free. 'Bang goes my Terry Waite book,' I said to myself. We followed him down the stairs and out into the crowd.

An astonished, incredulous and very astute Tony Birtley, who had a world exclusive in his camera, asked him, 'General, you have placed Srebrenica under the protection of the United Nations. What happens if it does not work?'

'Of course it will work,' he replied. The General went off on walk-about.

One of the young Canadians asked me, 'Larry, does that mean we are free to walk around among them?'

'No, my friend. It means that you are free to run around and protect them.'

Our next schedule with Kiseljak was interesting. The General sat in the vehicle himself. He spoke to a French colonel. I could hear the intake of breath as the colonel realised the implications.

By mid-morning New York time, the Security Council in New York knew all about their new UN Protectorate and had sat and discussed the policy of safe havens *vis-à-vis* safe areas. Meanwhile, mid-evening in Srebrenica, the General was mapping out his plans and had asked his deputy commander, the brilliant, irascible British Brigadier Roddy Cordy Simpson, to be at the other end of the radio at the next schedule.

The General sat in the vehicle in the seat behind me. I contacted Jeff, who handed over to the Brigadier. General Morillon began, 'Roddy, tomorrow I want helicopter flights into Srebrenica to evacuate the wounded.' There was a pause.

'That is not considered to be a good idea, sir.'

'By whom, Roddy?'

The Brigadier thought quickly. 'BH command, sir.'

'Roddy . . . I *am* BH command.' General Morillon had been able to leave Kiseljak to go to Konjevici and to Srebrenica only because he knew that in his absence his command was in the very safe hands of this British brigadier whose competence was respected by all sides and whose temper was feared by everyone.

I could hear the gentle, aristocratic intake of breath. The count to ten, then, 'Of course you are, sir.'

There were no helicopters the next day.

The General spent his time building up the confidence of the people. The town's authorities moved him out of the big room and gave him the two balcony rooms, one as his bedroom and the other as an office for Tucker and Mihailov. Furthermore, they installed a wood-burning stove. One of the women who had led the blockade was given the task of looking after him. She in turn employed two young girls who kept his suite neat and tidy. The ultimate accolade was the production of some fresh milk for his coffee. Not wishing to state the obvious, this did indicate that there was at least one cow hidden somewhere in the town.

Now that we had freedom of movement and were popular we could start doing our jobs. I had no aid to distribute but I met up with those responsible for the feeding of the town. I saw the empty warehouses, we discussed the distribution system. Everyone we met was courteous and kind. They had had no 'outside' conversations. They wanted to catch up on months of gossip. We were not much use on football or basketball, the two real religions of former Yugoslavia, but we were able to tell them about the world in general.

In the company of the two Americans, Major Rex Dudley and Sergeant Chappel, we met the military authorities to discuss the air drops which were the lifeline of the region. The problem was the collection. The town authorities wished to collect the aid so that they could distribute it equably. But in a town of tens of thousands of starving people, local initiative, survival, greed and other motives overtook common welfare. The air drops were carefully rationed. Srebrenica was the priority but if it got an air drop three times a week it was lucky. When the planes were heard in the sky, the streets filled with people rushing to the few likely dropping zones. We were told it was a free-for-all. That night we decided to see for ourselves.

It was much worse than we anticipated. We knew from our radio source, Michelle O'Kelly, where the air drop would be. We travelled in my vehicle without lights so as not to give the location away. We were on the outskirts of the town in a wooded area near to a clearing. We heard the drone of the aircraft coming closer. We also heard the sound of voices and the breaking of twigs and branches. Out of the dark we saw hundreds of people rushing towards the woods, men, women and older children. The aircraft passed overhead; all eyes looked skyward. As my eyes scanned the darkness I began to see the pallets of aid slowly and hauntingly swinging under their umbrellas of silk. I was not ready for what happened next. As the chutes approached the earth there was a whooshing noise, like a train going through a tunnel, the chutes collapsed and the one-tonne pallets slammed through the trees cracking off branches and landing with a shudder. There is no way you can avoid a pallet if you are standing in its path. They can demolish houses and squash people. As your eye is on one, another, unseen, is swinging menacingly towards you. There were shouts of warning, screams of pain, whoops of joy as individuals and groups seized, dodged, pursued these cubes of life-saving aid. Treat people like animals and they will act like animals. The strongest grabbed the biggest. Some hunted in packs, some as individuals. They growled, they barked, they fought. The cartons were ripped and torn, pulled and pushed. The innards spilled over the snow-covered, cold earth. Unlike the beasts of the jungle, these were the starving in Srebrenica. Within minutes all trace of the quarry was gone: the aid to be eaten, the boxes to be burnt, the parachutes to be made into clothes. There was nothing for the local authorities to collect. The fit and the brave had the aid. The weak and the vulnerable had nothing.

The following day we learned that during the air drop four people had been killed, three struck by pallets and one stabbed in a fight over the contents of a pallet. The UNMOs and the Americans recced the area and studied the maps. They came up with more isolated and more distant sites. This would assist collection. The Americans used their swish radio pack to inform their masters of the new locations and timings.

More people streamed into the town throughout the day, both from the west and from the south. Some came to Srebrenica because they had heard that the UN was in town, others because General Morillon was there. All had been forced from their homes. Some refugees had discovered a warehouse with a huge store of plastic crates, probably designed to hold one-litre soft-drink bottles; they were bright red. My first thoughts were that they were to be used as seats. But as night fell I saw that they were multi-purpose. Men and women were indeed sitting on them but as the temperature dropped their occupants rose and set fire to the crates. They burnt brightly and fiercely with an orange flame. They melted and dripped, heat and light. They quickly burnt to nothing. Leaving a black stain on the floor, a temporary warmth to the body, a dazzle to the eyes, then a return to the cold and the dark. It reminded me of bonfire night. Children roamed and ran from burning crate to burning crate. Each group had its moment of glory as its crate burned. The cautious waited until the night got colder and darker. Up and down the street the burning crates illuminated the family groups, like Indians on a reservation, like refugees from a previous war. The flames revealed the drawn, gaunt faces accentuated by flickering shadows. They revealed mouths smiling during a brief moment of relief, mouths displaying broken teeth, black stumps or dark gaps.

We wandered from group to group, ourselves drawn like moths to the flames. Every group we talked to had someone who cried, usually an older woman. Often the younger teenage children smiled when the elders cried, perhaps out of embarrassment, perhaps as their bewildered reaction to seeing a respected elder display an emotion usually reserved for themselves. Younger children clung tightly to the legs of parents or to their arms. Only when asleep did they relax and shudder. Some groups had food to eat and were warming it over a burning crate. Towards the end of the town was a group of the most recent arrivals. They were on the right-hand side of the road. There were seven of them, three generations. They had no crate. The men were sitting on the icy floor, the women on the small bundles containing all they possessed. The children were on the knees of the two men, father and grandfather, eating and passing something between them. They were picking at it, sucking on it, probing it; in the dark I could not see what it was. I moved in and greeted them, then I saw what the children were sharing. It was a horse's hoof. It was cold and uncooked. The men explained. They had arrived without food, someone had given it to them. There would not be enough for the adults. I wanted to be sick. I wanted to cry. But I was so stunned I did neither. I know that people do eat pigs' trotters and frogs' legs. Maybe cold horse's hoof is a Balkan delicacy. I doubt it. All these thoughts flashed across my mind. I really wanted to scream. I wanted to drag the people who were responsible for this from their offices, from their trenches, to stand and share this scene with me. I could not stay any longer with this family. I moved on.

As I walked back I tried to identify where I fitted in. We shared some of this hardship. We were cold. Our building was cold. In truth, I was hungry. But we were not them. We had good clothing, good boots. We had muscle, fat and vitamins, hope . . . and a ticket home. This was how and why we coped. We were tourists in their hell.

Back in the PTT building we huddled in our own groups and discussed what we had seen. In the vehicle we got into our sleeping bags and pulled the material as close to us as we could, leaving no channel through which the night chill could blow. Sleep came slowly, enveloping the images, blurring the scenes, dulling the sadness and calming the anger. But the mind had been scarred.

While we slept New York was awake. And in a flurry. The actions, the words and the decisions of *mon General* had slung the cat into the birdcage. The feathers of Boutros Boutros Ghali were ruffled with a wire brush. Shashi Tharoor was throatily singing his mellifluous, honey-coated words, ambassadors were explaining to their countries the nuances of what they had signed up to do; the UNPROFOR General in Sarajevo was defining to the press the connotations of 'safe' as in 'havens' or 'areas'.

Roddy Cordy Simpson was arranging helicopters for 'BH Command' *in absentia*.

The girls tiptoed in, lit the stove and General Morillon breakfasted on milk. Oblivious, maybe; impervious, certainly, to the new direction in which he had sent the United Nations. We woke and washed the sleep from our eyes. There was to be another air drop that evening. We had asked for one pallet for ourselves. We were running out of food and our Canadian warrant officer had decided to ration us to eating one meal every other day. Of equal importance, our glorious leader was out of Davidoff cigars. In our pallet there would be a carton of cigars for him and a bottle of brandy. The remainder of the pallet would contain medicine for the hospital. The UNMOs had recced a dropping zone on the hill at the back of the building where we were living. The aircraft would drop the aid for Srebrenica on the first pass, then turn and drop ours. Rex and Sergeant Chappel travelled out to the high ground to pass the co-ordinates to America on the singing, swinging, dancing phone.

During the day the UNMOs visited the southerly outer extremities of our newly designated 'safe area' and received a reminder of the presence of the Serbs. They were fired upon. I visited the hospital and the refugee centres. Laurence and I drew up a plan for the warehousing and the issue of food when convoys recommenced.

That day, lunch for us was very special. Murat's sister and brother-in-law had invited us to their home. We felt very guilty and had got together, as a contribution, the few remaining goodies that we had left. They embarrassed us with their hospitality. The table was set with the best china, the best glasses. There was soup and slivovic and she had cooked a pie. God knows what effort she must have gone to finding the ingredients. It was delicious. They wanted us to have seconds. But they did not eat with us. We guessed that they would have what we left. We declined seconds, but she insisted on wrapping the remainder of the pie for our colleagues.

If 'our' pallet arrived, we knew where some of our share must go.

Night fell. We were all excited. The military were in charge of the recovery of our pallet. We heard the drone of the aircraft. They were on time. We could see the Srebrenicans moving off to where they believed the pallets would land. We had a little chuckle. We heard the aircraft on its return approach. The military were off. Forty minutes later they were back with all that they have retrieved: a few strips of cardboard. The pallet was a few hundred metres off course. They were beaten to it. Somewhere in this starving city, somewhere very close to us, someone had his feet up with a glass of brandy in one hand and a Davidoff cigar in the other. Whoever you are, cheers! The following day the medicine arrived anonymously at the hospital. We offered a reward for the recovery of our goodies but what use is money when there are no shops?

So far, I had been sleeping on the floor in one of the rooms on the ground floor of the PTT with the soldiers. It is in the area of the post office where the counter service used to be. We used the counter as the distribution point for our food. We had only Meals Ready to Eat, plastic packets containing a mess or pottage of some flavour or other. Some menus were more popular than others, so in order to be fair, the good warrant officer devised a system whereby the packets were laid out on the counter face down so that you could not read the menu. We each chose one, picked it up, he noted who got what and threw the packet into the pan of boiling water. It was the individual's task to fish out his own packet, which at least warmed up the fingers. This ceremony took place at about seven every other evening.

Four rooms had been taken over as sleeping areas. There was a wash-basin and a toilet in one room with, of course, no water. Another, which was the manager's office, had a stove in it. This had become our main meeting room. We did not have enough wood to keep the fire going all the time but when it was lit there was a pan of water bubbling away. The Meals Ready to Eat packets contained sachets of coffee and I had tea bags. The soldiers collected water and wood from the nearby spa.

I found a small room at the side of the building which I appropriated in the name of UNHCR. It was three metres by two metres and contained what I believed was the automatic telephone exchange. I had also found four chairs. Standing them side by side, I now had a bed. True, they were not all the same height but at least I was off the floor. The room had one window which was shuttered. I therefore had no light but it was wind- and weather-proof. The exchange machinery was in the centre of the room and extended from ceiling to floor. I placed the chairs between the machinery and the inner wall to give me maximum protection in case of shelling. I did this without thinking. Later, I wondered to myself if I would always go through life applying war instincts and rules. The room was dirty and musty, but it was private. It became my own little safe haven. Over the next few days I learnt again that I did not need much to keep me happy. My torch was important but not absolutely necessary. I ate only with a spoon, but it was important that it was one that I brought with me. My little penknife kept my nails clean and my pencil sharpened. My sleeping bag was vital. I love my *New York Times* mug given to me by my daughter. I am fastidious about where my possessions are, each has its own place. I can find them in a hurry or in the dark.

The General had by this stage built up such confidence in the population that he could go anywhere. He was not happy with the tardy response to his requests for helicopters, so he decided to leave Srebrenica to pass through the Serb lines and to go back to Kiseljak. The Srebrenica authorities were happy with this, as long as the rest of us stayed.

He is definitely a charismatic leader. When he left we all felt vulnerable. To add to our vulnerability, the moment he was in their territory the Serbs shelled the city for the first time since we had been in it. They used multi-barrel rockets and killed one child and wounded a few others. My first experience of rockets was on the airport at Sarajevo. They are a frightening weapon. Six or twelve rockets are fired in rapid succession from the same launcher. They explode in the air with a puff of grey smoke, then throw out splinters of metal. The first burst takes you by surprise, the others follow so rapidly that you have no time to run or hide. If you are within its range you've had it. Just in case this shelling was a prelude to the Serbs taking the city, we had a meeting, a military 'orders' group and quietly we decided on a plan. We would abandon our kit and take to the hills. This was not Rorke's Drift and we were not the South Wales Borderers. As the oldest, the unfittest, a civilian and having had a look at the terrain around us, I decided privately on a little plan of my own: to shave off my beard and to take my chance mingling among the locals.

Every day I passed the school playground and watched the children playing football. The rag ball was getting smaller, so I contacted Michelle by radio. 'Larry here. On the next air drop can you include some footballs?'

'Some what?'

'Some footballs.'

'Sorry, Larry, reception is bad. It sounds as if you are asking for footballs [here I heard her laugh]. Can you spell what it is you want air dropping?'

I spell 'foxtrot oscar oscar tango brava alpha lima lima sierra'.

'Footballs. You want footballs?'

'For the children to play with.'

Michelle had fun with this one. Dietitians were agonising over the nutritional content of the food to be dropped. Doctors were debating the priority of medicines to be sent. Every milligram of air-drop space was argued over and prioritised. And the man on the ground wants footballs. She won. The next drop included a couple.

General Morillon was not having the success he wanted in arranging a helicopter evacuation. The Serbs were not happy. They suspected that 'war criminals' would be included in the evacuation. Their definition of 'war criminal' seemed to be any male between the age of sixteen and sixty. So parallel to his air evacuation negotiations, the General was pushing with UNHCR for the entry of an aid convoy.

Peter Kessler was in Sarajevo as the UNHCR spokesman. He is a little ferret. He gleans UNHCR news, then bites journalists until they have presented it around the world. We were now in contact every evening. He gave me the great news: 'Tomorrow you will receive a convoy.'

I then got a call from Karen in Zagreb. 'The convoy that comes in tomorrow will have Louis Gentile from UNHCR Belgrade with it. The trucks will off-load, then leave with the worst of the casualties. They must be women or children or men over sixty. Either you or Louis are to take the trucks with the casualties to Tuzla.'

I organised a meeting with the authorities and with Nedret from the hospital. Based on Simon Mardell's list, he chose ninety-seven patients. If we received ten trucks, that would be roughly ten patients per truck. The journey from Srebrenica to Tuzla would take up to eight hours. It would be a bumpy, miserable ride but ten to a truck would give them room to breathe.

I got on the radio. 'We need with the convoy at least one hundred mattresses and two hundred blankets.' Belgrade was quicker than I was. Each truck would have a co-driver with some medical training. They had blankets, mattresses, first-aid kits, water bottles all organised.

I went around the hospital with Nedret and saw the patients he had approved. I made two or three substitutions. 'Nedret, I do not want people who are going to die on the journey. Putting it bluntly, that will be bad publicity for the evacuation. Both the media and the Serbs would be delighted with such a story.' With some reservations, he agreed and so some of the weakest and most urgent were earmarked to die in Srebrenica. I passed on to the General that we would evacuate ninety-seven. This number formed the basis of his negotiations with the Serbs.

The atmosphere in the town was electric. I was starkly aware of the fact that we were to bring in at most one hundred tonnes of aid, sufficient to keep the town going for a few days. But the new spirit in the town had nothing to do with food. It was the fact that the outside world was coming into Srebrenica. That they were not abandoned or forgotten.

If the convoy came as planned, and if Louis stayed, this would be my last night in Srebrenica. So I was determined that I would make the most of it. After my meal I walked around the town. You could touch the excitement. Many approached me to confirm the news of tomorrow's convoy. They held my hand as they talked to me. They hugged me when I left them. I then went across to the hospital. 'Where is Nedret?'

'In the operating theatre.' I walked along the corridor expecting to find him carrying out some chore in preparation for tomorrow. I found him operating on a patient.

'Larry. Good. Please, have you a torch? Can you shine it in here?' he asked, pointing to the open stomach of the patient. He was assisted by another doctor. He had rigged up the operating light to the car battery but it was weak. Fortunately the operation was almost over. I spent the next half-hour with my eyes mainly closed. The patient was to have been one of our evacuees but complications had set in.

I returned to the PTT. The boys were chatting around the stove. Pat Hoorebecke, the Belgian UNMO, was, as ever, keeping morale high. He was an excellent officer. I realised that he had been a quiet but very positive influence here. I felt I knew him well. I knew about his wife and his dog. They were both very fond of England. I knew quite a bit about the personal lives of the whole team. We had all become very close. I wondered how much they knew about me. I made some tea and took it to my room. This might be my last night in here. It had only been home for a very short time but I was quite attached to it.

I awoke early and got up right away. Tonight I might be in Tuzla. In that case I could get a bath. So I decided not to wash, just to clean my teeth. I got on the radio. 'Peter, what news?'

'The convoy is at the other side of the bridge near Zvornik. It is all ready to go but we are awaiting approval.'

I spent almost a week at Zvornik trying to get in here but there was a big difference this time. New York was now aware of Srebrenica thanks to the action of *le General* and the man himself had gone out to meet the convoy to bring it in. Dirk, who spent so much time at Zvornik with me, had gone with him.

Throughout the day I kept in touch with Kiseljak and Sarajevo. The convoy moved very slowly. By late afternoon I made the decision that if it arrived it would stay overnight and we would carry out the medevac tomorrow at dawn. There was great disappointment among the patients but relief among the hospital staff that we were not attempting to out-load in the dark and the biting cold.

Darkness fell. The UNMOs told me that the convoy had passed the Serb lines. The tension and the emotion was overpowering. The majority of the population were out on the streets, waiting. The Srebrenica authorities were trying to keep the road clear. There were huge crowds outside the PTT building. I was first aware of the noise from the people as they heard the lead vehicles of the convoy. They were cheering and clapping. Then came the roar and the rumble of the lead APC. The chant of the crowd changed to 'Morillon, Morillon'. The APC trundled to a halt outside the PTT. In the cupola was the unmistakable figure of General Morillon. The crowd were wild with joy.

I was shouting into the radio for Peter Kessler and the world to hear, 'We have a convoy. We have a convoy.' I could feel the warmth of tears as they ran down my cheeks.

I left the vehicle to find Louis Gentile, the UNHCR man. He was a tough young Canadian diplomat on loan to UNHCR. I was thrilled to see him. Together we led the convoy down to the warehouse, where it was unloaded in the usual siege-town slow style. When the trucks were empty we took them back to outside the PTT. The drivers were given the big room on the second floor, where we began what Morillon called in his book '*la legende de Srebrenica*'. Louis and some more UNMOs had brought biscuits, sweets, fruit and booze. Someone had donated a bottle of wine. It was a strange feeling to share the 'stove room' with new people and with such food. Von Recklinghausen was like Ben Gunn. He had found some cheese.

I was up very early. I packed, said farewell to my little room and joined the drivers. It was still dark and the slope leading to the hospital was icy and treacherous. Removing stretcher-borne patients was not going to be easy. Inside the hospital, the staff had moved those who were to travel into the corridors. There was one big problem: a crowd of thousands outside the hospital. Whole families. Many with their possessions. I went to see the mayor and the military commander. He was saying farewell to General Morillon, who was leaving for the Serb front line to ensure that the convoy had no hassle there.

'Please move the crowd back. They are blocking the entrance to the hospital. It will be very difficult to load the sick on to the trucks.'

'We will try,' was the best answer I got.

We sent all the blankets into the hospital to wrap the patients. The drivers laid the mattresses on the floors of their vehicles. The co-drivers stood in the back to assist the loading. We reversed the first truck up the slope as close as possible to the hospital entrance. The first casualties were carried out and placed in the truck. Some were children. It had been agreed that wounded children would be accompanied by their mothers and that if there were other dependent children they would also travel with their mothers so that we could keep the families together. Whether it was the sight of fit women and children climbing on to the trucks or whether it was planned I do not know, but suddenly the crowd surged forward and within seconds the trucks were full of people; desper-

I adore this brilliant cartoon, drawn by an
eighteen-year-old working in the UNHCR office
in Zenica. His first published work! (*courtesy of Sinjin*)

A great moment – our first contact with Zepa. The Bear is on my left.
Pepe is on the left of the photograph (*courtesy of Risto Tervahauta*)

Risto is in the middle of the photograph with Benjamin, the mayor of Zepa
on his left. Then me, Pepe and Denisa, our translator. On the right of the picture
is Benjamin's father; to the left is his grandfather (*courtesy of Risto Tervahauta*)

This is the
'hospital' in Zepa
(*courtesy of
Risto Tervahauta*)

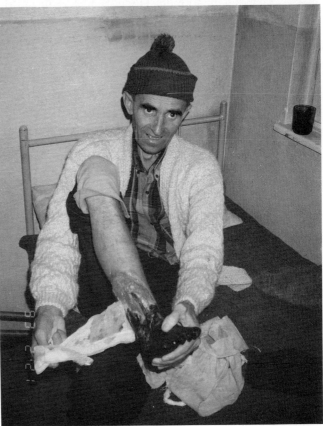

This man may
well smile. He will
be the first to have
his amputation
under anaesthesia
(*courtesy of
Risto Tervahauta*)

Pepe and me with the 'Hunter' and his wife in Pale

In Milenko's house in Zvornik. The boy is standing with his parents, grandparents and Risto. Jeremy Bowen is head of the table, with Pepe and the BBC camera crew (*courtesy of Risto Tervahauta*)

A funeral for a young boy in the icy overspill of Zvornik cemetery (*courtesy of Risto Tervahauta*)

Trying to keep warm in Zvornik around the dying embers of the French bonfire (*courtesy of Risto Tervahauta*)

An historic moment
– General Morillon
declaring Srebrenica
under the protection
of the United Nations
(*courtesy of Tony Birtley*)

Me with Dr Nedret
Mujkanovic, the
legendary surgeon
of Srebrenica,
after the war
in the safety of
Tuzla hospital

Me in my smoking jacket in Zepce, standing next to Harry Bucknall's driver Lieutenant Corporal Jock Davis, with Harry's father's Second World War 'Volcano' kettle (*courtesy of Harry Bucknall*)

(*above right*) Emilja and Kenan

With Emilja in the HVO office in Zepce trying to negotiate entry into Maglaj

Where there is a smile like this there must be hope

ate people, pushing, shoving, fighting, kicking, all of them deter-mined to escape from Srebrenica. Worse, the trucks were surrounded. We could not get the stretcher-borne patients any-where near them. They were shivering with cold. We sent them back into the hospital. I climbed on to the first vehicle and began to throw people off, physically. I was grabbing them by their limbs, their hair, and pushing them out. I was punched and kicked and bitten. As fast as I was throwing them, others were climbing up. Everything was out of control. There were thousands of people on the trucks. Women had thrown on babies and young children to give them the chance of escaping. The babies were howling, the young children were screaming, the women crying.

I jumped off. There was no one from authority in sight. I ran into the PTT and bounded up the stairs. The mayor was hiding in the room with the stove. I dragged him out and down the stairs. 'What the hell are you going to do about this?' I yelled. In his customary lethargic way he went back into the building and returned with a policeman who began firing into the air with a Kalashnikov automatic rifle. For maybe thirty seconds there was silence and peace. Then the mayhem broke out again as family fought family for a place on the trucks. The police tried another burst of fire. It was totally ignored.

I pleaded with the mayor to let us at least get the wounded on first, then we would fill up the vehicles. But it was a waste of time. He was powerless. We were all powerless. Mob rule had taken over. I stopped running around and told the drivers to move forward two hundred metres, to escape, at least, from the throng-ing crowd. This they did. The police tried to form a cordon behind the trucks but this was soon breached. I got on to the radio and talked to Kiseljak and Zagreb. 'Look, it is chaos here. I have hundreds on the trucks, maybe even a thousand. Few are the sick I intended evacuating. I can call off the whole evacuation and try again or go ahead with what I have.'

'You are on the spot. What do you think you should do?'

I had already worked this one out. If I called off the evacuation, eventually the people would leave the trucks. Would we then send the trucks out empty, after all the negotiations that had been conducted to get this far? If we emptied the trucks and waited, would the crowd go away? Highly unlikely. They had nothing else to do. Could the local authorities prevent the people from boarding the trucks? I felt that Naser Oric and his troops could, but that the rest could not. Would Oric? Why should he alienate his own people? A few less in the town would not detract from its defence. 'I think I should try to get as many sick on as is possible and then fill the trucks.'

'OK,' said my masters. 'But be careful we are not accused of cleansing the place.' I did not even deign to comment on this one.

I then spoke to General Morillon down at the Serb check-point. I explained what was happening: 'General, you have approval for ninety-seven. I can either cancel it or turn up with almost a thousand.'

'Larry, you come. We are waiting.'

'General, that does not answer the question.'

'Larry, you leave now.'

'OK, General. Leaving now.'

'Larry. No men under sixty, OK?'

So that was his answer. Get moving. Bring what you have. Make sure there are no men under sixty. I explained to Louis what I was about to do, shook him by the hand and wished him well.

I was just leaving the building when Tony Birtley approached me. 'Larry, will you do me a favour? Will you take my films out and give them to ABC in Tuzla?' I took them from him and stuffed them in my various pockets.

I climbed into the lead vehicle and left. In the rear mirror I could see women running alongside holding their children aloft and arms on the trucks pulling them aboard. I got the convoy moving at quite a speed because at every corner there were crowds waiting for the chance to go to Tuzla. We motored for about fifteen minutes. We were then out of the town, exposed to Serb fire but not to crazed crowds. I stopped the convoy and attempted to do a head count. I also made it clear that any males under sixty would be arrested by the Serbs at the check-point and that I would do nothing to help them. There were a couple on board.

'What can we do,' they asked.

'Get off and walk back,' was my reply. By now I hated Srebren-ica. I was extremely angry. These people had betrayed their own wounded. I reckoned that I had on board forty of the ninety-seven sick and about eight hundred sanctuary seekers. The sick were squashed and trampled under the fit. I tried to rearrange the trucks but this just caused more panic.

We stopped the convoy just before the Serb front line. I got out and walked forward and saw the General with Pyers. I explained what had happened. 'Will the extra numbers cause chaos here?'

'Larry, the Serbs would be happy if you brought everybody out.'

He was so right. I walked back to the convoy. There was a Serb officer standing by it. 'Mr Larry, I have some old people here from Bratunac. They are Muslims. Please take them to Tuzla.' I looked at them. They were old and bent and certainly more infirm than the majority of my convoy of so-called sick. 'Do you want to go to Tuzla?' I asked each of them.

'Yes,' they answered enthusiastically. I put them on board.

Despite the fact that we might have been doing the Serbs a favour, they took their time at each check-point. They counted and recounted and leered and threatened and provoked and humiliated my lot. It was early evening before I arrived with them at Tuzla. We were escorted by the police and a fleet of ambulances to the football stadium, which had been converted into a huge reception centre. There were hundreds of media people watching the convoy unloading its human cargo. As they were carried down and escorted up the steps to the line of doctors waiting to grade them, I realised that in truth they were all ill. The citizens of Tuzla had been affected by war but they were fit and healthy by comparison with those whom I had brought. 'My lot' were thin and emaciated; physically and mentally battle-scarred and weary. I felt better for this.

ABC news soon found me and took from me the Tony Birtley tapes – the first films out of Srebrenica. He was filming as the trucks were loaded. I hoped that there were not reels of me throwing people off them. I was taken to the main Tuzla hotel. I was desperate for a bath. There were no rooms. The place was full of journalists.

I was at my lowest ebb. And then I heard a voice I knew well.

'Larry, I have been looking everywhere for you.' It was Michelle. 'Did you get the footballs?' We both laughed. 'UNHCR has a party in its office. We are waiting for you.' At the party I met Rod Kay of UNHCR, a fellow Merseysider, who had a room in the hotel. He had twin beds and offered me one of them. The place was full of attractive women but Rod's was the only offer I received.

The following day the Serb radio vilified me for negotiating the removal of ninety-seven wounded and then evacuating 'almost a thousand'. They congratulated themselves on their compassion. The Bosnian government television vilified me for aiding and abetting the cleansing of Bosnians from Srebrenica. I could not believe it.

'Don't worry,' my friends told me. It is a game.

It wasn't to me. Ever.

I made my way back to Sarajevo and went straight to Simon's room to find out what had happened to him. He was back and safe. We swapped experiences over some rough red wine.

Deputy Prime Minister Zlatko Lagumdzija kindly hosted a dinner to welcome me back to Sarajevo. Murat Efendic, in the presence of several displaced Srebrenicans, presented me with a superb bronze picture and a thank-you letter from Srebrenica. I was very touched.

Later I learned that the order to detain us in Srebrenica had come from Murat Efendic. I bear him no ill will. In his shoes I would have done the same thing myself. Morillon's bold move to force Srebrenica on to the world scene needed an extra tweak. Murat provided it. His action kept the enclave alive for another two years, but sadly with disastrous results.

Only after I returned to Sarajevo did I begin to hear criticism of the actions of General Morillon. 'He abandoned his command.' 'He sought glory.' 'He had tunnel vision.' In my opinion he placed his head on the guillotine. He exposed his soul. He risked his reputation because he cared. By placing Srebrenica 'under the protection of the United Nations' he put the place on the map and forced New York to do something about it. What Morillon had asked for Srebrenica was a detachment of Canadians, an increase in the number of United Nations Military Observers and an air evacuation of the wounded. What he got was a cease-fire, the demilitarisation of Srebrenica, the entrance of the Canadians, an increase in the number of UNMOs and, amazingly, a UN Security Council Resolution declaring Srebrenica a 'safe area'. He also got an air evacuation, which included some of the victims of a vicious, barbaric, obscene shelling which took place on 12 April, in 'protected-area' Srebrenica and killed fifty-six including many children who were playing football in the school playground with the ball which had arrived by air drop.

Louis Gentile, brave, calm Louis, informed UNHCR that 'fourteen dead bodies were found in the school yard. Limbs and human flesh clung to the school-yard fence. The ground was soaked with blood. One child had been decapitated.' He concluded his gruesome, disturbing message: 'I will never be able to convey the sheer horror of the atrocity I witnessed. I do not look forward to closing my eyes at night for fear that I will relive the images of a nightmare that was not a dream.'

Simon Mardell and I attended the press conference in Sarajevo the following morning. I made the following statement. 'Simon and I wish to speak, as we have shared some of the anguish of the people of Srebrenica. When yesterday I heard the news about the shelling, my first thought was of the army commander who had ordered the shelling. I hope that he burns in the hottest part of hell.

'I then thought of the soldiers who had loaded the guns and fired them. I hope that they suffer from nightmares. I hope that their sleep is broken by the screams of the children and the cries of their mothers.

'I then thought about Doctor of Medicine Karadzic, Professor of Literature Koljevic, Biologist Mrs Plavsic, Geologist Dr Lukic and I wondered if today they will condemn this atrocity and punish the perpetrators or will they deny their education and condone it?

'I then thought about my Serb friends whom I have met on my travels. Do they wish to read in future history books that their army has chased innocent women and children from village to village, until finally they are cornered in Srebrenica, a place from which there is no escape, and where their fate is to be transported like cattle or slaughtered like lambs?'

The Srebrenica football pitch was designated as the landing zone. The first air evacuation of the wounded involved a very brave 'hot extraction'. The designated and agreed helicopter pad came under mortar fire and some of my Canadian friends were wounded.

I was supposed to travel in on that first helicopter but the Serbs were still smarting over my 'Hottest corner of hell' speech which had received a slice of media coverage. But in fairness to them, they let me travel on the first flight on the second day. We took in a 'Muslim' doctor from Tuzla and a Serb doctor from Zvornik. They were to examine the patients and to ensure that only seriously wounded would leave. The Serbs were still insisting that there would be 'no war criminals' among the wounded, which was supposed to eliminate all men between sixteen and sixty. Fortunately the Serb doctor whom we took in was kind, considerate and genuine. He was a doctor first and a Srpska Republika Serb second. He was also very kind to his 'Muslim' colleague. They were slightly wary of each other at first but soon swapped stories of colleagues and friends. The Serb gave some money to the 'Muslim' to give to a relative who was living in Tuzla. The 'Muslim' stood close to the Serb when the helicopter first landed in Srebrenica, when the Serb was at his most nervous and vulnerable.

It was strange to be back in Srebrenica. The UN crew seemed pleased to see me. Louis came to the landing site. He looked much older, the playground massacre had etched its mark on his young face. 'I have brought your vehicle for you,' he said, handing over the keys of my old companion. But going back is never the same. When you leave you cut the cord.

The negotiations with the Serbs had been for the evacuation of five hundred wounded. It was easy to categorise the first two hundred. They were stretcher-borne and painfully and visibly very sick. The remainder were a lottery. The amputees with suppurating stumps were an obvious category. Many had been identified by Simon Mardell, who was not allowed by WHO to go to Srebrenica for fear of reprisal for his previous behaviour.

He met the helicopters at Tuzla. He saw many of his patients from Konjevici Polje as well as from Srebrenica.

In Srebrenica, when the word got around that amputees were included in the evacuation, every amputee in the valley moved to the football stadium. They came on crutches, in wheelbarrows, in the arms or on the backs of friends. Some hopped, some ran, some shuffled. It was as if a Pied Piper had played a magic tune which attracted only limbless people. There were hundreds and hundreds of them; so many, that we had to modify our humanitarian action, by blocking off the road with barbed wire. Myself and a few soldiers were the keepers of the gate. For the first hour we were sympathetic as stump upon stump was unwrapped and raised for our inspection. But as we realised that we had few helicopters and jumbo-jet loads of applicants we became more ruthless. Fresh wounds, young children, women and Oscar-winning actors passed the first hurdle and were handed on to the doctors. There was good humour on both sides, so essential in so bizarre and tragic a setting. We knew that not only were we giving the chance of treatment but also the chance to escape from the risk of further shelling. We did not know then that many of those we left behind would lose their lives brutally two years later.

When Louis left Srebrenica he also brought out a convoy of wounded, more than I did. He had the same mad, chaotic scenes. So crowded were his trucks that some died for lack of oxygen as they fell to the floor of the trucks. He also had the one from which a little child fell. The picture of the child crying, as he watched his frantic mother waving as the truck she was on sped away, was in many newspapers. He was eventually reunited with his mother.

Back in Tuzla, this time I had a hotel room of my own. I found it very difficult to put the experience in context. It was as if I had been in a Fellini film or in a circus. My mind was full of images of bandages flying and crutches waving. I could not put a face to anyone, just a huge anonymous canvas of deformities. In and out weaved cameras and tripods and notebooks and questions; more compartments to close down.

I was glad to return to the measured insanity of Sarajevo. The city was abuzz with the news that the UN had granted 'safe area' status not only to Srebrenica but to Tuzla, Bihac, Zepa, Gorazde and Sarajevo itself. Apparently tens of thousands of troops would be requested for the task. We had had fun trying to get one hundred and fifty Canadians into Srebrenica!

My next aim was to get back into Zepa. I teamed up again with Simon Mardell. The rumour was that the Serbs had attacked the valley and the whole population had fled to the hills. We set off for Rogatica with a very hard Dutch colonel and a Norwegian UNMO. Our task was to get into Zepa and to ascertain the situation. We got a lot of hassle. The Serbs were very nervous and trigger-happy and singled out Zlatan, my driver, and the colonel's translator for their abuse. We therefore decided to send them back to Sarajevo under the protection of the Norwegian UNMO. It was not a good move. On the journey back the translator and Zlatan were arrested and the Norwegian forced to return to Sarajevo without them. The Dutch colonel was allowed to proceed to Zepa. Simon and I were delayed and then 'run out of town' by an arrogant young captain. At Lukavica, Brane stopped us and informed us that I had approval to try again, but Simon did not. Brane gave me a piece of paper stating that General Mladic approved my entry into Zepa. Foolishly I returned to Rogatica on my own. At the check-point I waved my paper and demanded to be allowed to motor on to Zepa. A soldier with a Kalashnikov was placed in front of my vehicle and I was told not to move.

The captain from yesterday then arrived. 'Why are you here?'

'I am going to Zepa.'

'I told you yesterday you are not going Zepa.'

'But,' I said, waving my piece of paper, 'I have the approval of General Mladic.'

'Let me see.'

Now the golden rule is never to let anyone take hold of your identity card, which is why we have them on a chain around our necks. And never to give anyone your approval to travel.

'Here it is,' I said, holding it up against the windscreen.

'Give me.'

'Terribly sorry, cannot do that.'

'Then sit,' said the captain. This was not in the rule book.

I started the engine and tried to move forward, but the Kalashnikov stood firm. 'I demand to see your commander,' I shouted. The soldiers laughed. The damn captain just drove away.

In the next hour Kalashnikov only moved once, to urinate on my front tyre. More menacingly, he was joined by a Serb soldier who was very much the worse for drink. He had a bottle with him which he shared with Kalashnikov. After a while I began to shout and wave my paper. They laughed. I was, in truth, worried. The longer I stayed at this check-point the later I would be leaving for Zepa, a long and lonely road, especially on your own. Also I did not fancy staying the night, on my own, at this check-point.

'Get me the captain immediately.' I waved my paper. 'Get me the major. Tell him that I have a piece of paper signed by General Mladic.' This time at least the soldier did something. He used a phone.

The captain returned. 'Give me paper from Mladic. I want to show it to major. If you do not, you stay there all night.'

Stupidly I gave him the paper. He grinned and the soldiers laughed.

He got back into his car and drove away. About an hour later he returned. 'Get out of the car,' he ordered, pulling open the door. Never leave the safety of a car – golden rule. But here I had no option; I was 'assisted' out of the car.

'I go to Zepa now,' I said, half as a statement, half as a question, with as much confidence as I could muster.

'Where?'

'Zepa.'

'Zepa. I told you yesterday you do not go.'

'But today I have approval from General Mladic.'

'Where?' He laughed. All the soldiers laughed.

'You took my paper from me.'

'No I didn't. What paper?' The soldiers were crowding around laughing, I could smell the alcohol fumes. They were enjoying this.

I could either be frightened or strong. 'Get out of my way. I am going to your headquarters to see the commander.'

I went to walk past him and to move towards my vehicle. The

captain drew his pistol from its holster. I looked at him. His face was white. His eyes were shining bright. He looked mad, nervous and very angry. The soldiers were suddenly silent, a very bad sign.

'I have approval from General Mladic. I have every right to go to Zepa.'

The captain aimed his pistol at my head. I stood still, very still.

'Sarajevo,' he said. 'Go.' He got hold of me by the shoulder and, still aiming the pistol at me, pushed me into the seat of the car. I remember that I needed to step back in order to get in but he was pushing me forward. I therefore struggled into the car. He slammed the door. I locked it. He still had his pistol in his hand. He pointed up the road with it. I turned the key, thank God the engine started. I knew that I must show no fear. This man was as hot as I was cold. He was dangerous. Slowly I moved forward. Kalashnikov moved out of the way. I turned slowly in order to make sure I could do the U-turn in one movement. I then moved away slowly, hoping that he would not fire. I was acutely aware that on my own I could easily disappear. I left and motored back in the dark to Pale. I was drained of energy and courage. I vowed never to travel on my own again.

Back in Sarajevo, I heard of the fate of Zlatan. I was furious. I promised myself never to let my staff out of my sight. Good old Tony got him out.

The Dutch colonel reached Zepa. There was no one there. He went into the hills. When the Bosnians saw that the UN was in the valley they began to return; first a trickle, then a flood. In heavy shelling in the city Zlatko Lagumdzija was injured. I went to see him. He was in an overcrowded ward. In Sarajevo, at war, the Deputy Prime Minister got the same service as everyone else. He was unconscious. His injuries were to his stomach. His bodyguard, blood-stained from the incident, was standing by his bed. I stayed a few minutes, gently touched Zlatko's hand and left.

PART TWO

II

To Banja Luka

I had a message from Zagreb. I was to fly there to see Neill
Wright. He was very professional. He took me to the bar in the
Intercontinental, bought me a glass of wine and suggested that as
I had been in Sarajevo for a year I should have a change. He
recommended the city of Banja Luka, the heart of Serb-held
territory, where we had no international staff member. It was a
critical spot. The minorities, the Croats and the Muslims, were
the most vulnerable groups in the whole of former Yugoslavia.
The UNHCR staff were constantly hassled by the authorities. We
did not have freedom of movement, no aid was moving into the
region and the international staff were withdrawn for their own
safety. The local staff were magnificent. They were keeping the
office open. UNHCR wanted to re-establish its presence. Would
I like to be the man to do it? I told Neill that I would very much
prefer to stay in Sarajevo but if I could not then I liked the
challenge of Banja Luka. I suggested to him that I should have a
word with so-called Prime Minister Lukic to see how *grata* my
persona was in Serb-held territory. Neill thought it a good idea.
Brane fixed me up with an appointment with Prime Minister
Lukic, who said that for a change he very much would like me to
work on the Serb side. I was not too sure what he meant by this.
The die was cast. In the last week in June I would leave my
beloved Sarajevo and go to Banja Luka.

Jerrie Hulme, who at that time was in the chair in Sarajevo,
expressed a wish to travel with me 'for the ride'. I was delighted
as up till then no one had motored from Sarajevo to Banja Luka
via Brcko, which was a Serb-held town of strategic importance

with Croat forces to the north of it and Bosnian government forces to the south. It was a hotly contested strip of land and a very active front line.

Jerrie and I went to Pale to see if we could get Serb approval for our trip. I particularly wanted to motor as I liked my vehicle, 333, and it was coming with me one way or another. At Pale we met with the Deputy Commissioner of Refugees, Mr Milan Simic, an interesting character who was making the best of a bad war. He is a small, neat, dapper man, who likes and is liked by the ladies. It is very difficult not to like Mr Simic and it is very easy to be carried along by his plans and sucked into his schemes. He thought there would be no difficulty in our motoring to Banja Luka, but he confirmed that the route was dangerous and difficult. He therefore very kindly volunteered to accompany us. We agreed to set off together the following day, *en route* via Pale–Brcko–Doboj, to Banja Luka. We left Sarajevo early, with 333 stacked to the roof with my kit and a bag or two of Jerrie's. I had to leave behind some paintings and some brass plaques. The plaques were gifts from the Bosnian army and the paintings, presents from the senior citizens of Srebrenica and Gorazde living in Sarajevo, bore inscriptions thanking me for my endeavours in breaking the 'aggressor' siege of those towns: items which I felt would not win the friendship of Serb fighters at the numerous check-points we would have to pass. It would be a year before I would see them again. My colleagues in Sarajevo looked after them, despite shellings, moves and covetous glances.

As befits two ex-military men, we arrived at Pale five minutes before time, entirely thanks to the discipline of ex-Major-General Hulme; a long beard is not the only unmilitary aspect of ex-Lt-Col. Hollingworth. Mr Simic was a little late and when he arrived he had one or two tasks to do before we left, a couple of hours late. We motored for two or three hours towards Zvornik on a beautiful, picturesque road with high, wooded hills on our right and the River Drinjaca on our left – real tourist country, if it were not for the war and the constant reminders of it such as check-points, burnt houses and men with guns.

Near Zvornik, Mr Simic asked me to take a left turn, down a narrow country lane 'where we could have a cool drink and if we wished a meal'. He was our guide, mentor and guarantee of safety; we were in his hands. We eventually came to a beautiful, idyllic country cottage at the side of the river. We were met at the gate and made very welcome by a family consisting of a mum, a dad, a young boy aged about fourteen and a girl of about eighteen. We were offered juice and coffee. Then Mr Simic announced it was time to go and, surprise, surprise, he and the young lady got into the vehicle. We had been, for the first time, 'Simiced', a new verb but one we were to get to know very well. The young lady was to travel with us to Banja Luka. She was to assist with translation duties. As 'yes' and 'no' and an all-encompassing smile seemed to be her limit, Jerrie and I did not use her services. From my occasional glances in the rear-view mirror she was better at saying 'yes' than 'no'.

The four of us proceeded in the direction of Zvornik, then on to Brcko. This was the dodgy bit, a narrow strip, heavily fought over. It was pretty obvious to me before we had gone very far that it was not a road which Mr Simic knew well. He was reading the rare road signs probably a fraction of a second before I was. If the road led us into culs-de-sac, then it led us into culs-de-sac. I could have done as well myself. We had a few false starts, but eventually we reached Serb-dominated Doboj, 'Cowboy Town'. Doboj is the Crewe of Bosnia. It is an enormous railway town. Like Brcko, it was a place of strategic importance, with a Bosnian government stronghold on one side and a Croat force opposing it on another. It was heavily fought over. He who had Doboj had the gateway to the south, to Zenica and to Tuzla. He also had the main entrance to a dense, difficult pocket of land, the Ozren with its Serb majority. If the Bosnian government forces could take Doboj, they could encircle the Ozren. If they could besiege the Ozren they themselves would have a large Serb enclave which they could use as a barter factor against the 'Muslim' enclaves of Gorazde, Srebrenica and Zepa.

All this we knew, but had not seen. Mr Simic first took us to the office of Mr Gogic, the Regional Commissioner for Refugees, a man whom I was to learn to admire as the bravest of Serbs in the so-called Srpska Republika; a genuine humanitarian aid worker and a man of immense courage. Mr Gogic had organised a translator, Lidija, a girl from Radio Doboj, very attractive and intelligent. Mr Gogic took us to see the mayor of Doboj. He was in uniform but had been the administrator in peacetime. I liked him. He made us very welcome. Our whole group then moved to the main hotel in town, the Bosna.

Not only is Doboj a front-line town, it is also where the Serb soldiers come out of the trenches and go for a little 'r and r', rest and recuperation. They are allowed to drink and to drink heavily. As we approached the hotel we could see on the left side of the road a small gathering of very, very drunken soldiers, shouting, jeering, fearsomely armed with weapons and bandoliers and heavily loaded with slivovic. We parked our vehicle outside the hotel and Mr Gogic warned us to take inside anything of any value. I valued first my flak jacket, then my helmet and last my sleeping bag. The rest I could live without. I was very pleased that I had not brought the Bosnian army plaques. They would have been a crimson cloak to a raging bull. We went into the hotel, where we found that we were the only occupants. We were booked into two quite small but adequate rooms. We met again down in the dining-room, where we were joined by two or three men in uniform. There was a strange atmosphere. The noise of the revelling soldiers outside contrasted with the contrived peace within. We were probably the first humanitarian aid people in Doboj for some while and we were not too sure how we would be received. We had promised Sarajevo that we would keep in touch and had arranged a radio schedule for 1800 hours. We were a little late. It was now 1810 hours, so we excused ourselves, explaining very clearly to all what we were going to do. We went outside, got into the vehicle, switched on the radio and tried to make contact. As usual, whenever you want to get through you never can. Mercury is the most overrated of the gods; and he has a twisted sense of humour. He allows trivia to pass with crystal clarity, then squelches or garbles words of import. Perhaps if we called him by his Greek name Hermes he might be more amenable.

We could not get through, so Jerrie suggested that I motored back and forth a few yards to see if it was local interference. For about ten minutes I moved the vehicle back 10 metres, forward 20, back 5 and in this manner we progressed up and down the street. Jerrie held the microphone to his mouth. 'Hello, Sarajevo. Hello, Sarajevo.' 'Hello, Zagreb. Hello, Zagreb.' 'Hello, Metko-vic.' 'Hello, Mum.' All to no avail. We parked back on the same spot and returned to the dining-room, where we were bought some wine. Delicious wine – Mr Gogic proved to be not only a splendid companion but also an excellent host.

We were drinking our wine, when my attention was attracted by some commotion on the steps by the main entrance. The soldier who had been making the most noise on the corner of the road, a young, ugly man with hardly any teeth wearing a red beret and fatigues, bandoliered and pistolled, was making some sort of protest.

Mr Gogic was called out; he returned and he looked serious. 'Which one of you was filming?' he asked.

'Filming?' we asked.

'The soldier, who I admit is drunk,' said Mr Gogic, 'is claiming that you were moving up and down the street filming the soldiers.'

We carefully explained that we had been out in the street, moving up and down trying to contact Sarajevo. Mr Gogic went out and explained to the soldier, but from the noise it was pretty obvious that he was not going to accept this.

Mr Gogic returned. 'The soldier wants the movie camera. He has both military and civilian police with him. They want to see the movie camera so that they can remove and view the film.'

Now here we were lucky, we were able to say to Mr Gogic, 'Dear Mr Gogic, if the civilian police, the military police, the drunken soldier, want to see the movie camera and wish to remove the film they are welcome to do so. But first of all they will have to find it. We do not have a movie camera. We were out in the car on the radio.'

Mr Gogic could tell that we were telling the truth, so he went out and brought in the military police.

We explained to them, 'This is our kit, if you wish to go through it you are welcome. If you wish to examine the contents of the vehicle you can look with pleasure. There is no camera and there has been no filming.'

The police were quite happy with our explanation but it was obvious that they were frightened of the drunken soldier. They left, but I knew that we had not heard the last of this issue. We continued to drink our wine.

I was casually looking out of the window when I saw a sight which I could not believe. I turned to Jerrie and said, 'Jerrie, I think we are about to lose our vehicle.' Jerrie looked at me, then out through the window. Our drunken soldier, red beret, no teeth and all, had returned. On his shoulder was an anti-tank weapon. *An anti-tank weapon!* He was pointing it at our vehicle.

I quietly motioned to Mr Gogic and asked, 'Do you think that man intends to destroy our vehicle?'

Poor Mr Gogic looked through the window and his face dropped. He hurried out to the steps. This was a lot of fun. We could not fail to see the funny side of it. This swaying, drunken soldier had this heavy anti-tank weapon on his shoulder, which was disturbing his ability to maintain his balance. It was easy to see that the military, the police and Mr Gogic were wary of him. The police would go nowhere near him. Mr Gogic approached him and told him that we were friends; here to bring in humanitarian aid. But the boy was having none of this, none of it at all. Mr Gogic did, however, appear to persuade him to put down the weapon. I felt a little relieved. I watched him through the window. He dragged a box across the pavement, opened it and took out an anti-tank round. He placed it on the ground near the anti-tank weapon. He then went away. Mr Gogic returned. We went back to drinking our wine. The incident seemed to pass. We were relaxing and musing on the event when all of a sudden the doors to the dining-room where we sat crashed open and through them came our drunken soldier with the loaded anti-tank weapon on his shoulder. He came across to me and pointed this lethal tube about six inches from my nose. If he had pressed the trigger, not only would I have disappeared, but probably half the street ahead of us as well. The back blast would have destroyed the hotel. Jerrie looked at me, I looked at Jerrie and no matter how frightening the situation was, we could not help but smile.

This drunken individual then accused me of having done the filming. If there had been a camera and a film, I was the one doing the driving, Jerrie would have been the one doing the filming. So this menace was wrong on all counts and without being disloyal to Jerrie I tried to tell him. He was not for placating and his finger was perilously close to the trigger of the anti-tank weapon with all its potential devastation.

The army officers around the table froze and did nothing. The only man who got up was Mr Gogic who said to the soldier: 'You have got to leave here. We will talk about this outside.' I do not know what else Mr Gogic said but he was firm, straight, direct, incredibly courageous and, most important, successful, for he managed quietly and gently to take the man away outside the hotel, where through the window we watched him put the anti-tank weapon down, remove the round from the tail, undo the wires and place the round back in the box. We then had the fun of watching him, guided by Mr Gogic, load into a car the anti-tank weapon, the round in the box and finally his drunken self. All bundled into one lonely little VW Golf. Mr Gogic returned and we congratulated him on his courage. After that we ate. (Later that night Mr Gogic's car was stolen. That was his reward from the locals for interfering. His car plus his possessions were never seen again.)

Jerrie and I then went to our rooms. Before we went to sleep we drained a bottle of whisky and recounted the story of 'the anti-tank weapon in Cowboy Town', a story and images which will stay with us for evermore.

We awoke early the following day and went down to breakfast, where we met Mr Simic and the two-word translator. After coffee we set off on the road to Banja Luka. Mr Gogic led the way in a Golf he had borrowed for the day. It was a very pleasant drive. It was obvious as we approached every check-point that Mr Gogic was well known and well respected by the soldiers.

I was thrilled when I arrived at the UNHCR office in Banja Luka. All the staff were at the window and as I got out of my vehicle they gave me a great round of applause. They came down to the car and helped us to unload. They were delighted to have a boss once again, a new head of the family. They gave me a lovely welcome. I saw my new office and knew I was going to be happy in Banja Luka. We had only time to unpack and say hello, before we were off to meet the hierarchy of the town. We called first at the office of the mayor, Predrag Radic, a man I was to get to know very well. We met him with Mr Simic in the mayoral parlour, a large open office in an old building which looked the part. We were about to commence our meeting when, for some strange reason never subsequently explained, the building was buzzed by a lone single-engined aeroplane. The first fifteen minutes of our meeting were drowned by the penetrating growl of this little plane as it lined up, approached, dived and turned away. The mayor told us he was pleased that we were back. He had great aims for us and great targets for us to achieve. He was very unhappy that HCR had fled, very impressed with ICRC who had stayed. We had a reputation to recover. He hoped that I was the man able to do it. After the meeting I went to the little house where I was to live. It was small and cosy, in the narrowest of streets. I was the sole occupant but if more staff came they would share the house. I chose as my room the main bedroom. The view was limited but the bed was comfortable. It had its own minimal wash-basin. The three bedrooms shared a tiny bathroom with a genuine hip bath, designed for sitting in only. For sitting on was a loo shoe-horned behind the door. The house smelt warm and welcoming. I knew that I would like it there.

My first days in Banja Luka were spent in assessing the problem and the players. The problem seemed simple. There were at least twenty-six towns with warehouses to which we could deliver aid. If, from these warehouses, the aid could be fairly distributed to all three communities, depending on their needs, then all would be well. I was assured by the Banja Luka representative of the Commissioner for Refugees (COR), a Serb of course, that all I needed to do was to hand the aid over to him and he would issue it fairly and squarely. The regional representative for the Red Cross assured me that his organisation had the best distribution network. He further confided in me that to give aid to the Commissioner for Refugees would inevitably mean a large percentage going to the fighting forces. The Catholic agency, Caritas, and the Muslim agency, Merhamet, both guaranteed to me that unless they were given their share direct, they would never see a kilo of aid. To complicate issues further, two local Serb charities, Dobrotvor and KSS, also demanded that their share be delivered directly to them.

I had come from Sarajevo where people were genuinely starving and where we were bringing in only a fraction of needs. I had travelled to Banja Luka through kilometre after kilometre of fields sown with crops. I had visited the market in Banja Luka, where there were items for sale which had almost been forgotten in Sarajevo. When you come from a place where there is nothing to a place where there is plenty, what hits you is colours: the yellow of the bananas, the greens and the reds of peppers and tomatoes, the orange of the citrus fruits. Banja Luka market was ablaze with colour. In Gorazde and Srebrenica people would fight for a cigarette. In Banja Luka you could buy cartons of two hundred. There were restaurants open where you could buy steak and for me, joy of joys, a bottle of wine.

I was here to deliver aid – valuable, life-saving aid. Was it really needed here, where the agencies were all in conflict and the odds on the minorities receiving their share were long? In my first week I visited and was visited incessantly. The office had been closed and many people wanted to express their delight that we were back in business, or their anger that we had left. I learned a lot.

Father Tomislav Matanovic, the representative from the Catholic charity Caritas, told me that he was bringing in aid from Zagreb on a weekly basis. He was giving a percentage of his load to the Serb Commission for Refugees for the privilege.

The main supplier of aid to the Muslim community was the charity Merhamet. I asked to see their director, only to find out that there were two Merhamets and that they were in dispute. Senad Sirbegovic was the deputy leader of Merhamet One. He was a professor of electronics at Banja Luka university, one of the few professional Muslims still to have a job. I liked him. He spoke very good English but preferred to go through a translator, which gave him time to think. He explained the rift between Merhamet One and Merhamet Two. The powers in Two had been expelled from One. There were hints of misappropriation and mismanagement. I was exasperated and told him that I could not believe that in the most dangerous environment in the whole of ex-Yugoslavia the Muslim community was fighting within itself. The ever reasonable professor agreed and hoped that I could solve the problem by closing down Merhamet Two. He then told me that until recently Merhamet had been able to bring in truck-loads of food from Zagreb. They gave twenty per cent to the Serb Commission for Refugees. What was left they gave to schools, public kitchens, social institutions and retired people. This deal had recently been stopped by the Serb army. He wanted me to get it going again and provide the balance to feed the majority of the Muslim community who were unemployed and dispossessed, a total according to him of ninety thousand. A further small task, which he gave me with a charming, disarming smile, was to recover 72 tonnes of food which had just been stolen from the Merhamet warehouse by the Serb army.

Within minutes of Mr Sirbegovic leaving, Mr Novalija arrived, the head of Merhamet Two. If it was by accident, the timing was remarkable, but I suspect that Davorka, the senior girl in my new office, is secretly a wonderful head of protocol! Amir Novalija is a tall, handsome man who arrived with two ladies. He was charming. He ran ten kitchens in the town and fed about seven hundred and fifty people every day, twenty per cent of them Croats and the remainder Muslims. We apparently had only helped him twice; he needed food or he was out of business. One of the women with him, whose name was Vesna, was a doctor of medicine. Vesna is an unusual name for a Muslim, presumably she was the product of a mixed marriage. She used to work within the government system but was now out of work, so she ran a clinic, which Bosnians call an *ambulanta*. She did house visits to the old and the infirm. All she could dispense to them was knowledge and sympathy. She really impressed me. I promised to help get some drugs for her from WHO or MSF in Zagreb. I talked at great length to Novalija, explaining to him that by running a splinter group he was doing the Serbs' work for them. Divided they would fall. United they would probably fall. I asked him if he would amalgamate with Merhamet One. Surprisingly, he said he would but that his management would want some positions of authority in Merhamet One. I first asked myself whether this petty squabbling could be true, then realised that when murder and mayhem are your constant companions, you need something else to occupy your mind. A good, simple dispute or argument with your neighbour could be therapeutic.

So far I had seen a Croat, and Muslim One and Muslim Two. I expected a Serb next but Davorka brought in the senior Croat politician Nicola Gabelic, senior of those who were left. He began by telling me that one-third of the Croat population had left the area and the other two-thirds wanted to leave. Fifteen Croats had recently been murdered in the Banja Luka region. He explained that the biggest nightmare was mobilisation. All males between the ages of eighteen and fifty-five were eligible. If men refused the draft, they were evicted from their homes; if they accepted the draft they were sent to the front lines. He told me that for two hundred Deutschmarks per person a family could get to Croatia, for four hundred and fifty they could go to Sweden. He concluded our first conversation with a heavy warning that the remaining Croats were ready to fight to the last man if they were pushed much further. He was doing his best to keep the lid on, but only because he feared massive reprisals. 'I want a Croat community in Bosnia. I want human rights. And I expect you to help. What can you do?'

The answer to his question was very little, except listen and report. But was that why we were there? Was the UN there to listen?

There was a lot of listening still to do. The visitors kept coming. Mr Muharem Krzic, the leader of the Muslim political party SDA, came with three friends. To the Serbs, Krzic was like a negro at a Ku Klux Klan convention. A sincere but difficult and demanding man, he began by telling me that although he represented the Muslim party he wanted a Bosnian state. He reminded me that the United Nations had accepted Bosnia-Herzegovina as a member state. 'Where are you? What are you doing for us?' he asked. He then asked for – no, this was Mr Krzic, he demanded – regular meetings with me 'as the situation for Muslims is so tense'.

Events proved him right. Of the four men present on that day, I was soon to spend a lot of time getting two out of jail, including Mr Krzic himself. He told me that of the seven hundred thousand Muslims who had lived in the Banja Luka region, only seventy thousand were now left. He told me the same story as Mr Gabelic, his Croat counterpart, only on a grander scale. The majority of Muslims were unemployed, many had lost their homes, many were beaten. He told me in detail of robberies, looting and rape that had taken place the previous evening in Gornji Seher, a suburb of Banja Luka city. He retold the story of the mobilisation rules. He outlined the plight of most of his people. 'Firstly, Mr Larry, the man is sacked. If he has no work he is deemed to be unable to pay his rent, so he and his family are moved to cramped shared accommodation. No job means no social security. No social security means no medical treatment.'

Mr Krzic was full of praise for the courage of Swiss ICRC Chief Michel Minnig, who had responded, after midnight, to a call from Mr Krzic and had prevented Serb violence on Muslims who had been herded into a local mosque. Krzic asked for my home number so that I could help when the next crisis happened. As he was leaving he asked me to support Merhamet Two, 'especially their soup kitchens'.

I needed a break from the office. Hannah, an UNPROFOR clerk in Sarajevo, had given me a little parcel to be delivered to her aunt in Banja Luka. She lived with her husband, Samir, in a block of flats in the centre of town. Samir is from the neighbouring state, Montenegro. He was then sixty-five and had had two heart attacks. He had been a very handsome man. On his wedding photograph he looks like Clark Gable. He came to Banja Luka at fourteen, found work, went back home and returned with his parents and his brothers and sisters. He believes passionately in communism and the old Yugoslavia. He had three sons and in the Montenegrin manner, when they married they brought their wives to live with him. In the flat below lived Samir's brother and his family who had worked in Germany and banked all his money in Belgrade. When the war broke out the government confiscated all hard currency. Samir's brother lost everything and his moaning could be heard blocks away. But at least his contacts in Germany got him and his family refugee status. For permission to leave, he relied on a local Serb army officer who, in return for this favour, accepted his flat and contents down to the last knife and fork.

Samir's sons did not want to join the army, certainly not on the front line in the Serb army, goaded and prodded to prove their loyalty to Dr Karadzic. The boys decided to leave with their families, one to Libya and two to Sweden. Leaving costs money. Samir had spent more than three thousand marks on getting his next generation out, more than his life savings. The colonel in his brother's old flat had friends who liked Samir's flat. They said it was too large for a man and his wife whose children had left. Samir was prepared to move if they would find a smaller flat for him. This would not prove difficult. The new flat would not be large enough for his furniture but the new occupants of his old flat would help him out there – Samir, sixty-five, his successful life crumbling around him. His error was that he thought he was a communist and a Yugoslav. His neighbours thought he was a Muslim.

I gave Samir the small parcel sent by Hannah. It contained some digitalis tablets. Hannah was curing the pain. Could we cure the illness? I knew there and then the answer was no. This was going to be a tour sticking my finger in the holes in the dyke. The torrent of ethnic abuse raged around us.

I walked back to the office, depressed. If you want to raise funds for refugees, show pictures of children. But my heart always bleeds for the older ones. The young have time to reassemble their lives. The old do not. Samir had completed his wheel of fortune, surely he would not have the strength, energy and time to go round again.

Davorka told me that Mr Spahic of the Red Cross was waiting for me. It was a courtesy call, but with an early request that I give all the aid to his organisation.

'If I do,' I asked him, 'can you guarantee delivery to Croats and Muslims? Can you guarantee to feed the minorities?'

His answer endeared him to me. 'No. But nor can you, or any other agency.'

Davorka had decided that my next call was to be on Michel Minnig, the International Committee of the Red Cross (ICRC) Chief Delegate so highly praised by the Muslim leaders. He offered me tea or coffee and I opted for tea. When it came it was herbal tea, bright red and horrible. Mental note, next time I ask for coffee.

I had been warned by my own office in Zagreb that Michel was not pro-UNHCR so I went in a little warily. I need not have worried. I found him to be open, frank and helpful. The UNHCR staff in Banja Luka was one international and five local staff. He had seventeen international and seventy-three local! He warned me of the security situation. His staff were frequently threatened by armed men, homes were burgled, cars broken into, some stolen. He said that all his staff had a freedom of movement certificate but its validity depended on the check-point commanders. 'All movement is difficult, unpredictable and dangerous.' We talked about the essential difference between his convoys and mine. ICRC world-wide refuses to be escorted by local uniformed or armed escorts. UNHCR had agreed with the Serbs that we would be escorted by a Serb military or a Serb police escort. Therefore theoretically we should have an easier passage than ICRC. Michel was sceptical. He emphasised that while convoys were vital, protection for the minorities was the number one task. For the most vulnerable, even protection was not enough; evacuation was the only solution. Evacuation needed greater ICRC–HCR co-operation. He could organise the mechanics of movement but they had to have somewhere to go. Resettlement was a UNHCR problem and in his opinion we were not providing enough overseas places for those who had to go.

He warned me that my number one task in Banja Luka would be protesting to the authorities. How right he was. We discussed aid. ICRC was bringing in almost 2000 tonnes per month and was not happy. The authorities wanted more and more, and he was convinced the aid was not going to the most needy. However, he was of the opinion that we had no option. If we wanted to feed any of the minority we had to co-operate with the Serbs. In my naivety I told him that I disagreed. I remember my words: 'When we have so little food I cannot see why we should feed people who are living in villages surrounded by lush green fields.' I was, of course, still conditioned by my Sarajevo experience.

'You will,' replied Minnig. He pointed out to me that to feed vulnerable minorities and not to feed the majority made the minorities even more vulnerable.

Minnig had taken a bold, controversial stance on the supplying of food to the prisoners in the infamous Manjaca prison. He refused, because the Serbs would not allow him free access to the prisoners. My first thought was that this was wrong, but on reflection I think he was right.

Finally we discussed whom I should see. We agreed that the big five were Corps Commander General Talic, Chief of Police Zupljanin, and Mayor Predrag Radic on the Serb side, and the Catholic Bishop and the Mufti on the minority side. Davorka decided that I should begin with the General. She told me that he had always refused to see my predecessor. I was luckier. I got into his small, neat office the next day.

General Talic is a large, benevolent-looking man: round, red, open face, gentle eyes and a relaxing smile; Pickwickian. If his reputation is anything to go by, his looks are very deceptive. I was told that he is a tough commander with a blood lust, who likes to be in at the kill. He welcomed me and praised the work of UNHCR. He said that he was very unhappy that we had left, that he knew of me by reputation and looked forward to working with me. I told him that in order to work at all we would need freedom of movement. This he immediately granted 'within the constraints of the security situation' – another document for my 'Neville Chamberlain' file. He then went on with words which were so significant that I have never forgotten them. 'HCR has saved certain areas from certain death. Thanks from me is not enough. Your thanks will come from God. But you can do more. Not only are there refugees but also the destitute, Serbs, Croats and Muslims.' Then came his best line: 'You are here to help all. I want all to stay. This land will be much richer if it has a multi-ethnic base.' My interview with him lasted ninety minutes. I came away believing him. Time and events would strain that belief.

I next went to see Regional Chief of Police Stoyan Zupljanin. He met me in his scruffy office in his scruffy building. He is an extrovert. He had with him his Banja Luka Chief and for some reason the commander of the Air Force base. He offered us drinks, said many things about UNHCR, all complimentary. Regretted the incidents against the minorities and promised to do everything in his power to protect them. He blamed 'uncontrollable elements' for the aggression. He brought to my notice the fact that the main

Muslim suburb of Banja Luka was on the outskirts of the town. 'As our soldiers return from the front, they pass through it. To some, who have just lost comrades, brothers and cousins in the trenches, killed by Muslims, the sight of the Muslim men lolling against their gates, idling away their time, Muslims who refused to defend the territory where they were born, is too much.' The Chief of Police said that he did not agree with the actions of the 'elements' but that he could understand them. During my interview with him there was much humour, much slivovic, many promises and very little sincerity.

There has been a Catholic bishop in Banja Luka since the twelfth century. The current incumbent was the right man at the right time. Franjo Komarica was a fighter. He was a Banja Luka boy, born and bred. He knew all the locals, the goodies and the baddies. He wore a well-made dark suit; his pectoral cross was small but good. He was neat and immaculately groomed. His wavy hair was greying slightly. After a few words of welcome and some comments on my 'prophet' beard we were straight into business. He was delighted we were back; we were needed, if only as an observer. But he hoped for more, much more. The war had hardly touched this area, therefore the cleansing, the beatings, the burnings, were out of character with the people and the situation. He was devastatingly critical of the international community. 'You watch them pen us like sheep and kill us like wolves.' And 'You are content to feed us to die. You should protect us to live.' He ended with two statements. 'The minorities here have not provoked the Serbs, they do not deserve the treatment they are getting' and 'The situation here is desperate. Do not be fooled by the calm outlook.'

He took me to an adjoining room where he had a large map on the wall, the map of his diocese. All his parish churches were marked on it. Some had 'x's covering the church, others a circle around the church. The 'x's were churches burnt down by the Serbs, the encircled were churches damaged. The Bishop had tears in his eyes as he gave me the numbers of parishioners who had fled. Komarica could be the last in a long line of Banja Luka bishops.

The key player I still had to see was the Mufti, the leader of the Muslim religious in the whole of the Banja Luka region. Mufti Ibraham Halilovic had his office in a building in the grounds of the Ferhadiya mosque. The mosque was built in 1574. In this century it had survived two world wars and an earthquake. It did not survive the night of 27 May 1993. This ancient, revered and UNESCO-protected building was dynamited. In the days that followed, bulldozers attempted to level the site. The window in the office of the Mufti overlooked the flattened mosque, a daily reminder to the leader of the Islamic community of the trials his people were undergoing.

Muftis and their subordinates, Imams, can be rigid, dour, humourless people and I was not too sure what to expect on my visit. I found a saintly man, one whom I grew to admire enormously. He had none of the fire and urbanity of the Bishop. He was more a cloistered academic, the scholar cleric. He is medium height, fit, with an open, smiling, slightly tanned face. His throaty voice has been trained by many packets of cigarettes. It is mellow, quiet and considered. His deep blue eyes twinkle in laughter and moisten in sadness. He carefully explained that he was the spiritual leader of those Bosnians who considered themselves to be Muslims. He made it clear to me that he was neither their political leader nor their cultural guide.

Humanitarian aid was the task of Merhamet, politics the domain of SDA. He recognised that he, his clergy and his religious buildings were the symbols of the Islamicisation so hated by the extremists on both the Croat and the Serb sides. He wanted a return to the multi-ethnic state that had been for most of his life Yugoslavia, and was now struggling Bosnia. We drank coffee. He asked me did I think that he should advise his people to leave. I told him that I did not, that I believed it was vital that they stayed. I reiterated the words of Dr Karadzic, Prime Minister Lukic, and at the local level General Talic that they wanted a multi-ethnic state. The Mufti was pleased with my words. It was what he wanted to hear. He would tell his flock that the new HCR man, the new UN man, thought it was safe to stay. At that time I believed what I told him, because I believed those who had told me. I soon had to revise my advice, my opinions and my judgement. We parted and I knew that I had met a good, honest, brave man. I hoped he would survive.

A few mornings later I arrived at the office and found a large group of Muslims waiting for me. They were committee members from Gornji Seher. Some of the men were crying. The night before, there had been an attack by armed men in their suburb. During it, one of their men had been killed and two were injured and were now in hospital, seriously wounded. Apparently, for weeks small bands of men had arrived in the village after curfew to loot the homes of the Muslims who had fled. The empty homes were now stripped so the bands were robbing from occupied homes. Any resistance was met with violence. The committee's request was simple: they wanted me to evacuate the whole population of seven hundred immediately. I tried to explain that to evacuate you have to have somewhere to go. Nations prepared to take seven hundred could not be found – a sad fact of life. After a terribly emotional half-hour listening to their sobbing and their dreadful stories, I persuaded them to return, with the reassurance that I would seek the intervention of the military and civil powers.

I contacted the General. I told him that I intended staying the night in the village and requested him to give me an escort. He was weary and I am sure genuinely concerned. He told me that it was a police matter, that my staying there could be considered provocative and, more importantly, that having reported the matter I should give the powers the chance to sort it out. He promised that protection would be provided.

I went back to the committee, explained what had happened and hoped for the best. I then went to my house, where at that stage I lived alone. I got into bed feeling really guilty. I felt that I should have gone and stayed in the village. I questioned why I had not. Was I scared? Did I believe the General? As darkness fell I heard shooting in the distance. I hoped it was not in Gornji Seher. If it was and I had been there, what could I have done? The next day I contacted the committee. They were very frightened. No government protection had turned up. At dusk a van-load of looters had arrived, attacked an occupied house and the son of the house was murdered. The Muslim community retaliated and in the ensuing gun battle one of the Serb criminals was killed. Serb reprisals were inevitable.

The General was not available. He was 'in the field'. Regional Chief of Police Stoyan Zupljanin was 'away'. The city police chief told me that the Criminal Investigation Department was handling the case and that the police were indeed fearful of reprisals and were attempting to ease the tension. I was told not to visit the area. He recommended that I take a food parcel to the family of the dead Muslim! I tried to get to the village but was turned back at the police check-point. 'Too much tension,' I was told. I went back to the office, contacted Neill Wright and asked him to send me urgently a protection officer, an international lawyer. He told me that an outstanding Sri Lankan lawyer, who had previously been in Banja Luka, was on his way back and that he was looking for another.

Mr Krzic and his gang of three turned up at the office to complain about the night's events. They were very critical. I was less than polite, but only because I did feel that I had let them down. By being there, we were offering a service. A service we could not fulfil.

It was beginning to look as if getting aid into besieged towns was far easier than achieving anything in Banja Luka. I prayed to God and to Neill Wright to send me reinforcements.

12

In Banja Luka

Neill heard my prayer. The arrival of Indrika Ratwatte was great news. I needed another international, for credibility, for the sake of the minorities and to have someone to discuss events with. He is from Sri Lanka. He is a clever lawyer, with a background spanning the quiet corridors of the World Bank and the violent world of the banks of the Jordan. He spent a few years in the UNRWA Palestinian refugee camps. He is a Buddhist, a very gentle man, outstanding at listening to the problems of vulnerable people, assessing what he can do and doing it with speed, courage and efficiency. He had been part of the old team who had moved from Banja Luka when our activities were temporarily suspended. He had not agreed with the decision. The staff loved him and the authorities respected him. I wanted more protection officers and was promised another 'soon'.

Out of the blue a Frenchman arrived. He had no experience in UNHCR. He was a doctor of philosophy, right-hand man to the Secretary General of the OECD and had volunteered his annual leave for humanitarian aid work in ex-Yugoslavia. Philippe Montigny had a Clouseau-like English accent, tremendous energy and enthusiasm. He rapidly became a vital part of the team. I made him a protection officer and under the guidance of Indy he was excellent.

Now that we were back in the protection business we had a constant stream of visitors, mainly Bosnians classified as Muslims by the local Serbs and under great pressure. They all wanted out. Sadly, more and more nations were closing their doors to refugees. The international community cannot have it all ways. The choices seemed simple. Either come in strong and sort out the situation or let the oppressed escape and give them somewhere to live. These poor people were stuck. They could not stay. They could not go. Meanwhile their nightmares were our breakfasts.

I arrived at the office, as ever, at about 7.15 a.m. There were a couple of men waiting for me. One was very distressed. The previous evening at dusk a car had arrived in his neighbourhood and four men in uniform got out. They walked up to his house, kicked open the door, came in and took away his seventeen-year-old daughter. It all happened very fast. He, his wife and his younger daughter watched her go. He heard her screams and her cries. He did not do anything. He said he knew that had he moved they would have killed him, probably killed his wife as well and still taken his daughter. She had not returned. Could I help to find her? And a second question: he wanted to know how he could explain to his daughter that he had let her go – heard her screams, her pleas and let her go without a fight. I was able to help find his daughter. My advice as to what he should tell her was irrelevant. She was pulled out of the river, naked and dead.

On the aid front we had success from the start. I issued the contents of the warehouse to the three towns, Banja Luka, Doboj and Petrovac. This meant that UNHCR convoys became high-profile. People could see the white trucks with the UNHCR logo. They annoyed some and were delayed at check-points and were stoned, but they thrilled others, especially Croats and Muslims who thought they had been abandoned by the international community. I appeared on local TV, on the radio and in the press. Wherever the convoys went an international staff member went. While the trucks were being unloaded it gave us the chance to talk to the local distributing agent, to assess his honesty and his integrity. We also tried to see the local community leaders. This was never too easy. If we announced our intention in advance we could get fobbed off with 'tame' minority leaders. When we returned we discussed our findings with Sirbegovic of Merhamet, with Krzic of the SDA and with any of the priests from Caritas. We were soon delivering aid to all the towns in the region.

But we were not winning on the protection front. On the night of 14 July two mosques in Banja Luka were blown up. This brought the total to eighteen destroyed in the previous year, which included five that had been built in the sixteenth century. When lives are being destroyed it may seem a little strange to get worked up about the destruction of buildings, but these acts indicated to the minorities that they were to be driven out and that all traces of their culture were to be removed. I knew that I could not get these poor people out. I was trying to persuade them to stay, quoting the words of the Serb leaders. How could I expect them to believe in a multi-ethnic state when gangs could turn up with explosives and blow up their mosques and their history.

I went to the site of the two mosques. From the stories told me, the *modus operandi* was the same. At dusk a van arrived, out got soldiers carrying boxes, they entered the area of the mosque, placed the charges, withdrew and up it went. These two mosques were surrounded by houses. At the first, three homes were damaged, one severely. There were only minor casualties. At the second location, one house abutting the mosque was no longer habitable. Two others had been shaken to their foundations and would need a lot of repair. I went to the destroyed house. The owner was swathed in bandages. When the van had arrived the villagers knew what was about to happen. So the men swiftly ordered their families into the fields, where they slept the night. The men stayed in their homes to prevent looting. They telephoned the police in Banja Luka, who said they would investigate the following day!

When the explosion went off, all the men were lucky. They had suffered only cuts from flying glass. As I walked around the shattered house, the wife of the owner was in what remained of the kitchen. She was washing the dishes – her way of coping with the loss of her family home, her possessions and life as she had known it.

I went to see the police chief. How could a van with explosives pass at least three police check-points? Why had the police not responded to the telephone call? What did he intend to do about the incidents?

His reply was truly Balkan: 'How do you know that the Muslims did not do it themselves?' He then went on to tell me that the Muslims had themselves destroyed the ancient Ferhadiya mosque in the centre of Banja Luka. The evidence was a masterpiece of detection. 'After the blast, we were very soon on the scene. We found no priceless carpets among the debris. The Muslims had removed the carpets before they blew it up and blamed the Serbs.' Dear Mr Zupljanin, one day when the war is over and I return as a tourist, will you tell me whether you expected me to believe you or whether you said it just to test my reaction?

General Talic was 'in the field'. Whenever there was a crisis, that's where the General was. I promoted him to 'field marshal'. More and more I was to deal with his staff officer, a polite, professional pre-war colonel, Vujinovic.

The market in Banja Luka was full of apples, fat and juicy. In the region there are many orchards. The crop is vital to the economy. The young men who would normally gather them were in the trenches and the barracks. Someone had to harvest. The Muslim and Croat men understood this. They accepted that they could not sit in overcrowded apartments, with no job to go to and watch the crop rot. They fully understood that the Banja Luka authorities had to call upon their services, that they had to do their bit for the war effort.

In Salisbury there are two Bosnian sisters, both doctors who qualified at Sarajevo university. They heard that I was in Banja Luka and asked if I would visit their Uncle Mustafa, a surgeon at Banja Luka hospital. They are in name a Muslim family. I went to see him. He was not at the hospital but I got his home address. He lives in a lovely old house in the centre of Banja Luka right next door to the mosque. He was playing pool with his friends. He had no shortage of partners: psychiatrists, lawyers, architects, all unemployed, all debarred from practice because they were Muslims.

Mustafa is a leading consultant bone specialist. He was not included in the first purge of Muslim professionals. With so many war wounded, it looked as if he would survive. In the second wave he was dismissed, but amazingly was reinstated. Some of his patients, wounded Serb soldiers, demanded his recall. But when they moved on he was out. He is a big, heavy man who has relished good food. He produced an excellent meal for me with lots of slivovic. He was a great, hospitable host. I enjoyed his company. When he was bused out to the apple orchards along with many of his friends, he must have felt that his soft, tender, caring hands could have been better used in the hospital than in collecting apples. On arrival at the fields his work group were allocated a 'norm' according to the good old communist system. The Serb soldiers, young, heavily armed men 'supervising' their work, made it clear that the norm would be multiplied by the number present and that they would not leave until it had been achieved and that tomorrow was another day and another norm. The farmers and labourers among them found the norm achievable; the doctors, dentists, lawyers, teachers, almost impossible. The soldiers encouraged them, shouting, pushing and occasionally beating. The soldiers were insistent that the apples were removed from the trees carefully. One university professor with an aching back and blistered hands constantly dropped apples, bruising them. He was singled out by a soldier as young as any of his undergraduates, told that he was clumsy and careless and ordered to extend his hand. He was whacked with a stick till his hand stung and his cheeks ran with tears. The soldiers laughed. His colleagues turned away in shame. At the end of the long day, norm achieved, they were bused back to Banja Luka for a short sleep before another day and another norm. I didn't see much more of Mustafa. He was too busy. I told the doctors in Salisbury he was OK.

Life went on in other parts of Bosnia – and death. On 30 July I received a message from Sarajevo. 'Message for Larry. Mrs Kira Sparavalo wants Larry to know that her husband, Veljko, whom Larry knew well, was killed by a mortar about an hour and a half ago. The children in England do not know yet.'

I remembered the last time I saw him, every inch the successful actor, immaculate. What would Kira and Denis, their son, do without him? Who would tell Aris and Enesa?

I found a little café on the bank of the river. No other aid workers went to it. It had no food but served wine. I sat with my translator on the patio which jutted out over the river, propped up by stilts and protected from the sun by a worn and torn canvas canopy. It was rickety and plagued by midges. But it was quiet and peaceful. We watched men fishing from the banks, cattle grazing and young children punting on the river, expertly manoeu-vring the flat-bottomed boats along the shallow river bed. As we became regulars we brought our own bread – wine, bread and pensive, precious moments. What were we doing in Banja Luka? We were welcomed by the Serbs for whatever aid we could bring in. We were welcomed by the minorities for whatever protection we could give them. But were we doing enough of either? Should we be busing people out and not bringing aid in? No. There were in the region about three hundred thousand displaced and vulnerable people, a third of whom were Serbs. Aid had to come in. Should we be bringing in aid *and* busing people out? Definitely. Were we bribing our way in? Was the aid really needed here. I could see green fields, cows and fish. If we were bribing our way in, what were we getting in return? What was the core problem? The abuse of the minorities. How can you stop that? Appeal to the better nature of the perpetrators? They have not got one. So what next? Bring in enough troops to prevent their action? Serbs will not let you, the international community will not produce them. Take all the minorities out? To where? No one will take them. Larry, eat the bread, drink the wine, bring in the aid, protest and shout.

On 1 August as we arrived at the office the phone rang and we had a strange message. A Serb woman in a place called Liskovac said that her Muslim neighbours had asked her to pass on a message. During the night there had been a massacre in the village. Could we get there urgently? We took two cars and raced to the place. There were few people about. One man who looked very scared told us to proceed to the top end of the village. Unfortu-nately, as we arrived there, a large group of police were walking towards us. They stopped our car and told us they were the scene of crime team and we could go no further. We argued and pushed. One man came forward. He was wearing blood-stained rubber gloves. He identified himself as a doctor and the local coroner. He quietly pointed out to me that if there was a murder inquiry in the UK, aid workers would not be allowed on the scene. I reminded him of my human rights responsibility. He promised that if I went to the police station in Gradiska he would ensure that I received all the information. Behind him stood a gorilla of a policeman whom Indy had clashed with before. We were not going forward. We moved slowly away. Some of the Muslim villagers approached us; they wanted us to stay. They were frightened. They told me there were five dead, two of them women. They were about to tell me more when the gorilla arrived and they all melted away. At the police station we met the chief and his deputy. He convened a meeting with detectives, doctors and police. He promised thorough investigations, prosecutions for the guilty, security for the minorities. We were in a difficult position with this man as he controlled the one and only entrance and exit from Zagreb to Banja Luka. All our aid convoys passed over the Gradiska bridge, metres from his office. Every refugee who left went out over the Gradiska bridge. He and his associates inspected the baggage of every one leaving. Few, if any, refugees got over the bridge without losing something. On his whim depended the food of many and the freedom of some. He promised to keep me up to date with progress. I called a meeting in the village for that evening.

I got the full story. At dusk a car had arrived. Out got the soldiers. They went to the first house where an old lady lived with her son and his daughter. They burst in and grabbed the girl. The old lady was brave. She fought them. One of them picked her up and threw her outside into the yard. She continued screaming so he shot her dead. Her son then tried to protect his daughter. He was also shot. The girl was repeatedly raped. Some of the gang moved next door. They killed an old man and his son and repeatedly raped the son's wife. They did not leave till dawn. Throughout the night other villagers had telephoned the police but they refused to come. I met the neighbour who had called the office. She described a night of screams and terror. The whole village asked for police protection for the night. The police chief promised to attend the meeting but did not, so when it ended I went back to see him. He said that he would happily provide police patrols in the evening but that he had no fuel for the police vehicles. I knew that this was another scam, another cheap, nasty way of getting something for nothing out of us. I also knew that no fuel meant no patrols. I further knew that if I gave fuel once I would have to give it for ever. And if attacks equalled more patrols equalled more fuel, would there be more attacks? Jesus, I hated this war. Moreover I was always short of fuel myself. I went back to the village and explained. They thanked me for my concern. For the rest of the summer as dusk approached they moved out of their homes and slept in the fields. I managed to convince myself that they would have done so with or without patrolling. Besides, I knew that the fuel would never have been used on police patrols. More excuses, Larry!

On 5 August another of our parked vehicles was damaged, a sure sign that we were doing our job well. A day or two later I received a real boost: two more protection officers, one a big, tough Greek, Georgios Karatzoglou; and a great surprise for me, Louis Gentile, who had worked so well out of Belgrade and who took over from me in Srebrenica. Louis was one of the best and if I could have chosen one person to join the team it would have been him. Sadly Philippe went back to the Ivory Towers where he has written an excellent book on Banja Luka. With the arrival of Louis I was able to reorganise the office. He ran protection, giving me time for everything else. My only problem with Louis was reining him in. He is a stocky, cocky, uncompromising fighter, with all the arrogance of youth.

Louis and his team were daily overwhelmed in their attempt to offer protection to increasing numbers in an ever worsening internal and external environment. I concentrated on pushing aid through. Only one Serb helped me unreservedly: Milko Gogic, the Commissioner for Refugees for the Doboj region, who was so brave on my first trip to Doboj. He is a humanitarian worker *par excellence*. He always wanted more aid than anyone else. If I sent a convoy to his area, he was always there to meet it. He knew where every kilogram had gone to and had accounts to prove it. More importantly, he fought for his beneficiaries. He is a Serb in a volatile front-line area. He had enormous pressures put upon him. The minorities in his area did not get all that they should have but they got as much as Gogic dared give them. He gave me total support and encouragement to attempt to reach besieged minorities. At the end of the war there will be rogues who must be punished and there will also be heroes who must be honoured. Milko Gogic deserves honouring, a brave humanitarian worker in a vicious and dangerous environment. May God grant that his health does not fail and his enemies do not succeed.

On 19 August as I arrived at the office I received a call from Colonel Vujinovic. The commander wished to have breakfast with me. I took Louis and we went to the corps headquarters to look for General Talic. However, the commander they had in mind was the Commander-in-Chief of the Army, General Mladic.

Seated at a large table in the dining-room were many of the top brass of the army of the so-called Srpska Republika. General Mladic was on top form. As I entered he got up and gave me a big bearhug. Then with a great flourish he introduced me to his top table. 'Gentlemen, my friend Mr Larry, the Muslim Ambassador to Banja Luka.' The joke was enjoyed by everyone.

As our activities expanded we needed more local staff but their recruitment was a problem. In Sarajevo the government complained that we had too many Croats or too many Serbs. In Banja Luka there were many hints that we had too many Croats. We had, of course, no Muslims. The locals seemed to be telepathic. The moment I thought about extra personnel, before I spoke to anyone, my staff were sidling up to me offering the services of their brothers, mothers, sisters, cousins. This was not surprising: we were paying about six hundred dollars a month in an environment where brain surgeons were on two hundred a month. I decided to rock the boat. I needed three extra staff. I informed the local authorities that I was about to recruit three people, one Serb, one Muslim, one Croat. The authorities came back to me very quickly with a statistical argument. The Muslim and Croat populations of the region represented less than ten per cent, my staff total was about to increase to nine, therefore I should employ less than .9 from the minorities. As I already had one Croat they wished me to take on three Serbs. And they would provide their names in due course. Right?

'Wrong,' I replied.

I had a novel plan of my own for the recruitment of my three. I went to Merhamet, Caritas and Dobrotvor and asked for a person from each. The qualifications were that the candidate spoke English and was prepared to work for one-sixth of the salary, the remainder to be distributed by the charity to the poor. I would hand over the money to a rep from the charity who would provide me with a breakdown, complete with signatures, of all those who received money. After a few false starts caused by nepotism I ended up with Igor, Aida and Sanja. Only Merhamet kept to its bargain and produced monthly accounts, but all three new recruits assured me that they only received a hundred dollars per month. Merhamet paid seven dollars each to forty-two families. Therefore, Aida kept forty-two families alive. I hope she felt as good about it as I did. The local authorities' response was interesting. You win one, you must lose one. They decided that I must pay for their services. Each convoy that entered their territory was escorted by one police car. In that car, they said, were five policemen. They demanded twenty Deutschmarks per person per day plus 210 litres of fuel per convoy for inspection teams. There was a cunning caveat to these charges. They were only applicable to those convoys which were passing through Serb territory, the implication being, 'Why should we Serbs finance in any way aid going to the enemy?'

I went to see Colonel Vujinovic. I explained that the bulk of the aid we brought into the so-called Srpska Republika remained there and kept his people alive. This aid came in through Croatia. The Croats did not insist on us having an escort and consequently there was no payment to them. I reminded him of the many promises, declarations and statements 'guaranteeing the free and unhindered passage of humanitarian aid' made by Dr Karadzic, his Vice-Presidents and his Ministers. Vujinovic refused to drop the issue. I refused to pay. The ever increasing bill became an agenda item at our weekly meetings but we never paid. They did, however, sting us for fuel for the escort vehicle, 20 litres per trip, and for a food packet if the escort was out late.

On 26 August some 'extremists' had fired seven shots from an automatic rifle into the Mufti's living-room. Amazingly there were no casualties.

The tenth of September started out a normal day. I left the house at 7.15 a.m. The office was very close, left turn, right turn, left turn, right turn and you are there. Not this day. As I took the second left there was a tank blocking the road. A second was manoeuvring into position. Troops were on the streets. Not the usual jaded, aimless, scruffy local soldiers but smart, fit, tough and surprisingly polite ones. I could see that they had ringed the military headquarters of General Talic. I could also see that they had blocked off the entrance to the municipal headquarters where I normally went to see the mayor. I found an alternative way to the office, radioed back to my breakfasting staff giving them the new route and waited for the local staff to come in, to see what they knew. When they arrived at eight, they were as excited and as amazed as I was. They told me that Radio Banja Luka was not broadcasting its usual programme and that the street rumour was that the town had been taken over by soldiers from the crack 16th Brigade. I knew the commander of this unit, Colonel Topic, a pre-war JNA regular officer. His troops had been in the front line since the very beginning of the war. He had fought against Croatian army forces before taking on the Bosnian army. He and his troops were considered to be the best. We were in for an interesting time.

We rang General Talic. He was 'on a conference'. I'll bet he was. It can't be much fun for a corps commander to wake up and discover his headquarters surrounded by mutinous troops. How had the tanks rumbled along miles of road at night, through many check-points without at least one officer checking with the headquarters?

We were unable to raise anybody. All our contacts were unavailable. The radio then announced that the town was under the control of a 'Crisis Committee'. The plot unfolded. The Crisis Committee was commanded by a captain. They had come from the front line and were refusing to go back until 'demands were met'. Basically they were fed up with fighting on the front line and returning home to find that their families had received little, but that some people were profiting very nicely from the war. One of their first actions was to close the restaurants and bars. The office girls used their contacts and found out what they could. There were two cordons, one blocking off the city centre and another on the outskirts of the town. We were scheduled to deliver aid, to receive aid and we had a convoy coming back from Zenica, which had told us by radio that it was stopped outside Banja Luka at a 'new check-point'.

The General was not answering his phone, neither was the mayor nor the chief of police. I decided to visit the Crisis Committee. I walked from the office with bold and brave Vesna. We got through two check-points and were close to the civic building opposite the municipal headquarters. It was in this building, facing the old seat of power, that the Crisis Committee had brazenly made its HQ. Here we were stopped. I explained that I wished to present my compliments to the commander. We were ushered into the building and told to report to his deputy.

We met him on the second floor. He was small, toothless and ruthless. We later learned that he had more notches on his gun belt than anyone else in the battalion. He told Vesna that he was pleased the UN was recognising their presence. I was not too happy with this interpretation but I needed them. Without their co-operation I was temporarily out of business. He took us in to see the captain, who looked worried, tired and not in command. I was amused to discover that his name is Zec, rabbit in Serbo-Croat. He looked like a frightened rabbit. I explained to him that if one of his aims was to stamp out corruption, he had my hundred per cent support. I outlined the aid which we brought in and expressed my doubts about the integrity of some of the distributing agencies. I then told him that I wanted the usual freedom of movement that HCR enjoyed. He told me that he would authorise the 'release' of the convoys returning from Zenica and that he would allow the freedom of movement of my convoys as long as they did not come into Banja Luka.

I asked about the freedom of movement of my staff, local and international. He told me that I had to submit an application for each vehicle and each staff member to him for his approval. I was quite happy with this. I returned to the office. My staff were not so happy; they were reluctant for their names to be given to the Crisis Committee. While I was discussing this point with them the phone rang. Colonel Vujinovic wished to speak to me. I went to see him but got no further than the 'rebel' troops.

Back in the office we spoke by phone. He had heard that I had been to see the Crisis Committee. He wished me to have nothing further to do with the 'rebels'. He told me that 'the corps commander is still in charge'. I gently pointed out that he was not even in charge of the access to his own headquarters, and explained all I had done and said. He asked me not to give legitimacy to the new committee by submitting requests to them. I promised to do my best.

The next week was fun. The Crisis Committee strong man proved to be a warrant officer. He upped his demands on a daily basis. Eventually he overstepped himself and asked for the resignation of the whole government. General Mladic came from Pale to sort out the situation. The rebels would not at first let him into the city. They demanded to see Dr Karadzic. General Mladic said that no way would he allow the President to suffer the indignity of having to pass check-points manned by dissenting troops. He invited the rebel commander to the airport outside Banja Luka to meet the President. The crafty warrant officer was not that stupid. He knew where his power base was. Eventually General Mladic came in and spoke to the troops. They were not as respectful as he expected. From this moment on they were doomed. The question was, would they be outmanoeuvred physically or mentally. Mladic decided on the mental approach. I think he chose this course because he was not too sure just how widespread this dissent was throughout the army. We had a good source of information from within the rebels, the boyfriend of one of our girls had served with them throughout the war and was manning one of their check-points. He believed that there were other battalions equally prepared to rebel. The sadness to me was that their cause for complaint was not the futility of the war but their disappointment at the behaviour of those who were not fighting alongside them in the trenches.

In the midst of all this excitement the deputy leader of the SDA party came to see me. Their leader, Mr Krzic, had disappeared. I immediately spoke to Michel Minnig of ICRC. He had also heard the news. We both tried all our contacts. The facts seemed to be that Krzic had left his house on the morning of 11 September, was seen heading towards the centre of town by some friends and then was seen in a police car by one man standing on a street corner near the military police barracks. We asked the legitimate authorities, but this proved difficult. We could not contact the mayor, apparently the Crisis Committee had placed him under house arrest. The General was too busy to worry about the safety of one Muslim activist.

The Chief of Police seemed to have lost some of his power to the Military Police, who looked as if they were leaning towards the Crisis Committee. I sent a polite letter to the Crisis Committee asking for their co-operation in establishing the whereabouts of Krzic. I never received an answer to this or to any other letter I wrote to them. Meanwhile my happy band of protection officers, led once again from the front by Louis, proved to be extra zealous in their investigations and were themselves arrested by the Military Police and carted off to the MP barracks. They were not to know it at the time, but they ended up only a cell or two away from Mr Krzic. When I arrived at the MP headquarters I was told the arrest of my staff was a misunderstanding. They were released immediately.

A few days later on the sixteenth at 1.30 p.m. we answered the phone, to hear the terrible news that the Mufti had been arrested. This made me feel sick. He was such a gentle man that I knew he would suffer mentally more than physically. I made the wisest decision that I had made for a long time. I rang Geneva and told Sylvana Foa, the head of UNHCR's Public Information department, what had happened. This was one of those days the phone worked when we really needed it. I then went to the old mosque to see Bedrudin Gusic, the head of the Islamic community. He was very frightened. The Mufti had been at home, a car-load of troops had arrived and arrested him and a young Imam from Srebrenica.

I left Georgios Karatzoglou with Bedrudin; if the soldiers returned to arrest any more from the Muslim community they would have a hard time with Georgios. He is a two-metre-plus, very stocky Greek with a bad temper, a short fuse and an over-inflated opinion of the value of a UNHCR card.

I went back to the office, wrote a protest note to the Crisis Committee and contacted Predrag Radic, the mayor, who, despite having problems of his own, promised to help. By three o'clock Sylvana had the news of the arrest of the Mufti on CNN, Sky and the BBC World Service. I spoke to Mr Gogic and to my contacts in Pale. By five o'clock the Mufti was free. He had been threatened but was unharmed.

It took Louis a further five days to get the Imam out, five days of constant aggravation. When he was released, he was in a bad way. Louis got him into the Banja Luka hospital, no easy achievement. Serb doctors are reluctant to treat Imams beaten up by Serb Military Police. It took seven days before the Imam could be moved. During this time the UNHCR protection team got him papers and a place on a convoy to Zagreb. Because he was then an ex-detainee he was able to find a third country to take him. Most countries, while not accepting refugees, will take as asylum seekers refugees who have been in prison. It is a cruel way to qualify. 'Every violent thunderstorm has a silver lining,' as I told each released prisoner, hoping that it translated into Serbo-Croat.

Getting the Imam out meant that we could concentrate on Mr Krzic. On the seventeenth, the rebel troops disappeared as quickly as they had arrived. Assurances were given that their leaders would be safe. I would not take a bet on the lives of the instigators at any odds. The Sarajevo-published pro-Bosnian government newspaper, *Oslobodjenje*, had an interesting theory. It suggested that the whole episode was organised by Mladic to prove that the troublesome independent Banja Luka corps commander, Talic, was not in control and therefore could be removed. Very Balkan. As Talic is still there at the time of writing, this theory was either incorrect or failed. Another mystery to be cleared up at the end of the war.

With the rebel troops out, the mayor was back in his office. We went to see him to discuss Krzic. He amazed me; he told me that Dr Karadzic was taking an interest in the case of Mr Krzic. He assured me that he did not know where he was but that he would do all in his power to help. Both UNHCR and ICRC spent hours of every day chasing up leads on Krzic or pleading his case with the authorities. I have to confess that I thought he was dead. But on the twenty-second he was released. I spent a fascinating, chilling couple of hours with him as he recounted his 'lost' days. He was a lucky man.

13

Tesanj and Maglaj

There should not be rivalry between aid agencies. We all share the same aims and the same goals. So, when I heard that ICRC had approval to enter Tesanj, I should have been happy. But I was not. I was fuming. I had put so much effort into getting in. Only the girls in the office knew how much it affected me. I rang Doboj. 'Mr Gogic, why ICRC and not me?'

'Mr Minnig never told the Serbs to burn in the hottest corner of hell,' replied the frank, honest and amused Mr Gogic.

The day arrived for ICRC to leave. I sat in the office. I rang them, wished them luck and watched them go. Early in the afternoon, I received a call from ICRC. Their lead vehicle had hit a mine. It was totally destroyed. No one was too sure about casualties. My first reaction was one of anger. ICRC in Banja Luka had limited experience of crossing active front lines. Of all the ICRC delegates that I have dealt with I liked Michel best. I hoped he was all right. News came back slowly. There were no deaths. Then we heard there were no casualties. Finally we heard that the convoy was returning.

Now I could smile. Sorry, but smile I did. The way was open for UNHCR. The Serbs had shown that they wanted a convoy to reach Tesanj. They were obviously claiming that the mine which blew up the vehicle was a 'Muslim' one. ICRC as an organisation was not going to race back in. I pressed hard. 'We have a convoy ready. We have experience. Give us approval.'

The following day I went to see Michel. He was OK. They had had a fright but were in good spirits. More importantly Michel was determined that I should succeed. He drew maps and briefed me as thoroughly as was possible.

Approval came for me to go to Tesanj, followed rapidly by approval for me to go also to Maglaj. Zagreb reacted rapidly: a Scandinavian convoy for Tesanj and a Brit one for Maglaj. I was to take the Tesanj one in, return to Teslic, then pick up the Brit one and head for Maglaj.

The convoy from Zagreb arrived in Banja Luka. The drivers were as hungry for success as I was; the chance of delivering aid direct to a besieged town was why they had signed up. MSF Holland were to join us. They had a vehicle full of vital medicine. Their team was a bright, happy, handsome and charming Dutch doctor, Bert Schilte, and a real character of a Brit, Peter Milne, whom I had met initially when he was a driver, part of the very first successful convoy into Sarajevo. He had motored from Split in Croatia with two of his trademarks: wearing a kilt and smoking a pipe. Peter is one of those men every small team should have, perennially happy and a fixer. Stowed away in their already over-crowded vehicle was Brian McCloskey, a World Health Organis-ation doctor, originally from traumatic Northern Ireland where, I think, he was a neuro-surgeon. He was now a public health special-ist in soporific Worcester, loaned to WHO. Brian, who is very much a hands-on doctor, had 'escaped' from the WHO office in comfortable Zagreb.

At the last minute I was called to the army corps headquarters. I went with trepidation. I knew that Colonel Vujinovic was away. Major King met me at the door with a sinister smile. The route was changed; no explanation. As I was expecting the bastard to cancel the convoy, my smile was much broader than his. New routes I could cope with. In fact it was awful. It would take us along a track with a very poor surface and some pretty wicked bends. The aim, presumably, was at best to slow us down, at worst to prevent us getting through.

After hours of driving, the Scandahooligans got us to the Serb front line at Vukovici. The track passed through a clearing in the woods. On both sides there were Serb soldiers in trenches, all members of the renowned 16th Brigade. They were quite friendly, but the convoy was halted. We had to wait for Colonel Topic, the legendary commander, to arrive. He is tough and independent. It was his merry men who had barricaded Banja Luka and his captain who was still incarcerated in some Serb military *kalaboos*. He is about five feet nine, solid, intelligent and quite a handsome man. He was obviously in charge. He greeted me courteously, I introduced him to Serb Vesna, they chatted and the ice was broken. We discussed General Mladic, Banja Luka and the war.

Meanwhile the convoy stayed in line, with engines running to keep the cabs warm. Colonel Topic asked me if I had been debriefed by ICRC. I told him I had. 'OK. I know I have orders to let the convoy through, so let's do it quickly and as professionals. You go forward about 50 metres, then you turn left. On the left you will see my front-line trench, in front of it are the remains of the ICRC vehicle. Immediately ahead of you is the road. That is no man's land. To the right is Croat and Muslim territory. Once around that corner they can see you. Do not be surprised if they fire on you. Once you pass my front-line trench I cannot guarantee your safety. I said the same to Minnig of ICRC. He ignored me and he lost his vehicle. He could have lost his life.'

'Will you accompany me to your front-line trench?'

His face broke into a big smile. 'Are you scared?' he asked me.

'No. Cautious. Are you coming?' I replied.

'No.'

Big smile from me. 'Are you scared?' I asked him.

'No. Cautious,' he replied and smiled.

I liked Topic.

I went forward wearing a bullet-proof jacket and a helmet. Vesna stayed with Topic. I noticed that they moved forward, keeping a safe distance but ensuring that Vesna was within earshot. As I turned left I saw the Serb trench. There were two soldiers in it. They were relaxed and smiling. One of them pointed over to my right where about 50 metres away I could see movement on the hillside. 'Muslims,' the Serb said.

In front of the trench were the remains of the ICRC vehicle. It was badly damaged. How they all got out safely I do not know. Immediately before me there was a large mound of earth half the width of the road. The remainder of the road was blocked by boulders. 'Mines,' said the Serb, pointing to the mound of earth.

It was obviously the route that Michel's vehicle had taken. There might be more mines, there might not. Just off the right-hand side of the road there was an unexploded hand grenade. A further 20 metres ahead there was a small makeshift bridge spanning a gap caused initially by subsidence, then enhanced by the Minnig mine. The left-hand side of it looked fairly solid but on the right-hand side the track and bridge disappeared in a heap of rubble, stone and twisted metal. I was hoping to send twenty-ton trucks over this.

From the right side of the tracks I could hear voices from the Bosnian-held hills. I shouted that I was UNHCR and raised my arms to show I was unarmed. Normally at this stage the Serbs would fire a single round. They would claim it had come from the 'Muslim' side. They would hope that the shot would frighten me off and that I would go back. They would also hope that the Bosnian forces would reply, thus allowing them to say, 'You bring a convoy here and they fire on you.' Topic was a thorough professional. He knew that one stray round would not frighten me away. He also knew that it could start a fire-fight, putting his soldiers at risk. When Topic decided to fight or to be difficult, he was vicious. War was no game to him.

I could see almost the whole length of the road between the Serbs' foremost trench and the first Bosnian post. The no man's stretch was about 100 metres long. I turned to walk back and found Topic and Vesna standing by the Serb trench. 'Colonel, I want to walk forward and make contact with the other side.'

'Fine.'

I walked back to the MSF truck, briefed Peter and the two docs, then called forward the convoy leader. I explained what I had seen: the destroyed vehicle, the mound of earth, the unexploded grenade, the damaged track and the proximity of the Bosnians. I told them of my intention to go forward. Vesna walked with me to the mound of earth. She was wearing her bullet-proof jacket and her helmet. She looked worried and very vulnerable. I asked her to wait at the mound, to watch, to observe and to try to hear any words shouted to me from the Bosnian side.

I approached the mound of earth. I could see the track taken by the ICRC vehicle. Where the thing had blown up, there would have been a fair bit of reckless movement, so I could safely assume that there were no anti-personnel mines in the mound. There might be more anti-tank but my 13 stone was not going to set these off. It was possible that the Serbs would place some anti-personnel mines there at nightfall. But I felt that I trusted Topic. Slowly I walked on to the mound. Step by step I advanced, carefully choosing a place to put my foot that looked 'clean' and firm. Once over the mound I walked to the point where the track was at its worst. I could see that this was going to test the drivers' skills. Once over this obstacle and round the corner, I was on a stretch of tarmac. Excellent. It is much easier to see mines in or on tarmac. At a glance I could see shrapnel and tails from mortars which had hit the road.

I walked very slowly, hands up in the air, shouting that I was 'UNHCR, Mr Larry'. It is a strange sensation. You feel like a ham actor in a 'B' film: conspicuous and slightly ridiculous. And you feel really, really high. One nervous soldier, one psychopath from either side, and you are dead.

I could hear words shouted back at me from the opposite hill. I looked back. Vesna was at the end of the road, too close for her safety but close enough for my morale. 'It's OK,' she said. Whatever was being shouted was not detrimental to my health.

I passed the half-way point and began to see soldiers at the Bosnian end. They were smiling. Any thoughts of quickening my pace were kept in check by the sight of anti-tank mines. The mines were wired together in threes on long, thin wooden boards which had been laid on the road to form a deadly zigzag chicane. I stepped over them. When I reached the Bosnian location I first saw a Croat flag flying from a house to the right down a lane. This was the Croat check-point.

But the first man to approach me extended his hand and said: 'Mustafa.' He was in uniform and on his sleeve was the Bosnian shield. He was a very tall, gangling, garrulous man with an almost overpowering friendliness. My first thought was that he was drunk, but I could smell no alcohol and he was steady on his feet. 'Bring convoy,' Mustafa continued.

'Yes,' I said with pride.

'Serbs OK?'

'Yes. I have a message from Topic for your commander. Where is your commander?'

'Comes.'

By now I was surrounded by Bosnian soldiers, all wanting to talk to me. 'Wait. I go get translator,' I said, accompanying my words with my best charades hand movements.

'OK.'

I walked back. No, I remember I strolled back. I felt good. Vesna was waiting with Topic. 'Come on, I need you,' I said to Vesna, then to Topic: 'Colonel, if the Bosnian agrees, will you meet him in the middle?'

Topic smiled. 'No weapons. No bodyguards.'

'I'll try.'

Vesna and I walked to the Bosnian lines. I introduced Bosnian Vesna to Bosnian Mustafa. She was then bombarded with questions from every direction, especially when they heard that she is from Sarajevo. It appeared that everybody had somebody living in Sarajevo. Apparently we were in the village of Kriz, a combined Croat and Muslim post.

Soon the Bosnian commander arrived, a very tall, handsome, intelligent-looking man. Younger-looking than Topic, but I sensed that they were equal adversaries. He was very pleased to see me. He knew that we were coming. He had hoped that we would not be put off by the ICRC incident. I asked him if the mine had been laid by him.

'Five metres from a Serb trench? I wish it had.'

'Have you planted any mines in the no man's land?'

'No.'

'Have the Serbs?'

'I do not know, but I doubt it. We dominate the road. But on a dark night . . .'

I put to him my suggestion that he and Topic should meet in the middle of no man's land. The Bosnian commander was agreeable. I left Vesna with them and walked down to Topic. 'OK. Let's go.' I said.

He called over his number two and handed to him his belt, holster and pistol. It was an understated, very professional and very brave gesture. We walked to the centre together. He stood in full view on the empty road. The Bosnian commander followed his lead and came with Vesna to the centre. He tried to come alone but Mustafa would not stay behind. They were both unarmed.

'Shall I send Mustafa back?' I asked Topic.

'No, he is harmless. I know him well.'

They all greeted each other, their first face-to-face contact for almost one year. I watched Mustafa, worried that he could become dangerous. They began to talk.

I left them. Vesna and I walked back. I collected a bottle of whisky from my vehicle and gave it to Topic's number two. 'Take this out to them.' He readily agreed. I was happier because then it was two and two.

Vesna and I discussed Mustafa. Her observation was much more accurate than mine: 'He's shell-shocked.' A diagnosis from a Sarajevo girl that I would never dispute.

After ten minutes and half the bottle I returned. 'Do you mind if I get my show on the road?'

Topic spoke to his deputy. He came back to the Serb lines with me.

The first problem was the 'blind' grenade. To my surprise it was no longer there.

Next problem was the earth mound, forward of the last Serb trench. Did it contain any mines? A few of us had now walked over it but that was not a sufficient test. I asked for volunteers among the convoy drivers to dig a path through the mound. I was swamped with volunteers but we had only two shovels. I asked the Serb deputy if I could borrow some shovels. His men were living in trenches, there could be no shortage of them. To my great surprise, not only did he provide shovels but men as well. This was a really good sign. If the Serbs had recently laid any mines in the mound, they were unlikely to stand over us as we picked our way through.

The ICRC mine was either laid by the Bosnians and their commander had denied it, or by the Serbs who had then forgotten it was there, or by the Serbs who knew it was there and had let Michel motor over it. The fact that they watched us dig led me to believe that they were pretty sure there were no anti-personnel mines in the area.

Digging the tracks was slow, hard work, and in truth the shovels soon all found themselves in the hands of the Danes. They cut through the mound of rocks, rubble and clay two tracks the width of the wheels of their trucks. We now had a path for our transport. But we still could not guarantee that under our newly made tracks there would be no mines.

I went to see both commanders and explained the next part of my plan. 'I am going to bring up one of the heaviest trucks, reverse it and motor it backwards over the tracks through the mound. Ten tons of flour will set off any anti-tank mine. With a bit of luck the driver will be sufficiently far away from the blast to be OK. Please warn your men, so that if there is a bang we do not start a war.' Both commanders thought it was a good idea. In truth I had hoped they would both agree that it was an unnecessary precaution, which would imply that they both knew there were no more mines. That they agreed with me implied that they did not. Neither of these commanders knew what their predecessors had left. I went to see the convoy leader. We chose the heaviest, longest truck. I suggested that I should drive it.

'You?' said the Danish driver. 'Not bloody likely. You might scratch it.' Wearing his bullet-proof jacket and his helmet, he reversed his truck up to the mound. We moved away. He backed his rear wheels over the tracks we had made.

Silence.

Back and forth went his rear wheels, defining a safe path for the trucks. He rejoined the convoy. We lined up. I shook Topic's hand, agreed a time of return – nine the next morning – and away we went.

The tracks of my vehicle and that of MSF were not as wide as the truck's, but my trip into Srebrenica had taught me that mine was not heavy enough to set off a land mine. The ICRC vehicle was armoured and therefore two tons heavier than mine. Peter Milne knew this, I knew this, the docs were not as convinced.

We paused at Kriz. A Bosnian soldier with a TV camera asked if he could travel on the bonnet of my vehicle and film the convoy. I thought he meant for the initial few yards, but he perched on the bonnet for the whole 10 or so kilometres. It was pouring with rain and he got soaked, but so did we. I could not use the windscreen wiper for fear of knocking him off. So we had to wind down the side windows and see through them. As we passed through tiny villages, the population lined the route and waved and cheered. Their waves were returned by our ecstatic acrobatic cameraman. I was really worried that he might fall off and end up under the wheels. We had two doctors in the following vehicle but we had come to save lives, not to hazard them. The Bosnian commander, in a battered police vehicle, led our way into Tesanj. By now it was late. They had chosen a warehouse on the outskirts of the town where we would unload. We motored the convoy in. This was a little disappointing as we were unable to see Tesanj itself or to meet many of the people. The drivers were undeterred; they knew they had brought in the first aid for five months. They unloaded rapidly and prepared themselves for the night. There was the rumble of distant shelling, but we felt safe.

On our arrival at the warehouse I reminded the commander that we had the MSF truck full of medicines for the hospital. A short while later, after darkness had fallen, a civilian came to collect us to take us there. It was a short distance away, but in the city itself. We were therefore able to see, by silhouette, the extent of the destruction. It was bad, but not as bad as I had anticipated. At the hospital we were met by the mayor of Tesanj, Muhamed Clanjak, who is a doctor himself, and his charming wife, a dentist. We were taken to the office of the hospital director, Dr Ekrem Ajanovic, who was formerly a professor at Tuzla university. He briefed us on the medical situation. They had wired up a bulb to a car battery to illuminate the office. They had had no visitors for more than four months, no supplies for ten. They were desperate to talk. Brian McCloskey and Bert listened patiently to their many tales. We met the two surgeons who had carried out two thousand operations in ten months. Their eyes were red, their faces drawn and lined, but as they recounted their successes and saw the wonderment and admiration in the faces of the visiting doctors their eyes sparkled with pride. Ninety-five per cent of the two thousand cases were caused by war trauma. An average day brought three deaths. Surprisingly there had been six hundred births in the past ten months, two hundred down on the previous year's figure. There were one hundred and thirty TB patients whose treatment had stopped for lack of medicines.

We then toured the hospital by candlelight. Nurses held make-shift lamps containing home-made rag wicks and burning oil. The hospital had been designed to have one hundred patients. It now had one hundred and fifty, the majority of whom lay in beds in the corridors. The wards had windows facing the Serb positions. Many Serb shells and sniper rounds had landed in the wards. The beds in the corridors, the burning oil lamps, the smell, the stained bandages, the blood, the gore, the shadows were how I had imagined hospitals in the Crimea. These latter-day Florence Nightingales took us from bed to bed. Accompanying and assisting them was a tall, slim young man, aged maybe sixteen. Gentle and innocent, his face untouched by a razor, his voice still not broken, he had volunteered for work in the hospital at the beginning of the war, almost two years before, and had never left.

We had been told that some of the patients were victims of mushroom poisoning. This was particularly poignant as these people are rural dwellers. They knew the risks, but preferred them to starvation. In one bed lay a very pretty ten-year-old girl. She had been brought in with mushroom poisoning. Her sister had already died. Her mother was at her bedside. As she lay sleeping, with her shallow breathing and her beautiful looks, I was convinced that she would live. She was surrounded by amputees and open wounds but in the flickering candlelight she looked like Sleeping Beauty. Sadly it was the Prince of Death who visited her in the night.

As we stumbled out of the hospital in the pitch dark, the doctors reminded us of their most urgent needs: fuel to run the generator, so that they could perform operations at night and run dialysis machines and incubators, anaesthetics, blood plasma, vaccines.

We returned to the warehouse. The drivers were surrounded by people from Tesanj, sharing their cigarettes, their food and their stories. We who had visited the hospital were quite depressed, but not for long. The irrepressible Peter Milne had found out before leaving Banja Luka that today was Brian McCloskey's birth-day – his fortieth. Peter produced a four-course meal which included salmon and was concluded by whisky. All that then remained was to find a place for Vesna to have her nightly ablutions and a discreet weewee; then sleeping bags out and the enveloping sleep of the emotionally drained.

The following morning we left at seven. I had said that we would cross at nine. We were at the Croat–Bosnian check-point at eight. Visibility was about 30 metres. I had no intention of emerging unannounced out of the mist at the Serb front line. The Bosnian commander had occasional radio contact with the Serb front line. The radio operators at each end were both local boys, had been to school together and were in the same class. The call sign of the Bosnian Serb was Geneva and the Bosnian Muslim Paris. Paris alias Hakija tried to raise Geneva alias Mirko, but the batteries were too weak.

In the meantime Vesna went off to explore Kriz and found a three-year-old boy called Mario. He lived in Kriz, in a house on the very front line. His parents, a young Croat couple, refused to leave their home. The detritus of war were the playthings of Mario. Vesna gave him cuddles and chocolate.

By eight thirty the mist had cleared sufficiently for me to feel safe in walking down no man's land. Vesna insisted on accompanying me. At the half-way point we were met by a happy, smiling Topic and his deputy. Topic invited the Bosnian commander for slivovic. I brought the convoy forward. There was much self-congratulation on all sides. For at least thirty minutes Serb-side soldiers mingled with Bosnian-side. I shook hands with all and thanked them, especially Topic. I watched as the Bosnian commander returned to his lines. I felt good, that I had broken the ice. We drove back to Banja Luka, arriving at ten thirty. By then the Serbs had shelled Tesanj.

Back in Banja Luka we had time only to write a quick report, make a number of phone calls, go to the loo, eat, wash and change. I said a fond farewell to the Danes and awaited the arrival of the Brit convoy, whose leader, big 'Ginger' Dawes, I knew well. 'Ginge' is an ex-warrant officer in the Parachute Regiment. Paras are either lean and mean like greyhounds, or big and square like bull mastiffs. Ginge is more than six feet tall, very heavy-looking, with a bright, cheerful, open face, topped by a good head of ginger hair. He has a ginger moustache, a Northern accent and a 'let's get it done, lads' attitude. He has a great sense of humour and a gentleness which belies his size and former training. I often watched him and found it difficult to see him as a bawling, beasting para senior rank. Also, with his size, it is not easy to imagine him dangling on the end of a parachute. Perhaps he has mellowed and spread with retirement.

The convoy drivers always fascinated me. The Scandinavians were young, smart, bright and arrogant. The German team were slightly older and a mixed but disciplined bunch. The Brit teams were special. They looked as if they had been recruited by a press gang touring motorway transport cafés. They were, in the main, ex-soldiers, tattooed, crude, rude and vulgar. They wore T-shirts bearing convoy logos or obscene graffiti, T-shirts which they pulled on over their eleven-months-pregnant stomachs. T-shirts which never quite managed to stay in their trousers and which therefore constantly revealed the first month or two of their brewery bellies. T-shirts which revealed in grotesque detail their belly-buttons, forced and stretched to protrusion by breakfasts at 'greasy spoon' caffs and the foaming brown contents of pint glasses.

The mere hint of a ray of the sun is a magnet to all lorry drivers. As it peeks through the sky, they divest themselves, the Scandinavians to turn their ski-toned muscles a subtle brown, the Brits to blur their tattoos a lobster pink.

'Are we going to get through, Larry?' asked big Ginge.

'No question, my friend. If the Scandies could get me into Tesanj, we can get into Maglaj.'

'My lads won't let you down. Just show us the way.'

We set out in the early afternoon with a Serb police escort of one battered Golf and two men. The police had been briefed by Major King and, surprise, surprise, we were going the scenic route – a route full of bends and pot-holes that would add on at least 25 kilometres – not the direct one. On the outskirts of Teslic we were stopped at the entrance to the military headquarters which were in a large house on the right-hand side of the road. A group of heavily armed and aggressive soldiers told our police escort that we had no approval to proceed and must return to Banja Luka. Their spokesman was a huge Serb with a shaven skull. He wore uniform but no hat, an aggressive brute with a smirk on his lips and the smell of alcohol on his breath. Our police escort were frightened. They did not want to be associated with us. With Vesna, I got out of the car and we walked over to the group of soldiers. They were all noisy and some were not sober.

The sneering giant barracked Vesna. 'Why are you, a Serb, helping them to feed the enemy?'

Whenever this happened, we had a pattern for defence. 'She is here to speak my words. Not to answer your questions. Get me your commander immediately.' Even translating someone else's words is not easy when the atmosphere is hostile and electric. She got back a stream of abuse. I waded in with very heavy words, demanding in the name of military discipline that I see the commander.

The harsh words, the tone and the noisy response eventually produced from the house a young officer, a captain, who was the adjutant to the commander. 'The commander is out. He will return late. Please go back to Banja Luka. By tomorrow the whole thing will have been sorted out.'

'Yes,' I said, 'but not to my satisfaction. Vesna,' I continued, 'tell him that I will stay here until I see the commander.'

The young captain was reasonable but made one telling point. 'I am sorry, Mr Larry, but I cannot guarantee your safety here, especially when it gets dark. Please return.'

'My dear friend, we stay.'

I walked away with Vesna and briefed Ginger and the MSF crew, Bert and Peter. Brian, the WHO adventurer, was returning to Zagreb with the jubilant Danes to inform the world on the conditions in Tesanj.

I returned to my vehicle. The large, bald Serb hurled an obscenity our way, which brought laughter and jeers from his companions. Vesna and I got back into the vehicle and locked the doors. She was white.

'Are you scared of him,' I asked her, nodding in the direction of the vulgar Serb.

Her answer was simple: 'Horribly.'

As we waited, the aggro built up outside the headquarters.

More soldiers gathered. More crowded around our vehicle and some banged on the bonnet and kicked the tyres. Eventually the commander and a number of his officers arrived in a convoy of three motors. He was briefed by the soldiery. Vesna listened to what was going on through our car window. She firmly warned me that the situation was explosive. I left our car and we approached. I offered the usual courtesies, but received a torrent of insults which needed no translation.

The commander was about fifty. He looked a petty but educated man. His message to me was simple: 'Go back. You have no approval. We do not want you here. Get out of here before it gets dark.'

I hate rudeness when I am trying to be nice. 'Commander, I have approval from Dr Karadzic, Mr Koljevic, General Mladic and General Talic to go forward. I have in my possession a piece of paper signed in Pale approving this convoy and this route. I respectfully ask for your co-operation in permitting the convoy to move forward.'

Now, I have to tell you that at this stage I was bluffing not only him but myself. I knew that, even if I got his approval, it was now too late to move off towards the Croat front line. It was too easy at night to lob a lone shell on to a slow-moving, unarmed, unescorted convoy, in a war zone at the front line. If he had been really clever he would have waved me forward. That would have tested the Hollingworth hot-planning facility! However, I judged that the battle was one between being forced back to Banja Luka or staying where we were till dawn. Back to Banja Luka would mean the end of this convoy's chances.

The commander taxed Vesna's vocabulary with a range of Serbo-Croat invective. She, poor girl, knows that English has twice as many words as German and four times as many as French, but has a paucity of swear words. She conveyed the mood, if not the mode. It transpired that this particular warlord, like so many others, had little respect for his seniors and superiors.

Time for me to huff and puff: white beard, white hair reflecting red cheeks, puce lips and green eyes. 'I am amazed by your disloyalty. What hope is there for you? You claim to be fighting for a sovereign state, Srpska Republika. You, you are a rebel commanding a rabble. This convoy is for women and children. Where is your Serb humanity? Where is your Serb chivalry? Where is your Serb loyalty? I have come here with approval, where is your famed Serb hospitality?'

Vesna translated all this, word for word. I knew she was frightened. Her face was white. She, of course, could hear the soldiers' comments, the taunts aimed at her Serbness or, more specifically, what they perceived to be her lack of it. She began by saying 'He says'. This was good as it at least slightly distanced her from me. If she had started to translate in the first person – I am amazed by your disloyalty – she might have got no further. Somewhat unfairly, I prefer a female translator. They can say far more than a male. The recipient is not likely to knock them down or arrest them. Also very few males have the courage to translate harsh words to men of violence in a dangerous environment.

The commander was shocked by the vehemence of my attack. It provoked much discussion among his colleagues. I pestered Vesna to tell me what was going on. She asked me to be patient. After a long minute or two the commander told me to wait and he entered the headquarters. Vesna advised that we get back into our vehicle away from the soldiers. Back there, in comparative safety, she briefed me on all she had heard. 'They do not want the convoy to proceed but they know that it has approval. The commander is being pressed by the toughs to send you back. The young officer is advising that we are parked here for the night. They have gone inside for the discussions to avoid pressure from the drunken soldiers.'

With the leadership inside, the soldiers moved around our vehicles. Using the radio, I advised all drivers to stay in their locked cabs but discovered that Ginge had already ordered this. Every fifteen or so minutes, Vesna and I got out and walked to the gate to find out if the commander wished to see us. It was important to show that we were not frightened and that we would not go away. After about an hour the crowd of soldiers had thinned out. It was cold and dark.

On our next visit to the gate of the headquarters we were invited in. The atmosphere was entirely different, the young officer took us into a room with armchairs in which were seated the commander and some of his officers. We were asked to sit down and offered slivovic.

'You cannot go forward tonight. You cannot stay where you are. You will have to park your convoy in the hotel car-park a few kilometres back at Banja Vrucica,' said the commander.

They all waited for my reaction. 'Very wise decision, Commander.' They were all delighted, not half as much as I was. But,' I continued, 'I have been guaranteed safety while on the Serb territory. I demand a guard, preferably police, to look after the convoy during the night.'

The commander told me that a police guard was beyond his ability but that he would produce soldiers. Reluctantly I accepted, knowing full well that they would be the same gang that had given us so much hassle already.

'Furthermore, I wish to leave for Maglaj at 0700 hours in the morning.'

The commander said, 'OK.'

The next problem was to turn the convoy round. The road we were parked on was far too narrow for the trucks to turn in. Ginge and I went ahead and found an entrance to a field, where each vehicle could drive past, then reverse. This we would have to do ten times. It was going to be a long, tedious night. While one of Ginge's crew sorted this out, we went off to the hotel, escorted by our police car which had reappeared. The hotel was a famous spa centre before the war and had some excellent buildings. I had been there on a number of occasions with Mr Gogic for conferences. The car-park was large and tarmacked. However, we were directed by the police and the soldiers to park on the far side of the empty car-park, furthest away from the hotel entrance and next to a line of trees. I made it clear to the police that they were to return to escort us on to Maglaj at seven the following morning. Slowly the trucks arrived and were parked up. Noisily the guards arrived, all tanked up and with a ghetto-blaster radio. They looked far more like the local street gang that they were, than the soldiers they pretended to be. The drivers began to cook and brew, the soldiers to cadge and barrack.

I briefed Ginge and Peter Milne, left the convoy in their capable hands and went with Vesna to the hotel. The manager met us, bought us a drink and offered us rooms – all of us. His offer was genuine, but I knew that if we left the vehicles unattended and at the mercy of the so-called guard we would have nothing left for Maglaj by morning. He was determined to be hospitable, so he invited Vesna and myself to his house, which was about 100 metres the other side of the line of trees where the convoy was parked. We went for one drink, but while there, discovered that his hobby was collecting mushrooms and that he had a fridge full of frozen dried mushrooms. He was insistent that we try them and his wife cooked an enormous pan of them. I still had the vision of the Sleeping Beauty in my mind and was not much in the mood for them. Also, I was not absolutely certain that all those he had collected were safe to eat. Some were enormous, some of strange shapes and colours. But once the smell wafted from the kitchen I threw caution to the wind. They were delicious. The manager then offered Vesna and myself a bed for the night at his home. I was already feeling guilty at having left the convoy for so long, so we declined but used the facilities. He kindly completed his hospitality by walking us back to the convoy.

The guard, by now, were dangerous. They had no officer with them, they were taunting the drivers and attempting to steal anything. Bert Schilte, the MSF doc, had pitched his camp bed on top of his landcruiser. One of our drivers in the vehicle next to Bert's found one of the guard attempting to steal one of his jerrycans and pushed him away. The soldier replied by loosing off a burst from his Kalashnikov. The hail of bullets whistled through the sky, the initial trajectory missing the reclining Bert by millimetres.

Ginge, Peter and myself reviewed the situation. The drivers were tough and determined to protect their load and their possessions, but we were all unarmed. The burst of fire had brought no visitors from the headquarters. We were on our own with a lawless, drunken bunch. I had the added complication of Vesna. Would they respect her? Should I take her to the house of the manager? Would we get there safely? What would we do if there was a serious incident and no translator? I had a lot of faith in her ability to charm and to tame.

I made a decision: all the drivers into their cabs. If they heard noises around their vehicles, they could shout and bang on the cab, but no one was to leave them. There was a quick flurry to the bushes, a return to the cabs, a clicking and locking of doors. The night air was frequently penetrated by shouts and bangs. Sleep came to few. By morning we had lost a hundred or so litres of fuel and four or five bags of flour. It could have been a lot worse. I cannot remember a time when I was happier to see dawn break. We were ready to roll by seven but there was no escort. The police eventually turned up an hour late and went directly to the hotel for breakfast. I was livid. I went in and bawled them out. But even the meek driver had been emboldened by the behaviour of the soldiers. He kept us waiting a further twenty minutes. I marked his card and had my revenge later.

We set off for Zepce. We had no trouble at the Teslic head-quarters. But the route was a killer, a track, barely the width of the vehicles, with some very tight bends. The first, a hairpin, was after only a few minutes of driving. The track was muddy and each of the vehicles had to run at it. The drivers, who had had so little sleep and so much hassle, were marvellous.

We eventually reached the Serb–Croat front line on the top of a hill at a place called Tadici. Why it was called anything I do not know, there was nothing there but a barrier. Going into Tesanj two days previously we had passed through the Serb lines to the joint Muslim–Croat post. The northern end of the pocket was defended by Muslims and Croats against the besieging Serbs. Here at the southern end of the same besieged pocket the com-bined might of the Serbs and the Croats was encircling the Bosnians.

Our police escort stopped on the Serb side and said they would await our return. Although here the Croats and Serbs were allies, there was not much love or trust between them. Our escort asked for some food, I refused, but this was not my revenge. That was still to come.

The Croats were not surprised to see us. The commander told me we had to wait, as the route into Zepce was blocked and he wished to send down a crane to clear it for our benefit. From the top of the hill where we were parked we could see the whole road. It was not blocked and traffic was moving up and down. At intervals I got out to talk to the commander about the progress of the road clearance. He kept a straight face as I became more irritated. Whatever plot they had in mind was now in place. We were free to find out and face it. The Croat army, the HVO, provided an escort. It sped away ahead of us. We followed at what was obviously too slow a pace, for after a short while the escort car stopped and told me to speed up the convoy. I replied that for the last hour we had proceeded at his pace, we would now proceed at mine. We turned left at Ozimica and headed towards Maglaj. The military escort vehicle was still pushing the pace. We passed the Catholic church on our right and turned the bend to approach the last Croat village, Brancovici, before the run into Maglaj.

As we came out of the bend, my heart sank. The escort car slowed. Blocking the road were a large group of women and children. The convoy came to a halt and the soldiers in the escort car disappeared into the crowd. I got out of my vehicle and approached the crowd. Through Vesna, they told me they were the wives, mothers and children of thirty-four Croats who had fought for Maglaj against the Serbs but had been imprisoned when the Croats changed overnight to the Serb side. They believed that the 'Muslim' action was treacherous. They had with them two soldiers who had been part of the group, but who had escaped. They told me stories of being used as forced labour, digging trenches on the front line and of collecting air-dropped aid which had landed in the minefields. The atmosphere was not tense. The women were emotional but rational. They would not let the convoy go through until their loved ones were released.

My first task was to make sure they understood that I had no intention of driving the convoy through them. I therefore turned my vehicle around, so that it faced away from Maglaj. The convoy, of course, remained facing it. I then went and explained to Peter and Ginge what was happening. I asked them to keep their drivers near the cabs but to make no forward movement. Friendly fraternisation was to be encouraged.

My next task was to try to find the decision makers. There was a Catholic priest among the crowd. I approached him and asked if he could find the leaders of the ladies so that I could meet privately with them. He agreed and quickly arranged a meeting. We met in the garden of a large house on the left-hand side of the road at the corner of the women's road block. We sat at a wooden bench and table. However, too many people gathered round and the proceedings were becoming orchestrated. The priest seemed to have a lot of influence. He was aged about forty-five, was the local parish priest and looked forceful and fit. He had a stentorian voice. I suggested that we found somewhere quieter. He had a word with one of the crowd and a group of about six of us were taken off to a building to the left of the garden. We went up a flight of stairs, entered a small room and sat at a table. Coffee was produced for everyone and for me slivovic accompanied it. I sat at the head of the small table, Vesna to my left and the women on my right. The priest, who was quiet, sat in between the women and slightly behind them.

One woman opened the talks, she was about thirty-five and very sincere. 'My husband is a prisoner in Maglaj. My children are downstairs. You can see them. They want their father. I want my husband. If he can come out, you can go in.'

A second woman interrupted: 'You can go, on your own, bring our men out and then take in the convoy.'

'I can't,' I replied. 'I cannot link aid to prisoners. I cannot buy my way in and buy my way out. I just want to take food in. You know they are starving in there; women and children, mothers like yourselves. They too are victims of the war. Please let the convoy go in, let me feed them. While I am there I will try to see your men. At least I can bring you news from them.'

The priest spoke to them.

'Can you negotiate their release while you are there?' one of the ladies asked me.

'I can try. I cannot guarantee that I can bring anyone out. But I can try. But to be able to try I need to go in and I can't go in without the convoy.'

They talked among themselves. The priest occasionally inter-jected. Vesna listened. I observed her. It seemed to be going well. Some of the women had tears in their eyes as they spoke. The priest seemed to steer the conversation but not to lead.

The priest then asked: 'Will you take in with you Father Stipo, who is the parish priest of Maglaj. We would like him to see the prisoners.'

I knew this could be a big problem. Implicit in the request was that I guarantee his safety. I could not guarantee my own. It had occurred to me and to my masters that the Maglaj authorities might take us hostage. To the Bosnian Muslim authorities in Maglaj, a Catholic priest could be an incentive or an added bonus. Furthermore, would Maglaj think that I was bringing a spy into their midst? Nevertheless, with the sniff of Maglaj air in my nostrils I replied: 'Of course.' I then rose from the table, determined to keep the initiative. 'I will do all I can for you,' I told the ladies. 'I can guarantee nothing. At least I will make sure that your priest sees your men.'

We left the room and I strode positively towards the vehicles to brief Ginge and MSF. 'I think we are on our way.'

MSF were looking very pleased with themselves. Peter had visited a house close by in order to fill up his water bottle and had found the lady of the house in bed. Her daughter was with her and she told Peter that her mother was dying of cancer. Peter went back and brought Bert. The old lady had had a breast removed and was in great pain. Somehow she also had a broken arm. She had been prescribed the drug Fortral, but none was available. Bert had some in his truck and had given it to her.

'She'll die soon but her last days will now be more peaceful.'

Taking in the priest worried me, so I contacted Zagreb. I asked them to get in touch with Tuzla and tell Maglaj a priest was coming with us. The word spread among the crowd that we were on our way. Some seemed pleased, others, mainly men, continued to look surly and to be obstructive. We waited for the priest to arrive, for the barrier to be removed.

While we waited, a family came across to us, led by a woman aged about forty-eight. 'Are you Vesna?' she asked of my translator.

'Yes.'

'Vesna Stancic?'

'Yes.'

'I am your Aunt Lucija. Here is your cousin.'

Vesna had found a long-lost branch of the family. The aunt had last seen her more than ten years before but had recognised the features and knew that we had come from Sarajevo. There was much cuddling and kissing and swapping of stories, which helped to pass the time while we allowed the locals to prepare for our departure at their own pace. I felt it was important that we left with dignity and accord. We still had to return and I was pretty certain that we would return empty-handed.

Interestingly, Vesna's relatives were hard-line and against the convoy, perhaps with good reason. They were refugees from nearby Zavidovici, until recently a happily integrated multi-ethnic town. When fighting broke out between Croats and Muslims, the Muslim son of a near neighbour was murdered. His family sought revenge and had attacked the house of Vesna's aunt, killing her eldest son and seriously wounding the second. Her husband had taken the wounded boy to Zagreb, leaving her and their youngest son to survive in Zepce. There were no bystanders in this war. Some were guilty, some innocent, but all were victims. We demanded a lot of loyalty from our local staff. We alienated them from their own. They wore our badge of neutrality and impartiality.

With the arrival of the priest, the convoy was ready and the barrier removed. A police car pulled out and we were off, Vesna and I leading, MSF behind with the priest, then Ginge and the boys. We approached the first Serb check-point. There were four Serbs in the middle of the road. To the left there was a house about 50 metres away. From the shattered downstairs window-frame a machine-gun barrel glinted. To the right was another house. In it, I could see both Serb and Croat soldiers. To our front was a barrier blocking the road to Maglaj. Lying on the road, clearly visible and menacing, were anti-tank mines. The leader of the group on the road was a middle-aged man. There was no bravado, no smell of alcohol. He knew we were coming. We smiled, shook hands. He raised the barrier. His soldiers removed the mines blocking the road.

'Are there any more mines ahead?'

'Yes. These here were laid by me. We are from Teslic. Further ahead there is the Doboj brigade. They have also laid mines. After that, you are in no man's land; there may be Serb mines, there may be Muslim mines.'

'Do the Doboj Serbs know I am coming?'

'I have no contact with them.'

I waved to the Croat escort, shook hands with the Serb. 'I will return at eight tomorrow morning.'

'*Sretan put*,' he said. 'Good luck.' Luck we were going to need.

Slowly, I moved the convoy forward, watching its progress in my rear-view mirror. I heard the voice of Ginge: 'Last vehicle clear of the barrier.' I smiled and stopped the convoy. Ten metres ahead of me I could see the first of the mines of the Doboj brigade. I got out of my vehicle and looked back. The Serbs at the first barrier were nonchalantly replacing their mines. Our little unescorted thirteen-vehicle humanitarian aid convoy was now mined back and front. The road was silent and still. It was fenced on both sides. I raised my hands in best B-movie style. '*Humanitarna Pomoc*. UN. *Komesarijat*,' I shouted. No reply. I tried again. I heard voices to the right but in the distance.

'I think there are Croats over there in the hills,' said Vesna.

I looked but could see nothing. To our left there was a small gap in the fence. It led to a path which crossed a stream by a makeshift footpath. The path was well worn and ended at a small house. I yelled my plaintive message in the direction of the house, breaking the stillness and the silence. The reply was deafening. From the woods behind the house a machine-gun opened fire. This brought a response from the right-hand side of the road, a more distant, more muffled rattle from another machine-gun. I stood still. I looked towards the vehicle at Vesna. I had left the door open. The bullet-proof helmets are heavy and large and Vesna looked tiny beneath hers. The helmet was white, her face even whiter. God knows what colour mine was. I repeated my message to both sides of the road.

Vesna called me to the vehicle. 'Someone is coming across the field from the right.'

In a short while a young, scruffy, tired but polite officer came to the road. After some persuasion he picked up just enough mines to permit the width of a truck to pass and said: 'When your last vehicle passes this point, you must stop the convoy and let us put back our mines before you go on. OK?'

'OK. Are there any more mines ahead?' I asked.

'I do not know. I'd be surprised if there weren't.'

'Thanks. We will return tomorrow at eight in the morning.'

The Serbs left. I moved down the road to tell Ginge to halt the convoy when the last vehicle had passed through the gap in the minefield. 'Then, my friend,' I said with all the false bonhomie I could muster, 'we will have two minefields behind us and the unknown ahead of us.'

We were not given time to dwell on this situation. Suddenly all hell broke loose. We heard the heavy crump of mortar fire from both sides of the road and in the near distance the shells exploding in Maglaj, as the Serbs detracted from the excitement of the inhabitants, especially those who were brave and foolish enough to be in the streets awaiting us. I walked back to my vehicle. Ahead of us there were approximately two hours of daylight and about 200 metres of tarmacked road.

I had not come this far to risk a vehicle on a mine. I had brought with me a six-foot-long thin twig. My aim was patiently and painstakingly to search every centimetre of the road. With twig lightly held between two fingers at the end of my outstretched left hand I slowly paced forward. I was looking for wires, anti-personnel mines, anti-tank mines. One, two, three, four, five paces. Eyes slowly scanning from left edge of road to right. If the twig brushed against anything, showed any resistance, I stopped. If there was a hole in the road I stopped, lay beside it and examined it. Mounds of earth, clods of grass, piles of stones, especially the edge of the road, all received the same concentrated attention. If at the end of my five paces all was clear, I laid the twig across the road. I stood and looked at the next five paces. I walked to both sides of the road, looked along the fence on both sides, all the time ensuring that I did not advance forward of my marker twig. Thus prepared, I physically advanced the next five paces, twig at arm's length. Forward, down, examine, up, forward. Vesna later described it as a 'bizarre, primitive, sinister ballet'. My actions may have been elaborate, even melodramatic. But I had been mined coming out of Gorazde and had lost a truck going into Srebrenica. Every twenty paces I called the convoy forward, ensuring that the lead vehicle travelled over the safest path. This way the trucks avoided the unexploded mortar bombs and the mounds of ammunition which my search uncovered.

Regularly, during our movement forward, there was heavy machine-gun fire from both sides of the road. At first I was worried, but I soon realised that the fire was parallel to the convoy. The Serbs were playing with us. They were not playing with poor Maglaj. Throughout the afternoon they continually shelled it. This arrogance made me even more determined to get in. At one stage, as I lay at the side of a large hole, I had the feeling I was being closely watched. God was not with me but his representative was: Father Stipo had decided to give me moral support. It was a genuine, sincere gesture, but it was reckless and in truth it made me feel quite foolish. Me in my helmet, bullet-proof jacket, complete with twig, ritual and gravitas. He in his shirt-sleeves, angelic smile and peaceful air. I sent him to my vehicle to be with Vesna. For the rest of the trip he looked after her. Ex-para Ginge visited me at several of my five-pace-break times. It was important that he always knew what I was doing, just in case anything went wrong. To better observe my actions he left his vehicle and drove mine, always briefing his patient, fascinated, determined drivers, who later irreverently referred to my actions as 'Larry's Papal impersonation'.

As we neared the Bosnian Muslim front lines, there was a derelict, destroyed café, outside which stood a large milk crate with bottles in it. I took some time over this. My fear was that they might be filled with petrol. A crate of Molotov cocktails we could do without. They turned out to be innocent.

Eventually I reached within 10 metres of the Maglaj front line. I could see the Bosnian soldiers in their trenches. I shouted to them. They shouted back. Vesna left the vehicle and came to say: 'They are telling you that there are no mines here.' The temptation to run forward to greet them was overpowering but I had not spent the last ninety minutes inching myself forward to throw it all away in the closing metres. My last pirouettes were within their enchanted gaze. As I reached their location I shouted a greeting. I was relieved and elated. They looked so young. They were down in a deep ditch at the side of the road.

I wanted to share this first contact. I waved forward Ginge. He came up to join me. The leader of the defenders, a boy who turned out to be eighteen but an already established front-line veteran, shouted something from the trench.

'Come up and join us,' I said.

Vesna translated and he replied, 'We can't; they can see us.'

'No,' I said. 'The firing is parallel to the convoy. We are OK.'

He and his number two climbed up on to the road. A hail of bullets came whacking in from the woods on our left. These were not parallel to us. They were aimed directly at us. They smacked into the tarmac and ricocheted around us, some hitting the canopies of the trucks. The two Bosnians leapt back into the trenches. Ginge and I did a little dance, a sort of retired military two-step. Poor Serb Vesna dodged the Serb bullets by taking refuge in the UNHCR vehicle, her own little safe haven. I clearly remember screaming into the woods, 'Stop that firing.'

I have no doubt that my words had no effect whatsoever on whoever had fired. He had achieved his aim by scuttling the Bosnians. But shouting made me feel better. I stopped and turned to my big companion. 'Ginge. What are we doing here?'

'I was just thinking that myself.'

We called the convoy forward and Ginge parked it along the road by the side of the Bosnian trenches. Thus protected, the defenders emerged once again. The Bosnians told us that we had to wait for an escort from Maglaj. They had had all day to get an escort there, but they waited until we arrived at the front line to call him forward. I was a little put out. We were parked in the middle of a very active front line. But it was easy for us to forget that being parked in such a spot was everyday fare for these boys. While we waited, the whole front line emerged from their various hidy-holes. They were desperate for cigarettes. The drivers looked after them. I had brought in many jars of coffee and I handed some out. Eventually one man walked in from Maglaj to escort us in – fuel and vehicles were for the seriously wounded, not to be spent on meeting convoys. He climbed into my vehicle and we set off for Maglaj.

No traveller ever approached Samarkand, no explorer ever entered Timbuctoo, with any less excitement than I entered Maglaj. This was the culmination of many requests, of pleading and imploring. I had been delayed, diverted, lied to, insulted, threatened. But we were here. We were not bringing much but we were here.

We passed the bridge where the last convoy into Maglaj had met its fate. They had parked for safety in the railway tunnel. The tunnel was mortared. Danish soldiers and a UNHCR translator lost their lives.

As we approached the outskirts of the town, the people came out of their houses to greet us. They stood by their garden gates; small family groups, children clinging to their mothers' skirts; dogs barking; mothers and sisters waving self-consciously; old men smiling toothlessly. As we advanced towards the centre the houses became apartment blocks. Their inhabitants stood in the narrow streets. There were tears, flowers, cheering and no shells. The Serbs had given their word that they would not shell Maglaj whilst we were inside. It looked as if they intended to keep their promise; the shelling had stopped as we left the Bosnian front line.

It was rapidly getting dark but still light enough to see the massive damage. Almost every building was hit. The people looked dirty, hungry, tired and confused. They wanted to get close to us but the town's military were in charge and kept them away. They seemed frightened of the military. Perhaps they were just too tired to argue, to press forward.

I halted the convoy, switched off the engine, climbed out of the vehicle and set foot in Maglaj. I know that my face broke into a big, satisfied smile.

'We've made it.' It was big Ginge, his smile as broad as mine. Peter was out of his vehicle, his craggy face puckered by a huge grin. He was shaking hands and patting heads. He'd make an excellent politician. Our Maglaj minder and guide pointed out the warehouse. Ginge took charge of the unloading. Vesna and I went off with Bert and Peter to meet the lady mayor and her team. On the steps of the building the first person we met was the Maglaj interpreter, Violetta. She was from Sarajevo and, amazingly, had been a student of languages at the university there in the same year as Vesna. They were old friends and colleagues. Violetta is a

Croat married to a Muslim. Sadly she was closely watched the whole time we were there.

The building in which the meeting was held was chosen for safety. It was protected by other buildings. Like the whole of Maglaj (and Srebrenica, Zepa and Sarajevo) it was cold and damp and dark. The meeting room was dimly illuminated by a bulb powered from a car battery. The room was crowded with dignitaries, some in uniform, some in civilian clothes, all active defenders of Maglaj. The seating configuration was two very long tables, placed at the edges of a smaller top table, making a large U.

We awaited the arrival of Aida Smailovic. There was a flurry of excitement and in she came. She is a tall, large-boned lady, in her middle thirties, with a beautiful head of dark hair. She has the presence and the bearing of a Margaret Thatcher. When she is in a room no one is in any doubt who is in charge. She took her place at the centre of the top table. I greeted her. She shook my hand and welcomed us. I immediately introduced my team and included Father Stipo. I explained that he was there to visit the prisoners and that I trusted he would be made welcome and given protection. I could see that some were not happy with his presence. Aida promptly guaranteed him both co-operation and safety. I placed some cigarettes on the table and a bottle of whisky. I was not too sure how the bottle would be received. I saw some of the men looking at Aida for guidance. She took one of the cigarettes but did not take any whisky.

She was straight into business. She handed me a many-paged letter which outlined, in English, the plight of the town. It gave details of the destruction of the buildings, of the shelling and the sniping and of a new hazard introduced since the commencement of the air drops over Maglaj. The Serbs were shooting at the townspeople, the starving townspeople, as they attempted to recover the life-saving packages. Ten people had been murdered in the past week. This crime I found particularly horrendous. The Serb snipers were in the hills, no further than 300 metres from the dropping zones. The snipers could hear the aircraft overhead, see the packages land, could hear the men, women and children racing out to recover them and their excited conversations, and yet could raise their weapons, focus their eyes through the sights, fire and cut down innocent, desperate, starving people. I find it hard to put a face to any man who could do this, who at 300 metres could listen to the screams, the cries, the panic, the despair and the agony inflicted by his squeezing of the trigger. Can these men ever be at peace with themselves?

Aida walked us through all these issues and concluded by giving me a list of the most urgent needs of the town, mainly food, medicines and fuel. It was explained to us that the wounded from Maglaj were taken to the hospital in Tesanj by night along a narrow but serviceable road. The road conditions were poor and many wounded died *en route*. Bert and Peter were able, with justifiable pride, to tell the assembled crowd what medicines they had taken to Tesanj two days ago.

Throughout her long diatribe there was no praise for the UN, no thanks for our coming. There was criticism, there were questions and there was regret – but no thanks. Later we were thanked profusely by the town administrator but Aida wanted to make it clear that Maglaj had come close to total destruction and that the world had stood by and listened to its plight and watched and waited. I had heard this in Gorazde, Srebrenica and now in Maglaj. Aida had run this town under unbelievable conditions. She must have had so much pent-up anger inside her and we were a justifiable target for some of it. At the end of the war I would like to see her confront the men who besieged her.

During her speech I heard the sound of shelling. It sounded to me very much like outgoing shells. I interrupted Aida and asked her military commander, Esad Hidic, if I was right. I told him that the Serbs had promised there would be no shelling on Maglaj while we were in. No incoming shells meant no outgoing shells. I felt bad in demanding this as I had seen and heard the pasting Maglaj had received while we were attempting to get in. The commander assured me that it was incoming shelling but sent a man to investigate. Within minutes the sound of shelling stopped.

The meeting was not easy. Aida was scathing about any linkage between future convoys and Croat prisoners. She could not understand why the UN did not blast its way in and lift the siege. At one point I foolishly mentioned that recently Croats in villages close to Maglaj had been murdered by armed groups from Maglaj.

My point was that defensive action by Maglaj was understood and accepted by all, but that offensive action, especially against civilians in neighbouring villages, placed them in the same category as the Croat and the Serb. This caused great anger, only a little ameliorated by the contents of a second bottle of whisky. The conversation mellowed. We agreed to adjourn until seven the following morning.

When we left the building it was very dark, there was no moon. I was asked if I wished to go to the warehouse to supervise the unloading. I didn't. Ginge was far more efficient at this than me. I was therefore escorted around the town to where we were to park for the night. It was in one of the main streets with high-rise blocks of flats on either side, thus giving us some protection from shelling. We moved without lights. The warehouse, which was quite close, could only accept one vehicle at a time so the whole convoy was in the street. The loaded trucks were at the front, those unloaded were already parked up for the night. There was a heavy police presence surrounding our location, preventing the people of Maglaj getting too close to us. I objected to this but we were told it was for our safety and protection. We would have welcomed a little fraternisation and an exchange of news.

I parked my vehicle at the head of the convoy and Peter and Bert parked theirs behind mine. They had Father Stipo with them. Now he was most vulnerable. Bert and Stipo decided to sleep in the back of one of the empty trucks where they could stretch out. Peter opted for staying with the still full MSF vehicle. They would not be able to unload until the following morning. It was too dangerous and too dark to do it this late at night.

I should have gone to visit Ginge but I felt very tired. I sent a message to him by the next truck to go forward. 'Ginge, do you need me?'

Vesna and I then got ready for the night. She moved into the driver's side. I moved into her seat. She is much smaller than me so she could cope with the steering wheel and the pedals. I could stretch out more comfortably in the passenger seat. Vesna unrolled her sleeping bag and snuggled down into it. I waited for a truck to come back with a message from Ginge.

Vesna began to talk to me about Violetta. 'She has a small child.

Her husband is not trusted because she is a Croat. He is sent to the front line and is used to collect the air drops if they are near the Serb lines. She is very frightened. I would like to give her any food we have left.'

We had brought in quite a bit of our own food to be given away. 'She can have whatever you like.'

As we were talking there was a tapping on the vehicle window on Vesna's side. I lowered it. It was Violetta. She looked scared. She began to talk to Vesna and I noticed the man in the leather jacket moving towards her. With a great flourish I got out of the vehicle and asked her to sit in the passenger seat. I could see that this did not please the policeman. I joined Bert, Peter and Father Stipo, who were rigging up beds in the back of a truck. They were also taking a surreptitious bite of food, hidden from view. In a besieged town with starving citizens you feel truly guilty if you eat.

Out of the dark a man approached me and asked if I had any spare torch batteries.

'No I haven't, my friend, and I will need my torch tonight, but tomorrow you can have the batteries out of it.' He beamed brighter than my torch could.

The next truck back had a message from Ginge: 'Unloading will take another couple of hours, but you are not needed. Go to sleep, you old bugger.'

While I was talking to the driver, the dark street was briefly illuminated by a red glow. It happened again and again. I suddenly realised it was the brake lights on my vehicle. I just got to the door before the leather jacket. I could hear laughter from within. As Vesna laughed, she was stretching out in the sleeping bag and hitting the brake pedal with her feet!

'Signalling, signalling,' said leather jacket.

'Rubbish,' I replied, opening the door. I explained to Vesna what had happened. She was blissfully unaware, but then saw the face of the chief of police. He spoke to her and accused her of signalling with the lights.

'To whom?' I asked him.

'To the Serbs,' he answered.

'Why?'

'So that they know where to shell,' he replied.

'Shell you, shell me, shell herself? Come on,' I said in exasper-ation. I looked at Violetta.

She was trembling with fear. 'I must go now,' she said, getting out of the vehicle.

'Just wait a minute, I will walk you home.'

I realised that I might have insulted the policeman in front of Violetta, which would not help her when we had gone. I therefore apologised, explaining what had happened. I gently rebuked Vesna. The policeman seemed happier. He agreed that I could walk with Violetta. 'But only to the corner of the street, for your own safety.' He left.

Vesna hurriedly got together a large bag of food which I stuffed under my jacket. I walked with Violetta a couple of blocks and in the dark gave her the bag. I turned to walk towards my vehicle and fell into a very large shell crater, scraping the skin off my knees. God loveth a cheerful giver!

I hobbled back to the vehicle, unfurled my sleeping bag and turned to Vesna. 'Good-night. God bless and no signalling to Serbs.'

It was a long night. I heard every vehicle return. Whenever I closed my eyes, images of the day filled them. At one stage I heard a mini-commotion around the trucks. Someone was looking for Father Stipo. They were not after his blessing. They were kept away by the police and an ancient, primitive Highland curse.

As dawn broke, the drivers awoke. Vesna and I were up quickly. The vehicle was freezing. As we clambered out, we met the man to whom I had promised my batteries.

'Come with me; I can show you where you can wash.'

'Great,' I said. 'Vesna, you go first.'

After a few minutes she was back. It was my turn. For some reason I thought he was taking us to his house, but he took me to a water pump in the square between the flats. There was already a large line of people. The chilly morning mist had risen only a few feet. I was taken to the front of the queue. A man pumped on the handle and a thin silver stream of water jerked out of the pipe. I cupped my hands and the water hit them. It was ice-cold. I splashed my face and was instantly awake. I stuck my toothbrush under the tap and wet it. I put a helping of toothpaste on it and realised that I was watched by every pair of eyes. Toothpaste, for them, was a long-forgotten luxury. I gave the tube to the woman at the front of the queue whose husband was pumping the water. As I left, I gave away my soap. I saw many sets of covetous eyes. I went back to the vehicle, where I had a carton full of soap. Vesna returned to the queue and handed it out.

The convoy remained in the street. Peter, Bert and Stipo left to visit the hospital, then to see the prisoners. I went back to the office of Aida. She was waiting for me. She took me round the town on foot. She pointed out the Serb gun positions. You could see the barrels glinting in the rising sun. She showed me the Catholic church. There was very little damage to it. She showed me the Orthodox church, which was badly damaged. 'Damaged by Serb shells,' she told me with a big smile. She did not tell me that it was in response to a mortar attack fired by her troops from the rear of the church. The Serbs told me that later. She walked over the bridge, defying the Serb snipers, to show me the damage to the ancient mosque. She pointed out aid pallets in the river. We went to see the hospital. There were few patients; during the night there had been an evacuation to Tesanj of the wounded. The hospital staff were unpacking the medicine brought in by Bert and Peter. They were smiling from ear to ear. I met the hospital director, Jasminka Smailagic, surprisingly not a doctor but a dentist. She thanked me profusely.

I saw the blocks of flats, all damaged. Children were emerging from the cellars. They were raggedly dressed and ingrained with dirt. They looked tired; old faces on young heads. They smiled and waved. We visited the collective centre which initially had been a school and then had become a centre for the elderly and the mentally sick who now mingled with the refugees. Each group looked bewildered; the patients whose lives were temporarily disrupted and the refugees whose lives had been shattered. The centre was also a soup kitchen and families were collecting their meal of the day. They carried all manner of containers from pans to jars. I watched the distribution. It was some form of greyish soup. It smelt terrible but those collecting it walked with care so as not to spill a drop. We walked back with Aida to the building where we had first met.

I turned to her. 'Aida, next time I come in I would like to bring something just for you. Something frivolous and personal. What would you like?'

Without a moment's hesitation her eyes lit up as she said, 'Make-up. I would like some make-up.'

So strong, so powerful, so feminine. I like you, Aida.

Time was running out. We had told the Serbs we would be there at eight. I said farewell to the mayor and promised that I would return in one week. I rejoined the convoy. Peter and Bert had been with Stipo to see the prisoners; they had seen twenty-eight of them. They were told that two had escaped and two were in Tesanj. The visit had not been without incident. The parcels had been 'examined' by the guards and some items 'confiscated'. But far more annoyingly, Stipo wanted to hear the confessions of the prisoners, prisoners who might die from shelling, gunfire, or be executed. The guards had refused. It was too late for me to do anything.

We had promised that we would take out mail, the first to leave the town for four months. Peter kindly accepted responsibility for it. There were sacks of it, urgently written messages to all corners of Bosnia, assuring the recipient that the sender was still alive. In Zagreb, Peter posted them all, presumably at considerable personal expense.

We left. We were escorted by a police car as far as the bridge. Then we were on our own again. We sped along the road, slowing at the Bosnian front line, where one young hoodlum threatened Father Stipo, drawing his hand across his throat. Then a sedate, slow drive down no man's land visually checking for mines. We found only those we had seen the previous day. We paused as they were removed by the Serbs who were waiting for us, first the Doboj lot, then the Teslic lot.

We returned to Brancovici. There was a group waiting at the barrier. It was clear they were at least hoping that we would bring some prisoners out. I could both sense and hear their disappointment. We took Stipo to the house of Father Simic, the priest who had been so prominent when we first were stopped.

He was very friendly and gave us coffee, food and slivovic. He seemed happy with the outcome of our convoy.

I then went to the office of the Croat senior administrator, Lozantic, and briefed him. I was convinced that I could get at least some of the prisoners out in the next few days and arrange for convoys in on a regular basis. My belief was founded simply on the fact that Maglaj needed all the aid it could get. I felt certain that for Aida principles would be second to survival.

We then headed back to Banja Luka. At the Croat check-point at the top of the hill we met up again with our Serb police escort. They led the way back into Serb-held territory. As we passed through Teslic they sped ahead to the junction to warn them of our arrival. I quickly spoke on the radio to Ginge. The convoy bunched together. As we approached the Y junction I could see our escort. Their vehicle was parked on the right fork, the road we had used to come in, the long diversion. They were out in the road talking to their colleagues. We approached the Y junction sedately, then I turned the convoy to the left along the direct and shortest route. I saw the police run to their car. I accelerated, the convoy accelerated and we sped along the narrow road. By the time the escort had started their car and turned it round it was too late. We were on our way. For the next few miles I could hear the police car hooting its horn as it attempted to overtake each vehicle. It received no assistance from any of our drivers. Perhaps one or two even used up a little more of the road than was necessary. We were well on our way before the police car overtook mine, blocking the road.

'You are on the wrong road. You have to go back.'

'No, we are on the right road.'

'You have no approval for this road.'

'No approval? I have a police escort,' I said, pointing to his car parked at the head of the convoy.

'We only have approval to use the other road. Major King will be furious. You must go back to Teslic and go the other way.'

'I am sorry but the road is too narrow for us to be able to turn the trucks.' This was untrue, as the Brit drivers can turn their vehicles on a sixpence.

'You must go back. We will be in trouble with Major King.'

'You are wrong. *We* are not going back and *you* will be in trouble with Major King.'

There began a discussion between the two of them which I cut short with a suggestion. 'If we get along this road quickly, Major King may never know. So let's move now.' I walked a pace or two, then stopped and turned. 'Next time when I say we move at seven, we move at seven. OK?' I got back into my vehicle, started the engine and watched with satisfaction as they slunk into their car. Revenge is sweet.

We returned to Banja Luka to a great reception from the girls. They met us outside the building. Big hugs, kisses and lots of praise. They were as thrilled as if they had been with us. They had shared every moment, listening to our radio contacts. Vesna was their heroine. Ginge and the boys stayed the night in Banja Luka and carried out a little quality-control exercise on the local beer. They left for Zagreb the following day. Peter and Bert had a small party in their Banja Luka house before also setting off for Zagreb, where their masters eagerly awaited them, delighted that MSF had been part of the team. We, UNHCR, all went to Adria, the restaurant with the largest choice. We ate and drank well.

I rang England and ordered some make-up.

Back in my room I had time to reflect. We had gone to Maglaj to take aid. Now we had to get back and take more aid, and try to release a group of prisoners. I now had more problems than I started off with. I was not offended by the coldness of Aida to the UN, but I wanted to understand it. Yugoslavs had watched and feared big-power intervention. Hungary and Czechoslovakia were the most significant role models. The Bosnians were now watching the UN beg from Karadzic permission to deliver aid to starving civilians. I could understand Aida not being able to believe this.

I was really pleased with the welcome home from my Banja Luka staff. They were an ace team in a great office.

PART THREE

14
Zenica

Neill Wright rang and asked me to go and see him in Zagreb. 'Larry, let's meet in the Intercontinental hotel for a glass of wine.'

Ugh, ugh. Last time I met him there I was moved from Sarajevo to Banja Luka. 'What is the plot this time?' I wondered.

'Larry, how is Louis doing?'

'He's great.'

'Is he Head of Office material? Could he run an office on his own?'

'No problems. He is a good leader, tough and a better administrator than I am. Where are you thinking of sending him?'

'Well, we are looking for a Head of Office for Central Bosnia. Which of course is the largest office and at the moment is the busiest and maybe the most dangerous.'

'Oh, he'll enjoy that.'

'No, Larry. We need an old hand. We think you could do the job well and Louis could hold the fort in Banja Luka. Another drink?'

Once again I took over a 'cold' desk. The previous Head of Office, Jorge de la Motta, had left before I arrived leaving everything in good shape. There were three internationals in the office: the brilliant, witty and laconic Canadian lawyer Steven Wolfson, who was protection officer and acting head; Mark de Guilio, an American field officer with a very high reputation for getting aid through; and Amir Saaed, a Pakistani in charge of administration. He is a fine example of the Raj legacy, a meticulous bureaucrat. Amir had a form for everything and could quote UN regulations including the punctuation marks. I may mock such men, but every office needs one. With Amir producing and controlling the paper mountain I would have time to get on the road and get aid moving. I looked forward to working with Mark but on the day I arrived he was in the Croat military headquarters in Kiseljak and read a few palms. He told a bombastic local commander exactly what he thought of his aid-blocking tactics. A source of information told the Brits that the Croat commander had left the meeting threatening Mark's life. The Brits recommended that he be moved for his own safety. Mark was happy to stay and brave it out, but field work involves a lot of travel. A single car is vulnerable. Also, if anyone is going to take out Mark they might include those travelling with him. Furthermore, I knew that he was engaged to an Irish girl and was soon to be married. His life was just beginning. I decided to move him on . . . to Banja Luka, where I knew he would fit in. Neill agreed. Mark moved the next day. Neill also agreed to my having responsibility for Maglaj from my new office.

Steven briefed me on the events of the past six months. He showed me the reports he had sent to Zagreb. They were like legal briefs, beautifully written, concise and accurate, all they lacked was a red ribbon. I discovered that Steven had an M.Phil. from Oxbridge, had worked as 'bright young assistant' to the most senior judge in Canada and was extremely good company. I installed him as Deputy Head of Office and put him in the second-largest office in the building. He would keep the reports flowing and make Zagreb and Geneva very happy. Amir would continue to control the administration. I could now concentrate on aid.

'Excuse me, Larry, may I have a word with you?'

It was Amir. 'Of course you may, my friend.'

'In UNHCR regulations there is no appointment Deputy Head of Office.'

'Amir, there is now.'

As I sat at my new desk I sent a radio message to all the other UNHCR offices: 'Greetings from the Master of Zen.'

The best reply I had was from Jerrie Hulme:

Welcome to your new appointment.

(To be sung to the tune of 'The man who broke
the bank at Monte Carlo')
Larry's song.

> *as he steps down off the antropov*
> *with his kit bag on his back*
> *you can hear his colleagues crack*
> *he's been through a lot of flak*
> *when the bullets fly he won't be shy*
> *he's certainly not afraid to die*
> *he's just the chap we want for old Zenica.*

There were no convoys coming in. They were suspended after an incident at Novi Travnik when convoys were moving across a front line which became active. One Danish driver, Bjarne Nielson, was killed and eleven Dutch soldiers injured. Despite no convoys, the UNHCR warehouse had some food in it, which surprised me.

I sent for the Acting Logistic Officer, Billy Bilic, a very bright and interesting man, a pre-war senior policeman. He is a Croat but his parents were clever. Instead of giving him an ethnic name they had called him Yugoslav Bilic – very clever until the break-up. Everybody called him Billy, I was tempted to call him former Yugoslav or ex-Yugoslav but he is a very big man with an uncertain temper.

'Billy, if we have had no convoys, how come we have food in the warehouse?'

'It's emergency stock.'

'When did we last issue any food?'

'Two weeks ago.'

'So some people have had no food for two weeks.'

'Yes.'

'How many weeks do they have to have no food before you call it an emergency, Billy?'

We emptied the warehouse. Billy proved himself to be an outstanding logistician.

House in order. Time to look outside and meet some of the principal players.

The Coldstream Guards had been in the Zenica region only a few days longer than I had. They were based in Vitez in the heart of the Croat portion of Central Bosnia. Their colonel invited me to his headquarters for a briefing. Peter Williams impressed me greatly. He is not a military martinet, nor a gung-ho cowboy. He is just a thoroughly professional, caring commanding officer. He told his men that there were three aims for their tour in Bosnia: to do the job well, to enjoy themselves and to return home safely. He ensured they achieved all three. He is tall, with fair hair and a neat moustache. He stands like a Guardsman: erect, shoulders back, head high. But from the moment you shake him by the hand and look into his eyes you realise that he is a warm and caring 'father' of his regiment. He explained to me the complexities of his patch.

Central Bosnia began the war with Bosnian Croats and Bosnian government forces on the same side. The common enemy was the Bosnian Serb. The alliance had always been shaky and had eventually collapsed into a war between Croats and government troops. The British battalion HQ sat in Bosnian Croat territory in what UNPROFOR called the Vitez pocket and the locals called the Lasva valley, named after the River Lasva running through it. The pocket was surrounded by Bosnian-government-held territory. He had a company at Gorni Vakuf, a front-line town and always militarily 'hot'. He had liaison officers in all the large towns. He patrolled the main supply route with Warrior armoured vehicles and wished to get it open for the passage of convoys which would bring in aid to all sides. Being Bosnia, there were a few complications. Close to his HQ there were two 'Muslim' enclaves within the Croat enclave. Also close to his HQ was an ammunition factory in Croat hands, which the Croats said they would blow up rather than see fall into 'Muslim' hands 'causing the biggest BBQ you will ever see'.

To ensure the closest co-operation, Peter offered me a liaison officer from his battalion. I accepted with speed and was allocated Captain Harry Bucknall, a tall, handsome, blond, archetypal young Guards officer – an Old Harrovian who hides a good brain and a fit frame behind a bluff personality. Harry was to spend four months shadowing me, overtaking me and standing on my toes. He kept me in the picture as to what the military were doing and by diligence and guesswork kept the military in the picture as to what I thought I was doing. Peter recommended that I visit the two local military commanders as early as I could. I motored back to Zenica, to find that I had visitors.

Before the war, the Iron and Steelworks in Zenica employed seventeen and a half thousand people. Which meant that with their families seventy thousand were dependent on a wage from this enormous conglomerate which belched huge clouds of smoke from its chimneys, which hung on the hilltops, polluted the air and gave Zenica the reputation of the dirtiest city in Bosnia. The war had changed all this. There was no fuel, production stopped, the clouds lifted, the air was clean and seventeen and a half thousand families were without a wage. The director of this giant industrial complex, Hamdiya Kulovic, was a short stocky man with dark hair, intense eyes, enormous energy and massive loyalty to his employees. When the violence began and war looked inevitable, he bought up three hundred thousand Deutschmarks' worth of food and stored it in one of his warehouses. While the roads were open, he organised convoys of supplies and brought in a further 20,000 tonnes of food at a cost of millions of marks. The roads were now closed. Mr Kulovic was keeping the factory canteen open. He was feeding as many of his employees and their dependents as he could. But his stocks were very low. Furthermore, all the high-rise flats in Zenica, where the majority of the citizens lived, were heated from a central plant within his complex. There was no coal to fire the boilers.

Mr Kulovic had come to see me. He had brought with him a request. Could UNHCR please get into Zenica 70,000 tonnes of coal, 80 tonnes of sodium, 50 tonnes of salt and 30 tonnes of hydrochloric acid. Once I had got this lot in, he would need 5 tonnes of diesel per month to remove the coal ash and 2 tonnes of diesel for transportation within the Steelworks. In addition to this, he wanted sufficient food to feed his seventy thousand. To make things easier for me, he knew where all of these items could be bought and the Steelworks had the money to pay for them and their transportation. He even knew where we could hire the trucks. All UNHCR, all the UN, had to do was to get it through the check-points. Then half the population of Zenica would be fed and two-thirds warm. So my bit looked the easy bit. 'And after all, Mr Larry, you are the United Nations.'

The president of the Red Cross of Bosnia-Herzegovina Zenica Region was a medical specialist, Dr Safet Zildzic, a jolly gentleman. A man who looks and acts like a successful country General Practitioner; in the UK the sort of doctor who would hunt with the hounds and be a guest at all the best dinner-tables. He was active and efficient. He was next in the office. He welcomed me to Zenica with a well-prepared brief. It began with extracts from the 'Principles of the UN World Health Organisation'. Very clever. Hang them with their own rope. The next page gave me the 'demographical data' for Zenica: population 145,577, refugees 49,500, children under fourteen 57,847. Other pages gave a host of fascinating information. In the year before the war, 4402 babies were born in the hospitals, last year only 1942. Infant mortality had risen from 16 per cent to the current 39 per cent. The last pages, the requests, were much more general than Mr Kulovic's. The good doctor just wanted enough blood, bandages, medicines, equipment and food to sustain the population. The actual amounts were left to me.

Branomir Ivanovic was responsible for Public Utilities: for garbage collection, funerals, fire brigade, sewerage, vermin control and road maintenance. His visit was short. He only wanted 240 litres of diesel a day.

As yet, I had not taken off my coat and hat.

Sanja was the personal assistant to the UNHCR Head of Office. Tall, elegant, dark-haired and uncompromising, she had arranged the really important protocol interviews: to see the Zenica authorities.

The mayor was Besim Spahic, maybe early forties, dark-suited, formal and suspicious. His humanitarian affairs co-ordinator was Mr Dzaferovic, who ran a successful garment factory which before the war exported ski clothing to Italy. He exuded the salesman charm and street credibility of a high-class car dealer. Together they outlined the problems of running a blockaded city at war with its neighbours. I was able to tell them that they were worse off than Banja Luka and better off than Sarajevo. They talked at great length on my least favourite subject: the inability of the

United Nations to have freedom of movement for its humanitarian aid programme.

'The United Nations has a mandate to operate in Bosnia. The mandate was approved by the Security Council and the member states. It specifically gave the task of co-ordinating humanitarian aid to UNHCR and the task of supporting UNHCR to UNPRO-FOR. That is the big picture,' said the mayor of Zenica. 'The little picture, as seen in Zenica, is even simpler.' He paused, then continued. 'Mr Larry, UNHCR is the appointed leading UN agency. There are twenty thousand UN troops in Bosnia. There are eight hundred British troops in Vitez, there are five hundred Dutch and Belgian in Busovaca, five hundred and fifty French in Kakanj and eight hundred Canadians in Visoko. These are all less than an hour away from here. We have no food, no fuel. You tell us that you cannot bring it in.' Then he twisted the knife. 'If you cannot bring it in, who can? If you cannot, why are you here?'

I gave him the party line. 'We are here operating in your war. We are doing our best. Your people, Serbs, Croats and Muslims, are all hindering us in different ways and to different degrees.' But I was reading from a script I did not truly believe in. I escaped before I got the 'Lifting of the arms embargo' lecture.

Harry, 'my' liaison officer, fixed up appointments with the top military men. First we went to the Croat side to visit Colonel Tihomir Blaskic, who was an old acquaintance. We had attended meetings together in Sarajevo and Kiseljak. He is a tall professional army officer, a sharp military man with a disarming ingenuousness, a man whose gentle frankness borders on naivety. Since I had last seen him, the massacre at the village of Ahmici had taken place. In this small village, a group of Croats had murdered men, women and children and burned homes. The aftermath of the incident was reported brilliantly by the doyen of television war reporters, Martin Bell. He showed film of the cellar of a house where five charred bodies lay, three women and two girls. Near the front door lay dead the two men of the house. As well as capturing the horror of the scene, Martin also filmed the frustration and fury of Colonel Bob Stewart of the Cheshire Regiment, who just after witnessing the scene was stopped by a Croat army patrol who asked him, 'Have you HVO permission to be here?'

'I don't need permission from the bloody HVO. I am from the United Nations,' fumed Colonel Bob.

Martin let the film roll as the HVO soldiers drove away, laughing and mocking the brave and gallant colonel.

Ahmici was in the area of responsibility of Tihomir Blaskic. He may not have had anything to do with the massacre but it was carried out by Croat soldiers operating on his territory. A vociferous condemnation of the massacre, followed by the pursuit, arrest and punishment of the perpetrators, would have absolved Blaskic from all blame and set a standard and a precedent which might have prevented future outrages. His handling of the Ahmici affair altered our personal relationship, but it could not be allowed to impinge on our working arrangements. For the resumption of vital convoys I needed him. He promised me maximum co-operation for their passage. He assured me that he was 'available twenty-five hours per day' if I had any problems. I left, after a promise of lunch in the future and a cordial hug.

The office of Commander Alagic, who commanded the Bosnian government corps operating out of Zenica, was near the Iron and Steelworks. He is very different from Blaskic. He is of medium height and stocky in a very physical, peasant way. He wore combat fatigues which emphasised his shapelessness and his strength. It is easy to imagine him as a partisan leader. He is not an easy man to get to know. He thinks in parables, speaks in riddles and is very stubborn. He quickly had the conversation around to the arms embargo, then to the inability of the UN to provide adequate aid. He made it very clear to me that, with or without the UN, the Bosnian government would sort out its problems. His adversaries were clearly the Croats. He intended to sweep them out of the Lasva valley. Time was on his side. Alagic moves and speaks at a frenetic pace. I found it impossible to relax in his company. I left, exhausted. He must be tiring to work for.

The next day, 12 November, there was great excitement in Zenica. President Alija Izetbegovic was visiting. It was not easy for him to get there. He is a brave man. He must have left Sarajevo by the tunnel, then used the mountain road. Some of the aid agencies went down to see the motorcade.

Solidarité is a French medium-sized charity. They bring in aid, mainly food, on their own trucks. They are independent and take more risks than most agencies. Recently they had had their land-rover stolen. They suspected it was taken by mujahedin. Some of their team were in the hotel which hosted the President. When the motorcade arrived they went out to see his arrival. They saw the President and they saw their landrover. Number three vehicle in the motorcade, it was complete with Solidarité sticker!

UNHCR is the lead agency. Solidarité may be reluctant to share all their successes, but they are quick to share their trials. They were banging on my office door asking for lead-agency intervention to get their vehicle back. Our points of contact were, of course, all involved with the visit. The head of Solidarité, a pugnacious veteran of other hard campaigns, wanted us to accompany him to the motorcade. In our presence he wished then to climb into his vehicle and motor away with it. I told him there were four snags to this proposal: each of them is large, bearded, heavily armed and sitting in the vehicle.

'If I had thought it was going to be easy I would have done it without coming here,' he replied. The portable radio crackled and we heard that the cavalcade had moved on.

I said a quiet 'Thank you, God' and sent Steven Wolfson down to sort it out, armed with chassis and engine numbers. He saw Ziad Imamovic, the exceedingly bright and helpful Head of Proto-col, who disarmingly confirmed that he too had seen the Solidarité vehicle. He promised to take up the matter with the Office of the President and the mujahedin. A few nights later Solidarité had another vehicle stolen. It pays to advertise . . . but not in Bosnia.

Each night I returned to the house where I lived. It was adjacent to the UNHCR office and warehouse. I had the top half, the owners the bottom. I had my own separate entrance. There was a tiny kitchen, a dining-room, a bedroom, a bathroom and a hallway. There was no electricity and of course no heating. I normally stayed in the office until I was ready for bed, then a quick dash up the stairs. The owners were smallholders and had a cow hidden away in a tiny shed. The lady of the house banged on the door every morning at six and produced a bowl of hot water and a mug of hot milk. Here in this corner of Zenica I got the Morillon treatment!

Her husband, who could see over the fence everything that went into our warehouse, had a word with Sanja. 'You have some wood-burning stoves in the warehouse. Send one over here and I will install it in the hallway upstairs. If Mr Larry buys some wood, he can be warm in the evenings.' Life changed. Every evening at six the owner lit the fire. I left the office earlier. The hallway became home to me. I moved into it cushions and my sleeping bag. I boiled water on the stove for tea. I sat beside the fire, lit a candle and read books. The hand-held radio kept me in touch with my fellow internationals and with our radio room. Not for the first time, I realised how little I needed to make me happy. I was so cosy I resented the thought of the arrival of spring. But that was a long way off.

We still had no convoys. The lack of food was a serious problem for the local authorities. There were demonstrations outside the offices of the mayor and a real risk of a breakdown of law and order. A group of civilians marched from the centre of the town to our warehouse. They were stopped at the gate by the guard. I invited them in to inspect the warehouse. It was clean and empty. They left, sad and weary.

But the unrest spread. Kakanj is a coal-mining town near to Zenica. I was invited by the mayor to visit him to discuss his disappointment at receiving no food. We had no convoys but I agreed to see him and we fixed an appointment as soon as we were both free. But this was not soon enough, for that very day our senior driver, Emir Kratina, a pre-war veterinary surgeon, was visiting Kakanj in a clearly marked UNHCR vehicle and was set upon by soldiers who told him they were starving. They had been to the municipality buildings begging for food and had been told that there was none 'because UNHCR has failed to deliver any'. As he motored away they fired into his vehicle. He was very lucky he had been hit by only one bullet in the shoulder. The rest miraculously missed him.

The next day, 18 November, the representatives of the warring sides agreed, in Geneva, to 'The freedom of movement for all UNPROFOR and UNHCR accredited convoys'. This declaration brought some hope and the strong rumour that soon we would be able to start convoys again, with the result that the office was harassed by the mayors, dignitaries and men of influence. They all wanted the first convoy to come into their fiefdom and hinted darkly that if aid travelled through their area without stopping and delivering, the trucks would be hijacked. We in UNHCR therefore worked out a master plan. The first convoys would drop off aid as a rolling barrage. They would move forward so that the nearest villages on the route got fed first and the most distant last. This way we would in effect 'buy' our way in. I visited all the local warlords. They all signed up to this. However, Brigadier John Reith, late of the Parachute Regiment, who had run ten thousand trucks in the Gulf, bombasted his way into Central Bosnia with twenty-eight UNPROFOR trucks carrying humanitarian aid. He was successful but unfortunately for me buggered up my arrangements and confused the locals. We, UNHCR, brought a ten-truck convoy into Travnik from my old stamping ground of Banja Luka and picked up the pieces of my plan.

Now that we had convoys we had to have deliveries. We felt that an early convoy must go into the 'Muslim' enclaves within the Croat enclave: Kruscica and Stari Vitez, especially Stari, a pathetic little island within an island. It had a population of twelve hundred and was very close to the Croat ammunition factory, which was unfortunate. The Croats were short of shells but not short of gunpowder. Therefore they shelled innocent Stari Vitez with any heavy chunk of metal they could stuff into a piece of tubular metal. The heaviest calibre was a fridge-freezer. An engine block was a common missile. This would be very funny if it were not true. We persuaded Croat Colonel Blaskic that we should link deliveries, one mini-convoy into Croat-dominated Vitez Colonia, one into Muslim Stari Vitez and another into Muslim Kruscica. After some hard bargaining Blaskic agreed, but we lost on the division of aid. The Croats got seven vehicles, Stari one and Kruscica two. Not perfect but better than nothing.

The convoy was scheduled for 25 November. We had a great day. I led the Stari vehicle in. The commander, Sevkija Dzidic, is a character. His enclave was so small he could hear the Croats breathing heavily as they loaded their weapons. He showed me the scrapyard of metal which the Croats had aerially delivered. It really was a black comedy.

The highlight of the day for me was a visit to the home of the lady who was responsible for the distribution of the aid within Stari Vitez. This involved a run through a garden exposed to active sniper fire. Blaskic agreed that we could go in, but said nothing about a cease-fire. The lady's old mother had insisted that we visited her for coffee. The roof of the house had a shellhole in it, the walls were bullet-scarred, but the house was immaculately clean and tidy.

At the doorway the daughter shouted to her mother, 'Mother, it is Mr Larry.'

Mother came to the door, welcomed me and invited me in. I stepped forward into this little war-damaged gem and received a tug on my sleeve.

'Take your muddy shoes off,' demanded the old lady. I did as I was told. Here was someone who did not compromise, war or no war, siege or no siege.

Stari was surreal. I am convinced that if the British battalion had not been in Vitez, Stari would have been eliminated in one blood-curdling night. Their morale held because of the leadership of Sevkija Dzidic, who might never have read any of Baden-Powell's books but who knew how to defend his mini-Mafeking. They were a closely knit society and they shared the food and the hardship. Their spirit was much more buoyant than that which I had seen in Gorazde or Srebrenica. It was on a par with Zepa. Stari Vitez was such a plucky place. A microcosm of the war, it had had, in miniature, all its share of the tragedy of a besieged enclave, but so much more personal and tangible and emotional.

One swallow does not make a summer. For months to come, convoys were to be infrequent and the result of bargaining. For Stari, convoys in were one problem, sick and wounded out another. They were caught up in pathetic point scoring between the Bosnian government authorities and the Croat authorities. The Bosnian government insisted that casualties from Stari should be taken to Zenica. Although there is a small, adequate Croat hospital at Nova Bila, in the Vitez pocket, the Bosnian government did not want any of its casualties to go there. The Croats insisted that they would only permit 'Muslims' to go to 'Muslim' Zenica if Croats could be taken to the large Croat hospital in Kiseljak, a journey through 'Muslim' check-points.

For me this idiocy came to a head when the British battalion were informed that a wounded child was desperately ill and needed surgery. They tried every Croat avenue to get approval to take the child out to the hospital in Zenica and failed. The child died. It must be very hard to lose a child. But so much harder when you know that treatment is available but that you can't get the child to it because someone is blocking you for political reasons, that your child is a pawn in petty power politics.

After the death of the boy we went to see the leaders on both sides. Dario Kordic was the political master of Croat affairs in the Lasva valley. A tall, thin man with bright eyes, he looks like a Jesuit missionary; an image he encourages by wearing an oversized set of rosary beads like a bishop's pectoral cross.

'Mr Kordic, can we not isolate dying children from political point scoring? The UN is prepared to collect and transport the wounded. Could you just allow the UN to use its discretion as to where patients go?'

'Mr Larry, you do not understand.'

Mr Kordic, you are so right. I fared no better with Alagic and Spahic. They insisted that Stari Vitez patients must be taken to Zenica. The mother of the little boy who died would have accepted treatment from an itinerant quack.

Such squabbling, linkage, bartering, bargaining, went on throughout the hostilities: water from the 'Muslim' side for access to the road on the Croat side; live prisoners for dead bodies; aid for prisoners. Sickening, demeaning negotiations.

November ended. We had managed to issue nine per cent of needs this month. Nine per cent of the minimum food needed to keep people alive: 1.7 kilograms per person. Think positive, Larry. It is 1.7 more than they would have had if the UN had not been there.

It was approaching Christmas, there was talk of a cease-fire. But the omens were not good. This time the Bosnian government forces seemed to be to blame. They attacked and overran a number

of Croat villages. Rasim Delic, the Bosnian government Commander-in-Chief, was reported as saying there would be no cease-
fire as 'there is too much unfinished business in Central Bosnia'.

Colonel Blaskic was not taking any chances either. He sent me
a note: 'Since the cease-fire is only verbally agreed it is not
advisable that the International Agencies put themselves into
danger. We are warning you that the fighting is going on inten-
sively. You move around at your own risk between 23 December
and 1 January.'

On Christmas Eve, I received in one envelope three more
messages from Tihomir Blaskic. The first, a letter, stated:

> Respected Gentleman
> As you know . . . a special Muslim unit has
> broken into the villages of Dubravica and
> Krizancevo Selo where they set on fire several
> houses, murdered ten civilians and captured or
> killed thirty-three. We request you to visit the
> Muslim prisons in Zenica and Travnik so that
> you can register the imprisoned.

The second, another letter:

> Respected Gentleman
> HVO Officer Fabijan (Ivo) Tadic has been
> murdered in the recent attacks. Muslim soldiers
> have cut his head off. . . .
> Since the above-mentioned officer is to be
> buried very soon we request you demand III Corps
> of the Bosnian army to do their best so that the
> head of the officer is urgently brought back to
> us.

The third is a Christmas card:

> Merry Christmas, Mr Larry.

In the centre of Zenica there is the Catholic church of St Elias.
Attached to the church is a small religious community. One of
the priests, Father Stipo Radic, was very active in Caritas, the
Catholic charity, and worked hard to bring food aid into the region.

Zenica, of course, had minorities, Croats and Serbs, and while there was not the evil physical violence against minorities that there was in Banja Luka, there was discrimination. Father Stipo, despite his faith and his background, was as near to being neutral as was possible. He helped the needy. By pulling strings, calling in favours and using everyone, he managed always to have something to give away.

On Christmas Day he invited a large number of aid workers to the religious house for Christmas lunch. Altogether, with the religious community, us and some locals, we numbered perhaps thirty and others dropped in, stayed a few minutes and left. It was a great day. He laid on wine and slivovic. The food was all home-cooked and served by a delightful team of nuns. I particularly liked the senior of them, busy, efficient and always happy. When we were leaving I thanked her.

'What for?' she asked.

'For looking after us.'

'That's what God put me here for.'

I was often invited back. Father Stipo and I became close friends.

There was, of course, no Christmas cease-fire.

The Bosnian army corps headquarters blamed mujahedin for the beheading. I have to confess I pursued it no further. I was fearful that if successful I might have to go and collect it. That I could not do.

Another year began; the war continued. Morale among the team was surprisingly high. True, we had convoys arriving and we were distributing, but for December we achieved only twenty-one per cent of needs. I myself was depressed. It was not good enough.

I received a letter from the refugee groups that they would again demonstrate outside my office in one week's time. The demo took place – peaceably. I brought the leaders in to see the empty warehouse. The Bosnian police, however, kept the main group out of my compound with a whiff of CS gas – effective, but not good PR.

Not only did we have civil unrest, but we had it on our convoy routes. At a place called Lisac there is a sharp bend at the bottom of a hill. The trucks must slow down, especially if the roads are icy or wet. Traditionally, the local kids have gathered at Lisac corner and begged. Traditionally, the generous convoy drivers have thrown sweets to them. Lisac corner therefore became known as 'Bonbon Corner'. Convoys at Bonbon Corner were then surrounded not by children but by adults hijacking the contents of the trucks. This self-distribution did not help me. If we lost the food before it arrived we would have even more trouble in the cities.

Trouble in the cities and trouble on the convoy routes was serious enough, but not as serious as the reports coming out of Maglaj, which I have not forgotten.

15
Maglaj Two

As so often happened, the relieving of a besieged town was a momentary joy. The minute the convoy left Maglaj the siege was reimposed, the shelling began and life for the inhabitants returned to its previous perilous tempo. Getting into Maglaj in October had achieved nothing more than a quick feed. We took in three days' worth of food. In November all convoys were stopped because of the death of the Dane at the crossing point near Travnik. In December we tried to make amends but the co-operation of the Croats was minimal. In the accessible areas we were only able to bring in 1.7 kilograms per person. Inaccessible Maglaj got nothing . . . in a month when the temperature fell to as low as $-22°$ C.

Maglaj began to look possible again in January. As ever, my first aim was to get the media interested. Media pressure was always more successful that my words in the wilderness. Louis Gentile, tough 'pull no punches' Louis, was a great ally. He was equally as determined as me to get into both Maglaj and its neighbouring besieged town of Tesanj. Together we bombarded the Bosnian Serb and the Bosnian Croat authorities to give us approval. The Serbs in Pale gave Louis approval to mount convoys from Banja Luka, but refused permission to me. Louis made a few attempts but failed because of the usual Serb disjoint between approval and intent. Eventually we agreed to try to have a combined 'go' at Maglaj. Louis would bring the Maglaj convoy from Banja Luka, from where it would have Serb approval. I would come from Zenica with a matched convoy for Croat Zepce, to be delivered if the Maglaj convoy went through. The Croats would not like this distrust, but that is war. I would also bring an agreement from the Bosnian government forces that they would cease firing as the convoy approached and, more importantly, that they would not antagonise the Serbs in the run-up to the convoy's arrival.

At the end of the first week in January Louis set off from Banja Luka with a convoy of Danish drivers whose leader was Ole, a short, heavy, red-bearded man. I went to Zepce to deal with the local commanders: Mayor Ivo Lozancic and Commander Niko Jazinovic. I took with me a much larger group than I would have liked. Lt-Col. Hap Stutt, the Canadian senior ECMM officer, was very influential in the region. He had set up the meeting. He brought two other ECMM monitors, a Greek and a Dane. The British liaison team, a trio from Hereford, also came in with us and we had the local UNMO team. All in addition to me and my interpreter, the attractive Emilija, and my Britbatt LO, Harry Bucknall. To make matters worse, my driver Kenan, a Muslim, was not happy to sit in the vehicle in Croat-held territory, so he stuck to me like a limpet. Lozancic saw us all in his office, a spartan room and, like all Croat headquarters except Mostar, dirty and untidy. He sat at the head of a long table. I explained my aim: to take the convoy, Louis's convoy, which was about to arrive from Banja Luka, into Maglaj. I told him that 'his' convoy, containing an identical load to the Maglaj convoy, was on its way from Zenica and that it would park up in Bosnian government territory, close to his front line and cross into his territory when the 'Maglaj' convoy entered Maglaj.

Lozancic smiled at my caution but was most co-operative and friendly. 'No problem,' he said. 'Maximum co-operation,' he said and continued, 'As long as you have approval from the Serbs, you will have no problem.' Serb approval we had. He concluded by asking me to liaise with his military commander.

We left his office and I said to Emilija, 'I do not like this. It is too easy.'

'You are right.'

'But I am certain we will succeed.'

'Would you like to bet on it?'

'Definitely,' I said.

She set the stakes as a dinner in Zenica.

We then went off to the military headquarters, another unglamorous Croat location. Jazinovic always met me in the same place, a grotty conference room dominated by a round table with tatty chairs which were too large for the room. At one end there was a small cigarette-stained table on which stood a telephone. There was always a soldier sitting at the table manning the phone, always a different one, but all had the same habit of chain smoking. This phone was what passed for the 'hot line'. Jazinovic sat with his back to the wall. On it was 'the map' on which were plotted the Bosnian and the Croat dispositions as known to Jazinovic. It was never the most accurate of maps.

We all trooped in and Jazinovic immediately began to berate me. He accused me of breaking my word to the people of Zepce, referring to the fact that on my successful visit to Maglaj in October I had 'promised' I would bring out the thirty-two Croat prisoners. He went on to accuse me of having smuggled in weapons on my last visit. 'How else can you account for the fact that immediately after your convoy the Muslims were able to attack our villages?' He concluded, as ever, by calling me a Muslim sympathiser who had starved the population of Zepce. I heard this from him every time I saw him and reacted in my usual manner. A slow start, thanking him for seeing me, asking about his son and his family, then gently refuting each accusation, building up to a climax where I questioned his intelligence for making such ridiculous statements, then slowly defusing all by explaining away his accusations as the understandable actions of a tired military commander carrying such huge responsibilities. Jazinovic was always accompanied by Zoran, a tall, dark, pleasant-looking man who spoke excellent English. His task was to listen to conversations and to pick up our asides. He also interrupted if he felt that his commander's words were being misinterpreted. I never knew if I trusted him or not. He would frequently whisper and smirk during these exchanges.

After the usual opening session we got down to business. Jazinovic informed me that the convoy would have to be inspected to ensure that it contained no contraband, i.e. no weapons. I agreed and on this happy note I left to meet up with Louis and the convoy.

The inspection went well but was done at a pace to ensure that we could not leave for Maglaj that day. The HVO had therefore achieved their aim for one day. I contacted the 'Zepce' convoy which was parked near the front line. This was military. It was accompanied by my logistician, the Dane, Steen Fredriksen. He was disappointed. He made the wise decision to return in one hour to Zenica, sleep the night in the warehouse and come out again the following day.

There was a small restaurant near where we were parked. The journalists told us that it served wine, a then forbidden substance in Zenica and my favourite libation. Louis, Hap, Harry, myself and interpreters hotfooted it there to discover that the journalists had drunk the place dry. Fortunately the resourceful Louis had a bottle of whisky with him. We ordered a meal and were tucking in happily when Zoran, the English-speaking HVO, entered, called me to one side and said that he had been sent to invite our group to a meal that evening in the same restaurant but in a private room. I needed all the co-operation I could get, so I quickly accepted. Two meals in one day was never a problem in a place where tomorrow might bring none. We met the HVO crowd at about seven. They produced Stock brandy, a local sweet not too strong version of the French variety, and the inevitable slivovic. The meal was large gobbets of lamb. The anti-freezing effect of the pure alcohol loosened up our hosts and I was able to gauge who was for me and who against. The boss, Lozancic, seemed sincere. He was worried that we might have problems with women demonstrators, but felt that we would get through. The military commander was still difficult with me. He was forever cursing Muslims and constantly referring to a Muslim massacre in one of his villages. The Military Police chief, Dragan, I watched with interest. He said little to us, but spoke in whispers to Zoran, who behaved like a giggling schoolgirl. I got the impression that we were being set up. I did my best to keep the small talk going and ignored the provocations of Jazinovic. I was impatient to get outside and talk to Emilija. I wanted to know from her the gist of the Dragan–Zoran conversations.

We left at about nine and returned to the car-park. It was yet another bitterly cold night. The drivers had a fire going. We parked our landrover and prepared for the night, agreeing that the convoy should move at 0700 hours the next morning. Emilija was to sleep across the two front seats; Kenan, the driver, and I would sleep in the back, one down each side. We wriggled into our sleeping bags, tossed and turned to establish where the bumps, ridges and edges were. Emilija thanked her petiteness as she negotiated steering wheel and gear lever, Kenan had the driver's side of the back. He had the task of switching the engine on whenever he awakened during the night, just a few minutes of heater to chase away the sharp cold of night. We slept in most of our clothes. The last drill for me was mentally to check where my helmet, flak jacket and boots were; then glasses off, find somewhere safe for them and close my eyes.

Dawn broke and woke me. Found glasses, donned shirt and pullover, got out of sleeping bag, boots on, out of vehicle, morning wee, cleaned teeth, rolled sleeping bag and was ready for the day. The only other vehicle awake was Harry's. The Brits had a fire crackling and were drinking tea. Harry gave me a sip from the cup of his flask. Kenan was a slow starter. Ole, the Danish convoy commander, was up and doing the rounds of his trucks, banging on cabs. The Brits and the Danes were into making some form of breakfast. We in 'Refugees' didn't run to breakfasts. At a quarter to seven the boys from Hereford arrived, bright-eyed and bushy-tailed. Louis and Nidal awoke last. By seven we were ready but with nowhere to go. We had no Croat escort. I contacted Zenica. Steen and his 'Zepce' convoy were on the way. They would, as yesterday, halt near the front line. By seven thirty we were joined by Dragan, the Military Policeman. We could go.

Now the adrenalin ran, the stomach twitched. This was why I joined. We moved out slowly, sedately. I led. So much could go wrong but we were on our way; we were moving towards Maglaj – towards besieged, hungry Maglaj. Out of the car-park, left turn, round the sharp bend, up to the junction, left on to the Zepce–Maglaj–Doboj road. Past the church of Father Simic who assisted me last time in a strange way. On to Brankovici. I looked in the mirror. The convoy was spread out behind me. We turned the bend into tiny Brankovici.

The road was blocked again. On it there was a line of women

and elderly men. They stood behind logs laid on the tarmac. It was so cold that they had lit a fire at the side of the road. I slowly took the convoy right up to the barrier. They stood firm. I told Kenan to halt, he did and the convoy stopped. My experience told me to sit in the vehicle; not to get out; just sit and watch; observe the mood; see who talks, who moves, who sneers, who laughs. I could see the village idiot, the drunk, the shrew. I would avoid these. I saw some of the women from my last attempt. I looked for the woman who, last time, was the most compassionate. She was there. I was prepared to sit a little longer, but glancing in my mirror I saw that the Hereford boys were out of their vehicle and advancing with Harry towards the barrier. They were accompanied by at least two TV camera crews. It was very import-ant that this civilian barricade saw this convoy as a United Nations humanitarian aid convoy, not as an UNPROFOR siege breaker. I opened my door, went to the back of the vehicle, collected Emilija and walked towards the barrier, heading for the compassionate woman. There was barracking from the crowd but it was good-natured.

I heard my name mentioned. I wore my broadest front-line smile. '*Dobar dan*,' I greeted them. My arm outstretched, I stepped over the logs. I told Emilija to tell them that we were headed for Maglaj and that I had approval from both the Croat and the Serb authorities. She got no further than the word 'Maglaj' and I did not need to be a linguist to know that they were not happy. At this stage we were surrounded and many people were tugging or pulling, attracting my attention to give me their version. I asked Emilija if she could arrange for them to elect a few spokespeople to meet me. There was a hum of discontent and Emilija said that they did not wish to discuss anything with me. I decided that the best course was to return to my landrover and sit and see what happened. I quickly briefed Harry and Louis, everyone was to stay in their vehicles. Back in mine I was able to watch the reactions to my proposal. I saw the key player, Father Simic, arrive. A car pulled up. Dragan, the Military Policeman, and Zoran, the English-speaking Croat, got out and passed easily through the crowd. I decided that it was time for me to emerge again. I approached Father Simic and asked if he could organise a meeting with the leaders of the barricade. He agreed to have them together in fifteen minutes. I watched from my vehicle whom he contacted. Certainly some of the women seemed powerful, some just vociferous. What I did not like was that there were two or three mouthy men in civilian clothes. One was armed. The two military took no part in the organising but Zoran was into a lot of whispering and smirking.

I attended the meeting with Louis, Harry and some of the media. We sat on one side of a wooden garden table at wooden benches. The home team was in two groups. Seated were two of the women who had led the barricade during my successful October attempt and Father Simic, and standing a group of women plus the two male agitators. Hovering close by were Dragan and Zoran. I outlined what I wanted: a convoy into Maglaj to feed starving civilians. Significantly, Simic began the reply. He accused me of having betrayed the women of Brankovici on my last visit. He told me that I had promised that if the convoy went in, I would bring out the prisoners. They had allowed me in, the prisoners were still there. The women, who had tears in their eyes, stated that they wanted their men out. The male agitators were muttering that no convoy to Maglaj would pass. I explained that I had the full approval of the Serb and the Croat authorities to go to Maglaj, that I objected very strongly to any accusation that I had betrayed the women. I outlined the chain of events following my successful October attempt; the death of the Dane near Travnik resulting in the complete stoppage, for more than a month, of all convoys in Bosnia-Herzegovina. The subsequent refusal of the Serbs to permit a convoy to cross their front line into Maglaj.

I reminded them that the only hard knowledge they had of their loved ones was from my October visit, that I had taken in with me Father Stipo, that I had arranged with the Maglaj authorities the deal 'Convoys in, some prisoners out'. It was not my fault that I had been unable to get back into Maglaj. There were no convoys followed by no Serb approval. Both events were out of my power. I reminded them that I was here now in good faith, ready to take a convoy in and to see what I could do for their men. The women, through tears and emotion, stated their position: they wanted their men out. The male agitators insisted that I listen once again to the story of how their men had become prisoners through Muslim treachery. I agreed with them that their men had gone from being defenders of Maglaj to prisoners in Maglaj and that it was very unfair on them.

But it was at times like this that I felt cheap. For the real reason why the Maglaj Croats suddenly became prisoners was simply because the Herceg-Bosna Croats changed sides and stabbed the Muslims in the back at their hour of weakness and need. However, explaining this truth was not going to advance matters. I appealed to the women to permit the convoy for the sake of the women and children in Maglaj, many of whom they had known as neighbours. This brought more tears and the women replied by saying that they understood the plight of the residents of Maglaj but that I must see their side. They had children who needed their fathers. They were not preventing the convoy, they just wanted their men out. I agreed. I told them that it was expressly forbidden for me to link convoys with prisoner exchange. That I had written agreements from all sides for the unhindered access of convoy, but that as I felt an obligation to them for their kindness in the success of my previous convoy I was prepared to discuss with the authorities in Maglaj the release of their men. I was prepared once again to take in Father Stipo and that together we would see their men. I seemed to be getting somewhere with the women, but the priest cut me short with 'Prisoners out. Convoy in.' I said, 'Sorry, no can do.' I explained in words of one syllable that I was not permitted to accept 'linkage'. 'Prisoners out. Convoy in' was direct linkage and unacceptable, but 'Convoy in. Discussion on prisoners leading to prisoners out' was not direct linkage. Slowly but surely I was becoming Balkanised! We had reached impasse one, so I called a halt to the meeting, told them that I would refer the matter to Sarajevo and Mostar, but that the convoy would remain on the road where it was, facing Maglaj.

I returned to the convoy, briefed them and the press and sat in my vehicle and observed the crowd. They were good-humoured. It was a cold day, they had lit fires, they had no television, this was the nearest event to a village fête since the war began. They were settling in to enjoy it. After a few minutes Military Policeman Dragan came to my vehicle to inform me that he wanted the convoy to return to the hospital car-park as he could not guarantee my safety where we were. In my gravest voice I reminded him that, in accordance with the agreements signed in Mostar and Sarajevo, he was responsible for our safety. I further reminded him that I had the full approval of his military and civilian leaders for this convoy and that it was going only one way and that was forward. He did not seem best pleased. We were then into the inevitable waiting game. Bluff and bravado would decide the outcome.

I contacted Zagreb and spoke to Karen Landgren. As ever, she was fully supportive and quick to act. She got Jerrie Hulme, late British Army, retired major-general, and UNHCR incumbent in Mostar, to speak to General Roso, late French Foreign Legion, retired colonel, and incumbent Herceg-Bosna military commander. Jerrie's feedback was not good. Roso was supporting the local line. It was time to bluff. I left my vehicle and headed off to meet with Lozancic. I informed him that General Roso had assured UNHCR that he agreed with the principle of unhindered access for humanitarian convoys and respected the agreement to which he was a co-signatory. I told him that I presumed that his communication link with Mostar would confirm this and that he would assist us to move forward. The pear-shaped ex-military leader, now mayor, wore his most sincere look and explained to me that the influence of Mostar diminished in proportion to the distance from Mostar. 'Ah,' I said, 'thus giving you, the senior man on the ground, greater power.'

'No, no,' said Lozancic. This apparently was not what he meant. I have to confess that he was reasonableness itself. He agreed to come with me and help me to plead my case with the committee. I returned to the convoy to await him, briefed everybody and started on the next chapter of my book. The convoy drivers were in good spirits; by now those civilians not actually manning the barrier were chatting, smoking and drinking with them. The local children were being well provided with sweets. The press were happy. They were carried along by my enthusiasm, thought we were going to get in and that they would be able to file a good story. They were a little worried about whether the Serbs would allow them to proceed once we passed this Croat barrier. I reminded them of the words of my favourite hymn: 'Lord, for tomorrow and its needs I do not pray, keep me, Oh Lord, just for today.' On the side of the road near where we were parked there was the small farmhouse, where the old lady with cancer had been treated by MSF on my last visit. Outside the house was a large Dobermann dog chained to a kennel. This Dobermann hadn't read the dog books, he was soft as a pantomime horse. With the man from the *Independent* I visited the house. The old lady, sadly, had gone. Her husband was there, he produced some coffee and some slivovic. I gave his daughter a jar of Nescafé and we were allowed to use his loo, a vital negotiation, especially for the female translators and the ladies of the press. The old man thought we would get through to Maglaj but insisted that I would have to do something about the prisoners.

In the afternoon Lozancic duly appeared. He told me that he had not yet received any orders to co-operate. We met with the ladies and the priest. Lozancic was excellent. The priest was becoming more obviously the leader of the opposition. I also began to suspect that two of the women could cry to order. At this meeting it was suggested that I go to Maglaj on my own to see if the Maglaj authorities would agree to releasing the prisoners. My first thought was that this would be a great idea. With luck I would get the Croats to agree to the medicine that was on the convoy going in with me. But I was very wary of the linkage problem. I said that I would have to refer this to Zagreb.

Lozancic left. Jazinovic arrived. He demanded that the convoy returned to the car-park immediately. Tempers were high, he could not guarantee our safety. I told him I had no intention of moving but I thanked him for his concern.

In my vehicle I mulled over the prospect of a trip to Maglaj on my own. I could see one big danger. Here was I, going in, saying 'Prisoners out. Convoy in.' What would happen if the Maglaj authorities said 'Convoy in. Mr Larry out'? I could be there for a long time. The rest of the day passed with radio calls to Zagreb, Sarajevo and Banja Luka. By 1600 hours the light was beginning to fail. Even if the barrier were removed it was too late to cross the Serb front line with the likelihood of mines. I saw Lozancic and Jazinovic. They invited a group of us to dine with them in their headquarters.

They asked me to move the convoy back to the car-park, as they could not guarantee that we were not in range of the Muslim artillery fire from Maglaj. I was more concerned about the safety of the convoy from looting by locals. Furthermore, I wanted us to appear to the locals to be the good guys, so I proposed that we would guarantee not to move forward so that the locals could go home to bed. But they were in carnival mood and made it clear that they would man and woman the barriers throughout the night. To the annoyance of Jazinovic and the amusement of Lozancic, I insisted that the convoy stayed where it was. The boys from Hereford organised a guard from among the Brits and the ECMM. I decided that I would go to Maglaj but that I would take two vehicles. Then, if I was taken hostage, we might get one vehicle back with the latest news and the conditions. We might, of course, also lose two vehicles and provide two sets of hostages. The joy of command. A real plus about going in was that we would be a recce for the convoy. We would establish the attitude of the Serbs and the condition of the road in no man's land. We would also get the medicine in. The Croats were delighted with my decision.

I got on to poor Steen. He and his convoy had sat the whole cold, bone-chilling day waiting for us to move forward so that they could enter. We agreed, 'Same time, same place, tomorrow.'

In order to go into Maglaj without a convoy we needed to do some liaison with Maglaj itself. The Croats had a radio in Ozimica post office. They monitored Amateur Radio Maglaj, knew the time scheds and the frequencies. Dragan and I went, together with Emilija. With very little difficulty we were through to Maglaj. I briefly explained the position and asked their approval to come to Maglaj without a convoy. They were not happy. There were silences and the request eventually was put before Mayor Aida Smailovic. She came to the radio and spoke with me. She could see no reason why I could not bring in the convoy and discuss other subjects while there. Eventually she agreed that I could come and that she would warn off her front-line troops. We agreed I would enter her territory at eight o'clock. Dragan promised that he would go and see the Serbs. I returned to the convoy.

I took particular care to ensure that Kenan did not park opposite an exhaust pipe. The air was already thick enough with diesel fumes to make your eyes water. Within minutes of unrolling our sleeping bags we were all asleep. The noise from the barricade could be heard all night. Occasionally a villager strolled across and banged on the side of one or other of our vehicles, innocuous enough in a war zone.

I was one of the first up and about. Our military guard had done well. We were all safe and sound. There were a few bleary-eyed civilians still at the fire next to the barrier. The moment we stirred children appeared, hoping for the odd goodie. It is a little disconcerting to be cleaning your teeth and spitting when surrounded by kids. Teeth cleaning is important in the field, washing isn't. Not that I have much face to wash. Teeth cleaned, hair combed, beard brushed, I was ready for action. A quick call to Zenica and Steen was on his way. A quick touch base with Sarajevo and Kiseljak.

The Maglaj group was two vehicles: the senior SAS man, Harry, Hap, Louis, myself, Kenan, Emilija and Nidal, the medicine and, as agreed, Father Stipo. Dragan was always a good timekeeper. We set off at 7.30. The barricade was removed sufficiently for us to weave our vehicles around. There were hugs and smiles from those already up and about. As we pulled away, following Dragan in his red Golf, I got that exciting feeling again. I also knew how the others would feel; for them it was new ground. Emilija was also excited. Maglaj had been her patch before the place became besieged. At the Serb front line they were expecting us. I got out, greeted them and handed out a couple of jars of coffee, while Dragan spoke. I could see the mines on the road. There was some negotiation and a phone call before a path was cleared for us.

Once through the first barrier I knew from previous experience that we had cleared only the Serb Teslic command barrier. We still had to go through the Serb Doboj one. There is a mere 100 metres between them, but on a bad day they could be on different planets. At this stage my vehicle took the lead. Dragan sensibly became number three. We proceeded very slowly, stopping regularly, me getting out, looking for trip wires. The Doboj Serbs gave us no trouble and we were then on our way through no man's

land to the Bosnian government front line. This was where Ginger
Dawes and I had danced during my October outing.

When we reached it I stopped and got out. The leader of the
defenders was still the bright young nineteen-year-old. Dragan,
with a lot of courage, left his vehicle and came up to join us.
Dragan is about six foot two, thin, dark and was wearing Croat
HVO uniform. The Bosnian defenders were a motley bunch in a
variety of clothes. They carried a selection of weapons from hunting rifles to Kalashnikovs. Dragan had the gall to ask the Bosnians
why they did not surrender instead of living like rats. The young
man, whom I liked more and more, asked Dragan why the Bosnian
Croats did not return to fight on the side of Bosnia. Dragan was
put down by these remarks. From his lofty height and his
besieger's position he thought that the Bosnian would be at least
apologetic, if not afraid. This young man was neither.

Dragan agreed to return at one. He left. I gave the Bosnians
some coffee. A man from Maglaj squeezed into the vehicle and
we headed for Maglaj town under his direction: straight down the
road, then a turn to the left. 'The Serbs now have you in their
sights at a distance of no more than 200 metres,' our guide
gleefully told us. Then we drove under the bridge, past the tunnels
where 'the Dane and the UNHCR interpreter died' (more tourist
info from our guide). Along the river bank, one left turn, then
destruction was before our eyes on both sides of the road. Every
house, every building, was damaged, no glass anywhere. The guide
took us to the same building where the majority of the leaders
were waiting for us. As last time, they had rigged up a source of
light using car batteries. There was lots of backslapping, handshaking and tears. Even Father Stipo was greeted warmly. It was so
good to see them again. I handed over some jars of coffee, put a
bottle of whisky on the table, a single malt provided by Louis,
and some cigarettes, the first they would have seen for three
months. They all looked thinner and wearier.

We sat down and awaited the grand entrance of the Lady Mayor.
Aida Smailovic was, as ever, immaculate even in besieged Maglaj.
I greeted her with a kiss. She sat and presided. She welcomed us,
reminded me that last time we met I promised I would return
one week later. She outlined the present troubles, told me of their

needs, their hopes and their fears. She then invited me to explain my absence, presence and lack of convoy. I suggested to her that the military with me should be given the chance of seeing the town, that Louis should see the hospital and deliver the medicines, Father Stipo see the prisoners and that she and I should discuss the answers to all her questions. She agreed. My companions went, leaving Aida, Emilija and myself. I gave her the small parcel of make-up which I had carried around with me for quite a few months. I said nothing. She peeked in, smiled, leaned forward and kissed my cheek. No words were necessary.

Then we got down to business. I explained to her everything that had happened: cessation of convoys; no Serb approval. She winced. I made a great point of explaining that it was not my habit to link convoys with prisoner exchanges. That if she wished I would say no more about prisoners but that I felt I was not going to get a convoy through Zepce unless there was some co-operation from her. She started to give me the rhetoric. Where is the strength of the United Nations? Why must the Bosnians be the victims of aggression?

I cut her short: 'Aida. Do you want a convoy in this week? If you do, then compromise some way, somehow, on the prisoner issue and I will guarantee a convoy. If there is no give from you I do not believe that I will get a single truck up the road.'

'What is the best deal I can hope for?' she asked me. I had pondered over this long and hard.

I suggested to her, 'What about three prisoners per convoy? You have thirty-two prisoners. If I can get in eleven convoys then you can feed your population with the World Food Programme suggested minimum every day for the next two months.' By even mentioning this I was breaking every rule in the aid delivery handbook. I was leading with my chin and risking a knock-out blow on it. The flaws in my proposal were numerous. Was I setting a precedent? Gorazde, for instance, had Serb prisoners. Our convoy was of nine vehicles. Was I establishing a rate of three trucks per prisoner? Was the rate two trucks of flour and one of tinned meat or two of tins and one of flour? If the exchange went well and we stockpiled eleven convoys' worth of food in Maglaj, was that an extra incentive for the attacking Serbs? Would the

Serbs let eleven convoys in to release thirty-two Croats? If I did not make a proposal and no convoy came in, had I done my best? If there were no convoys and many people – innocent women and children – died of starvation, was that better than compromising our rules? Why, oh why, could I not just deliver aid without all this hassle? Every bloody time there was a catch, a compromise, a condition.

Aida listened. She told me she would have to discuss the issue with her military commander. She is a tough woman. 'I want to negotiate from strength. The message you take back is, "Convoy in. Discussion on prisoners. No convoy, no discussion." Understood?' This was fine by me. It meant that I could bring the convoy in without any obvious previous precedent-setting deal. I was also optimistic enough to think that the women in Brankovici might see a glimmer of hope for successful negotiations. I agreed with Aida that I would return the next day, early, with or without a convoy, to bring back the reply of the Croats.

Aida then took me on a walk-about around the town to show me the damage that had occurred since my last visit. Maglaj had a Lowry look about it: matchstick men and women against a backdrop of snow and grey and cold. Aida is a born leader. She wore an expensive fur coat, black high-heeled shoes and walked like a retired ballroom dancer. The Serb positions were visible. She advised that we should not stop as we crossed the bridge into the old part of the town but she did not quicken her sprightly step. The Serbs appreciate strength, they must admire Aida. Few seemed to live in the old town, it was too exposed and too vulnerable. The mosque had received a few more hits since my last visit but it still stood. Back we went, over the bridge and a quick visit to the hospital. The lady dentist remained in charge and was still sending the badly wounded by night to Tesanj for treatment.

They were overjoyed with the medicine we brought, mainly anaesthetics and antibiotics – so pleased with so little. I knew that if I could get the convoy in tomorrow I would bring in ten tons more. I discussed this with the hospital director. She assured me that she would send the majority of it on to Tesanj. I told her that Louis, with his terrier-like tenacity, would try to get into Tesanj from Banja Luka. It was now time to meet back at the municipal building to return on schedule at the Serb check-point.

Everyone was happy. The SAS man had done a good recce, Louis had visited homes, centres and the hospital. Stipo had seen twenty-eight of the thirty-two prisoners and could account for the others. ECMM had had a good look around and I had shuttled the Croat proposal and was about to bat back the Bosnian reply. The most important fact was that we were in Maglaj. We could see on the faces of the locals that they were delighted we were there, even though all we had brought was hope. They all enquired about the convoy. We were saying 'tomorrow'. Emilija was still convinced she was going to win a dinner. I hoped she was wrong. I had lots of cigarettes in the car and I wondered whether I should give them all out then, or wait until tomorrow. With or without a convoy, I decided I would be back, so I took the cigarettes with me.

Our return was easy. Dragan met us at the Serb check-point. He was disappointed that I had brought no prisoners out with me. I could sense the anticipation as we approached the barricade. People were looking in our vehicle to see if we had any released prisoners. We stopped at the convoy, quickly briefed it and the press, then proceeded to the office of Lozancic to give the Maglaj reply. *En route* we stopped at the house of Father Simic and dropped off Father Stipo.

Lozancic was glad to see me. I tried to be at my most enthusiastic. I explained to him the conditions in Maglaj, the scale of the suffering, the responsibility which he bore, his chance to demonstrate to the world, via the media with us, the humanity of the Croats. I was carried along by my own enthusiasm. I told him that I was certain that a convoy going in would return with some gesture from the Maglaj authorities. Lozancic listened politely. He then informed me that he had been told by his headquarters that he was not to use force on the local population. I asked him whether he had any objection if I organised another meeting with the leaders of the Brankovici barricade. He seemed relieved. I think he had feared that I might ask him to address them.

On returning to the convoy I contacted Zagreb and Sarajevo. Karen Landgren promised to talk again to Jerrie Hulme to see what the latest was from the Croat General Roso. She gave me every encouragement to succeed. She told me that Nicholas Morris, the Special Envoy, had spoken to the office of the Croat leaders in Croatia and in so-called Herceg-Bosna. She outlined the media interest, which was considerable. Tony in Sarajevo was fuelling it. His Public Information king briefed the pack twice a day. Jerrie came back from the HVO side in Mostar with the distinct feeling that it would be 'no go' without the prisoners being released.

Time to put words in the General's mouth again. Back at the barrier, the committee was waiting for my brief. Simic had orchestrated the meeting. He was to chair it, sitting opposite me at the end of the wooden table. Next to him were the women with the best tear ducts. I described the town of Maglaj, the condition of the people and the vital need for a convoy. I told them I had full approval from General Roso to take in the convoy. I pointed out the presence of the world's media hovering by, the opportunity for the women of Brankovici to show to the world their compassion, their humanity. As I talked I could sense the meeting dividing into two camps. I could see the disapproving glances of the priest as the women warmed to my words. The priest had a hard face, his dark eyes were neutral, his power was in his voice. It was deep but flat, clear and loud. For the first time I realised that those around the table feared him. He demanded the return of the prisoners before a truck entered. He accused me of betrayal, of being a 'Muslim sympathiser'. The mood changed for the worse. The women cried, the priest ranted, the other men jeered. I called an end to the meeting and returned to the convoy. I briefed press and convoy. We stayed close to our vehicles.

Father Stipo visited me quietly and told me that we were unwelcome. He advised me to be careful. This he did as a friend. Suddenly there was trouble near my landrover where a crowd had gathered. I pushed my way through it to find my driver Kenan very frightened. I could hear in the crowd the word 'Muslim'. Kenan told me that he had been identified as a Muslim and that men in the crowd were threatening to kill him. Emilija heard the name Nidal also mentioned. She was the Banja Luka interpreter with Louis. She too is Muslim. The crowd jostled us, men shook their fists. One drew his hand across his throat and pointed to Kenan. I got everyone into their vehicles. We sat tight; we stayed still. I made up my mind that we would move back to the hospital car-park but I would let some time pass first. I did not want the crowd to feel that it had routed the United Nations. My dilemma was solved for me with the arrival of Jazinovic. He told me that once again it was not safe to stay where we were and this time insisted that we returned to the car-park. I made a pretence of weighing up his words, then told him that as a mark of respect for him I would agree. He was amazed.

The SAS boys turned the convoy round in a dignified and unhurried manner. We returned to Ozimica. That night we refused the invitation of the HVO for a meal, but we were pressured into accepting an invitation for a drink. I did not want to offend at this crucial stage. Lozancic told me that he thought we would not get through, but that he supported us staying and trying. I suggested that I go into Maglaj the following morning on my own to have a final discussion with Aida. They were all very keen on this. Dragan agreed to do the liaison with the Serbs and Maglaj. Lozancic asked me to tell Aida that he could send at least eight hundred Maglaj people living in Zepce to Maglaj, all of whom wanted to return. 'Eight hundred Muslims for thirty-two Croats.' The Croats seemed to be pleased with this ratio. I was irritated by the conversation. Firstly, very few Maglajans in Zepce wanted to go back, knowing full well that the place was starving and constantly shelled. Secondly, I knew that Lozancic had recently forced thirty-six old people to return to Maglaj on foot against their will and without negotiation, a heartless and reckless act. Surprisingly, Lozancic did it believing it to be a conciliatory gesture to Maglaj. Thirdly, these numbers were people – people like me and you. We were in our sleeping bags early.

Leaving Louis in charge, I departed from Ozimica at 7.30, just myself and Emilija. At the Serb check-point they were very friendly and happy; they knew that we were coming and they knew that I was going up to discuss 'prisoner exchange'. They had a neat little request all of their own. There was a Serb in Maglaj. He was confined to a wheelchair. Could I bring him out today? Aida was going to like this one!

We drove directly to the usual building. The translator, Barbara, was present. I liked her, she is full of life. The one we met on our first visit was not around. Questions about her were ignored. Barbara is also a Croat. She must be vulnerable too. I asked her if she could get any information for me on the Serb in the wheelchair. She promised to do her best.

Aida arrived. The works: lipstick, powder, eye shadow! I summarised events in Zepce. I was frank: without prisoners out, there would be no convoy in. Before her tongue went into condemnatory autopilot, I told her that I had a short time only and that I wanted to see the prisoners and compile a list of their names. I mentioned Lozancic's offer. She gave me a quick burst on the elderly thirty-six he had 'expelled' from Zepce earlier in the week. But she seemed interested in getting some people from Zepce. This was the first 'bite' on this hook. She knew that I wanted to see the prisoners. They were ready and waiting. Dragan had done well. She promised that she would have a list of people she wanted out of Zepce on my return from seeing the prisoners. A soldier took me to the place where they were detained. It was close to the Catholic church. Emilija and I entered the prison through a small door which led into a large open courtyard. All the prisoners were there, lined up, waiting for us. They were all clean-shaven, wearing clean clothes and among them there was a great air of anticipation. I quickly addressed them as I did not want them to think that I was there to release them. I told them that I was about to bring a convoy in, that I hoped they would be released soon. Emilija compiled a list of their names. In an attempt to verify who each was I asked them to give me their names and their next of kin in Zepce. There were twenty-nine of them. Two were mentally disturbed. The remainder seemed as fit and as alert as any other occupant of Maglaj. We handed out cigarettes and smiles, hope and heartache. We left and raced back to Aida. The prisoners looked to me as if they were ready for handing over. Why else make them look so presentable?

Aida took us into her little office, the first time I had been in there. We went straight to lists.

I asked her, 'Are you prepared to release any prisoners?'

She replied, 'Yes.' A sweeter word I have never heard.

Her military commander then joined us. He had a list of those Maglaj men whom he wanted out of Zepce. It was twenty strong. Aida agreed to five Croat prisoners out. She and her commander were not happy that the Croats should chose them from the list of twenty-nine.

Here I began to shout. 'You want to choose your twenty and they cannot choose their five! Why don't you take any twenty and they take any five?'

Aida was amused by my temper. The military man was not. He started to accuse me of being more interested in prisoners than aid. I hit the roof. I told them to stick their prisoners. I got up as if to go. Poor Emilija was half-way through trying to find a Serbo-Croat equivalent of 'Stick your prisoners' and I was on my way.

Aida called me back. She agreed that the Croats could choose their five, as long as they got their twenty plus a convoy. I was so elated I could not get out quickly enough. If we really moved we could do convoy and exchange this day. As we were leaving, one of the military handed me a letter from the Serb in the wheelchair to his relatives in Zepce. I still had a large quantity of cigarettes left. I was so convinced that I was coming back I did not give them out. At the Serb check-point they were pleased with the letter from their man in Maglaj until they opened it. It was one long plea to come out.

On my return, I headed straight for Lozancic's office. He was pleased to receive the list of Croat prisoners. He was not happy with the list of twenty 'Muslims' wanted by Maglaj. They were 'all war criminals'. He promised to talk to his military leaders and to the authorities in Grude.

I was deflated. I tried to push him. It was 'Convoy in, five prisoners out, then twenty in'. Surely this was what he wanted? Whilst the convoy went in he would have time to discuss and arrange the twenty. 'Just get the women off the streets, remove the barrier, get the convoy moving,' I pleaded. 'Euphoria will do the rest.'

No. I had to wait. He promised he would come to the car-park. I returned to Ozimica, briefed everyone and waited and waited. On a reporter's phone I spoke to Karen in Zagreb. She was still prepared to support the convoy. We both hoped that if it succeeded the press would ease off on the prisoner exchange angle. I was convinced that if we could get them in they would have a big enough story. We both agreed that morally our job was to get aid to the desperate and that there was no community more desperate than Maglaj.

Lozancic turned up with all his henchmen. He said he had orders that the convoy was not to move until the prisoners were released. I was furious with him. I tore into him. He seemed genuinely shocked by the force of my invective. I accused him of deceiving me all week. I summarised our efforts. We had risked our safety by going into Maglaj without a convoy. We had gone against our principles and discussed prisoner exchanges. I concluded that we had a right to deliver aid, a right accepted in written agreements, signed by his so-called President and his military commander. Lozancic looked guilty and left meekly.

We sat in our vehicles and waited. I knew that this could not be the end of it. Lozancic returned. The convoy could go, furthermore the convoy waiting in Bosnian territory to deliver aid to Zepce could also go to Maglaj. The prisoner exchange was off. There was no obligation to bring back Croat prisoners. He was not offering the release of the twenty but 'all those Muslims who want to return to Maglaj are free to do so'. This reversal was too quick, the concessions too dramatic. But it was not an opportunity to be missed. I informed Zagreb. I spoke to Steen still sitting on the front line with his convoy. He later told me that when he told his drivers they were going into Maglaj there was cheering, clapping and even some tears.

We lined up, revved up and set off. The excitement among us was tangible. Our smiles could have melted ice. I kept the pace slow and dignified. We had no police escort. At the crossroads we turned left and I watched in my mirror as each vehicle rounded the corner. We drove past the church of Father Simic and on to Brankovici. As I turned the corner I could see that the barrier was no longer there. My heart raced. Where the barrier had been was the detritus of the picket: ashes where the fires had burned, broken chairs where they had sat.

I looked up from the scene of so much hassle at the road to

Maglaj. One hundred metres ahead a large blue truck was reversing into the road. A small car overtook the convoy at great speed. I recognised its occupant as Father Simic. The driver of the truck jumped out of the cab and abandoned the vehicle in the middle of the road. I slowly brought the convoy to a halt and sat and watched. The priest, Father Mathias Simic, Man of God, was barking orders to a small group of men. Father Simic, Catholic priest, directed the placing of oil drums on the road to complete the barrier. The spiritual leader of the parish approached my vehicle and banged on the door. 'What do you think you are doing?' he shouted in his most dramatic pulpit manner. 'Where do you think you are going?'

I got out. Simic looked violent. The small crowd that had gathered were very noisy, angry and aggressive. I tried to explain that I had approval from Lozancic. His name brought jeering and spitting. I was pushed and jostled, there was lots of arm-waving and shouting. The message was clear: 'Go back.' I returned to my vehicle and by radio I told the drivers to stay in theirs.

Jazinovic, the military commander, was next on the scene. His attitude was, as ever, that he could not and would not remove his own civilians by force. He warned me that the mood was the worst it had been. I asked for Lozancic, who eventually came. He was wearing a fawn raincoat which for some reason has always seemed to be significant. Perhaps it made him look ordinary and vulnerable.

I may never know if I was conned from the start on this particular convoy, nor whether Lozancic and Jazinovic played me like a fish on a hook. I do know that when Lozancic arrived he was worried. His actions over the next half-hour were, I am certain, genuine and brave. He moved into the crowd, which by now was larger than it had ever been and contained far more men than women. We opened our door so that Emilija could hear what was said and translate.

Lozancic told the crowd that the convoy had approval to go to Maglaj and that it was the duty of everyone to obey that decision. He told them that I was a good man, that I had a duty to deliver to Maglaj, that the press were present, that the world should see how honourable Croats were. He was shouted down. He raised his voice. The crowd began to push him, to assault him.

Throughout this, the priest, Simic, was rabble-rousing. He was muttering to some, prompting others. I watched him malevolently pace back and forth on the periphery of the crowd. I saw him push people towards where Lozancic was speaking. I have no doubt that the leader of this blockade, the force behind the stoppage of this convoy, was Catholic priest Father Mathias Simic.

The final words of Lozancic were, 'If you do not accept the orders to permit this convoy to go to Maglaj I resign.' This provoked a howl which drowned any further attempts at translation. Lozancic turned towards his car and climbed in. I got out of mine and thanked him. He left. We were now the sole focus of the crowd's attention. There were many threats, much drawing of fingers across throats, a lot of banging on my landrover.

I thought that we should sit it out. Harry Bucknall and the SAS man approached us. The latter told me that he was responsible for the security of my convoy, which was news to me. He informed me that he was ordering it to turn around and to head back to the car-park. I was not happy with this. I will never believe that the UN should be seen to run. I preferred to sit it out a little longer. I knew that we would have to move but we should do it at our pace in our time. This was neither the time nor the place for there to be division in our ranks. I therefore reluctantly agreed. I insisted that the convoy be turned around in a slow and orderly manner. During this manoeuvre I went across to talk to the senior man from Hereford. He was rude and vulgar. He is off my Christmas card list.

I had a conversation with Louis. He was all for staying in the car-park for another attempt the next day, but was prepared to look at alternative solutions. Next to Maglaj, the place that most needed aid at that time was Central Bosnia. So the choice seemed to be another day with two convoys trying to get into Maglaj or to release both convoys to Zenica and Central Bosnia. We decided to cut our losses and to opt for Central Bosnia. Our suspicion was that the Croats would not let our convoy back into Bosnian government territory, but would insist that we gave it to them. We therefore decided on a quick run straight across the front line.

No asking permission, just go. Go we did. The Croats at the check-point were a little confused and let us pass. We sped to Zenica, where we met up with an equally disappointed Steen.

Back in the office there was lots of 'Well done but hard luck', which I hate. As we unpacked my vehicle I saw that I still had the cigarettes with me. I remembered my promises to Aida, to the doctor in the hospital, to the people in the streets of Maglaj. I left the office, went to my house and quietly wept.

I added Simic to my list of those who have a lot to answer for.

16
Sad and mad

27 January. The blackest of black days.

'Mack' Court travelled down from Tuzla where his ODA convoy, the 'Nomads', was based. He came down with three trucks and his own landrover. An ex-marine, he was one of the most respected convoy leaders. The vehicles arrived in Zenica in the early evening. They were parked in the compound of the European Community Task Force (ECTF) close to UNHCR, to be unloaded. The team then left to book into the Metalurg hotel. This was not the usual hotel for the drivers but was used when the two better hotels were full. The food in the Metalurg was not to the liking of the team, so they moved to the best hotel for the evening meal. Shortly after seven they received a call that two of the vehicles were loaded. Mack took in his landrover two of his drivers, Paul Goodall and Simon King, to the ECTF compound to place the loaded trucks in the parking bays. An hour later they left the ECTF compound and set off back to the hotel. They slowed down at a notoriously bad patch of road where the surface had been washed away. As they slowly bumped over the corrugated road surface they were overtaken by a green Volkswagen Golf car, which cut in front of the landrover.

It stopped and four men leapt out of it, three from the rear and one from the front passenger seat. They were carrying Kalashnikov rifles. 'Get out,' shouted one of them. The ODA team got out. Mack Court immediately offered the keys of the vehicle to the gunmen, as is the training and practice in such a circumstance. We can always buy a new landrover. He noted that all of them were wearing some sort of uniform, were dark-haired and that three of them were bearded. There was some confusion among the men with the guns as to what was to happen. They ordered the British drivers back into their own vehicle but in the rear passenger bench seat: Simon first, Paul in the middle and Mack behind the driver. One of the gang sat in the back behind the team and two others sat in the front. The team were told to put their heads in their laps and their hands behind their backs. The man in the front passenger seat then said, 'You are to be taken hostage to exchange for one of our people who is being held prisoner.' What thoughts went through the minds of the team I do not know. But they now knew that this was not a robbery. The gang spoke among themselves. Mack believed it was in Arabic.

The landrover travelled about three kilometres, was halted and parked off the road. They were told not to look up. The one who spoke English told them not to worry as they were to be exchanged. The driver, however, was more agitated and shouted at the interpreter. The team sat, looking at the floor. A second car arrived, there was some conversation and they followed it a further two or three kilometres. The team were ordered out of the vehicle. They were taken forward to the side of a small hill. Ahead they could see and hear the River Bosna. They were told to kneel, were searched and lost their wallets and valuables. Then they were moved down to the bank of the river and again told to kneel. A few paces below them the thirty-metre-wide River Bosna flowed fast from left to right. It looked deep.

Facing the river, Paul Goodall was on the right, Mack Court on the left and Simon King in the middle. There was silence behind them, then footsteps, then a sharp bang-bang as two pistol rounds were fired into the back of Paul's head. At the sound of the first of these rounds Mack leapt forward and threw himself into the river. His action was followed by Simon. The attackers fired their weapons at the two escapees. Mack was hit in the back and Simon in the arm and the leg.

Both normally good swimmers, they attempted to swim across the river but the current was too strong. They were carried downstream towards Zenica and away from their captors. They swam under the icy water to avoid being seen. Mack was the first out of the water. As he stood on the river bank he was alarmed to hear footsteps behind him. Peering into the darkness, he discovered it was Simon. Both were wet and exhausted, but the icy water had staunched their wounds. They walked towards Zenica, fearing pursuit, and arrived at a small group of houses. They knocked on a few doors before finding one that answered. It is not surprising in a war zone that people in houses without electricity, peering out through their windows late at night and seeing two men wet and wounded, do not answer. Eventually, the people in one house did show courage and let them in. They sent a member of the family to the telephone to call the police. The police arrived and took them to hospital. Amazingly Simon was bandaged, discharged and sent to the Metalurg hotel! Mack was admitted to the surgery ward. The police rang me from the hospital. They told me two British drivers were there and a third was dead. I contacted John Adlam, the head of the ECTF and *de facto* head of the Brits. Together we went to Zenica hospital where we saw Mack. He was only concerned about Paul. In his usual gruff manner he told me to go and find him. I did not tell him Paul was dead. The British battalion in Vitez were informed and they were excellent. It was after eleven, but they sent an armoured ambulance which had to cross a heavily mined Croat check-point.

They collected Mack from the hospital and Simon from the hotel and took them back through the minefield to Vitez, where they were treated by the outstanding Royal Army Medical Corps Lt-Col. David Jackson. Britbatt sent a Warrior armoured vehicle to pick up Paul's body. He too was taken to the Brit battalion to be with his own. John Adlam and I had one more task to do. We phoned England and told Jack Jones of ODA what had happened. ODA sent a man to Paul's home to inform his family. He was the father of four beautiful girls.

The next day Tony Winton, the extremely caring and sensitive boss of the ODA in Zagreb, arrived with the equally caring, equally sad, Karen Abu Zayed, the UNHCR Chief of Mission. Tony went to see his boys, all three of them. Then Karen and Tony, with John and myself, attended a meeting with the authorities in Zenica. They were shocked and expressed genuine and deeply felt condolences. They were extremely worried that the murder would cause the aid programme to stop. They assured Karen and Tony that every effort would be made to find the 'terrorists', as they called them. The chief of police made it clear that the aim of the crime had been to murder, not to rob. He believed it was a political crime. The one slightly annoying note was that a man calling himself the Head of the Military Court was critical, saying that we, UNHCR, had hindered the investigation by removing the three victims to the British battalion.

Within a few days the police had found the Golf and detained some suspects for questioning. The ODA landrover was discovered, involved in a strange incident. It was spotted trying to cross into Sarajevo. The police chased it. There was a shoot-out and all the occupants were killed. Many letters of condolence were received by the office from various Bosnian authorities and from Bosnian members of the public.

I got together all the aid agencies in Zenica and told them everything I knew. Most were stunned by the fact that murder was the motive. All of us knew that the hijacking of vehicles was a likelihood. It had happened to many agencies. But to be stopped with murder in mind was new. Regardless of this, all agencies agreed to stay on, although all appreciated that there were few safety and security precautions that we could take.

The greatest tribute to Paul was that the Nomads, his team, took a convoy from Zenica to Tuzla within hours of his death. They stopped at the site of his murder and laid a wreath. It was not the first. Many citizens of Zenica had left small posies of flowers.

The suspects arrested in the Golf were released except one who was positively identified by Mack and Simon on the morning they were evacuated to Britain. Bizarrely and ominously, he was being transported to Sarajevo in police custody to be a witness in another case when he 'escaped'. He was a Saudi member of the mujahedin. The case was closed.

Two other incidents arose from the case. We received a phone call in the office purporting to come from the Turkish mujahedin threatening 'to kill a member of UNHCR by 1100 hours'. This I gave maximum publicity. The result was a request from the local mujahedin commander for me to visit him at his headquarters in an isolated part of Zenica. I sought advice. The Zenica chief of police thought that to go would be extremely dangerous. His relationship with the mujahedin was not cordial. Karen in Zagreb was clever. 'Invite him to our office,' she suggested. Surprisingly he agreed to come.

I had to clear the compound. I sent the staff home early and we awaited his arrival. He arrived with a small but well-armed bodyguard. He was a Turk, but he spoke Arabic. No problem, our ace convoy controller, Nijaz, has a degree in Arabic. He translated.

The mujahedin commander was thin and tough. His message was heartwarming: 'We, the Turkish mujahedin, have never issued any death threats against you or your staff.' Then the bit I really liked: 'You and we are here for the same job. You are supporting Bosnians, so are we.' Then the real beauty: 'And we are having the same success. No matter what we do it is not enough. If anything goes wrong we get the blame. Neither of us gets any praise or thanks – only criticism and blame.' In a strange way I liked him.

Zagreb had decided it was time for Steven Wolfson to move. He was replaced by Mark Cutts. I was really lucky with staff. Mark has a degree from Durham University in Theology and is the son of the former Anglican Archbishop of the Argentine. Tall, dark-haired, his looks make women stop in the street. He is a fluent Spanish speaker. He has a studied, measured hesitancy in his speech delivery, a man who weighs his words but brings them from his soul. A passionate humanitarian aid worker, he too writes excellent reports. He also enjoys chairing meetings. Mark will rise to the top. With him as Deputy Head of Office I was still free to roam.

The piracy of our convoys was increasing. At Lisac, at Opara, at any place where there was a sharp bend which slowed the convoy, the trucks were swarmed and emptied on the move. We gave an ultimatum to the Bosnian authorities: 'Stop it happening or we stop the convoys.' They said they had no fuel. 'Give us fuel and we will do our best to patrol the danger spots.' We gave them fuel, some of which was spent on the problem.

The UK charity, Feed the Children, were doing a great job. They were delivering their aid to the children on the hijacking route, trying to persuade them to leave the convoys alone, an initiative much appreciated by UNHCR.

January achieved twenty-three per cent of the minimum needs of the population of Central Bosnia.

'Are you content with twenty-three per cent?' asked a petulant, new-kid-on-the-block reporter.

'If you joined the team now you would not be happy with twenty-three per cent, but if you were here when we issued nine you would be overjoyed.'

February was bleak. The UN New York announcement of the use of NATO airpower in support of the troops on the ground had caused a panic among many agencies. They feared being caught in an air strike or being taken hostage. The British government Overseas Development Administration had stopped its convoys running and withdrawn some of its advisers to safer Split. When the biggies do this it has a knock-on effect. The smaller agencies feel obliged to follow. I called an inter-agency meeting. It was well attended. I explained that we UNHCR were here 'for the duration'; we would not be pulling out. ICRC was equally determined to stay. Unfortunately most agencies were thinning out. The stopping of the convoys was a real blow. Commander Alagic told me he had arrested twenty-one people for bushwhacking our convoys. Now we had no convoys to bushwhack. You take one step forward and two backwards here. I was fed up.

I sent a radio message to Enda Savage in Metkovic: 'Convoys to Zenica. Please be assured there is no extra danger to convoys entering or operating in Central Bosnia. There are more than fifty internationals who live and work here including twenty females under thirty-five. No one has expressed a wish to leave. We desperately need the convoys. Please continue to send them.'

It was true that no one had asked to leave, but many were ordered to leave by their masters who were out of the theatre and did not understand the play. By the end of the week we were no more than a handful.

Eleventh of February was the first day of Ramadan and I had just been told a Sarajevo joke: 'What is the difference between a Muslim in Saudi and a Muslim in Sarajevo?'

'One fasts for Allah, the other for UNHCR.'

I did not laugh until I was on my own.

Saint Valentine's Day, but not a lot of love was shown at the village of Opara. A courageous British aid convoy escorted through this Bosnian-government-controlled village by a Bosnian police escort was attacked by civilians who stole from the trucks more than fifteen tonnes of aid. The Bosnian police fired into the crowd. What a place! There were Croats firing on Bosnians and Bosnians firing on Croats and now we had Bosnians firing on Bosnians!

That night the Coldstream Guards mess had a St Valentine's party which was like having a funeral without a body. I was glad I went, as I had a long conversation with Darko Galic, the Croat staff officer at the right hand of Colonel Blaskic. Darko speaks fluent English. He is a tall, taciturn man. He had fought at Vukovar, one of the earliest and most vicious battles of the war in the whole of former Yugoslavia. The city was totally destroyed. We had just done Darko a little favour: by pulling in favours in our turn we had been able to reunite him with his family. I asked him the name of his son.

'Amarillo.'

'I have not heard that one before. Is it Croat?'

'No. It is Spanish.'

'But you and your wife are Croats?'

'When I was in Vukovar I fought alongside a Spanish mercenary. We were there for the whole battle. We shared everything. The Serbs took the city street by street, house by house. The Spaniard and I were like brothers. We fought from house to house, we retreated from house to house. The last days of the battle were the worst: so many of them, so few of us. The Spaniard was hit and died in my arms. I had no time to cry over him, to bury him. I left him. He gave his life for our most precious possession, my country. I have given his name to my most precious possession, my son.'

Two days later, a small agency, Sans Limites, tried its luck and tested its courage with a convoy escorted by a British battalion armoured vehicle. At Bonbon Corner the convoy was plundered. The Brits fired into the air but the crowd took no notice. What a dilemma. Was the answer to shoot dead some of the looters? Was the safe arrival of a convoy worth the loss of a life? Were these people starving or profiteering? The truth is they were thieves. They were trading with their ill-gotten gains. They were stealing food destined for their kith and kin who were starving. They were guilty, but a Bosnian civilian problem needed a Bosnian civilian solution. We had little food. What we had we could not afford to lose so I cancelled the distribution of food to towns along those routes where we had trouble. In the company of Peter Williams, the Brit CO, I visited the Bosnian and Croat commanders and told them I would start deliveries again when they could guarantee their safety. This had the opposite effect to what I had expected. The bandits of Bonbon Corner and Opara, who by then must have had more stocks than I had, panicked. They picked clean the next convoy through their location; a Dutch *military* convoy carrying food for UNPROFOR and escorted by Britbatt armoured troops! As before, the thieves ignored the shots in the air. I felt sorry for poor Oxfam. They had risked sending a convoy believing it would be safe in such heavy company. They were wrong. They lost their aid.

That was it. On Saturday, 19 February I cancelled the distribution of aid in the whole region. Not out of pique – the warehouse was empty. The word got around rapidly. An empty UNHCR convoy returning from Zenica to Metkovic was hit by sniper fire. Fortunately no one was injured.

Throughout all this hassle with the 'Muslims' the Croats were not snow-white. It would not have been Bosnia if they had been. As each and every convoy emerged from Bosnian government territory into the Croat Vitez pocket it was stopped and searched by Croat police and customs. Few convoys passed without long delays, arguments, hassle and petty pilferage. This was not fair on drivers at the end of a long journey.

Peter Williams, who was as fed up as I was, decided on a head-to-head confrontation with the leaders of the Croat and Bosnian authorities. He drew up a chronicle of all the hindrances, objections and incidents that had stopped the free and safe passage of humanitarian aid. Our first call was on the Croats. We were a large delegation: Peter, Sir Martin Garrod of ECMM, American Jay Carter of UN Civil Affairs and me. They were Dario Kordic, Colonel Blaskic, Chief of Police Rajic and a man representing the

Mostar authorities, Marinko Bosnjak, a straight, honourable man whom I liked. Peter hit them hard, reading out the litany of sins. I went for cajoling and humour, Jay for straight, curt common sense. We received an act of contrition and the immediate agreement for us to medevac two wounded from Stari Vitez. We came away at least feeling better.

We called on Bosnian Commander Alagic. He got the 'Muslim' version of the chronicle. He was tired, bored and uninterested. He listened and nodded and smiled. He was a bey, a pasha, listening to a petition. Where his mind was, what he was thinking about, I did not at that time know.

Two days later, 23 February, a Peace Accord was signed in Zagreb between the Bosnian government military commander, General Rasim Delic, and the Chief of the Bosnian Croat forces, General Ante Roso. The deed was under the chairmanship of General Cot, the head of UNPROFOR. A cease-fire would take place at midnight on the twenty-fifth. Alagic had no time to lose. There were a fair number of scores to be settled in those remaining twenty-four hours!

On the day the Accord was signed we received twelve convoys without hindrance or hassle. We began to distribute immediately.

With food in the warehouse, I turned my gaze once again towards Maglaj. If the Croats were back in bed with the Bosnians I had only the Serbs to worry about. I spoke to Peter Williams. He agreed to mount Operation Lawrence: a heavy escort from the Coldstream, a transport platoon from the Dutch–Belgian battalion and UNHCR. It was the usual formula: two convoys, one for the Croats in Zepce and the other for Maglaj. Despite the new wind of change, in Zepce the trucks for Maglaj were inspected in such a casual way that I knew we were not going to get in. I left the convoy and motored forward with just my own vehicle.

Sure enough, the road was blocked with women and children, supported by some drunken men in uniform. The men were very abusive. They again tried to drag poor Kenan out of the vehicle. I got out to try to reason with them. It was a waste of time and it was degrading. A grandfather who was with his grandchildren squared up to me with his fists clenched and attempted to provoke me into a fight. I was sorely tempted to lay him out but instead turned away. The crowd jeered. The grandfather pulled on my arm and drew his hand across his throat to signify that he would like to cut mine. It was his moment of glory with his grandchildren.

I motored back to the convoy. 'Turn around. Let's go back,' I said forlornly.

The military were openly critical of me. 'Don't know why you brought us here. Nothing has changed since last time,' said one officer.

'You are making a fool of us,' said another.

I bit my tongue. It would not be right to vent my anger on the wrong group. 'We are here because Maglaj has not been fed by convoy since October. They will know that we have tried today. That will help them to hold on.' I knew I was right but I also knew that I had not convinced them. A very dejected convoy returned to Zenica. I was reminded by a number of people that food and resources were still scarce and that we could not waste them on personal quests. For the first time I began to wonder if I had been here too long.

Back in the warmth and familiarity of my office with my loyal staff, I got my confidence back and realised that my detractors had not been here long enough. February had ended with a cease-fire, a convoy route open and, despite everything, with thirty-one per cent of needs delivered. My staff had worked their socks off. I hoped that now routes were open I could get some of them away to the coast for a break.

I was beginning to annoy the Zenica authorities. They were pestering my male staff. They wanted them in uniform. They wanted to conscript them. If only they knew how much war effort my boys had put in. They also did not like the composition of my staff. I had a good sprinkling of Croats and Serbs. They preferred me to employ only Muslims.

> Dear Mr Larry,
>   We would appreciate it very much if you could send us a list of all your local staff for the purpose of our keeping a record of your employees nationality structure.
>   Signed Minister Fuad Djidic.

I whanged back by return:

> Dear Sir,
> All my local staff are Bosnians.
> Signed Mr Larry.

Doctor Djidic, who has a doctorate in Marxism – a qualification as useful as a comprehensive knowledge of the common diseases of the dodo – was not pleased with my reply. My staff were.

The reports coming out of Banja Luka were as horrendous as ever. Having left did not prevent me from reading them with anger at our impotence. I decided to go and talk to Mayor Besim Spahic. I outlined to him the latest report and asked unofficially for his advice. 'Would the Zenica authorities wish to help the Muslims in Banja Luka? If I could get them out, would Zenica offer them accommodation?'

The mayor was not enthusiastic. 'You will have to go and see Mr Djidic. He is the Minister for Central Bosnia.'

Not the answer I wished to hear but. . . 'Dr Djidic, I have come to ask your advice. I have not discussed this subject with my masters in Zagreb nor with my colleagues in Banja Luka, but could Zenica take any displaced from Banja Luka? If so, how many and how soon?'

I had to listen to the history lesson and then the diatribe: 'If UN were stronger . . . If UNHCR were more aggressive . . . If the Aggressor . . .' Eventually he told me that Zenica already had its fair share of displaced persons and was not prepared to take any more.

'Look, UNHCR could provide more money, for refurbishment of accommodation, for food.'

'No. I am sorry.'

'Thank you. I will not report our conversation to my masters. I was just after your advice.'

The next morning, just after eleven my phone rang. It was friends. 'Have you or any of your staff listened to BiH radio?'

'No. Why?'

'Mr Djidic was on. He said that he had been visited by that well-known humanitarian aid worker, Larry Hollingworth, who has proved to be a hypocrite by attempting to persuade the authorities to ethnically cleanse Banja Luka.'

I rang him up and thanked him 'on behalf of the people of Banja Luka'.

My staff were very protective of my privacy. That evening I received a note:

> Dear Larry,
>   I have been trying to reach you for a couple of
> days but your staff protect you far better than
> Mr Clinton's. Can you spare a couple of minutes
> for an old wounded compatriot?
>   Tony Birtley.

It was marvellous to see him again. He told me how, after I had left Srebrenica, he had pursued the story of the aerial bombing of the border villages. One fine day he had lingered too long, too far forward. A Serb mortar man landed his bomb close enough to bite a sizeable chunk out of Tony's calf muscle. Two UN soldiers were also wounded. A helivac saved his leg, perhaps even his life. After such an incident any sensible journalist would switch to fashion correspondent or religious affairs – not Tony, the original ace cameraman reporter. He was back, limping around front lines, hobbling across check-points, filing the best stories. I briefed him about the little Central Bosnian picture. He briefed me on the big Bosnian picture. We had a drink or two and he left . . . for the front.

On 4 March General Sir Michael Rose, who had demilitarised Sarajevo, went into Stari Vitez, with a UNHCR convoy close behind.

I began to hear whispers that Lozancic was meeting with Commander Alagic and discussing Maglaj. Rumour had it that they had met on 1 and 2 March, in Zepce. I rang Alagic to see if he could give me any advice on getting in.

'I will be there before you,' was his cryptic message.

On Sunday, 6 March my day was dominated by news from Maglaj. First I heard that the Bosnians there had released the Croat prisoners; thirty-two out, safe and sound. Then news arrived via the UNMO net that there was a massive realignment of the front-line trenches. The Croats were disengaging and moving back and the Serbs moving into the Croat trenches to maintain the stranglehold on Maglaj. This was bizarre. Did the Croats wave or shake hands when they left and changed sides? Did the Serbs spit on them? ECMM then rang with the news of a massive explosion in Maglaj. It was believed that the main bridge over the Bosna had been destroyed. First reports blamed Serb aircraft. This was disproved by NATO watchdogs in the sky. The next guess was a Frog missile. Whatever, whoever, aerial reconnaissance photos showed that the bridge was damaged but not down.

Finally I had a visit from Martin Dawes of the BBC and John Pomfret of the *Washington Post*. They are both old friends so they levelled with me. 'Larry, we have found a way of getting into Maglaj. We are going in tonight. Can you give us a briefing? Whom to see? Where to go?'

I was amazed. They were serious. They are two excellent reporters. They both look like teachers. They are very low key. They do not wear reporters' jackets bulging with torches and knives and water bottles like some of their colleagues. And here they were telling me they were going into Maglaj that very night. They were going to infuriate their fellow hacks. I briefed them and wished them luck. I never mentioned to anyone the purpose of Martin's visit. But the following day my office was full of journalists. The word was out. Dawes was in. Everyone wanted to know how they got there. Two days later Martin and John were out with excellent footage. They were taken in by the Bosnian army, presumably through trenches which had once belonged to their enemies the Croats, now their friends the Croats.

The scene was changing fast. Journalists visiting me asked if I had seen an announcement by the British Ministry of Defence that sixty SAS were now operating in Bosnia. I was more surprised that it was in the press than by the fact or the numbers. The MoD would be selling videos next.

Two days later two teams from Hereford were flown into Maglaj at speed, by courtesy of a helicopter of the Nordic Air Wing. They were fired upon by SA 7 missiles, which thankfully missed.

Later that day a third team went in on foot. Maglaj was now on General Rose's agenda.

I went to see Peter. 'Peter, Hereford is in. The BBC have been in and out. Soon there will be guided tours of Maglaj. We have got to get in.' I passed the same message on to Zagreb.

The twelfth of March was the end of Ramadan. The commander of now free Stari Vitez, Sevkiya Dzidic, threw a party and arranged a football match against the officers of the British battalion. Stari won.

I received a visit in my office from the squadron commander of the boys now in Maglaj. He asked me to brief him on everything I knew about Maglaj, Tesanj, Doboj and the Ozren. He assured me that I would soon be in Maglaj.

'If I helilift in any more of my men, are you prepared to go with them?' He did not need an answer, he saw the sparkle in my eyes.

'OK. I will let you know then.'

I was now really excited. But I heard nothing for more than a week.

Meanwhile there was more excitement in a different direction.

17

Split and back

I heard a buzz that a VIP was soon to arrive. No one would confirm who it was but he or she was obviously very, very important, so much so that they were given a code-name. I was intrigued.

I was even more intrigued when I received a message from Brigadier John Reith inviting me to dine with the code-name. The dinner was to be in his headquarters in Split the following day. This left me with two options. The first was to motor to Sarajevo and try to get a flight to Split, which was the easiest, but had that element of doubt of no airlift, no flights, no time to reach Split, read about code-name in the paper. The second option was to motor myself to Split. This involved an early start but almost guaranteed me getting there. I asked my staff to prepare my vehicle 333. Vesna was to accompany me. I packed the car with a change of clothes.

Vesna asked, 'Where is your suit?'

'My suit?'

'Your Karadzic suit.'

'I have given that up.'

'Where is it?'

'It is in the flat.'

'Give me the keys.'

'No. I don't need it.'

'Why did you bring it to Bosnia?'

'For special occasions.'

'You are going all the way to Split to dine with a code-word. Do you know any occasion more special than that?'

'Code-name.'

'Code-name, code-word. Go and get the suit.'

I went and got the suit.

Normally, I would travel to Split behind a convoy. It is easier, no map reading and there is the safety-in-numbers factor. But convoys are much slower than free-running vehicles, so I decided to go it alone. The trip down was hot, dusty, sticky and uneventful. In Split I went to the Brit headquarters where I was expected. A WRAC captain gave me the details about the dinner, the time and the venue but she said that she did not know who the code-name was.

I booked into a local hotel and washed off the grime of the day. I changed into my lightweight suit. This was its second airing in almost two years. I felt strange in it. I wore a bow tie. This is a little game that I have with myself. When I left the army I threw away the razor. When I joined UNHCR in the field I determined to give up ties. However, thirty years of conforming make it difficult for me to be the only person without a tie on. Hence the bow-tie. It is there but you can't see it, the beard obscures it.

The dinner was in the HQ senior dining-room, a sort of combined senior NCOs' and officers' mess. When I got there, the early arrivals already had their first round into the bank. Everyone was looking smart. They were all wearing their code-word suits. Vesna was right. Over my glass of wine I spoke to Andy Bearpark of ODA. He confirmed that his boss, Linda Chalker, was one of the guests. There are not many people senior to her so that narrowed down the mystery. The room filled with people, chatter and excitement. Then the guests arrived. First through the door was Prime Minister John Major. He was the one I had put my money on. I was near the door and was introduced to him. He very kindly said that he had seen me on the tele. We talked about the recent arrival of the second British battalion. Somewhat presumptuously I thanked him for this extra support to the humanitarian effort. It was a great gesture by Britain and as a Brit I felt proud and pleased by it. Mr Major seemed genuinely happy with my comments.

He was then whisked away and I saw Baroness Chalker. She was smashing. She came across and gave me a kiss and asked me how things were. Choosing her to head the ODA was a master-stroke by someone. She has the respect of everyone in the international humanitarian aid business. She is hands-on and caring.

I next spoke to Mr Rifkind, the Minister of Defence. I had seen him in Bosnia on a number of occasions, including the time at a private party in the house of the CO of the Coldstream Guards in Vitez when I asked him if he had ever wanted to be anything but a politician. He very gently reminded me that he was a successful lawyer and a Queen's Counsel.

At the dinner I was seated at the top table, a small, intimate group of eight, including Mr Akashi, the special representative of the United Nations Secretary General. I could not believe that I was so lucky and remain to this day in the debt of John Reith for this honour.

I had a great time. The PM began by saying that everything we said was to be in private and off the record. I detected a little glance at me here. In two and a half hours we discussed many, many topics. I learned a lot. I asked the PM how important Lord Whitelaw had been to Margaret Thatcher. He thought he had been very important. I asked him if he had a Willie Whitelaw. He said, 'No.' I then asked him if he would have liked a Lord Whitelaw. He said, 'Yes.' He also told me that his favourite writer at that time was Joanna Trollope. He said that her characters fascinated him. My revelations are not up to the tabloid diaries but I can say that I thoroughly enjoyed the evening and especially the company of Mr Major. He was charming, easy-going, frank and very patient with me.

There was lots of buzz and hum from the other tables. It was an informal and happy evening. The food was excellent. I do not know how it compared with Number Ten but it was better than anything in Zenica.

The following morning I left Split to return to Zenica, but not by the route by which I had arrived. I had to pass through Metkovic, as I wanted to visit Enda Savage who ran the UNHCR warehouse there. Enda is an ex-Irish Army officer. He is very straight, a direct talker and a good friend. I underestimated the journey. We left Split at eight. I intended filling up the vehicle with fuel early in the journey but forgot and very nearly got caught out. The coastal route is super-scenic. The views of the mountains on the left side and the Adriatic on the right are stupendous. But having constantly to keep one eye on the needle of the fuel gauge and another on the road ahead searching for a fuel station detracts from the view. At the same time I kept up an endless chat with Vesna, not wishing to let her know that I had been such a dunderhead as to have set off without fuel. Future tourists, fellow travellers, take my tip, fill up in Split. To the best of my knowledge there are no petrol pumps between Split and Makarska, and you have to leave the main road to enter Makarska, where the pump is at the far end of town.

From Makarska I was a different man. The feeling reminded me of being a boy on a coach trip to see the lights at Blackpool, after the coach had pulled over and we were able to relieve ourselves. This anecdote was wasted on Vesna.

Metkovic did not seem to come any closer. I began to get slightly worried. From Metkovic to Zenica was at least six hours, the last two through some notoriously dangerous Croat territory with a reputation for hijackings. I did not fancy being a lone runner on a dodgy road late at night, especially as my translator was female. We eventually arrived at Metkovic to discover that Enda was in bed with the flu. To his great credit he got up and came in to see me. We discussed warehouses and auditing and distribution. I suggested that Enda sent his second-in-command to Zenica to look, check and recommend. With this he agreed and it was done.

There are three main ways of getting into Zenica from Metkovic. I asked Enda's staff which way was the best. I was told that the only safe one was via Medugorje, Mostar (Croat side), Jablonica, Prozor, Gorni Vakuf and Travnik. There was a snag. The road from Mostar to Jablonica was via a new mountain route. 'The best views in Bosnia . . . for the passenger,' I was told by Enda's convoy controller, who advised that we stayed overnight in Metkovic and followed a convoy the next day. He also told me that he believed that the new mountain route was signposted, protected and patrolled by the Spanish. From their territory we would pass into the hands of the newly arrived Malaysian battalion. We all agreed that time was our enemy if we were to clear lawless Prozor before dark. I did not want to stay but I was uneasy about going on. I decided to leave, with a little twinge of reservation. We left Metkovic at about two thirty. It was a hot, hazy, sticky day.

Our trip through west Mostar brought back some memories for me of my time there. It caused Vesna great pain. It was the first time she had seen Mostar since the war began. It was an ancient city she knew well. Being a Sarajevo girl she was used to destruction, but this made her silent and sad.

We found the road out of Mostar, with no thanks to the Spanish. There was not a single sign anywhere and we were well on our way along a rough, zigzagging track before we came upon one lone Spanish APC. We had passed a number of forks in the road and by good luck had managed to choose the right ones. At first the terrain was dreadful, huge boulders and barren hills. We began to climb, the views became spectacular and the track narrowed.

At the peak of this mountain road there was a check-point manned by ten or so Croats, heavily armed and in uniform. They were a friendly, happy bunch. I clearly remember thinking, we were only two, we had a vehicle they would like and they would guess that we had money. They could easily have thrown us over the side and no one would have been any the wiser. I very rarely had worrying thoughts, but on this day I did.

As we began the descent my admiration for the convoy drivers increased. It was a hairy run with tight bends, fast descents and no barriers. Lose control and dive down, down, deep into the reservoir. When we reached the bottom we crossed the reservoir by the bridge which is not many miles north of Mostar. In two hours we had advanced no more than 15 miles. A section of the Malaysian army were manning the bridge. I was delighted to see them. They were very friendly. They assured us that the road was secure between themselves and Jablonica. We moved on in a far more relaxed manner. I felt safe once again.

In Jablonica I checked in at the Malaysian headquarters. A fairly abrupt, uninterested colonel told me that to the best of his knowledge there had been no incidents on the road recently. This next bit was for me the most dangerous stretch. We were tired. It was getting late. Once we set off there was no turning back. The next friendly forces were the Brits in Gorni Vakuf.

The 25-kilometre stretch of road from Jablonica to Prozor is tarmac. It is in a valley. There was no traffic on it, none, not even a Malaysian vehicle, nothing to boost morale or bolster confidence. Nothing passed us; we passed nothing. We tried to radio Zenica. We had tried all afternoon with no success but we were now that much closer. Nobody could hear us. We could hear other channels and lots of inconsequential chat. Good reassuring stuff if we had known that they could hear us. But no one was acknowledging our call.

It was early evening as we approached the outskirts of Prozor, which is the Croat equivalent of Doboj, another cowboy town, fiercely Croat, strongly HVO, anti-UNPROFOR. Coming up from Jablonica you do not have to go into the centre of the town. You enter the outskirts, then take a right turn on to the Gorni road. I knew that this next bit of road was our most dangerous stretch.

At this turn we saw the first vehicle we had seen for half an hour or more. It was a landcruiser with some HVO soldiers in it. There were a couple of other cars about and we set off along the road. It is carved out of a steep-sided valley with mountain ranges on both sides. Immediately out of Prozor the road twists and turns quite dramatically, then there is a steady climb up to a café at a barren outpost called Makljen. In October and November of 1992 I had stopped on a number of occasions at the café. This was before the Croats and the Muslims had torn at each other's throats. It had never been a friendly place. It always had just a few surly HVO soldiers in it. It was certainly not a place to stop, on your own, or worse still, with a female translator. As we approached the summit of the road and the café I noticed that we had a vehicle behind us. Although I was going slowly it made no attempt to overtake us. At the crest of the hill outside the café it surged past us, then slowed.

Vesna was quicker than me. 'That is the landcruiser we passed in Prozor,' she said with only a trace of fear in her voice. I told her to get on the radio and try every call sign we knew.

The road out of Makljen is a very steep descent. Initially, there are few bends. The car ahead was going no faster than us. We were not wearing our flak jackets. I said to Vesna, 'Get the jackets from the back, try to put yours on, put mine behind me.' Flak jackets are very difficult to put on in the confines of a moving car. She put both hers and mine on our seats behind us. She was still trying to raise a voice on the radio. I was watching the car ahead, which was trying to close the gap by slowing, but as it slowed so did I. I thought about a quick turn around. I had the space but where was I to go? To the 'safety' of the café? With the car ahead I at least knew how many we were up against. There were three of them. Also, as long as we were moving we had as much of the initiative as they did.

To the left of the road was the mountain, to the right it varied between a drop or the other mountainside. It was obvious to me that the driver ahead knew the road and knew when he was going to move. Sarajevo had taught me that when there is danger about you sit up straight, hands firmly on the wheel. It is a strange feeling. Every muscle is alert. You are aware of your toes and your fingers. You almost feel as if you are outside your own body. Somehow you can see your own face. Time does stand still. Adrenalin definitely flows. You can feel it coursing through your veins. I was waiting for him to make his move. Our lives might depend on my reaction to whatever he did.

Suddenly we approached a twisty section. I could see in the distance a turning off to the right. We were in the deepest part of the valley, the most isolated section. As I followed him around the bends, he was able to dictate the distance between us. We were closing all the time. Then he moved. He indicated that he was pulling over to the right and braked sharply. I went to the left as if to overtake him. He swerved into my path to head me off and tried to push my vehicle into the side of the road. I was now completely in command of myself. I swerved to the right. He did likewise. I swung the wheel to the left again but he anticipated this and once again my path was blocked. I switched to the right, to the open side of the road. He did the same but his vehicle reacted more slowly. The front of my vehicle was centimetres from the rear of his. I was heading for the edge of the road. I saw the gap was closing. I accelerated. The front side of my vehicle was alongside the front passenger wing of his. The gap between him and the barrier was just enough for me to get through. I could see his passenger, who was shouting to him. Despite the bend I went like the wind, foot hard down, great sweeps of the steering wheel. Our kit tumbled around in the back as the car swayed from side to side. I expected shots. I hoped that the flak jackets would stop them, but the bends presumably prevented them from aiming. They gave chase for only a few yards. In the mirror I could see we were pulling away. I could feel myself tingling. I looked at Vesna. Her shoulders were hunched in anticipation of bullets, her face a stone mask of fear and concentration. We sped away. Vesna pointed out to me, in the distance, the village of Gorni. We hammered on until at the bottom of the hill we arrived at the check-point. There was a Brit APC. I stopped the car and a Coldstream Guards officer approached. He could see at a glance that we had been in trouble. Vesna and I were ghostly white. I told him what had happened. He sent the APC back up the road as far as the café but they saw no one.

On reflection, I should have gone with him. I knew what and whom we were looking for. I motored on to the Brit camp. When we had parked we got out of the car and hugged each other for a long time. No words, no tears. We had time to motor on to Vitez but we could not have made Zenica. We decided to stay in Gorni. We had had enough excitement for one day. The Brits gave us a meal. We then returned to the vehicle, unrolled our sleeping bags and I remember saying, 'The least that would have happened is that we would have lost the vehicle and our possessions.' What thoughts went through Vesna's mind I do not know. She is pretty and a Serb.

18

Closing down

Back in the office, my first call was to Peter Williams in Britbatt. 'Any news on Maglaj?'

'No firm news but lots of gossip. The Croat news agency "Hina" is quoting a UN source as saying that the siege is soon to be broken either with Serb consent as a result of Russian pressure or by it being declared a "safe area" and occupied under NATO air cover or through a cease-fire and a total exclusion zone.' He concluded with a twinkle, 'We thought you might be the UN source.'

Melisa was our medical doctor who organised medical evacuation. She is a tall, attractive blonde girl who qualified in Sarajevo. A special skill she has is to twist men around her little finger. She has had great success in getting Britbatt to evacuate sick and wounded for whom UNHCR have found places in overseas hospitals. Her patients were taken by UNPROFOR helicopter to Split, then onwards by commercial aircraft.

She came to my office and looked sad. Her charm had just failed. She had been dealing with a young man in Bugojno who was badly wounded in a mortar attack. He had lost one eye, could only distinguish light in the other and had also lost a hand. Melisa had worked hard for weeks to get him a sponsor nation and had succeeded. A hospital in Denmark was prepared to take him. There was a complication: we needed to send a relative with him. His wife was the obvious choice. She loved him dearly and was marvellous with him but she was now nine months pregnant. When Melisa had begun her search for a hospital the woman was in her eighth month. When she went to send him and his wife to Split the helicopter crew refused the wife. Their action was understandable. They had a minimum crew and no facilities for childbirth. It was a war zone. Furthermore, as they rightly pointed out, when they got the couple to Split for transfer to a commercial flight to Denmark no airline was going to take her. A decision was therefore made to postpone the medevac until after the birth of the baby. The woman was devastated. She feared that her husband would lose his place, that we would say she could not go with an infant. On this latter point she could be right. She would be going to look after and to support him. Could she do this with a tiny baby? Would the baby be OK? Would Denmark take an extra person? Would the airlines take a days-old baby?

The helicopter team left with promises to return. Melisa had spent a lot of time trying to reassure the woman that she would be OK. The couple had left for Bugojno. Melisa promised to get them out immediately after the birth. She had spoken to Zagreb and Sarajevo. They would try to clear the way with Denmark and the commercial airlines.

I was summoned urgently to the radio room. A message from Britbatt. The British cavalry unit, C Squadron Light Dragoons, patrolling close to Maglaj had discovered that the Serbs had withdrawn from Ljesnica, the approach road to Maglaj. The way in was open. Peter was rapidly resurrecting Operation Lawrence. We were off. I took with me 'signalling Serb' Vesna, who had been with Ginge and me on the first successful attempt. Major the Hon. Richard Margesson was in command of the military, one of the most professional officers I have ever met. With him, everything is planned to the last detail. The mission was to be achieved without hesitation or deviation. In an idle moment I discovered his grandfather had been the MP for Salisbury and that his Australian wife is an airline pilot.

However, Commander Alagic was determined that he was going to be first into Maglaj and had done a deal with his new-found allies. When we arrived at Zepce we were delayed, held at the side of the road for almost an hour. During this period Alagic led a joint HVO–BiH convoy into the town. He sent me a message by radio, 'Alagic first. UN second.'

'Where were you five months ago?' I replied, further cementing our relationship.

The convoy of ten vehicles driven by Dutch and Belgian drivers came behind me, following the new Earl of Maglaj, Richard Margesson. There were no mines on the road, just SAS troopers. This was very different from my previous attempts. At the spot where Ginge and I did our little dance to the tune of machine-gun fire we stopped the vehicle and Vesna and I posed for a photo. There was no one in the trenches. The sun was shining. She pointed out to me a flowering cherry tree. The siege of Maglaj was over.

As we entered the town we saw more people than we ever had before. They were lining the streets, on the balconies, waving and cheering. This was the relief of Maglaj. They knew it. Vesna and I smiled and congratulated each other, proud to have been part of it.

Commander Alagic was basking in his success, his laden convoy parked at the side of the road, his drivers receiving their accolades. We quietly overtook him and went directly to the warehouse and unloaded first. We sent two trucks up to Tesanj with a Hereford escort. So we relieved not only Maglaj, but Tesanj and Maglaj on the same day.

Aida greeted us warmly. She looked as elegant as ever and wore a nice line in make-up, I noticed with pleasure. At our meeting in the municipal hall she was full of praise for the SAS.

The great joy of the day was the fact that Richard and his boys stayed in Maglaj. The siege was indeed over. The Brits kept the road open. For the rest of the war Maglaj would not be an encircled pocket but a finger along which convoys could pass almost unhindered.

Vesna met up with the translator Barbara. You could have lit the town with their smiles. Violetta had gone to Zepce. At the hospital we met our dentist director friend. She made a great fuss of Vesna. She looked well and was overjoyed to see us. We attended a lunch in our honour which must have used up the rations we had brought in. Music was played, songs were sung.

While we were in Maglaj, General Sir Michael Rose was celebrating in Sarajevo with a football match in the stadium. Music was by courtesy of the band of the Coldstream Guards resplendent in their red tunics. What a day.

We returned to the office. The staff were waiting for us and excited to hear the news from Maglaj. Then they told me the news from Bugojno about the pregnant girl and the blind husband. Our reassurances had not been enough; they had committed suicide. She lay alongside him and pulled the pin out of a hand grenade. He was twenty-six, she twenty-three; so close to a new life. In her final moments of despair whom did she blame? Why does good news here have to be followed by such bad news? I wanted to celebrate Maglaj.

The competition for local staff to get a job with the UN was always fierce. The salary was not fantastic but it was money when none was about. Which made it very strange when Leyla in the office asked to see me and explained that she wanted to resign, leave Zenica and go back home to Sarajevo.

'Leyla, of course you can go. And I will help you to get there safely. But why do you want to give up the money and the better guarantee of safety that there is here?'

'Larry, my daddy is blind. Before the war he knew his way around his favourite haunts. He could go out on his own. During the war he has not been able to go anywhere; shelling, craters, tram wires down, rubbish everywhere, snipers; not the place for a blind man to walk. Well, now it has changed. I want to go back and hold his hand and guide him through the new routes.' She returned to her daddy.

March ended with us having achieved seventy-five per cent of needs. The roads were full of convoys, the warehouses almost full of food.

The scene had changed. We were not yet in the plains of peace but we were over the top of the mountain of war. It would get better. I had no confidence for the future of Srebrenica, nor Zepa nor Gorazde. They were 'safe areas' only in files in New York and Geneva. They were Bishop Komarica's 'penned sheep awaiting the hungry wolves'.

For my little mind there were so many experiences, too many compartments to close down. It was time to go home for a break and with luck for pastures new. Mark was to hold the fort.

   Father Stipo brought me a small hand-made table and a beautiful crocheted tablecloth to cover it, made for me by the nun.

   The staff, whom I would miss enormously, gave me a great farewell barbecue party and a fantastic present, a huge hand-made model boat which I treasure. It was a warm day. There was lots of booze, thanks to Britbatt; lots of food, thanks to my staff. The car-park was clear of vehicles. Someone had rigged up music. My memory is of burning coals, grey smoke, sizzling meat; dancing and singing; party dresses and perfume; wine, beer, cokes; kind words, swapping of addresses; intimate conversations, cuddles, kisses, lipstick stains; handshakes and hugs; speeches and tears.

   My dear Bosnian friends, my dear friends in Bosnia. I was with you long enough to be able to see what was going on. Long enough to know that I would never understand. Long enough to see moments of tragedy and of happiness, to hear laughter and crying, to condemn and to praise. To do my job was a privilege. I thank all who gave me the chance.

19
Epilogue

I am not a gardener, but within hours of my return from anywhere I like to sit in mine with a glass of wine in my hand, and
look at the colours, listen to the birds, and think. I try to put
recent events into perspective. Bosnia will take a lot of time in
the garden.

The question I am most often asked is whether being in Bosnia
changed me: meeting a priest who delays and prevents the delivery
of food to a starving community; meeting a doctor who delays and
hinders the delivery of medicine to a clinic performing operations
without anaesthetics; meeting senior military men who have
ordered the mortaring and the shelling of villages, towns and cities
crowded with civilians; seeing snipers carrying telescoped weapons
through the streets on their way to their eyries to fulfil their
murderous work. This has all changed me. What I wanted to
see were priests demanding convoys for the innocent; doctors
demanding the free, unhindered access of medicines; military
men fighting on the battlefield with valour and honour; outraged
civilians denouncing the men of violence.

Another question I am often asked is if the United Nations did
enough. It can only be the sum of its parts. Some nations
did nothing, which I think is preferable to some other nations who
voted for action and took none. Some nations voted for action
and took action. I once said that the architects in New York had
drawn up plans for a house and provided materials for a shed.
But the shed did save hundreds and hundreds of thousands of
lives. Wise old Tony Land says it better. 'Debit all those who die
to the war; credit all those who live to the humanitarian effort.'

The question I ask myself is whether I could kill my neighbour. Do I understand the action of the Muslim father in Zavidovici, whose son was killed by Croats, who in retaliation murdered the Croat son of his next-door neighbour? Do I understand the action of the Muslim soldiers in besieged, starving Srebrenica who attacked Serb civilians on the outskirts of Bratunac? I understand, but I still condemn the action. I also ask myself whether I could forgive my neighbour. That is the question that will keep me in the garden for a long time.

Since Bosnia I have witnessed the conflict between the Hutu and the Tutsi, the Georgian and the Abkhazian, the Chechen and the Russian. I give many lectures and I am often asked if religious and ethnic conflict could happen in the UK. I have not yet been invited to lecture in Northern Ireland.

I have been back to Bosnia four times. Srebrenica has fallen. Zepa has fallen. Benjamin is OK. I can't find the Bear. Avdo, they believe, is dead; Zlatan, Nonjo, Sejo, Mica in America, Pepe in Canada, Meliha in Sweden. Zlatko is fit. Leyla is still in Sarajevo, Una in Prague. Vesna is in England.

Tony Land is in Geneva. Jose Maria Mendiluce is a European MP. Risto is back in Finland, Simon is a GP in England. Brane is OK, so is Mr Gogic. Mark Cutts is now in Cambridge, Steven Wolfson in Afghanistan, Louis Gentile in Djibouti, Indy in Hong Kong. Sylvana Foa is now the spokesperson for Boutros Boutros Ghali in New York. Jerrie Hulme wore himself out in Mostar and died of a stroke. Enesa and Aris are in Bourne End with their new baby . . . a boy.

Index